Kate Griffin

Fyneshade

VIPER

This paperback edition published in 2024
First published in Great Britain in 2023 by Viper,
an imprint of Profile Books Ltd
29 Cloth Fair
London
ECIA 7JQ
www.profilebooks.com

Text Design by Crow Books

1 3 5 7 9 10 8 6 4 2

Printed and bound in Great Britain by
CPI Group (UK) Ltd, Croydon, CRO 4YY

A CIP catalogue record for this book is available from the British Library.

ISBN 9781788168779
eISBN 9781782838838

FSC
www.fsc.org
MIX
Paper | Supporting
responsible forestry
FSC® C171272

Fyneshade

For Stephen

'It may be, of course, above all, that what suddenly broke into this gives the previous time a charm of stillness – that hush in which something gathers or crouches. The change was actually like the spring of a beast.'

Henry James, *The Turn of the Screw*

Wolf Moon

I

Grandmere died in the midst of a winter white and hard as the alabaster monument marking the entrance to the Van Meeran family crypt. Death took her slowly, gnawing her flesh to the bone before casting her aside. It was cruel that her mind was sharp until the end. Her eyes, black like mine, refused to shut even when the last breath left her body.

I was safe while Grandmere was alive, but as I listened to the Reverend Van Meeran wheeze through the liturgy in the church-yard beside the rimed hole that swallowed her coffin, I knew that my days in the village would soon be over. Aunt Clare would see to that. And so would the Reverend, who had noted the way his son looked at me during his interminable sermons.

I glanced up from the frosted earth piled at the edge of the grave. Nathaniel Van Meeran was staring at me now. Just for a second, the tip of his tongue appeared between his lips. I cast my eyes down, stepped forward and scattered a handful of dirt onto the coffin below. It pattered across the brass nameplate attached to the wood. I slid a look at the Reverend to reassure myself that he hadn't noticed Nathaniel watching me today.

If he knew the truth, I would have been sent from Croyle a long time before Grandmere died.

For my part, I liked Nathaniel well enough. I liked his stiff red hair, his soft pink mouth and his hard green eyes. But most of all I liked the fact that one day he would be rich.

Nathaniel was not destined for the Church. He would, in due course, inherit the family estate and a title. When his father's older brother died without issue, the Reverend and his family would leave the flint-walled rectory and move to the fine old manor house on the hillside above the village.

There had been Van Meerans in Croyle since the days of William and Mary. In six generations they had become prosperous without ever achieving anything of note, although I believe that many years back a variety of tulip – a startling shade of crimson – had been named after a distant female cousin in Leiden. I imagined the girl as a blowsy creature, topped with the vivid red hair that suited Nathaniel but made his three pale, plump sisters look tired and cheap.

When we retired to the cottage after the funeral, Judith, Caroline and Susannah crammed themselves into the window seat overlooking Grandmere's herb garden. They clashed with the improvidently early daffodils fluttering beyond the glass. The day was unexpectedly bright and the low sun made the yellow flowers glow with a delicate beauty the Van Meeran girls could never hope to attain. In the sky, the sliver of the new moon curved like a jewelled hairclip above Susannah's head. Grandmere had died with the waning light of January's Wolf Moon. In the last days her body had been devoured swiftly and mercilessly by the scavenging beast within her.

Fat Judith had already eaten her slice of mourning cake. Now she was chasing the crumbs around the plate with a stubby finger. The way her small eyes darted to the funeral breakfast laid out along the parlour table told me that she was wondering when it might be permissible to pay a second visit.

I watched my aunt move among the mourners. Our little parlour was rank with the musty smell of cloth dragged from the back of dingy cupboards. I'd always thought it an irony that the stiff black dresses and dusty coats carefully hoarded for the most formal occasions became shabby through underuse. I would never keep things for best. I knew I was born to feel the finest cloth next to my skin.

Most of the village had come to see Grandmere buried. I suspected that some of those present were there to reassure themselves that she was truly dead. The fact that she was French by birth and had never lost her accent had always been a cause for mistrust, but it was mainly her skill with herbs that caused people to whisper.

Aunt Clare had no interest in Grandmere's recipes. In truth, I knew she was more than a little frightened that the villagers might regard her with the same suspicion.

I heard the word 'witch' only once when I went out with Grandmere. It was when she took me to visit old Mrs Canvin of Lytes Farm, who had been struck by palsy. I was around ten years old and thought it natural that a woman should prepare tinctures and syrups of ease. In the centre of the village a group of boys, simple lard-faced fools, gathered under the thatched roof of the butter cross and watched us as we walked by. They were silent, but I heard the crunch of their boots on the stones as they turned to see where we went.

'*Witch*.'

The word was hissed at our backs, but Grandmere did not react and neither did I. Later, after we had left Mrs Canvin's bedside and were returning to the cottage as a full moon rose over the roof of the manor house, Grandmere stopped and cupped my face in her hands. Behind her the empty butter cross was a mound of shadow. Her black eyes caught the silvery light.

'What do you think, *ma petite*?'

'Think of what, Grandmere?' I knew very well what she meant. Until that day, I had never heard anyone call her witch to her face, or even to her back for that matter, but from the mutterings and occasional raised voices I heard through the boards of my attic room, I knew Aunt Clare was fearful for our reputation.

Grandmere smiled. 'Am I a witch, Marta?'

She always said my name in the French way.

I thought of the farm boys at the butter cross and shrugged. 'Witches exist only in stories for children.'

She ran an age-smudged hand over the shawl covering the pots and herbs in her basket and nodded. '*Bien*. Then neither are you, *ma petite pie*. But stories have a great power. They often hide a truth. Always remember that.'

I did. And sometimes I wondered if her words were a warning or a simple statement of fact.

I watched Aunt Clare batter flies from the funeral baked meats. There was nothing of Grandmere in her form or her thoughts. My aunt was small, stout and pink. The buttons down the back of her black crepe mourning gown pulled and gaped across her wide shoulders.

Looking back, I believe Grandmere must have known about that little tin hidden beneath a board in the corner of my bedroom, but when she first gave me that French pet name, *pie*, I simply saw myself as the magpie to her crow. I never met my mother, she died before I could form a memory of her, but I imagined she was also a crow or perhaps a rook. Or maybe a jackdaw.

Aunt Clare was a hen, but not the maternal kind. Here was an ordinary domestic fowl that scratched and quarrelled. She disliked me and I think she also feared me.

Now she turned from the baked meats and flapped a small puffy hand at the Reverend and his wife. They were talking to Mr Colson, a farmer, and his wife Rebecca, who was standing half in the room and half in the hallway. The dark bulge of Rebecca's belly, the only part of her visible through the doorframe, announced the imminent arrival of another Colson child. This would be her fifth. In six years, I'd seen Rebecca's neat body spread. Now her pretty features were blurred by the flesh of childbearing.

'Reverend.' Aunt Clare called across the room and waved again. Her wrist was red where the crepe caught too tight.

I felt a hand on my arm and turned. Nathaniel offered me a thin slice of crumbling mourning cake on a small china plate.

'Sweets to the sweet,' he bent to whisper in my ear. I took a currant and pushed it between my lips.

'Shakespeare.' I looked up at his wide green eyes. 'That line is also spoken at a funeral – or did you think it to be a compliment?'

His grip tightened on my arm. 'I have to speak to you, Martha. In private.'

It was too late for us. Nathaniel Van Meeran had thrown away his chance to make me his wife, and less than a month later, I'd thrown away his child. Besides, I knew that we were not destined.

'Not here.' I shook my head and drew back, aware of a flutter of interest from the window seat. I glanced at Judith, who was staring at us. A fresh morsel of cake between her fingers hovered before her open mouth.

'Martha!' Aunt Clare's voice was shrill above the dismal murmurings. 'Join us.'

I freed my arm from the pinch of Nathaniel's fingers and walked slowly around the table. Aunt Clare was standing with the Reverend and with his sour-faced wife, Agatha. Her grey eyes travelled from me and back to her son on the far side of the table. For once she looked almost happy.

'Martha, I have some news for you. Away!' The beads on Aunt Clare's gown rustled as she batted at yet another fly. Agatha Van Meeran's eyes locked on mine as the fly fell to the white tablecloth. Some of its legs still moved.

My aunt dabbed at her fingers with a square of cotton and gave me a small, tight smile. 'Reverend Van Meeran has an old friend in Derbyshire in need of a governess. We have decided that this position would be most suitable for you.'

Bone Moon

2

The Pritchard carriage was fine enough but it reeked of dog. It was too cold to open the window for fresh air so instead I held a square of cologne-soaked cotton to my nose as I watched the landscape harden into the north. We had passed through the last village some time ago and now we were rumbling along a rutted track. Beyond the glass, the world was blank. The craggy hills that rose and fell beside us were smothered by snow and the twisted branches of trees that sometimes scratched across the top of the carriage were black as the cane Grandmere had used in her last months.

If Aunt Clare had expected me to argue against the plans so carefully laid to remove me from Croyle – and from Nathaniel Van Meeran – she must have been disappointed. I made no objections to the position offered and within a fortnight the Pritchard carriage was sent for me. An honour, according to Agatha Van Meeran.

The lane to the cottage was narrow, so the carriage waited by the butter cross while the groom – a dark, stooped man – came to collect me. When I followed him to the square Aunt Clare did not accompany me. In fact, no one came to see me off on that frozen February morning. Winter had returned to snuff out the heralds of spring two days after Grandmere's funeral.

The carriage was darkest red and its lacquer reflected the snow that lay thick on the ground. It was grander than the Van Meerans' landau and more elegant. On the door the letter 'P' was painted in scrolls of gold. Before I climbed inside, I traced the outline of the letter with the tip of a finger.

Nearly everything I possessed was packed into the leather-bound travelling trunk the groom had strapped to the back of the carriage. Occasionally, when we juddered over a furrow in the road, the trunk bumped hard against the wood behind my head. My old life knocking.

I smiled at the thought, folded the scented cotton to a square and tucked it into my sleeve where I had hidden Nathaniel's note. I slipped out the little square of paper and flattened it over my knees. He had passed it to me two days ago when Aunt Clare and I left the last Sunday service I would ever attend in Croyle. His hand had brushed mine as we stepped out into the porch side by side. A small hard parcel had been pushed into my palm.

I stared at the paper scrap, stark against the black bombazine of my skirt. It was fortunate that mourning became me so well.

'Not long now, miss,' the groom called from the box. 'You'll see her down in the valley after the ridge.' I heard the crack of a whip. The carriage veered left and started to descend as I tore Nathaniel's passionate declaration into strips. Sliding the glass, I let the papers fly away. His bleating promise disappeared into the snow. The sudden sharp chill caught my breath, but I thought of the flush that would come to my cheeks and left the window slightly open.

I linked my gloved hands together and rested them in my lap. Through the thin leather, I felt the little stone in the ring Nathaniel had pressed upon me. It was a simple thing – a gold band set with a ruby. I wore it on my smallest finger and saw no reason to cast it to the snow after the note that had wrapped it.

The carriage lurched and the trunk bumped again at my back. I wondered about Grandmere's bowl. It was wrapped in my shawl and tucked into the folds of my second-best gown, but if it was to crack would it still serve? I moved closer to the window and scanned the pallid landscape for the house. The carriage was moving faster on the decline. The horses in the traces, two fine bays, whinnied – a sure sign that they were nearing their stable.

And what was coming to me?

My employer was a widower. His wife Sophia had died ten years ago in childbirth. I gathered, despite Reverend Van Meeran's delicacy on the subject, that the child was unexpected given Sophia's age. Now the girl required a female companion. At Grandmere's funeral breakfast, I had watched Agatha's fingers pluck at the black ruffles of her bodice while her husband talked about his old friend. Occasionally her eyes flicked to my face and then quickly away. She seemed uneasy. I decided that she thought I might make a scene, or worse, that Nathaniel might disgrace himself before the better half of the village.

In truth, I *was* angry that day. I was furious to think they had decided my future. Without Grandmere to protect me, I was to be packed off to Derbyshire like a chattel. But as I listened to the Reverend describe his friend's simple requirements and then his estate and house – one of the finest in the county – I began to reconsider. I knew I would accept the offer when Reverend Van Meeran said his friend was Sir William Pritchard.

The trunk thumped loudly as the carriage pitched forward. We were rattling down from the ridge at a sharp angle.

The groom called again. 'Down there, miss. Through the trees to the right.'

I moved to the edge of the seat. It was late in the day and the light was failing. The snow on the hillside was bruised with purple. In the valley below, snow-shrouded trees huddled beside a frozen river. At first there was no sign of the house, but then, just as the groom had said, it appeared through a break in the woodland.

It was huge and grey. More like a fortress than a house, it marched in a disorderly fashion along the curve of the river. I saw three square towers, turrets, a wide stone gateway and a multitude of tiny windows, but then it disappeared from view again behind the trees as the carriage turned on the zig-zag track.

It was several minutes more before we clattered under the arch of the gatehouse and came to a halt. The groom opened the door and I stepped down to a stone-paved courtyard. I stared up at the building that loured above me. Crenellated towers nibbled the sky.

'Your things will be sent up, miss.' The groom nodded and went to the back of the carriage. I heard a dull thump as he hauled my trunk down to the stones.

I hoped I had done enough to protect the bowl. It was, in a way, why I was here.

The water whirled about. Grandmere sprinkled salt on the surface and then I handed her a small glass phial. I watched as she poured the sticky blood from my monthly courses into the bowl. As the milky water stilled, the blood pulled itself into the shape of a letter. It was clear as the moon that shone through the open window of Grandmere's bedchamber.

'There is your fortune, little pie.' She smiled and raised a finger to her lips. 'Your fate will turn on the letter P.'

I watched the carriage rumble across the courtyard and disappear through another arch in the furthest wall.

'You're here at last!'

I turned at the voice. A woman was standing in the shadows at the top of a ragged flight of steps leading to an arched doorway beneath the central tower. It was too dark to make out her face as she spoke.

'I wondered if you might have to break the journey, with the snow and all. The nearest inn is six miles off and that's an afternoon's ride in this. Come inside then, Martha.' She bustled down the steps and now I saw that she was a homely woman wearing the simple clothes of a servant. The ribbons of her white cotton cap flapped in the wind.

'Marta,' I corrected her. 'My name is Marta.'

She halted for a moment and stared at me. 'You're a mite ... younger than I was expecting.'

I had the impression that 'younger' was not the first word that had come into her mind. I smiled and waited her for to continue.

'Well, no matter. Miss Grace has been looking forward to meeting you. She's been watching the ridge from the tower room all day.' The woman's accent was as broad and flat as her face.

The deep bark of a dog echoed from the doorway. There was scuffling and a moment later a huge grey hound bounded down the steps. It ran in a wide circle around us, swaying its massive shaggy head from side to side, and then it came close to snuffle at my skirt. I stepped back and held my hands to my breast. I was not fond of dogs.

The woman smiled. 'He might be the size of a pony, but Lancer wouldn't hurt a fly.' She gripped the dog's collar and scratched the wiry fur at its neck. 'Did she send you down to greet her new governess, my lad?'

Lancer yelped once and lolloped back up the steps.

The woman pointed at my trunk. 'I'll have that sent to your room. Now, you follow me.' She started back up to the door. She paused just before the entrance and turned to me.

'Where are my manners? I'm Mrs Gurney, the housekeeper. Welcome to Fyneshade, Miss ... *Marta*. Welcome indeed.'

3

At the top of the grand wooden staircase that rose from the centre of the hall Mrs Gurney turned right and set off down a dark panelled corridor lined with sombre paintings in heavy frames. Generations of Pritchard men and women leaned out from the wall, watching me.

I bit my lips and, when Mrs Gurney wasn't turning back to offer some prattle on the house and its treasures, I pinched my cheeks hard between my fingers and thumb. Not that I needed the sting to bring colour to my face. Money was not wasted on the heating of Fyneshade. My breath misted the air and a chill was trapped beneath the bell of my dress. The house was not unkempt, but it was – in some way – forgotten. Like the clothing worn by the mourners at Grandmere's funeral, it had grown stale through lack of wear.

But as we walked, I came to see that Mr Pritchard was indeed rich.

The corridor was lit by scores of candles clumped together in the branches of ugly wall brackets. Aunt Clare would never have permitted such wanton extravagance. Thick rugs muffled the sound of our footsteps and forced flowers tumbled with voluptuous ease from china basins, filling the air with the sweetness of wealth.

Mrs Gurney was not leading me to my room, I was certain of it. Flowers would not be wasted on a governess.

Halfway down the corridor she paused before a painting of a young woman with a child in her lap.

'That's Lady Sophia, Miss Grace's mother.' She sighed. 'A good woman and a fair mistress.'

I stared up at the painting. Sophia Pritchard was pretty in a pallid manner. Her fair hair, caught loosely with a yellow-striped ribbon, tumbled over one shoulder and a rope of pearls gleamed beneath the gauzy neck of her dress. Her large eyes were blue and her lips were very pink. She looked younger than me and the fat infant on her knees was no longer a baby. The way the child leaned and stretched a hand towards the small dog hidden in the folds of its mother's skirts suggested that it would rather be crawling and playing.

Reverend Van Meeran had said that Mrs Pritchard had died in childbirth. I was also quite sure he had suggested that she was an older woman, not the cream-faced girl on the wall above me.

I wondered if perhaps this was some sort of memorial, a sentimental fantasy created to flatter and soothe the grief of a widower and, in time, his motherless daughter. I glanced at Mrs Gurney, who seemed lost in thought as she stared at the painting. She shook her head again and the little jet earrings dangling from her ears twinkled in the candlelight.

'I sometimes think I catch a sight of her in Grace. But it's a fleeting thing. Poor lamb.'

She turned from the painting and carried on along the corridor. At the end we passed through an archway draped with heavy red curtains and came into a small panelled lobby.

'Here we are.' Mrs Gurney gestured at a pair of double doors. They looked too grand for the bedroom of a governess. Clearly it was just as I had hoped: I was about to be introduced.

I smoothed the line of my skirt.

'I am to meet Mr Pritchard now?' I looked down and secretly bit hard again on my lower lip. Nathaniel always said it was slightly too full and too wide to be a perfect match. He liked to crush it against my teeth with the fleshy pad of his thumb before kissing me.

'Dear me, no.'

I looked up. According to the chimes of a golden clock we had passed in the passage – Mrs Gurney had pointed it out as a particularly valuable French timepiece – it was not yet seven. Surely it was too early for Mr Pritchard to retire?

Now she was holding a silver chatelaine close to her eyes and sorting along the keys on the ring.

'It's late for Miss Grace, but I promised her that as soon as you arrived, I'd take you to her.'

There was a thumping sound from the corridor beyond the velvet curtains. The large grey dog appeared and nudged between us to scratch at the doors.

'Here we are.' She found the right key and bent to fit it to the lock. As I stared at her rump, I wondered why it was necessary to lock a child of ten in their room.

The dog pricked its ears, yelped and bounded through the open door. I followed Mrs Gurney, who rustled ahead.

'Grace.' She tucked the chatelaine away, planted her hands on her hips and called again.

'Come now. Don't be a silly girl.' She glanced at me, in a way that seemed almost conspiratorial, tutted quietly and took a lighted candle from a table just inside the door. She held it aloft. 'You've been looking forward to meeting Miss Martha . . . Marta,' she corrected herself, 'and now you won't show yourself.'

She walked a little way forward. Her sturdy body blocked the light from the fire blazing in a wide stone hearth, but the candle in her hand and the flickering glow from several others set about the room showed that we were in a library. Rows of books climbed into the shadowed gloom of a vault so high above us that I could not clearly see where the shelves ended and where the ceiling began. Heavy curtains were drawn across three tall windows set at intervals between the volumes lining the wall opposite the door.

The room was very long and filled with furniture: couches, tables, chairs and desks were arranged at irregular angles and positioned to create smaller, more intimate spaces. As my eyes grew accustomed to the light, I saw stacks of books set out on some of the tables. The air was warm and smelt of applewood and leather. It was the retreat of a gentleman.

'Miss Grace!' There was a sharpness to Mrs Gurney's voice now. 'Come out!' She looked at me and shook her head. 'Not two hours earlier she had her nose pressed to the glass in the tower to catch a glimpse of you.'

The child was obviously playing a game. It occurred to me that it would be best to make Grace Pritchard my friend from the beginning.

'Is this hide and seek?' I went to stand beside Mrs Gurney and scanned the furniture. I stretched my mouth into a smile that shaped the appealing tone of my next question.

'I am fond of games too. Do you want me to come and find you, Grace?'

The answer was a muffled giggle from the shadows at the far end of the room. I heard footsteps, the sound surprisingly heavy, and the scratch of the dog's claws on wooden boards. A moment later there was a shimmer of sound.

Mrs Gurney gasped and started off up the room, picking her way through the maze of furniture.

'You come here this instant, Miss Grace. If you touch that harp—'

I stood by the fire wondering whether to follow. I caught a muttered conversation during which the word 'naughty' was repeated three times, then, after a moment more, Mrs Gurney returned. The dog, Lancer, padded at her side. The wagging of its great grey tail caused a draught that made the flame of her candle dance on the spines of the books.

Mrs Gurney's left arm was caught behind her back. She turned to speak to the girl she had, presumably, dragged from her hiding place.

'Step out now and say hello to Miss Marta, just as we practised.' She shook the hand caught fast in her own and yanked hard. I heard a snort and something like a word. Then Grace shuffled out from behind the ample shield of Mrs Gurney's body and stared frankly at me.

Her large face was round and pale as the moon. Her nose was small, but splayed wide, her mouth hung open and her mild pale eyes tilted oddly at the edges. The only resemblance between Grace Pritchard and Sophia, her pretty mother, lay in the mass of fair hair that tumbled over the child's pudgy shoulder. There was even a ribbon attempting to detach itself from the remains of a plait.

The girl made the noise again. I could not describe it as an identifiable word, although it must have been meant as a greeting. She stared at me while she dug a finger into her nose. Then, shyly, she grinned and offered her hand.

4

We had little to say to one another. It was quite clear that the pretty speech I had prepared for my new charge – promises of friendship, companionship and pleasurable entertainment – would be wasted. A few minutes after our meeting in the library, Grace was collected and led away to her bed by an elderly woman introduced as Old Maggie. The girl turned to look back at me as she went out through the door.

The dog padded over to snuffle at my skirts. When I did not pet it or acknowledge its existence in any way, it gave a snort of disappointment and trotted after Grace and the ancient nursemaid.

The girl's ribbon had slipped to the floor. I let Mrs Gurney stoop to collect it. 'Well, that went as well as to be expected.' She wound the pink satin around her fingers and glanced at me. Briefly, I saw appraisal in her eyes. 'Before I take you up to your room, I daresay you must want something to eat, Miss Marta?'

We went down to a small parlour where cold meat, bread and cheese and slices of dense dark fruit cake had been laid out. There was also a teapot set ready over a copper burner. The room was plain but neatly furnished. A fire glowed in the hearth. I recognised it immediately as the domain of the woman who settled herself at the plain oval table.

'Sit.' Mrs Gurney reached for the pot. 'You didn't know about Miss Grace.' It wasn't a question.

I watched her fill my cup and busy herself with the bread.

'There.' She pushed a plate towards me. 'The bread's fresh baked today but I recommend cheese with the cake. I daresay it's not regular but that's how we like it here.'

I took a small piece of cake. Mrs Gurney was wrong on one count. Hunger was not what I felt.

She placed a thin slice of cheese next to the cake on my plate and carried on: 'I could tell, as soon as you looked on her. Your face told a tale.' She helped herself to a corner of pale cheese and pressed it to a square of cake. 'That's not right – not for you or for the little one. Right from the start, I told him . . .'

She stopped herself. The parlour was silent except for the crackle of the fire. She meant Sir William, I was certain. I wondered *what* she had told him, and whether it might be useful. I waited for her to continue but when she started again, she was on a new track.

'Now you're here at Fyneshade . . .' she smiled at me, '. . . I hope you'll make the best of it. For all her . . . troubles, Miss Grace has a loving nature and she deserves kindness. We've done our best but we're old women and she needs a young lady, such as yourself, to help her find her way.'

At Grandmere's funeral breakfast Reverend Van Meeran had

told me that my particular skills had 'impressed' his widower friend. What use would French and music be to a girl like Grace? I crumbled cake between my fingers. I had no appetite for sweetness tonight.

I found I could not look across the table in case the woman read my features a second time.

'Can she speak, Mrs Gurney?'

'Sometimes. Not always and not always so as you'd understand, but yes, she does . . . talk. Mainly to the dog.'

'Has she had any lessons before? Or a companion?'

'No, none at all. I hold myself responsible there, mind. I tried, but . . .' She paused again. 'He wouldn't accept it . . . accept *her*. After the mistress died, he wouldn't so much as look on her, poor mite. And then, when it became clear to us all that she . . . she was . . .'

'That she was . . . different?' I prompted.

Mrs Gurney nodded. 'Yes, that's right . . . *different*. It was as if she didn't exist for him. But that's not right. We agreed.'

I took a sip of tea. 'You mean you eventually managed to persuade Sir William to engage a . . . companion for his daughter?'

'In a manner of speaking.'

Quite suddenly, she leaned across the table and caught my hand. 'She's no trouble, Miss Marta. Little Grace deserves better, poor lamb. You'll help us, won't you?'

I watched the sky lighten from the window. My room faced due north and looked out across a rounded inner yard at the back of the house and onto a hill shaped like the back of a bull. Brackish light slowly defined the snow-covered flanks of the brooding creature as I considered my position.

I had slept little that first night. The bed was comfortable, the room was grander than I had expected, well appointed and warm – a fire was already burning in the massive stone hearth when I retired a little after eight o'clock – and my trunk was waiting for me as promised.

It was a relief to find that Grandmere's bowl had survived the journey intact. I would use it again as soon as my courses came in time with the full moon. Now it was wrapped in a shawl and stowed safely with her spice box and my tin of stolen treasures beneath the hinged panel at the centre of the window seat in front of me. I had placed a pair of tapestry cushions on top of it.

I felt cheated.

I had seen children like Grace Pritchard before. A boy in Croyle, Jim Padfold, had shared her distinctive features. The Padfolds had already produced several healthy children before the arrival of Jim, whose slow manner and odd appearance marked him as different to the rest of them. He died young. According to Grandmere this was to be expected for '*un enfant touché par le fées*'. In the next village an older girl called Tally Hess still worked as a dairymaid. The men took advantage of her soft mind and soft body. There was something of Grace in the cast of her eyes.

I remembered the way that Agatha Van Meeran had fiddled at the ruffles of her bodice and failed to catch my eye while her husband talked about the requirements of his fine friend in Derbyshire, and I knew that I had been tricked.

The Pritchard girl didn't need a governess, she was in want of a nurse. For all Mrs Gurney's misguided optimism, there was little

I could do. I thought about our conversation in the parlour. After catching my hand in her own, the housekeeper had released me with an embarrassed apology. We had sat in silence for a minute or two more and then she had offered to show me to my room.

We were at the second landing of the staircase when the sound of many clocks chiming the hour filled the gloom. Jingling, jangling, chinking and the deeper strike of bells came from all around.

'You'll have to get used to it.' Mrs Gurney had raised her candle to show a particularly fine longcase patterned in the chinoiserie style on the landing just above us. 'There are more than fifty of them throughout the house. I should know, I'm the one who winds them. A deal of trouble they've caused me.' She shook her head. 'Sir William's father had a fascination for all manner of clocks and such.'

At the mention of my employer I had asked, again, if I was to be introduced the following day, but the housekeeper's answer was blunt.

'No. No you will not, Miss Marta.'

I turned from the window, huddled my nightgown around me and went to poke at the embers of the fire still glowing in the hearth. I knelt on the rug and watched tiny golden flames flower anew beneath a half-charred log.

Grandmere had promised to teach me to read fortunes in a fire, but she had passed only the most basic principles of the skill to me before she died.

I plucked five hairs from my head and plaited them together. This was simple country divination, the sort that clucking girls might use to question the intentions of a lover. I cast the black twist into the fire, inscribed the shape of a five-pointed star in the air with my thumb and whispered my question.

The sudden brilliant blue flare that leapt from the left of the hearth was my answer. Surprised, I sat back and considered the message. There was no mistake. The colour and the position of the dancing flame was explicit. I was, indeed, meant to be here at Fyneshade.

5

Grace sucked her thumb and scribbled on the paper I'd put before her. The sound of the pencil set my teeth on edge. I wanted to beat hard on the desk to stop the squeak of the lead, but instead I moved my hands to my lap and tightened my fingers into fists.

The schoolroom was midway up a winding staircase in the eastern tower. It was plain and clean. Four small wooden desks with bench seats attached told of Pritchards long past who had submitted their infant minds to education here. One of the drab women who flitted through the passages had lit a fire in the tiled hearth. The crackling of the logs, the scratching of the pencil and the continual sucking were the only sounds.

My own larger desk was next to a long window that looked down over the front of the house. Snow had fallen throughout the night. Flurries still danced in the air like feathers plucked from a goose. The courtyard below was smooth and white as a bedsheet. Any trace of carriage wheels or footsteps were long gone. Nothing marked my arrival.

Grace made a new noise. I turned from the window to see her waving the paper at me. Another animal: this time a horse. So far, she had produced a dog, a cat, a fox, a mouse, a ram, a bull and a long stringy hare with strange, watchful eyes. She drew surprisingly well. But that was all she did.

When Mrs Gurney led me to the schoolroom earlier that morning, I felt obliged to respond to her hopeful questions about the lessons a young lady might reasonably expect to be taught. As she opened the door to my new domain, she patted my arm and repeated a version of her plea from the previous evening. 'You'll do your best for her, won't you?'

Grace was delivered by Old Maggie a few minutes after Mrs Gurney's departure. The girl's white smock, trimmed with lace and fastened down the back with ivory buttons, was crisp and fresh as the courtyard. The old woman led her silently by the hand to the side of my desk and bent to smooth her neatly plaited hair before leaving us alone.

Once the door closed, I smiled.

'Good morning, Grace.'

She made a mewing sound, ran to the back of the room and refused to look at me. After some cajoling, which sounded false even to my ears, she finally turned from the wall.

'Will you sit here?' I pointed at the little desk in front of my own.

The girl didn't answer. She brought her thumb to her mouth and stared at the window. In the cold clear light, I saw that her eyes were an unusually pale shade of blue.

I began again. 'Do you remember my name, Grace?'

If she did, she did not care to repeat it. The wet sucking noise grew louder as she worked at the thumb. It was defiant and repulsive. I looked at the clock on the mantel. It was barely ten. I was expected to remain here in the schoolroom with my dull charge until midday and then, after lunch, we were to spend three more hours in each other's company.

Wondering what to do with the girl, I went to the little bookshelf behind my own desk. Perhaps I could read aloud to her? A romance or fable would fill the hours – for me, at least.

'Do you like stories?' I scanned the shelves for a suitable collection and found only dry ancient volumes of Latin, Greek, French and German alongside grammar, history and geography; nothing that would hold any use or appeal to either of us.

There was a scratching noise behind me. I turned from the shelf to see that Grace had sat down at a desk and was now scribbling furiously with a pencil over the polished surface. Head bent low, she was completely absorbed in this desecration.

'No!' I ran to take the pencil from her. We wrestled with the wretched thing – Grace was surprisingly strong – and then when, finally, I prised it from her grip she started to wail. The sound came as a single high-pitched note, repeated again and again. It was so acute and piercing that I was certain it would carry down the stone stairs of the tower. Soon Mrs Gurney or one of the others would come running.

There was a pile of paper on my desk. I snatched up several sheets and laid them in front of her.

'Here, draw on these.' I forced the pencil back into her wet hand. 'Not on the desk.'

After almost two hours, Grace and I had achieved a sort of truce. Her once-pristine smock was smudged with grey, but as long as I allowed her to scribble, she seemed content. I had already decided to visit the library before returning to the school-room that afternoon. While I read, Grace could draw whatever she wanted.

Now she squirmed on her seat and held the paper out to me. I stood and went to her side. The horse was running: its mane and tail, caught in a series of looping scrawls, gave the drawing a sense of urgency and movement. Because of the skewed positioning of her composition and the boldness of her lines, the creature looked as if it might gallop off the side of the page.

I nodded. 'Very good, Grace.'

She scratched her head where the plait pulled tight, pushed the paper to one side and started on a fresh sheet. The pencil squealed again. I glanced at the clock to reassure myself that this torture would soon end and went to stand at the window.

There was a tallow quality to the flat grey sky that suggested the lacy wisps of snow falling now would soon thicken to a blizzard. I pulled at my cuffs to cover my wrists and rubbed my hands together. The heat from the fire did not reach this corner.

The courtyard was still an oval blank. It was clear that no one had left the house today – or come to it for that matter. I thought about what Mrs Gurney had said when I arrived.

'The nearest inn is six miles off.'

As I watched, the gateway through which I had arrived began to disappear, the outline smudged from view by snowfall. After a minute or two I couldn't see the courtyard at all. It seemed an age since I'd been deposited there yesterday with my bag. Fyneshade's many clocks caught time in their hands.

At noon, Grace was collected by Old Maggie – whose most notable feature, apart from that dismal name, was her silence – and taken to her room. I went down to Mrs Gurney's parlour as arranged. After a plain meal, for which I had little appetite, I asked if I might visit the library before returning to the school-room.

'Looking for a particular book for Miss Grace, are you? That's good.' Mrs Gurney sounded relieved.

During the last hour, she had asked very little about our morning in the tower. I imagined it was because she already knew very well how it had gone. Instead, hardly pausing to draw breath, she had enumerated the many trials of running a house the size of Fyneshade with diversions on the shortcomings of tenant farmers on the estate. The woman rattled on like a button tin.

The only time she faltered was at the end of our meal when I asked again about Sir William. Now that Grace and I were fully acquainted with one another it was surely time for a proper introduction. Mrs Gurney's round eyes slipped from mine. She dabbed the side of her mouth with a napkin and busied herself with the cups on the table. 'More tea, Marta?'

As she poured, I waited for an answer. She pushed my cup towards me and coughed daintily.

'I can't seem to shift this. It's sat on my lungs since Christmas.' Her hand fluttered to her breast. I had not noticed this affliction before. I assumed the cough was a topic designed to deflect my attention. I tried again, framing my question so simply that she could not avoid a direct answer.

'When will I meet Sir William?'

She sat very still. 'Master's not here. He's gone away.' She stiffened her back and stared at me across the table. 'The light won't last in this weather. You'll be wanting to get back to the school-room. You'd best be on your way if you're to visit the library first.'

I passed the afternoon in tolerable comfort. Grace, dressed in a fresh clean smock, continued to draw while I sat close to the schoolroom fire and read a French novel. I discovered that the library included a small selection of surprisingly piquant works, hidden behind a dusty curtain on the lowest shelf on the fur-thest wall from the door. I could not imagine the saintly Sophia with these books – even as a cow-eyed girl – which prompted me to think again about her husband.

'Master's not here.'

Where was he then? It was clear that when Mrs Gurney could no longer avoid telling me the truth, my swift dismissal was intended to close the matter. She was uneasy each time I asked about my employer. More than that, she seemed guarded when I mentioned his name. Why?

I rested the book on my knees and looked over at Grace, who was hunched at the desk scrawling circles. The pencil screeched as she carved at the paper.

What a disappointment she must have been. Sir William Pritchard owned the finest house in the county, but his child would never be an ornament to his name.

I remembered what Mrs Gurney had said last evening. 'It was as if she didn't exist for him.'

And something else came back to me too.

'But that's not right. We agreed.'

I sat up straight and the book tumbled from my lap to the

floor. Grace turned to stare at me. She fiddled absently with the tip of her plait, then went back to work.

I had thought Mrs Gurney to be talking about Sir William. I had imagined that '*we*' to refer to an agreement between them, but now I understood something quite different. The women of Fyneshade cared about Grace. The way they dressed her, petted her and worried for her future were evidence of deep concern. Perhaps even love.

They had employed me as her governess. Sir William had nothing to do with it.

Grace's father, wherever he was, had no idea of my existence.

6

We dined in Mrs Gurney's dim parlour again that evening, waited on by a scrawny maid I had not seen before. The girl's thin, dun-coloured hair was knotted on the top of her head and there was a prominent, disfiguring mole on her cheek. She was plain; not that it mattered here. Apart from the stoop-backed groom who had conveyed me from Croyle to Fyneshade, I had yet to see another man.

As the senior servants, it was natural that Mrs Gurney and I should spend time together, but it would be on her terms. Fyneshade was costly to run, she explained at great length, and – although, as governess to Miss Grace I was welcome to use the library, long gallery, drawing room and salons – heat and candlelight throughout the winter months would be confined to the most frequented parts of the house. My dreary world shrank even more when I learned that the north wing, the oldest part of the house facing directly onto the moors, was completely closed. The doors were chained and bolted.

As I sat there moving a cutlet around the plate, I imagined a succession of tedious days plodding from the schoolroom to the housekeeper's parlour and back to my bedchamber.

Surely this was not the fate intended for me?

I spoke little during our meal. I could not trust myself to engage Mrs Gurney in conversation for fear of saying something I might regret. The certainty that I was right about her secret conferred a sort of power upon me and I wanted to consider how I might use it to the best advantage.

'I wish you'd take a little more, Marta.' She pushed the meat dish towards me. 'You need some fat on your bones.'

I shook my head and laid down my knife. 'I have had enough, thank you.'

She prodded her fork at another greasy cutlet. 'You're in mourning.' It wasn't a question, but I knew an answer was required.

'Grandmere died in January.'

Mrs Gurney looked up from her plate, confused.

'My grandmother. *Grandmere* is French for grandmother.'

'Ah.' I could see her thinking about it as she chewed. Her teeth, which were surprisingly large and even, made a clicking noise as she worked at the meat.

'So, you're French then?'

I shook my head. 'My grandfather was English.'

'He's dead too?' She didn't butter her words. And neither did I.

'Grandmere was widowed young. My own parents died of fever before I was a year old. I never knew them. Grandmere raised me.'

There was little point in telling her more, though the story was rich indeed. Grandmere had been born to an aristocratic family. At two months old she had been hidden from the mob and sent to be raised in an isolated convent in the Arrée Mountains near Morlaix. The Melusine Sisters were an ancient and unusually learned order and Grandmere had learned *much* in their care. Mrs Gurney would not have understood or approved of their teachings. My grandfather had been an English merchant. Grandmere had fallen in love with his wild heart and golden hair. He, like my parents, died young.

I did not mention Aunt Clare. I did not regard her as a part of my family or my story. When I looked into a mirror, I saw a younger version of Grandmere and beyond her generations of high-born women. When I looked at Aunt Clare, I saw a peasant.

Like Nathaniel, she was nothing to me now.

Light from the single candle between us flickered on Mrs Gurney's flat face. I had the impression she was assessing me. She swallowed and returned her attention to the cutlet. The sound of her sawing on the china made me want to pluck the knife from her hand.

'Well, you're not what I expected, Miss Marta.' She did not look up. I was interested to know what that meant. Exactly how had I come to be here? What dealings had there been between Mrs Gurney and the Van Meerans?

I was about to say something, but the door opened and Lancer pattered into the room followed by Grace and Old Maggie. The dog came close to the table and stared at the dish of cutlets. The creature glanced at Mrs Gurney, brown eyes full of appeal, and nudged forward to rest its shaggy head on the cloth.

'Away with you!' She swatted Lancer's nose and turned to the door. 'What are you doing here? It's past Miss Grace's bedtime.'

'She won't settle.' Old Maggie's voice was a crackled, thicker version of Mrs Gurney's. 'She's been a devil for the last hour. I only turned my back on her for a minute. Then I looked back and she was gone. Vanished into . . .' The old woman faltered, then rallied. 'You know how it is.'

I saw a look pass between them. Old Maggie nodded and continued, 'Took me an age to find her and now she won't lie quiet. All because of the young lady, there.'

'Marta?' Mrs Gurney turned to me, accusingly. 'What did you read to her?'

I could hardly admit that I had not read anything to Grace at all. I smiled at the girl, who was now wearing a long white nightgown. Her hair was freshly tied in a neat plait that draped over her shoulder. She rubbed a hand across her face and made a noise, something between a snort and laughter.

I sat upright. 'Good evening, Grace. Or, in French, *en Français*, we would say *bonsoir*.'

I slid at look at Mrs Gurney, to see if she approved of my evident devotion to the child's education. She glared at me, no doubt imagining I had spent the afternoon stuffing the girl's head with fairy tales of the most gruesome and vicious variety. There were plenty of them, after all.

'Come, lass.' Old Maggie removed Grace's hand gently from her face and led her to the table. Lancer lost interest in the meat. The dog butted its head against the girl's stocky white body and allowed her to weave stubby fingers into the scruff of grizzled hair at its neck. The ancient nurse shook her head.

'It's the monkey. She wants to show the lady. Don't you, Grace?'

The answer was a snuffle.

'Is that it?' Mrs Gurney turned to me. 'She must like you,

Marta.' I thought I detected a note of surprise in that. Her expression softened as she continued, 'The monkey's a great favourite. Well, as it's a special night I see no reason why not.' She reached out to stroke Grace's cheek. 'But only the once, mind.'

I frowned. 'Monkey, Mrs Gurney?'

Was this another pet? I remembered that Jim Padfold had a tame rabbit that followed him wherever he went. Children like Jim and Grace often had an affinity for animals. Grandmere said that creatures were *attirés par l'innocence*.

'You'll see.' Mrs Gurney rose from the table. She wiped her fingers with a napkin and put a hand to her belt. I heard the jingle of the keys on the chatelaine. 'Grace, you can lead the way.'

The girl gulped like a carp and clapped her hands. She spun around and clumped to the parlour door. The blue and white china on the dresser chinked and jittered at her heavy tread. Lancer yelped and followed. I heard the thud of their feet on the wooden stairs.

'Careful now!' Mrs Gurney called after her. Counting along the keys, she exchanged another look with Old Maggie. 'Once that child gets a thought stuck in her head …' She sighed and gestured to the door. 'Come along then, Marta. Miss Grace won't rest tonight until you've seen him.'

I followed the housekeeper and nursemaid up the broad oak staircase to the first landing. This time Mrs Gurney did not turn off into the portrait-lined passage leading to the library; instead, she raised the candlestick taken from the parlour and went to the left through a curtain tortured into swollen curves by gilded swags.

It was so cold in this new passage that I could see my breath. More paintings – mainly of a pastoral variety, as far as I could tell – lined the panelled walls here and a variety of clocks jostled for space on tables set at intervals between a dozen doors. The ticking was like a thousand beetles busy in the wood.

Somewhere ahead of us, Lancer barked.

'We're coming.' Mrs Gurney raised the candlestick and turned to me. 'Grace knows every inch of this house. She could find her way round it blindfolded. Especially this room.'

She sallied ahead and I followed with Old Maggie. The old woman had yet to direct a single word at me. In a few moments we came to Grace and Lancer waiting outside a door set midway along the chilly passage. The girl clapped again as Mrs Gurney handed the candle to Old Maggie and lifted the chatelaine. She went directly to a small key with a square-shaped bow and fitted it to the lock.

Before she opened the door, she caught hold of Lancer's collar and bent to talk to Grace.

'What do we always say?'

Grace smiled and shook her head. To my surprise she managed a word.

'Touch.'

Mrs Gurney nodded. 'Good girl. That's right. Don't touch.' She looked up at me. 'That goes for you too, Marta. In you go – not far mind, just in case. Stand still and I'll light some candles.'

The room was as dark as the Van Meeran crypt. The musty air held a tang of metal and there was also a deeper note – a little like Grandmere's spice box, but not as bitter. I stood quite still, my arms wrapped around me against the cold, and watched Mrs Gurney light candles in wall brackets. As she worked, reflected light bloomed from mottled mirrors arranged about the room.

And now I saw the monkey.

This was no living thing. Set on a plinth before a curtained window, it was a golden statue, almost as tall as Lancer's shoulder. The animal was seated on a gilded cushion speckled with scores of gems that glittered in the candlelight. The monkey's fur had been cast in whorls and curves that suggested muscles beneath. Its long tail curled around its feet and its fore paws were raised to cover its eyes.

Grace came to stand next to me and tugged at my folded arms. I allowed her to hold my hand.

Mrs Gurney nodded approvingly at this, to her eyes, charming tableau and pointed at the monkey.

'What do you think of our Panjan?'

I stared at the figure. It was finely wrought and studded with more precious stones than I had ever seen. Sir William was a man of inconceivable wealth. I smiled at the housekeeper.

'I have no doubt that this is one of Fyneshade's greatest treasures. It is an exceptional statue.'

Grace squealed and squeezed my hand. Mrs Gurney chuckled indulgently and glanced at Old Maggie, who now had charge of Lancer. The dog's extravagant tail swished perilously close to an arrangement of porcelain ornaments on a low table.

'Oh, he's much more than that. Shall we show her, Miss Grace?'

Eyes locked on the monkey, the girl nodded vigorously and started to suck on the thumb of the hand not clasped in my own. In a mirror I watched the housekeeper go to a spindle-legged table next to the door. She lifted the lid from a small octagonal porcelain box and took out something that glinted in the candlelight. She held the object close to her eyes and peered at it. Satisfied, she came back to stand beside the plinth.

'I usually do this once a month, to keep the mechanism in order ...' she raised a tiny golden key, '... but seeing as Miss Grace wanted you to see him ...' She ran her hands along the edge of the cushion and bent to fit the key. She twisted it several times, producing a loud metallic click on every turn, and finally when the clear note of a single bell sounded, she straightened up and stepped away.

'Now watch.'

At first nothing happened, but then tinkling music – a pretty pattering tune – began. The end of the monkey's tail started to twitch in time to the rhythm and then its head turned from side to side. The tune grew louder, and slowly the monkey's paws moved apart to reveal eyes – two massive rubies set in circles of white in a pointed face. Grace gripped tighter.

'This is the bit she likes best.' Mrs Gurney patted the child's shoulder.

Suddenly the glowing eyes moved. They swung slowly to the left and to the right. And then the monkey's mouth fell open. A tiny golden ball dropped to the cushion and zig-zagged along a path carved between the gemstones. It circled the monkey's haunches twice before disappearing into a hole beneath the twitching tail end.

The ruby eyes moved again. Now they seemed to be looking down, searching for the ball. The jingling music took on a sadder, more stately tempo and then it stopped.

Slowly, silently, the monkey's paws shifted back to cover its eyes once more and then it was still. The performance had lasted a minute.

Mrs Gurney stroked Grace's head.

'What do you think of that then, miss?' I wasn't sure if the question was aimed at me or the child. Grace span away from the housekeeper's touch and hugged my legs through the bombazine.

I decided the question was for me.

'It is extraordinary, Mrs Gurney. Grandmere told me about such things. Is it French? I believe the finest examples were made in Paris.'

'That may be, but our Panjan came all the way from India. Sir William's father bought him as a wedding gift for Miss Grace's grandmother. I told you he was fascinated by all manner of clocks and mechanical things. This goes by the name of an automatory. And you love him, don't you?' She tugged Grace gently from my skirt. There were tears in the girl's large blue eyes.

'There, there. Don't fret now. You'll see Panjan again, but not tonight. We made a pact, remember. Just the once.' Mrs Gurney leaned close to me and whispered, 'Sometimes I wind him up when we want her to do things. It always works.'

She went back to the delicate table by the door and slipped the little key back into the octagonal box. Then she started to blow out the candles in the brackets. Soon the golden monkey faded into the gloom.

'Maggie, you'll take Miss Grace up to the nursery. Lancer too.' Mrs Gurney blew again. Without turning to look at me she continued, 'Take that last candle to light yourself to bed, Marta.'

I opened the door to my bedchamber and was grateful to see a fire burning in the hearth. The mourning gown was elegant, but thin. Cold had bitten into my bones as we stood below admiring the automaton. Or 'automatory' as Mrs Gurney would have it.

I knelt before the fire and warmed my hands. Within a minute blood pulsed in the tips of my fingers. It had been an interesting evening after all. My knees cracked as I stood and went to the window seat. Moving the tapestry cushions aside, I opened the hinged lid. The tin box was wrapped in a shawl. It rattled as I wound it free from the wool.

I flicked open the lid to look upon my treasures: a single pearl earring; the locket from Aunt Clare's necklace; three gilt buttons; a tiny china figurine of a shepherdess; a lace-trimmed handker-chief so fine it was transparent; a silver coffin plate.

Such small things. Trinkets easy to steal. Aunt Clare had been most distracted by the missing earring. I remembered her cup-ping its pair in the palm of her hand and asking in that querulous voice, 'What is the use of a single pearl? The set is quite spoiled.'

Taking out the lace handkerchief, I wrapped the little gold key to the automaton in its folds, then I closed the tin and returned it to the box seat. The theft had been a simple matter; too easy. Tedious. I'd found long ago that the thrill of discovery was almost as important as possession.

I drew the curtains across the window and turned to the bed. Although there was little light in the room, I could see that there was something square and white on the pillow. I went over and took up the sheet of paper. Grace's strange, wild-eyed hare stared back at me. I remembered Old Maggie's complaint.

'Took me an age to find her.'

Now I knew where the girl had been.

7

Snow continued to fall throughout my first week at Fyneshade. Sometimes it came in blizzards that blanked the view from the windows and stained the daylight green; at other times tiny flakes fluttered and danced beyond the glass. When the snow came lightly, the pale landscape sharpened to something resembling an engraving.

It was impossible to leave the house, not even to walk in the courtyards. Mrs Gurney said the snow had settled to the height of Dawson's thigh – he being the groom who had collected me from Croyle. Fires were only lit in the rooms of necessity and curtains were drawn across the tall windows in most of the passages, sending Fyneshade into a permanent dusk.

Days were bounded by the frigid track from my chamber to the parlour and to the schoolroom. Occasionally, during this dreary round, I would encounter one or other of the maids who flitted through the passages like moths. They were all young and silent. Once, I passed an older woman, the laundress I supposed from the pile of folded linen in her hands. She was tall with a large nose and angular jaw. I caught the tang of carbolic and lavender as she stepped aside on the landing to let me pass into the schoolroom corridor.

I did not trouble myself to speak to any of them, not even Jennet, the dunnock with the mole, who served Mrs Gurney in the parlour and who came to my room with hot water each morning.

The only time the whole household gathered together that first week was on Sunday. Mrs Gurney explained that the nearest church was too distant for regular attendance, but that instead, the diocese had given permission for informal worship to be held in Fyneshade's ancient chapel.

The service, the first of many similar occasions, was a short perfunctory affair and the chapel, a vaulted chamber jutting from the east wing, had no pews or chairs. We stood close together in that plain musty space listening to Mrs Gurney read aloud from the Bible, her breath quite visible above the large pages open on the lectern before her. As she droned feeble platitudes, stammering over the more difficult words, I studied the memorial tablets on the walls and the carved marble figures piously reclining in niches beside the altar.

On the right, a veiled woman holding a child in her arms knelt before a large urn from the top of which crisp little flames sprouted like ferns. The name 'Sophia' was inscribed in bold letters across the urn and there was something else below – a line of Latin cut into the veined stone. Sir William's deceased wife had been given pride of place. I thought of the Van Meerans hiding their dead in a musty crypt and, quite suddenly, I thought of Nathaniel, of his hands and his tongue. I forced the thought of him away.

Head bowed, I covertly examined my dreary companions. To the right, Old Maggie held Grace's hand. My pupil fidgeted and stared open-mouthed at the eagle lectern behind which Mrs Gurney mangled the words of the Lord. To my right, Jennet and several other maids stared at their polished brown boots. There was not one among them I might consider an equal. Not that it mattered. I was not here to make friends with servants.

Soon, I came to prefer the time I spent alone with Grace. Mrs Gurney's prattle was as numbing as the snow. I'd made a mistake in telling her about Grandmere. The woman's attempts to wheedle more from me about my French blood were at best an irritation and at worst an insult. I guarded my tongue and reflected that there were likely two of us with secrets. It was best, I decided, to wait and see if Mrs Gurney betrayed herself about the terms of my engagement. Information was always useful.

Grace demanded nothing more from me than pencils, paper and the occasional word of praise. Once, when my legs ached for lack of use, we ventured up the tower stairs to the long panelled gallery that stretched the entire width of the house beneath the south-facing battlements. While I strode up and down, arms wrapped around me against the cold, Grace sat placidly on a broad windowsill drawing circles on the glass misted by her breath.

In the main, we were confined to the schoolroom. The fire gave out a fair heat if I sat close beside it and the books I had discovered on the lowest shelf in the shadows of the library filled the hours. Sir William's hidden collection revealed him as a man of singular tastes.

I took care. A large Bible was always at my feet when I read by the hearth so that I could hide my guilty pleasure in the excesses of the Old Testament. I sat with my back to the nursery door. If someone entered the room, it was the matter of a moment to slip one of these slim black volumes between the pages of Leviticus.

Today I did not trouble to guard my reading. The book had been printed in France and I was certain that no one apart from me would understand the words on the pages. The illustrations, however, were more incriminating. I looked up and stared into the flames. The orange glow reminded me of Nathaniel's hair. I twisted the cheap ring on my smallest finger. The little ruby caught the fire.

Perhaps it was Juliette's adventures that brought him to mind now. For a moment I allowed myself to imagine his hands on my flesh, the sharpness of his teeth on my lips and elsewhere, the drip of hot candle wax on my stomach, the scrape of my naked back against the cold stones of the Van Meeran crypt. The stolen silver coffin plate was a trophy of victory – over Nathaniel, over his family and over the small ways of Croyle.

But now?

I might as well be buried in that crypt alongside generations of Van Meerans.

I snapped the book shut and stood up. Grace turned and put her finger to her lips. Sudden noises seemed to disturb her. She stared at me, pale eyes full of unspoken reproach, but a moment later she returned to her scrawl. The only sound in the room was the crackle of the fire and the scrape of a pencil.

I wanted to scream. I held the book so tightly that my knuckles showed white through the skin. All I had to look forward to each day were a few hours by the fire in the company of my imagination. Surely I was meant for more than this? Fyneshade was not the fortune intended for me. It was a living death.

My throat tightened beneath the high-buttoned collar trimmed with beads of jet. I pulled to loosen the constriction and tiny beads scattered to the boards but it did no good. My lungs were stone beneath the bodice of my dress.

I ran to the window and threw open the casement. Snatched by the wind, it flew from my hand and battered against the wall. One of the diagonal panes cracked, a thin line zig-zagged across the glass, but it held its place in the metal frame.

I leaned out and gulped the frozen air. Snowflakes melted on my tongue and caught in my eyelashes. Hair came loose from the twist at the nape of my neck and whipped around my face. It was thrillingly cold. In a moment the skin of my cheeks burned and the bones beneath ached. Arching my neck, I allowed the chill to circle the skin of my throat like a pair of hands. Like Nathaniel's hands. Oh, we had played such dangerous games. He would never find another like me in Croyle, or in the genteel airless houses of the families where Agatha hoped to find a docile brood mare to ensure the Van Meeran bloodline.

But Nathaniel Van Meeran had not been a gentleman and I was certainly not a lady. Not one his mother approved of, at least.

I rested the book on the sill and breathed more steadily. Grey, fat-bellied clouds rolled overhead, but there was a glint of palest gold on the edge of the crags to the south. I looked down at the courtyard expecting to see the same oval of virginal white. Now there were tracks in the snow below. Two sets of footprints crossed the courtyard – one led from the gateway to the steps and one, perhaps made by the same person, retraced the way back.

I felt a small hand slip into mine. Abandoning her drawing, Grace had come to stand next to me at the open window. She dipped a finger into the puddle left by snowflakes that had melted on the sill and put it in her mouth.

'Cold.' She sucked the finger and smiled up at me. Then she repeated the word. 'Cold.'

The child loosened her hand and wrapped her arms around her stocky body. She was wearing a white cotton smock over a blue woollen dress. If she were to take a chill, these bearable hours in the schoolroom would be lost to me. I reached for the casement latch and closed the window.

'Come.' I led her back to the hearth. I knelt, held my hands to the flames and encouraged her to copy my action. She sank into a lumpen heap on the rug next to me and drew a circle with her fingertip in the ash fallen on the tiles. I shut my eyes as the warmth tingled through my body.

Five minutes later, Old Maggie found us seated companionably side by side when she came to take Grace to her midday meal in the nursery. The old woman's face, usually so solemn and grim, softened as she stood in the doorway. What a charming picture we must have made.

Old Maggie called Grace's name and held out a hand. At first the girl didn't move, but then she hauled herself to her feet and went to the door. There were smuts from the hearth on the hem of her smock now.

I rose and followed them into the dim passage, bracing myself for another hour in the company of Mrs Gurney's ill-fitting teeth. Halfway down the corridor I remembered the book on the sill. Although the words were French, the illustrations were perfectly comprehensible. What if it were to be found by one of the maids or even, by some ill chance, Old Maggie when she delivered Grace back into my care?

I returned to the schoolroom. Snatching up the book, I searched for somewhere to conceal it. A narrow cupboard in the wall beside the chimney breast offered a likely place. The door hadn't been opened for a long time. I pulled hard and as it came free dust pattered from the lip of a shelf onto my black skirt. I was glad to see the space was already filled with withered educational volumes. I pushed the plain black novel into a pile of Latin primers and stepped back.

Bending to brush my skirt, I noticed what Grace had been drawing in the ash on the hearth. In a few bold lines she had caught the hunched shoulders and curved beak of a hawk. It stared up at me from the tiles, black eyes worked with the tip of the child's finger. Just for a moment I felt that the creature *knew* me, that it was looking, not so much at, as *into* me. And I too felt a shudder of recognition, a connection to the bird that plucked at something deep within.

I gasped and put my hand to my breast, where a sudden sharp pain bloomed. Then, just as soon as it had come, the stabbing sensation disappeared. I frowned and ran my fingertips over the smooth seams of my bodice, pressing to see if a pin left in the material by the careless Croyle seamstress had worked loose. I felt nothing.

Before I left the schoolroom, I rubbed away the bird in the ash with the toe of my shoe.

As I neared the landing at the top of the stairs, I heard Mrs Gurney's voice from below.

'The roads to the south are clearing. Paskin's lad from The Angel brought word this morning. Took him four hours to walk here, mind. I sent him away with half a cheese for his trouble.'

I paused behind the curtain at the entrance to the passage and thought about the tracks in the courtyard.

'Everything is to be ready,' Mrs Gurney continued in a lower voice. At the same moment the longcase clock on the landing began to chime. I strained to hear.

'Same as usual. He'll take her on, that's what he said. He'll be here by Wed—'

Lancer's bark stopped her. I heard the scramble of the dog's feet and the ticking of claws on the wooden stairs. The yelping came again, close by.

'Who's there?' Mrs Gurney called loudly. Betrayed by the dog, I could not remain hidden. I stepped through the curtain.

'Grace has just gone up to the nursery with Old Maggie.' I started to make my way down. Lancer followed, herding me as if the beast were bred to be a sheepdog.

Mrs Gurney was in the hall below with Dawson. The groom was swathed in a thick dark coat that reached his ankles. Snow crusted his boots. It was the first time I had seen him in the house. His domain was the rambling stable block visible from my room. He stepped quickly back from the tiled hall to stand beneath the arched porch just inside the doorway. He nodded at me and moved his wide-brimmed hat from hand to hand.

'Well, that's settled then.' Mrs Gurney's remark was addressed to Dawson, who shrank even further into the shadow of the porch.

He glanced at me again. The hat moved back and forth. 'I'll be certain to ... to ...'

Mrs Gurney raised a hand to silence him. Her eyes locked on mine. I knew she was trying to divine whether or not I'd been eavesdropping. She pursed her lips and seemed to be on the point of asking outright. Instead, she turned to the groom.

'That will be all. You'll see to it, won't you?'

'Aye.' Dawson nodded, flattened his hat to his head and reached for the iron ring at his back. A flurry of snow skipped across the threshold into the hall as he opened the door wide. The cold came with it.

'Wednesday, then,' Mrs Gurney called after him as he trudged out onto the steps.

'Aye.' He didn't look back as he closed the door behind him.

The housekeeper rubbed her hands. The lace lappets at the sides of her cap flapped like the ears of a spaniel. She slid a glance at me and adjusted the shawl round her shoulders.

'Dawson's going into Tideswell for me this week. The weather's changing at last. We should be glad of it, Marta.'

'It is coming from the south.' I smiled, knowing it would throw her into a muddle to think I had overheard.

Mrs Gurney's eyes widened, but I continued smoothly, 'The schoolroom faces south. The air over the hills seems clearer.'

'Ah.' She looked away but not before I'd seen relief soften her flat face. She nodded, her jowls quivering with the lace. 'Just today I wrote out the order. The boy came on foot, but soon we can send Dawson out with the cart. Haven't been able to do that for days. Not since you came.'

The housekeeper turned sharply from me and headed down the passage to the parlour stairs. Lancer plodded after her, eager for a scrap from the kitchens. I followed.

'I saw the tracks in the courtyard from the schoolroom window.' I spoke to her back. 'That must have been your messenger.' I measured my words, wondering if she would offer more. She didn't. She paused halfway and ushered me before her down the narrow stairs to her quarters.

'You really should eat more, Marta. You're nothing but skin and bone.'

The smell of stewed lamb oozed from the crack beneath the parlour door, fugging the little space with the sour miasma of wool fat. Today it did not revolt me for I knew without a shadow of doubt that on Wednesday Sir William Pritchard was coming home to Fyneshade.

8

'You'll take a little cake tonight.'

Mrs Gurney went to a cupboard beside the parlour door. She produced a dark cake on a large china dish and set it on the table between us.

'Dawson brought back some dried fruits yesterday.' She cut a thick slice and eased it onto a saucer. I stared at the cake's glistening interior studded with dark currants and fat sultanas and my mouth watered. I had a fondness for sweet things. Mrs Gurney slid the saucer towards me.

'Won't you take it, Marta? We haven't had the like of this since the night you arrived. I've watched you at table and I reckon you're the sort who prefers dainties.'

'There's cheese too.' She pushed another dish at me. 'If our ways are to your taste.'

It was true that I had barely touched the bowl of stringy meat and gravy set before me earlier that evening. All day I'd been waiting for the sound of Sir William's coach in the court-yard beneath the schoolroom window and all day the hours had passed much like any other at Fyneshade.

I was wound tight as a cat ready to pounce. When I had lin-gered behind the curtain at the top of the staircase Mrs Gurney and Dawson had been discussing arrangements for the arrival of the master. She had even mentioned me. Surely I had heard correctly? There could be no other explanation for:

'He'll take her on, that's what he said.'

If Sir William Pritchard was now aware that his daughter had a governess, there was no reason for any further delay in my introduction, other than the fact that it was now late on Wednesday and he had not come home.

As I looked at the cake, my stomach mewed like a kitten.

Mrs Gurney grinned. 'There's my answer. Eat up, lass.'

I broke off a tiny corner and put it in my mouth. It was good; the sweetness – laced with spice – dissolved on my tongue. I crumbled off a little more, eating the fragments slowly and carefully.

'That's more like it.' Mrs Gurney winked at me across the table. 'I've discovered your weakness.' She leaned forward. 'Tell me, how goes it with Grace? She's taken to you, according to Maggie. That's good.'

'She is . . .' I searched for the right answer, '. . . most amiable.'

I looked directly at the housekeeper's face, but she was staring intently at my saucer. Without raising her eyes, she continued, 'I thought you might be able to . . . well, that's to say . . .' She shook her head, stood and went to the hearth where the teapot was warming. While her back was turned, I tore the cake into two and held out the larger part beneath the table. In a moment I felt

Lancer's nose press into my hand. The titbit was licked away in a second.

'These are early days,' Mrs Gurney went on. 'As I told you, she's never had lessons before.' It came to me that the woman's expectations were higher than I had imagined. I addressed her back as she busied herself with the tea.

'I fear that I will never be able to teach her to speak French, if that is what you wish. Grace finds speaking in English difficult enough.'

Mrs Gurney turned from the hearth, her large eyes full of sorrow. 'She is a good child. We had ... *have* such hopes for her. Surely the company of a young woman such as yourself must be beneficial. Perhaps it will take time?'

It would take a miracle, I thought, to make Grace Pritchard anything more than herself, but I knew that was not what Mrs Gurney wanted to hear, especially if she was to justify my appointment to her master. Indeed, when the time came, it was important that she made my case. I needed to give her the affirmation she clearly sought.

'I cannot promise I will make a lady of her.' I spoke gently. 'I think you already understand that, Mrs Gurney. She is, as you say, a dear, sweet girl and I believe the hours we spend together are ... worthwhile. Her drawing shows great promise and that is something I encourage. I would go as far as to say she has a talent any young lady of quality would envy.'

'There now!' A wide smile spread across the housekeeper's face. She came back to the table with the brown glazed teapot and set about filling the cups.

'Isn't that something? Miss Grace an artist.'

I nodded and took up a little more cake. 'I'm sure that Sir

William will be interested to learn of her gift. Perhaps we can show him some of her work?'

The flow of tea from the pot in Mrs Gurney's hand quivered for a moment.

I tried again, testing my suspicion of a homecoming. It was as good a time as any to play my hand.

'I have collected all her drawings together in a binder I took from the library. Earlier this week I heard you discussing Mr Pritchard's return with Dawson. Would tomorrow be convenient for a presentation?'

She finished filling her own cup and leaned over the table to attend to mine. In the flickering light of the candles set on brass sticks at the centre of the table, her shadow billowed on the parlour wall.

'I'm afraid it would not be convenient.' She shook her head as she sat down again. 'No. It would not.' Taking up a bone-handled knife, she carved a slice from the cheese.

'But when . . .?' I tried again, but a look of startling ferocity from Mrs Gurney stopped me. The subject was closed.

We sat in silence broken only by Lancer's grunts – the dog was now slumped in front of the fire – and the moist clacking sound of Mrs Gurney's assault on the cheese.

I took the last morsel of the remaining cake between my fingers. It had an aromatic, almost bitter flavour I couldn't quite place.

'You've eaten it all.' Her eyes scanned the last few crumbs on the saucer. 'Good, very good, Marta.'

I awoke with a start. The curtains were not drawn and starlight spilled across the boards.

I was marrow-cold and lying on my bed still in my dress and boots. Both the fire and the candle on the bedside table had burned out. I sat up, but instantly my head spun. A dull, thumping pain muffled my thoughts and a clammy chill gripped the base of my spine before clawing its way to my throat.

I rolled from the bed. Kneeling on the boards, I reached for the chamber pot and voided the contents of my stomach. I swiped at my mouth and retched again, but nothing came. Taking a deep breath, I pushed my hair from my face and stood up, steadying myself against a bed post.

Gradually the lurching of my stomach ceased, although the thudding in my head continued. I looked at the candle stub beside the bed. The last thing I remembered was lighting it in the parlour and going to the stairs.

I ran a hand over my forehead. I was cool, not feverish; my skin was a little damp to the touch but the nausea had passed. My back was stiff and my feet ached with the cold. As I bent to unlace my boots, the hammering in my head came again.

Once, Nathaniel and I had shared a whole bottle of Reverend Van Meeran's finest port in the burned-out ruins of the old farmhouse on the western edge of Croyle. The house had an eerie reputation and people feared it. Nathaniel and I met there often. The port was rich and sweet, but next day I was sick and my head was cleft in two.

I thought about that ringing pain as I changed quickly into my nightshift and burrowed beneath the chilly sheets and blankets of my bed. I had not taken port this evening. Or on any evening since I had come to Fyneshade. Alcohol was rarely served in Mrs Gurney's parlour and then it was watered. And yet . . .

Suddenly my stomach clenched and my mouth flooded with bile that left the taste of spice and something more. A sour, faintly medicinal tang coated my tongue. I sat up again as I recognised the taste. Grandmere had used an elixir when the people she tended were chained to their bodies by pain. It was a last kindness to help them slip the shackles of disease. Near the end, in lesser quantities, I knew she used it herself.

Wrapping a blanket around me, I went to the window. The Bone Moon of February had not coincided with my courses, but I was hopeful that soon I would be blessed. I looked at the waxing, near perfect moon rising above the ridge and whispered a greeting. Her light was strong and cold in the clear star-pocked sky.

I knelt to open the seat. Grandmere's spice box was tucked into the folds of my red silk petticoat. I took out the box and sat with my back to the glass. Long, narrow and made of dark wood inlaid with ivory figures, the box had belonged to generations of women in my family. Often, I could sense them when I touched it. Tonight, distant voices scuttled through my head like withered leaves as I slipped the metal clasp to open the lid. Carefully I lifted out the first layer; beneath it were several blue glass phials labelled in Grandmere's neat script. I took the one I wanted and eased the stopper free. A pungent scent filled my nose. Deep and bitter, opium was like fresh-stripped willow bark dipped in incense. It was the taste that lingered in my mouth.

I turned the phial between my fingers and thought about the way Mrs Gurney had urged me to eat. The way she had watched the crumbs on my saucer was like a miser counting gold. And I remembered that all the while she had not taken a slice of cake for herself. The only thing she had eaten after the greasy stew was a hunk of cheese. She did not know I had given more than half of my drug-laced portion away.

Opium was dangerous in unskilled hands. I wondered how it might affect a dog. Lancer was probably still twitching and dreaming in front of the hearth in the parlour. If the creature was even alive.

I put the stopper back and returned the phial to the box.

My aching head was full of questions, but one thing was plain: Mrs Gurney had intended me to sleep soundly this night. There could be only one possible reason: the master had returned while I lay senseless on my bed.

Then why had she drugged me? Why go to such trouble to hide his arrival? Especially as it seemed that he had agreed to my employment.

The window was cold at my back. Shivering, I pulled the blanket around me and scanned the corners of the room for an answer that did not present itself. My head was heavy and dull. Tomorrow I would ask myself these questions again.

I stood, opened the seat and tucked Grandmere's spice box beneath my linens. Eerie brilliance spilled across the snow-covered yard below my window. It was as if the world had been dipped in milk. Grandmere said it was bad luck to look at a new moon through glass, but tonight she was almost full. Besides, the superstition was for women who carried.

As I watched, a low dark shadow stole along the edge of the furthest wall and disappeared beneath the stone archway leading to the stables. Cats were not to be admitted to the house. Their presence was suffered in the outbuildings to combat the nuisance of mice. Mrs Gurney had told me several times that she did not like them.

'Such nasty, evil things. And the way they look at a person!'

The woman was ridiculous, but tonight she had outwitted me. When my head was clear I would have to consider this with care. I reached out to close the curtains, but as I caught hold of the tasselled edge a rumbling sound came from below.

A carriage rolled into the yard. Moonlight gleamed on the polished square of its roof and on the backs of the greys that drew it as it circled the oval yard and passed beneath the archway leading to the stables.

I pressed my hands on the window and my breath misted the pane. This was the sound I was not intended to hear. The sight I was not supposed to see. He was here. Sir William had come home!

Drawing the blanket around me, I darted to the door and hurried along the deserted passage to the landing above the hall. I hid myself behind the same curtain from which I had overheard the conversation between Mrs Gurney and Dawson and waited.

I expected voices – words of welcome, orders, the clatter of servants' footsteps, the thump of baggage dragged across the threshold. Apart from the ticking of clocks, the house was silent.

I listened for such a long time that when, confused, I finally went back to my room, I could hardly walk for the blood frozen in the veins of my bare, numb feet.

9

Mrs Gurney did not breakfast with me in the parlour the next morning. Jennet said she had taken a chill and was resting. I suspected that she was avoiding my company and my questions.

Her absence was useful. I left the table and went around the house searching for any signs of my employer's return. I went to every corridor leading from the first and second landings, to the library, to the drawing room overlooking the river and up to the long gallery. I even went to the stone archway leading to the shuttered north wing. The great carved door was still chained and bolted.

Nothing had changed. Fyneshade was exactly as it had been every day since my arrival. There were no trunks left out in corridors to be hauled to attic storerooms. I did not meet the laundress carrying cloth-bound bundles to the wash. Fires were not lit or even set ready in salons, and if Sir William had a valet or personal man, his discretion was admirable.

The only slight difference I found was that the flowers in the corridor where the painting of Grace's mother hung had been replaced. I had noted that this was the only part of the house where such extravagance was allowed. Given the fact that Mrs Gurney seemed to revere Sophia Pritchard as a sort of saint, it was, I supposed, to be expected that her portrait was a shrine. I wondered if there might be a hot house in the grounds dedicated to the production of mourning blooms.

I paused in front of this insipid icon during my discreet investigations. The infant Grace nestled on the young woman's lap was vivacious and lively. I thought once again that it was odd to paint a dead woman and her damaged child in such a fanciful manner.

That morning in the schoolroom I studied Grace as she scrawled, all the while breathing heavily through her mouth. Apart from her flaxen hair and the blue of her eyes I could detect no resemblance between my pupil and the pretty child in the portrait.

When Old Maggie came to collect Grace from the schoolroom at midday, I asked if I might take the girl for a walk in the grounds. I pointed at the schoolroom window. The sky was enamelled blue and sunlight sparkled off the snow that still lay thick on the roofs and turrets.

'It would be good for us both to go out this afternoon. Fresh air and exercise would be beneficial after so many days inside,' I ventured, adding, 'Not far, I promise. And I might set Grace some drawing lessons from life.'

I saw immediately that Old Maggie liked that. She smiled and nodded, casting a look of dog-like devotion towards the girl, who scribbled at the desk. It proved to me that my encouraging comments regarding my pupil's artistic abilities had already been discussed.

As for herself, Mrs Gurney had no say in the matter. At noon she was still absent from the parlour – I ate my thin brown soup alone – and there was no sign of her when Old Maggie brought Grace back to the schoolroom at one o'clock prompt, buttoned to the nose in a good woollen coat, her large hands encased in knitted mittens.

We walked down the great staircase hand in hand and crossed the hall to the main doorway. I was bitterly aware that my black cloak was worn at the hem, but I possessed no other. Had it not been so cold, I would have draped a shawl around my shoulders and worn three cotton petticoats under my dress instead. From a distance, I hoped my cloak would not appear to be shabby.

As I opened the door, Lancer joined us. I was surprised. I had looked for the dog earlier and called its name, but when it failed to answer my summons it occurred to me that it might have curled up in a corner to die. Now, Lancer's head was low and the tip of its tail brushed the tiles. The creature whimpered as it pressed its nose into one of Grace's paddle-like hands.

'Come with.' Grace tugged at my sleeve and giggled as Lancer padded unsteadily out onto the steps, long legs splayed like a foal's. The dog gaped wide and its flanks moved quickly as it guzzled fresh air. Today I had some sympathy for the animal. Its sorry condition confirmed my suspicions.

I nodded and pulled up my hood. 'Yes, Lancer can come with us.'

Indeed, it was perfect that the dog should accompany us. What could be more natural or more pleasing than the sight of the governess out walking with her pupil and that child's beloved pet?

We went down the steps together and met the tracks left in the snow of the courtyard by Paskin's messenger boy. The air was flint sharp. When I breathed, my nose stung and my lungs ached. I caught Grace's hand and we crunched towards the archway leading beneath the west wing of the house and out into the stable yard under my window. My intention was to confirm the existence of the carriage and the greys. After finding no evidence of Sir William's arrival this morning, I was beginning to doubt myself. Opium dreams brought strange visions.

The dog paused to relieve itself against the dripping wall. A cloud of steam rose from the yellow puddle in the snow. Above the acrid scent, I detected the faintest lace of the drug that had affected us both.

I pulled Grace across the yard towards the second archway leading out to the stable block. Lancer trotted quietly ahead, turning occasionally for reassurance that we were still there. The dog seemed to have recovered a little from its ordeal. Its half-mast tail was wagging again and its nose scented the air. The animal's breath billowed around it like a little cloud.

Halfway across I looked up to confirm that it was possible to have seen the carriage last night. I shielded my eyes against the brilliant sunlight glancing off hundreds of diamond-shaped panes. The wide-set mullions of my window gave a perfect vista of the stable yard.

Two crows circled overhead. I watched their shadows swoop over the oval of pristine snow and I realised something was missing. Where there should have been carriage tracks, the yard was white and fresh as a laundered sheet except for a single track of steps heading towards the stable arch. I hesitated, let go of Grace's hand and turned to look back. These tracks and the fresh marks we had left were the only signs of disturbance.

I rubbed my gloved hands together and searched the snow for signs of deception.

At a rusted metallic clanging, Lancer barked. Footsteps crunched behind me. I twisted about to see the tall, hard-faced laundress setting a key to a heavy lock in a gate drawn across the archway leading to the stables.

I stepped forward. 'Good afternoon.' My breath rose in front of my face.

The woman turned from the gate, picked up the cloth bundle at her feet and nodded as she passed by. I called after her.

'Wait. What is your name?'

'Eavis.' She didn't look back as she trudged on through the archway leading to the main courtyard. 'Mrs Eavis to you.'

While Grace and Lancer played in the snow, I went to the stable gateway. I tried the lock and pushed uselessly at the ornate metalwork that now barred my way. Stepping to the right, I craned to catch a glimpse of the stable block beyond the stone arch, but the brick wall curved, revealing nothing but a narrow slit of light a dozen yards ahead.

I bit my lip and span around. 'Grace! Come here. Now.' I spoke sharply. The girl shook her head and backed away. She rubbed her mittened hands together beneath her chin and stared at me. I forced a smile and a softer tone.

'Shall we go to the gardens, with Lancer?'

I held out my hand and after a moment she plodded to my

side. We retraced our way and crossed the main courtyard to the wide steps leading back into the house. If it was possible to reach the river on the eastern side there might be another way to the stable block by following the bank along the outer walls.

I dragged Grace across the hallway and down the pantry stairs used by the servants. Lancer trotted after us.

In the low dingy kitchen, two scullery maids, hands and forearms raw from pan-scouring, stopped their chatter and watched in silence as we made our way to a stone archway beyond the range. A purple stain bloomed across the forehead of the smaller girl. It ran down across her left eyelid and fell from her cheek to her chin like a trail of dripped paint. Her fair companion was even-featured, but a twist in her spine raised her right shoulder to the level of her ear.

I felt their eyes on me as we passed into an echoing passage that would have been the domain of the butler if Fyneshade were not a convent.

A door at the end led out across a small cobbled yard and hopefully, if my sense of direction was true, to formal gardens. My interest lay beyond the frosted ornamental beds and clipped trees. There was a gate at the far end of the topiary avenue; I had seen it from the library window.

❦

Grace and Lancer chased each other through the snow. The dog yelped and ran in circles around the large trees planted at the corners of the terraced lawn and the girl laughed and tried to catch its tail. Despite the garden's evident neglect, years of pruning had forced the snow-capped evergreens into the shape of cones, each one tapered from a broad base to a point. The girl and dog were happy playing an inexhaustible version of hide and seek. I left them and went to the gate in the wall furthest from the house. Through the bars, I saw the ice-stilled river, mirror-flat and fringed with frozen osiers.

The gate creaked as I pushed it open. I glanced back at Grace, who was kneeling to catch her breath. Her round face, usually so pale, was pink and alive with pleasure. She waved at me and then she stumbled to her feet and skidded after the dog, who was now loping up and down the snow-crusted gravel walkways between the lawns and rose beds.

The pair of them would be happy without me for a few minutes. I looked up at the house. Curtains had been drawn across the windows of the library and the drawing room was shuttered. No one was watching.

Stepping through the gate, I followed a barely visible path down to the river. As I had hoped, there was a walkway following the course of the water, but it was treacherous and in places overgrown. I went carefully, steadying myself against the trunks of willows whose bare drooping branches were held fast in the ice. When I had gone a fair distance, I paused to confirm my direction. I was standing in the lee of the north wing now, the oldest section of Fyneshade.

Yellow-tinged sunlight fell across the jagged battlements, giving it the look of a row of rotten teeth. Blank windows stared back at me and a ruined tower, circled by crows, marked the end of the range. If I was able to continue along the river's edge, the path would bring me around the crumbling north wing and to the rear of the stable block. I pushed back the hood of my cloak for a better view of the way.

'You there!'

I turned. A man stood on the opposite bank. Visible through a gap in the osiers, he wore a long grey coat and a tall hat to match. He held out an arm as if to point at me and I saw a leather glove that almost reached to his shoulder. I was too far away to see the man's features plainly, but I had the impression of pallor, dark brows and a pointed chin.

'Who the devil are you?' His voice was clipped and hard.

My hair was flying loose around my head. I raised a hand to push it back and stared boldly at the man across the water. From his clothing, bearing and the tone of his voice, I knew he was gentry, but he wasn't old. This couldn't be Sir William. Puzzled, I went to the river's edge.

'I might ask the same question. I have every right to be here. Do you?'

I thought I heard a snort of laughter before the reply came.

'More right than any other man.' He turned from me and his coat flew out around him.

'Dido!' he called loudly. I heard a long, low whistle and then the papery beat of huge wings as something flew very close over my head. The man raised his gauntleted arm and a great grey hawk, talons extended, swooped to grip the leather at his wrist. The bird's outstretched wings flapped wide and it arched its neck to call just once before it settled.

'Good girl.' The man seemed to offer something. Dido – for that was, I assumed, the creature's name – lowered her head and tore at his leather-clad fist.

He bound the bird's trailing ties to his wrist and turned to face me again. I saw the hawk's white breast banded with black and the powerful grey wings folded to its sides. The vivid yellow of its talons and around its eyes and beak was the only colour in the day. It watched me and I thought of the drawing Grace had scribbled in the ash.

The man stared at me too.

'She is a beauty.' He raised his arm a little and the bird spread her wings and stamped on the leather. 'Dido is a champion. There is not another in the north to match her.'

He moved through the rushes to stand closer to the river edge and his long shadow fell across the ice. Now he was closer I could see the angles of his face framed by the brim of the hat and upturned collar of his coat. The man was of an age with me, perhaps a little older. His face was too jagged and creased to be called handsome in the milk-soft way admired by the Croyle dairymaids. As I looked at him, I felt a faint but familiar tug deep in my belly.

I raised my chin. 'You did not answer my question, sir.'

He smiled. 'Neither did you. No matter. I was told that Grace had a new governess, but if that's who you are then you're not what I expected. Not at all.' The lazy tone of his voice suggested that he alone was privy to a great jest.

He continued, 'Where is she? I imagine my sister is very poor company for you, madam. Have they let you out?'

'Sister?' I blurted out the word in amazement.

The man made a little bow. 'I am Vaughan Pritchard, heir to Fyneshade. Grace is many years younger than me and she is a murderer.' He smiled at my confusion. 'That is to say, her arrival led to the death of our mother.

'Now, you will excuse me, Marta? That *is* your name, I believe?'

I nodded, too surprised to think of a clever answer.

He started to walk swiftly away along the opposite bank,

the hawk hunched on the crook of his arm. As he moved, I felt myself drawn in his wake.

'Wait!' I kept pace with him on my own side. 'Will you be dining this evening?'

'I am leaving early tomorrow with Dido. We are travelling on to Carlisle.'

I did not know what to make of his drawling answer. I tried again. 'You came late last night in the carriage, is that not so?'

He stopped and turned to me.

'Were you watching, governess?' He smiled. Beneath those dark brows, his eyes were a very pale shade of blue. The distance between us seemed to narrow.

I nodded. 'Yes ... no, I mean. I heard the carriage from my room, but you did not ...'

I could not admit that I had gone out to listen on the landing.

The hawk watched me as closely as her master. 'I did not *what* precisely, Miss Marta?'

'I did not hear you welcomed into the house. It was late, but no one went to greet you or tend to your things.'

'And what does that tell you?' His words were brittle as the ice between us.

I shook my head.

'I thought governesses were clever. Then again ...' He paused and his cool eyes locked with mine. 'I thought they were plain.'

Blood rushed to my cheeks and I pulled up the hood of my cloak to mask the tell-tale flush. From the shadow I threw him a challenge. 'You must decide on my qualities for yourself, sir. As I have already decided on yours.'

'Ma'am.' He tilted his head.

'Tell me,' I continued, emboldened, 'if you are truly Grace's brother, why did you not enter the house and go to your own rooms last night?'

The man's pale face clouded. 'That is a question for my father. Good day, governess.'

His grey coat flew about him as he turned sharply and walked away. I tried to follow, but the path on my side of the river disappeared abruptly into a tangle of willow and bramble.

'Then I will ask,' I called to his back. 'I will ask that very question when Sir William returns to Fyneshade.'

Laughter came back to me on the wind.

IO

Returning to the formal gardens, I was glad to find Grace and Lancer unscathed by my absence. This small relief soon turned to irritation as the pair continued to pursue each other in a frantic game whose rules were only comprehensible to the participants. My pupil's shrieking excitement proved difficult to manage and it was not without pleasure that, a short while later, I returned her to the care of Old Maggie.

The unexpected meeting had given me much to consider and it was for that reason that I went to the passage leading to the library.

I raised my candle to examine the portrait of Sophia Pritchard and thought I understood. The sturdy child wriggling in the young woman's lap was the man I had seen at the riverbank. He had been born when she really was the insipid, peach-skinned beauty captured in oils. The man I had met earlier today must have been almost adult when his mother died. The arrival of

Grace, many years after the execution of this painting, had been too much for the older Sophia to bear.

'Murderer' was an interesting word, but there was an element of truth in it. The birth of Grace Pritchard had killed her mother. *Their* mother.

Vaughan Pritchard's short bitter statement was, in fact, very rich with detail. How must it have been for the pampered only son to be deprived of his mother and his unique position on the very same day? I tried to imagine how he might have felt: the maids clucking over the orphaned baby; a house thrown into mourning while the cries of a newborn echoed in the corridors; a father lost in grief; and at the centre of it all, a furious boy.

I stepped back and looked up at Sophia's mild blue eyes. Her son's eyes were also blue, but where the painted woman's gaze was full of warmth and maternal affection, Vaughan Pritchard's eyes were pale and cold as the ice-stopped river. I remembered that last bark of derision as he strode away and wondered if he also held his father responsible for Sophia's death.

'What are you doing here, Marta?'

Mrs Gurney was breathless. She glanced up at the portrait and then at me. Guilt mingled with suspicion on her face. She need not have worried on my account. I had decided not to test her on the opium. I pointed at the fresh blooms spilling from the basins nearby.

'I came to see the flowers. The scent reached all the way to the stairs.' I smiled blandly. 'Is there a hot house here at Fyneshade?'

Mrs Gurney seemed relieved that I had not asked another question. She nodded.

'Yes, there is indeed, along the south wall beyond the kitchen garden. It was the late mistress's great pleasure.' The woman

almost bobbed a curtsey before the painting. 'But these did not
... that is ... no. No.' She broke off abruptly and looked down
to count through the keys on the chatelaine in her hand. Despite
the cold, I noted a fine sheen of perspiration beneath the lace of
her cap.

'How are you this evening, Mrs Gurney? Jennet told me that
you were unwell.'

Her eyes flicked quickly to mine and then back to the chatelaine. 'I've been better, to speak the truth. If you'll excuse me, it's
winding day. I'll see you in the parlour at seven as usual.'

She rustled past me and began to make her way along the
candlelit passage.

'Wait.'

She turned at my call.

'Is there anything I can do? You do not seem to be fully recovered from your chill.'

'It's not that.' The jet earrings quivered above her starched
collar as she shook her head. 'I've lost Panjan's key and I can't
think where it can be. When Grace came with Old Maggie to
the automatory room an hour back for winding day, it wasn't in
its place. The poor child is in such a state now. I don't think she'll
settle tonight unless I can find it.'

I arranged my features with care. 'But how can that be, Mrs
Gurney? Surely you have the key there.' I pointed to the silver
chatelaine at her belt. 'And I have never seen you without that
pretty thing.'

She shook her head. 'Panjan's key isn't here. It's always been kept
in a special place, although I did wonder if I'd slipped it on here by
mistake when I last started him up ...' she rattled the chatelaine,
'... but it's not here. And I couldn't find a copy in the library.'

This was interesting.

'Do you mean there are copies of all the keys?'

Mrs Gurney stared dismally at the chatelaine. 'Not all of them, just the best of the clocks and most of the house keys. All labelled and written out neat they are, but nothing for Panjan. Years ago – it must have been before he married and bought the monkey – Sir William's father paid a Sheffield watchmaker for them.'

I was glad to hear that a copy did not exist.

'I am sure you will find it. It was late and dark when you took us to Panjan's room. Perhaps you merely misplaced it.'

It occurred to me that it might be unwise to remind her of that visit. I offered her something to take her mind in a new direction.

'Grandmere always said that lost things love to be found. *Les choses perdues aiment être trouvées.*'

She sniffed. 'French, is it?'

I nodded. 'An old proverb. I am sure you will find Panjan's key.'

'Well, I'm not sure of that at all, Marta. The trouble it will bring …' She glanced apologetically at the portrait. 'It's the one thing that we can rely on to calm Grace down when she's taken bad.'

Now we moved closer to my interest.

'Then we must hope the key is found as soon as possible for her sake.' I continued pleasantly: 'Indeed, I wanted to ask you about Grace. We had such an invigorating walk in the gardens this afternoon. With the improvement in the weather after so many days inside, I thought that fresh air would be beneficial.'

Mrs Gurney stared at me. 'I heard you'd gone out. You really should have asked me first.'

Her lips puckered as she realised her mistake. It was difficult to ask permission from a woman in hiding.

I pretended to be unaware of her discomfort. 'I think it was good for Grace. She seemed to enjoy herself.'

Mrs Gurney grudgingly agreed. 'Old Maggie said it was a long time since she'd last seen the child looking so well. It's a pity that this evening changed that.'

The nursemaid was almost mute in my company but she tumbled like a fountain when it came to discussing her charge with the housekeeper.

'I am sorry about the key.' I smiled sympathetically. 'But it is good to hear Old Maggie's report. From now on I will ensure that we take regular walks outside on fine days, for the good of Grace's health. We all have the child's welfare close to our hearts, I think.'

'That we do.' Mrs Gurney's face softened.

'There is something else.' I pounced, confident that she was not expecting my next question. 'I met Grace's brother this afternoon.'

Flustered, she started to gabble. 'You shouldn't... He shouldn't ... It's not ...' Exhausting any further prescriptives, Mrs Gurney gave up and glared at me.

'Where?'

I had practised this part. My face was a mask of innocence as I answered.

'We were walking in the formal gardens. I thought I heard a noise beyond the wall and I went to investigate. I'd gone just a little way along the river path when I heard the sound again. Mr Vaughan Pritchard was across the ice from me, with his hawk. Dido, is it? I think that is her name.'

Defeated, Mrs Gurney stared at the boards. 'He was not to go out. It was agreed.'

'But surely this is his home?' I pressed my advantage. 'I see now that this was the arrival you discussed with Dawson. Why didn't Mr Vaughan come into the house? There were no preparations for his arrival. Indeed, had I not met him by the river I would have no idea of his existence. Yet he knew me. He knew I was Grace's governess.'

'Eavis.' The housekeeper whispered the name to herself and sucked her teeth.

'It was most odd . . .' I started again but the woman held up a hand to stop me.

'No more.'

This was *infuriating*. Raising the candle to flood my face with light so that she might see my distress, I continued, quite certain of the moral altitude from which I spoke.

'I am companion to his sister, Mrs Gurney. It was most humiliating to meet the son of my employer without knowing who he was.'

The candle flames were the only things that moved in the passage.

After a moment Mrs Gurney spoke. 'Well, now you do, Marta.'

She pulled her plain woollen shawl about her shoulders. 'I am going to my room. I don't believe I've shaken off this chill after all.'

The woman set off. After a few steps, she turned, her plump face hollowed out by the glow of the candles. 'Mr Vaughan keeps his damned bird and a room in the stable block. He is not, on the orders of the master, to be admitted to the house.'

Worm Moon

II

The knot of dark blood in the bowl glistened in the moonlight. I licked the tip of my finger and swirled the water around, whispering the words that Grandmere had taught me. I raised the bowl and offered it to the full moon through the glass of my bedroom window.

The Worm Moon of March was named for the life beginning to coil beneath the frosted soil. The last full moon of winter, she marked a boundary between the dead and the living, and she was powerful. This year she had ripened early in the month.

My courses had come that evening. I took it for a sign that the blood coincided with the full moon and that meeting at the river. The time was right.

In accordance with the ritual, I had knelt before the window waiting for the rising, and now the moon hung like a lantern in the clear starry sky. Cold light flooded my room, sharpening angles and deepening shadows. Grandmere said that the moon was envious of her brother the sun, so she stole colour from him.

My limbs were white as bone and my hair flowed black to my waist. An hour back I had loosened the cords of my shift at the neck and allowed it to fall to the boards before stepping naked to the window.

I bowed my head and whispered the greeting again. Closing my eyes, I bent to place the bowl before me on the boards. I brought the tips of my fingers to my forehead and concentrated. The faint, familiar thrum of power began to tremble through my body. My hair crackled and I felt it rise. My lips parted to form the words of supplication.

At the same moment there was a loud bang on the door. The intrusion cut into the ritual like a knife. Gasping with pain, I snatched my white shift from the floor and held it to my breast.

I was certain I'd locked the door, but if someone was to walk into the room and find me, it would be difficult to explain myself.

I turned and watched the handle move. The door shook, but it did not open. Someone outside in the passage beat twice more on the wood. The pounding had such a force that the door juddered in its frame. Then, nothing.

I crept closer. The passage beyond was quiet. Aware of the thumping of my heart, I rested the palm of a hand against the wood and listened. After a minute I heard creaking boards, more footsteps and a woman's voice, urgent but low.

'I found her. She was trying to get to him.'

Scuffling was followed by a muffled yelp from nearby. To be more precise, it came from the direction of the nursery. Mrs Gurney's fears about the consequences of her failure to make Panjan perform had clearly been proved correct. The child had not settled this evening and had escaped the confines of the nursery.

A door slammed. The sudden absolute silence told me that Grace's escapade was over.

I went back to the window and the bowl. My blood had stained the water but there was no message tonight. Grace had broken the ritual. If she had been here in the room with me, I would have slapped her.

I snapped my fingers to break any lingering threads of power – it was ill luck to leave a working unfinished – and bent to take up the bowl, intending to rinse the failure away with water from the jug on the washstand. As I straightened up, I heard the grate of rusted metal and the crunch of wheels on snow. I watched from the window as a small, smart black carriage, slicked silver by moonlight, emerged from the stable-yard archway. It was drawn by a single grey horse that tossed its head as it circled the courtyard.

'I am leaving early tomorrow with Dido. We are travelling on to Carlisle.'

I gripped the bowl as the carriage rolled under the arch leading out to the main courtyard and disappeared. The man I had met by the river was gone.

I would have flung the bloody water at the window had I not looked down.

My question had been answered. The letter P, formed from my own blood and clear as if a lawyer's clerk had written it, floated on a pool of liquid silver.

Grace breathed heavily as she hunched over her drawing. Although the girl showed no outward sign of her nocturnal adventure, the shadows beneath Old Maggie's eyes told another story. The old woman had looked more haggard than usual when she delivered my pupil to the schoolroom after breakfast. Mrs Gurney had been absent from the parlour again this morning. It was not a chill that detained her. I had no doubt about that.

I rested my stockinged feet on the fender and tried to concentrate on the book, but this morning not even the adventures of Juliette could divert me. Every time I read to the end of a paragraph the letter P floated on the page before me.

When I had finally lain beneath the covers of my bed last night I thought about that message and the day on which it had come to me. And I thought about the other message that had come unbidden when I stood across the river from the man with the hawk on his arm. I had learned many years ago what the twist in the depths of my belly meant. Nathaniel had not been the first, although he had been the—

No! I would not allow that thought to take form. Nathaniel Van Meeran was not worthy of my consideration. He was not my destiny. I held the book to my lips, tasting the age of the leather, and stared into the flames, my vision blurred. At first, I was reminded of wild red hair, but I forced myself to see another face where pale blue eyes burned like the heart of the coals.

Why was Vaughan Pritchard banished from his father's house? And why, for that matter, would Mrs Gurney go to such lengths to ensure that I did not know of his existence?

Grace squawked at her desk. I looked over and she waved a sheet of paper at me.

I smiled and nodded. 'Good. Very good.'

Usually this was enough to satisfy her, but this morning she continued to flap the paper like a flag, all the while rocking to and fro. Old Maggie had tied a fat pink ribbon in her hair; the colour matched the girl's large wet lips.

I put a finger to my own lips and made a hushing sound. Grace pouted as I returned my attention to the novel. Moments later she snuffled at my shoulder. A single long grey feather, tipped with black, fell onto the page.

I took it and looked up. 'What is this, Grace?'

'Present.' She wiped the back of her hand over her nose.

I twirled the feather. 'How pretty it is. Did you find it yesterday in the garden?'

She shook her head and fumbled with the sheet of paper clutched to her smock. I saw that the lines of a drawing were scrawled over handwriting. Grace could not, as far as I knew, write a single word, and besides, the paper I had given her this morning had been blank, as usual.

Intrigued, I reached out to take it from her, but she moved away. I watched her flatten the sheet on the desk, patting it like a kitten, before seating herself and going back to work.

'Grace, what do you have there?' I stood. Now she was humming tunelessly as she scribbled.

I went closer and rested a hand on her shoulder. 'Please let me see your drawing.'

She shook her head and bent forward. The pencil shrilled as she worked at the paper. The writing – a firm sloping hand – reached the edge of the sheet. I saw the word 'Marta'.

I tightened my grip a little. 'Grace, you wanted me to see your drawing and now you won't let me.'

'Mine.' She squared her broad shoulders against me. I wound my hand into her thick blonde hair and pulled hard.

'Give it to me!'

Instantly, she stopped scribbling and clapped a hand to the back of her head. She twisted to look up at me, pale eyes full of disbelief and confusion. I seized the paper and moved swiftly away to examine it by the window.

I was distantly aware of Grace sobbing and snuffling as I tried to read the words that were not obscured by heavy black spirals.

----rness Marta

-- --- an unexpected pleasure to ---- your acquaintance -----. I hope my presence at the --ver did not alarm ---
I must thank you for the ---- you have shown to my ------. Grace appears to be ---- of you, although I ------- that it is often difficult to discern the extent of her aff------ and understanding.
She has always ---- - ---- useful and biddable friend to her brother. I ---- ---- you and I should be friends, Ma---. God knows there ---- be little in that cold house to divert a woman ---- ---. It is my ---- that we may become better acq---nted when I return to ----shade.
If --- wish this, --ve my sister the feath-- enclosed with this ---- and she will return it. Grace knows all the ways. In time, I trust she might be persuaded to reveal them to you.

Yours
V------- -ritc----

I read the note three times to be sure I understood. It was intended for me, a message delivered by Grace from her brother. But how had she come to receive it? I stole a glance at the girl, who was still snivelling and rubbing the back of her head. The ribbon had fallen to the floor. I needed to be careful.

'Grace,' I cooed softly. 'I think this letter was meant for me.'

She shook her head and turned away. I watched her reach for a fresh sheet and begin to draw. I scanned the note again. It was an offer and an invitation. I had seen the wolf behind Vaughan Pritchard's cool eyes and I knew him for a hunter. The bond I had felt between us was an affinity. I remembered how he had praised the beautiful hawk on his arm.

There was a new champion in the north now.

I folded the note, tucked it into my pocket and went to Grace's side.

'I am sorry that I spoke sharply.' I took up the ribbon and smoothed her hair. 'I didn't mean to hurt you. Not at all. You are my friend.'

She refused to look at me and concentrated on her drawing; another horse galloped across the page.

I knelt and stroked her head. 'This ribbon is very pretty, isn't it?' I pushed it onto the desk in front of her. 'Grandmere, my grandmother, loved to dress my hair. It is very long, just like yours, when I haven't tied it up, but not such a lovely colour. Your hair is like fairy gold, Grace.' The pencil stopped. I continued to stroke her head, running my hands down over her shoulders, soothing.

'I know, shall I braid your hair? Let me try one of my Grandmere's special plaits. I can make you look so beautiful, Grace.'

I slipped a little bone comb from my pocket and began to run it through the springy hair at her temples. Soon she was sitting back in the chair, swinging her feet and tilting her head to the deft touch of my fingers. For all that she loved her charge, I could not imagine that Old Maggie was so gentle.

'Doesn't that feel good?'

The answer was a deep sigh of satisfaction. Grace raised her hand to mine and rested her fingers on my knuckles as I combed. I hummed a tune, an old French ballad, while I gently freed the knots.

'There, all the tangles are gone and we are ready. Sit up straight now, little one.' My voice was soft as the down at the base of the feather Vaughan Pritchard had sent to me. The feather I needed Grace to return to her brother as my answer.

There were a thousand questions I wanted to ask, but now was not the time. Patience was my sole virtue. I divided her hair into sections and set about plaiting. I purred into her ear, 'We are such friends, you and I, Grace, aren't we?'

She giggled and nodded. I started to bind the ribbon into the thick braid. 'I think you are a good girl to have brought that message to me from your brother.'

Wriggling on her seat, she turned to look at me.

'V.' She sounded the beginning of his name. 'Help.'

I nodded. 'Vaughan asked you to bring me the feather and the little note, didn't he? You have been a very clever and helpful girl.'

Grace sat quite still and then she slid a glance at the door. She raised a finger to her lips. 'Shhhh.'

I had her confidence. Careful not to look at her face, I tied the trailing ends of the ribbon into a bow. 'Yes, that's right. It is a secret. Our secret, the three of us. He wants to be my friend too, just like you.' I sat back and pretended to admire her.

'Look how pretty you are.' I brought my hand to my mouth. 'Oh. You can't see, can you?'

Grace shook her head. I smiled and took her hand. 'Well, come with me.'

I led her to the door. We went out into the empty passage

and along to the stairs. On the landing below, a long gilt-framed mirror stood behind a table bearing a collection of small porcelain figures, little gilded clocks and enamelled boxes. I moved Grace to stand in front of me and rested my hands on her shoulders.

'There we are.' I smiled at her reflection in the glass. She pulled the plait over her shoulder and patted the elaborate pink ribbon. A grin spread from ear to ear.

'Do you like it, dearest?' I asked.

She twirled around and hugged me, burying her face in the folds of my skirt. In the glass my long black arms held her close. I bent to whisper, 'If you take the feather back, just as your brother asked, I will make Panjan play for you again, Grace ... because you are my friend.'

The girl looked up me, her eyes filled with a desperate, hopeful plea.

I raised a finger to my lips. 'Shhhh.'

12

Another day passed before I met Mrs Gurney again. If she had her way, I imagine that a week would not have sufficed. We came upon each other by accident in the library. It was the time I had grown to see as my own – the twilight hours after the daily purgatory of the schoolroom. Since I had made my pact with Grace, she had become cloyingly attentive. This morning my pupil had insisted on sitting at my feet near the hearth, resting her head against my knees.

Without further interrogation I had given her back the feather and simply asked her to return it, and I had promised that very soon Panjan would perform again. The question was how? I could not satisfy my part of our bargain unless I gained the key to the automaton's room, and that was on Mrs Gurney's chatelaine. It would be difficult enough to take that key under usual circumstances, but now that the housekeeper was avoiding me, it was impossible.

I was returning *Juliette* to the low-curtained shelf and flicking through the spines of the books to find a new diversion when the doors opened. Mrs Gurney's shadow advanced into the chilly room, followed by the woman herself.

I moved softly along the wall to the window and pretended to be studying the garden. The day had been fine again and there was a band of gilded violet to the west. Feigning surprise, I turned and stepped into the circle of light cast by the candle in her hand.

'Oh! Mrs Gurney, you startled me.'

Even in the gloom, I saw the blood drain from her cheeks.

'I hope you are recovered.' I smiled.

'Whatever are you doing here at this time, Marta?' Her eyes darted to the door, seeking escape.

'I come here most evenings when Old Maggie takes Grace to the nursery. I like to look out over the gardens to the river and to the hills,' I lied. 'The days are growing longer. I believe I am searching for spring.'

Mrs Gurney swallowed and her candle quivered in the brass chamberstick. 'I thought that perhaps you were here watching for . . .' She faltered, but I knew what she had failed to say.

'Watching for Mr Vaughan over at the river?'

When she didn't answer, I continued smoothly. 'He told me that he was intending to travel on to Carlisle. The day after I met him, I heard his carriage leave early in the morning.' I stepped closer. This was my opportunity to test her.

'From our brief conversation by the river, I now understand that Sir William Pritchard has been absent from Fyneshade for some time.'

No such conversation had taken place – but if Mrs Gurney believed me then she would have to answer. The housekeeper cast another stricken look at the door. How she must have regretted this chance encounter. I reached out to rest a hand on her arm. The woman was shaking.

'Please, Mrs Gurney, if we are to be friends – and I think we must be for the sake of dear Grace – tell me the truth. I have come to think that *you* employed me out of the goodness of your heart. But ...' I paused, '... I also believe that Sir William does not know I am here.'

She stared at the rug and cleared her throat. 'It was for Grace I did it. My sister is in service to the cousin of the woman who recommended you. A foreign name it was. Von ... Von ...'

I frowned. 'Van Meeran?'

'Yes.' She nodded. 'That was it. In her letter she said you ... that you ...' Mrs Gurney looked at me. 'Well, you're not what I expected. Not at all.'

On that point, I was quite certain she was speaking the truth. Agatha Van Meeran would have sworn that the moon was made of cobweb and curd if she thought the lie could part me from her son. No doubt Mrs Gurney had been expecting a plain, pious matron. I considered this not entirely unexpected revelation and patted the housekeeper's arm.

'I hope I have not proved to be a disappointment.'

'No, indeed no. Grace is very fond of you.' Mrs Gurney's jowls wobbled. For a disconcerting moment I thought she might weep. 'It's just that you're not ... It's not s ...' She pursed her lips to hold back whatever it was that she was about to say. After a moment she began again, her voice almost a whisper. 'It's not so wrong, what I did. Any good Christian would do the same by her. And you're right, Marta. Sir William has been away for a long time. It *was* I who employed you.'

She glanced warily at the door. I imagined that she did not wish to be overheard. It was unusual for a servant, even someone as senior as Mrs Gurney, to employ a governess without permission.

I sensed that she needed reassurance and perhaps an ally. 'And you are a good woman to have done so. I am glad to be Grace's help and guide.' I smiled and pounced again. 'But tell me, why is Mr Vaughan barred from the house . . . and from his sister?'

'Because he is a devil.' The words escaped before Mrs Gurney had a chance to stop herself. She brought her fingers to her mouth. She was shaking so much that wax dripped from the candle and onto the back of her thumb. She gave a little cry of pain.

'Now look!'

Gently I took the jittering candle from her hands and placed it on a table nearby. A sudden draught from the loose panes in the old window moved the curtains and extinguished the flame. As we stood in the twilight, a discord of notes strummed from the golden harp in the corner. Doubtless it was the effect of the gust, but Mrs Gurney gasped again. I heard her fumble with the chatelaine and the strike of a Vesta.

She bent to relight the candle with an unsteady hand.

'Do you think the dead come back and watch the living?'

This was not a question I had ever expected to hear from such a plain, practical woman. I watched her light three more candles in a silver stick on the buffet.

'Well, do you?' She turned to face me. The light had restored a little of her usual command. 'Do you believe in ghosts, Marta?'

Now it was my turn to be wary. The question was ridiculous. Of course I believed in ghosts. It was like asking if I trusted the sun to rise and the moon to set. But it was dangerous for me to answer truthfully.

I was not gifted like Grandmere and she had died too soon to complete my education, but when I chose to, I could hear the echoes of long-dead souls. I knew there were many types of ghost. Most were harmless. The ones who had lingered too long when the last breath left their body wandered like shadows. Usually they did not even realise they were dead. Others were so strongly connected to a person or place that they simply refused to leave. Gradually their spirits wore thin as time parted them from the object of their obsession. Some were compelled to play out a grief or tragedy again and again in the theatre of their drama. Their unhappiness was imprinted on stone, wood or dust like a fading illustration in an ancient book.

The worst – and thankfully they were rare – were angry. Their souls were consumed with bitterness and hatred so heavy that it chained them to the earth. The more these dead saw of the living, the more powerful they became, feeding on their own envy.

This was not the answer Mrs Gurney would expect. I knew too much about the dead to satisfy her. It was, nevertheless, an interesting question. I clasped my hands before me and looked down at the rug.

'I do believe such things may be ... possible, but I have never seen a ghost, and I would not wish to.' I allowed my voice to break a little. 'Not even my Grandmere, whom I loved very much.'

My playacting had the required effect.

'Forgive me, Marta. I forgot about your recent loss. I did not wish to cause you pain.' Mrs Gurney rested a hand on mine. 'I was thoughtless.'

Under all that starched cotton and bantam hen bustle, she was a good woman. Her desire to see the best in everyone – except, it would appear, Vaughan Pritchard – was helpful.

I shook my head. 'No, it was I who was at fault. I should not have reminded you.' I looked up. 'I was unprepared for your question. Do *you* believe in ghosts, Mrs Gurney?'

She made to move away but I caught her wrist. 'Please, tell me. Was it the sound of the harp? It seemed to disturb you.'

The housekeeper was silent for a moment. She gazed at the beautiful golden instrument and frowned.

'It belonged to Lady Sophia,' she began. 'She brought it here to Fyneshade on her marriage and played it nearly every day. Such an ear she had, such a delicate touch. You might have thought her an angel. After what happened, I often think—' She broke off. 'No, no. It's just an old woman's imagination.'

When she added nothing more I prompted. 'What *do* you think, Mrs Gurney – is it that Sophia Pritchard haunts Fyneshade?'

The old woman freed her hand and busied herself with the keys on the chatelaine.

What did she mean by '*after what happened*'? I tried again. 'Was it Lady Sophia you spoke of when you asked me about ghosts?'

'Maybe.' The answer was barely audible. 'I must be getting on now, Marta. I came here to look through the spare house keys again, just in case, for the sake of Grace.'

She took up the brass chamberstick, went over to a large mahogany desk and bent awkwardly to the lowest drawer. There was a click and a tray at the bottom of the left-hand side sprang open. I heard the chinking of metal as the housekeeper sorted through a collection of keys.

This accidental meeting was proving to be informative in several ways. 'Devil' was an oddly potent word and I was not prepared to allow the subject of Sophia Pritchard's shade to vanish so easily. Grace was my way back. I formed an acceptably benevolent explanation, intending to lead Mrs Gurney into further revelation.

I waited for a minute while she scraped and tutted over the drawer.

'Ah! I think I see.' I clapped my hands lightly. 'Lady Sophia returns to watch over her daughter. After her sudden and untimely death, the strength of her love, a mother's love, draws her back.'

The housekeeper stopped sorting and shook her head so vigorously that pins fell from the grey hair gathered under her cap. I heard them patter into the tray.

She closed the drawer and put a hand to the small of her back. I heard the dry clicking of her bones as she stood. A clock on the mantelpiece began to chime the hour and soon it was joined by the sound of dozens of clocks throughout the house tinkling tunes and striking six times.

'The key's not there. I'd best be getting on. I'll see you in the parlour later, Marta.'

'But you did not answer me.' I tilted my head. 'I think I have it. Sophia returns to watch over the child she never knew. It is a charming notion.'

Mrs Gurney snorted. Now she stared directly at me.

'It's him she looks out for – her son. There's nothing charming about it.'

The woman's watery eyes locked on mine and I saw her make up her mind. She took a deep breath. 'And you should look out for him too, Marta. Vaughan Pritchard is not ... a gentleman. That's why he will not be permitted to cross the threshold of this house until the day his father dies.'

13

Grace could scarcely contain her excitement. She hopped from foot to foot and rubbed her hands as I fitted the key to the lock. I glanced back along the passage and mimed that we should be silent. She nodded and plucked at the long cotton sleeves of her nightshirt. It was past midnight. Apart from the ticking of her great grandfather's clocks and the settling of ancient timbers, Fyneshade slept.

It was cold in the passage. The frigid air carried the heavy scent of the flowers from the floor below, the aroma laced with beeswax and smoke from the fires permitted in a few of the rooms.

There had been no fire in the library yesterday. After Mrs Gurney left me there, I went to the mahogany desk. At first it was difficult to find the secret tray, for the join was almost invisible. I knelt to run a hand over the lowest drawer and then I felt beneath the edge. To the right, beside a clawed foot, there was a small metal lever. When I pulled, the tray sprang from the desk and all the doors to Fyneshade were opened to me.

The distinctive square-headed key, labelled *Study North-West Corridor* in a neat, cramped hand, had been easy to find. And now it turned easily in the lock to Panjan's room.

I pushed open the door and stood back to allow Grace to go first. I watched her pad barefoot to the monkey. In the dancing light of the candle in my hand, his golden fur seemed to shiver. She stood in front of him and I heard her breathe very deeply, then she turned to me, eyes shining with expectation.

'Now.' It was a demand. Pulling the grey feather from her sleeve, she laid it, like an offering, at Panjan's feet.

'Good. That's right, Grace.' I smiled and closed the door. Using my candle to light two more in brackets on the wall, I spoke softly. 'If I bring Panjan to life, you will return the feather to your brother. It is our promise.'

She nodded and clapped her hands.

It was a simple bargain, made in the schoolroom earlier that day. At first, I was not sure that Grace had understood when I asked her to come to my room once everyone was asleep. I carefully explained my plan several times, but the girl ignored me and concentrated on another drawing – a flock of crows whirled on the paper in front of her. Eventually, believing this to be a futile exercise, I went to the fire and stared into the flames seeking a better plan.

'Dark.' I turned at her voice. Grace rose awkwardly, laid down her pencil and came to my side. Reaching out, she patted my hair and ran a sticky hand over the black coils of the braids curled above my shoulders.

'Pretty.'

Annoyed, repulsed even, I was about to push her away, but she dropped to her knees, curled on the floor at my feet, closed her eyes and pretended to snore, presumably mimicking the sounds made by Old Maggie, who slept soundly in a room connected to the nursery.

'Secret.' She looked up at me, her eyes suddenly – and surprisingly – shrewd, and placed a finger to her lips.

I began to think that my pupil's powers of comprehension were greater than I had suspected.

Now she waited for me to bring the automaton to life. She giggled and reached out to touch the creature's tail.

'No, Grace!' I remembered Mrs Gurney's warning. Presumably the monkey was fragile and the clockwork finely balanced. The child was not delicate. She paused, her hand suspended in mid-air.

'Touch.' She shook her head. The movement reminded me of Lancer shaking the snow from its nose.

'Good girl.' I spoke softly. 'Shall we make him play for you?'

She nodded and clasped her hands together.

Setting down my candle on a small table, I went to the side of the automaton and studied the golden jewel-studded cushion where I had seen Mrs Gurney fit the key. A tiny lock enclosed in a filigree heart was set halfway along beneath a row of glittering red and green jewels.

I fished in the pocket of my wrapper and took out the tiny stolen key. There was a faint gasp from Grace as she recognised it. I concentrated on fitting the key into the lock, twisting gently until I felt the mechanism resist.

'Now!' I whispered and smiled at my pupil. Tinkling metallic notes began to play and the tip of the monkey's tail beat time.

As I stood back to watch the performance, a damp hand crept into mine.

It was an object of extraordinary value. The gems scattered across the cushion were fine enough, but the monkey's huge ruby eyes swimming in discs of mother of pearl were magnificent. Just as before, the jingling music ran faster and then Panjan's mouth opened. The golden ball dropped and followed the grooved channel expertly incised into the gilded cushion. As I watched it roll around the monkey's haunches, I saw that even this ball was studded with brilliant faceted jewels that captured the light from the candles.

The ball disappeared into the hole beneath the twitching tail. The tune grew louder and Panjan brought his paws slowly together to cover his ruby eyes.

'Again.' Grace tugged at my hand.

I looked down at her eager face. 'We are friends you and I, aren't we?'

She nodded.

'Well, in that case, I will allow Panjan to perform for us one more time. But . . .' I knelt so that I could look into her eyes. They were almost black in the dimly lit room, but circling those black pools, I recognised the same odd pale shade of blue that I had seen in her brother. A fleeting resemblance, no more.

I took both her hands in mine. 'You must not tell anyone that you have come here tonight, little one. If Mrs Gurney or Old Maggie, or anyone here at Fyneshade, were to know they would be very angry with you, Grace, and they would not allow you to see Panjan ever again. Do you understand me?'

The girl's eyes widened. She looked at the monkey and then back at me.

'Secret?'

I nodded. 'Yes, this is our secret and if you keep it, we can come here many times to see Panjan, just you and me. I promise. Do you want to see him again now?'

She nodded fiercely and licked her lips. 'Promise.'

I smoothed her hair and smiled. 'And there is another promise, Grace. Will you take the feather to your brother?'

In answer she pulled away and snatched the grey feather from its place of veneration.

'Wall.' She ran the banded tip of the feather back and forth across her palm.

As I turned the key again, I wondered what she meant by that, but it was not the time for questions. Gaining the child's trust was enough, for now. If she delivered the feather to her brother, I would learn more. His message had been admirably, scandalously, clear.

It is my ---- that we may become better acq---nted when I return to ----shade.
If --- wish this, --ve my sister the feath-- enclosed with this ---- and she will return it.

When I allowed myself to dwell upon becoming 'better acquainted' with him – for that was clearly the meaning of the words obscured by his sister's scribble – I thought about the proud hawk tethered to his arm, and imagined myself in her place. I suspected that we would make a good match for each other.

I stood listening to the pretty tune once more and thought about the pale eyes of the man at the river. Until the return of

Vaughan Pritchard's father, as foretold, it would be a pleasure to become *better acquainted*.

I locked Panjan's room and shepherded Grace along the passage. I hoped that Old Maggie was still soundly asleep, but if she had discovered her charge was missing, I had prepared a pretty story about hearing footsteps outside my room and going out to find my pupil at liberty in the house. Given what I knew, it was credible.

At the landing I raised my candle and listened. Our shadows, suddenly black and huge, billowed up ancient, musty tapestries that swayed gently in a draught.

There was a sound from below. The oak stairs creaked at the thump of a heavy tread. I forced Grace behind me and peered over the bannister. A shadow moved on the stairs. Shielding the candle flame, I watched a dark low shape round the landing. Claws scratched on wood. Lancer looked up and wagged its tail. Relieved, I turned to take Grace by the hand once more, but she was gone.

'Grace?' I whispered as loudly as I dared.

I held the candle higher, but there was not a sign of her. I went to the dark entrance of the corridor leading to Panjan's room, thinking that she had gone back to the automaton.

'Grace, come here!' I hissed again, but silence was my answer.

14

I made a frantic and increasingly desperate search of every floor and passage, but I could not discover my pupil. I went to the great locked door of the north wing and tried the chains. I ran down to the library and raised my candle to light the shadows beyond the golden harp. I even went to the chapel where mice scuttled in the dark, but she was nowhere to be found. Grace had disappeared like a fairy child. Finally, frozen and wretched, I returned to my room where I lay awake until dawn, waiting to hear Old Maggie raise the alarm.

When she did not, I splashed my face with water, dressed, pinned my hair and went to breakfast. Ignorance was my best defence, I decided. Before reaching the lower hallway, I had prepared a speech of surprise and concern. As a further surety, I practised an expression of alarm in the long mirror over the great marble mantel in the hallway before going down to the parlour.

I opened the door to find Mrs Gurney already seated at the

table. Sturdy in her striped dress, her broad face framed by the starched lace of her cap, she nodded at me, scraped butter onto her toasted bread, stirred sugar into her tea and complained about the dilatory work of the scullery maids, but she showed no sign of distress at the loss of her beloved child.

And why should she? For, in truth, my pupil had not disappeared at all.

One hour later that morning, Grace Pritchard – neat in a clean white smock and with her flaxen hair brushed and plaited as usual – was delivered by her nursemaid to the schoolroom.

When we were alone together, she sat at her desk, stared at me and placed a finger to her lips.

'Secret.'

She whispered the word and, reaching for a fresh sheet from the stack, began to draw. I wanted to swipe the pencil from her hand and box her ears for the alarm she had caused me, but it would not be profitable. Instead, I knelt at her side and stroked her hair.

'Where did you go last night, little one?'

She concentrated on filling the dark eyes of the dog-like creature forming on the sheet.

'Please tell me. You gave me such a fright.'

The girl stopped scribbling and slid an odd look at me. 'Wall.' She nodded as if the matter was perfectly understood between us and returned to her drawing.

The same word again? I rested one hand on her shoulder and smoothed the springy hair at her forehead.

'What do you mean by that, Grace?'

The answer was a muffled giggle. I felt my temper rise and drew my hand from her shoulder in case I gripped too hard.

'Friends do not keep secrets from one another. I wish you would tell me where you went, my dear.'

Grace ignored me. The pencil squeaked on the paper and her head lolled to one side.

Mastering my anger, I stood and went to the window. The snow was melting now and the courtyard was pocked with pools of grey water. I opened the window and allowed cold air to flood into the room. Perhaps that would sharpen my pupil's dull wits.

'Grace!' I called sharply and at last she stopped scribbling and looked at me.

I smiled. 'If you do not tell me where you went last night, I will not make Panjan perform for you ever again.'

She shook her head and opened her mouth.

I folded my arms. 'I mean it. I will count to five and then you will tell me, otherwise . . .'

I let the threat linger in the frigid air for a moment and then I began.

'One. Two. Three . . .'

Grace's eyes filled with tears.

'Wall.' She said it again and then she repeated the word over and over until it became almost a howl. She began to rock on the chair, gulping the air and pulling at the neck of her smock. The girl's distress was loud and persistent. The peculiarly high note of her wailing carried. If it continued it would certainly bring faithful Old Maggie to the door.

Bridling the bitter words on my tongue, I went to my pupil's side.

'Hush, hush now.' I knelt beside her again and spoke soothingly. 'You know I would never do anything that made you sad.' I leaned closer and whispered into her ear. 'Of course I will take you to Panjan again, dearest.'

The effect of this was instant. Grace stopped keening and turned to me. For a fleeting moment I thought again that I glimpsed something in her eyes, an intelligence I had not expected. It was almost as if someone else was looking out.

'Promise.' Grace rubbed a hand over her wet cheeks.

I nodded. 'Yes. I promise. But in return, will you tell me your secret. Where did you go?'

She took a deep breath and reached for my hand. Her fingers were hot and moist and I smiled with difficulty, hoping to persuade her to confide in me.

'Soon.' She grinned, sat back and looped her feet around the lowest rung of her chair.

'Soon, Miss Marta.' The deep, mocking masculine voice with which she had answered was not her own. I dropped her hand and sprang to my feet.

'What did you say, Grace?'

In answer she put her thumb into her mouth and began to suck loudly. After a moment she returned to her drawing. I stared at her broad, white back and felt a chill whisper at the nape of my neck where the hair was drawn up into a coil.

I went to the window and pulled it shut, all the while hearing Vaughan Pritchard's voice on his sister's lips. Surely I was mistaken? I fitted the metal hook into its ring to secure the leaded pane and turned to study my charge, who was engrossed in her scrawl once more. Occasionally she snuffled or sighed as she worked at the page.

I brushed a hand across my forehead, pushing back strands of hair that had come loose from the pins. It was ridiculous; I had heard no such thing. I had not slept and my fatigue was, no doubt, the cause of this delusion.

I went to the cupboard by the hearth and slipped the latest volume I had found in the library from its hiding place. The book was a tepid tale of a pure, unblemished girl stolen into slavery and seduction by Barbary pirates. Before I settled, I glanced at Grace, who was also a picture of innocence as she swayed on her chair and circled her pencil.

I had gone too far with her earlier. My threat had not produced the answer I desired. Indeed, it had almost called the household to the schoolroom. I needed to tread more carefully. Grace was my ally and my messenger. If she had, somehow, returned the feather last night, then what next?

The thought brought more heat to my body than the little fire that crackled in the hearth. I watched my pupil for a moment, noting the row of bone buttons down the back of her smock and the tidy plait that hung to the seat of her chair. Old Maggie had washed and dressed her charge this morning with her usual care and without any suspicion that for much of the night Grace had not been sleeping soundly in the room adjoining her own.

'Wall.' I turned the word in my mind and an answer opened to me. Fyneshade was ancient and built to defend. Old houses kept many secrets. I thought of Vaughan Pritchard's message.

'Grace knows all the ways. In time, I trust she might be persuaded to reveal them to you.'

At last I came to an understanding. I had been too harsh. My pupil was telling me her secret after all, in her own way.

As I watched, the girl scratched her head and reached for another sheet. She tucked a leg beneath her on the seat of the chair and settled into a new position. Both she and the day ahead were much like any other at Fyneshade.

No. I was quite wrong. I had not heard Vaughan Pritchard's

voice. It was a fantasy wrought by weariness and perhaps by desire. I tried to read but my eyes skipped over the words on the page without lodging in my mind. In the secret part of my body a familiar ache told me all I needed to know about Grace's brother. When he returned to Fyneshade, I would be ready.

15

Vaughan Pritchard returned to Fyneshade one week to the day
– or more correctly, to the night – his sister vanished. This time
I was told he was coming.

'We've had word. Paskin's lad came from The Angel this
morning.' Mrs Gurney reached for the knife by her plate. 'Mr
Vaughan's asked for his rooms to be made ready. According to
the lad, we're to expect him this evening.'

She put the knife to the wheel of cheese on the dish between
us and carved out a chunk.

'You'll take this, Marta. You've barely eaten this last week.'
Reaching for my saucer, she pushed a crumbling wedge from
the knife onto it and I thought about the drugged cake she had
fed me when Vaughan Pritchard last came to Fyneshade. She
cleared her throat.

'And you'll take my advice too. Don't go out into the grounds
while he's here. He never stays long at Fyneshade. I'll let you

know when it's ...' She stopped as the door opened and Jennet entered with a tray. She nodded at Mrs Gurney and set about clearing the table. The fatty meat – lamb again, I think – was cold, congealed and almost untouched on my own plate. The mole on Jennet's face seemed larger than ever today. When she ducked into the light to take Mrs Gurney's empty plate, I saw a dark hair growing from it.

'Leave the saucers, girl. I'll take some cheese too.'

Jennet bobbed again and headed for the door as the housekeeper cut a second grey-tinged slice for herself. When she took a large bite from it, I knew she was not trying her trick a second time.

I sat very still, waiting for her to continue, but there was nothing apart from the sound of chewing. Eventually I prompted, 'You were saying, Mrs Gurney, you'll let me know ...?'

'I'll let you know when he's gone.' Her jowls rippled as she swallowed. 'Mr Vaughan has a reputation. Not a good one, if you take my meaning. A young woman like yourself ...'

She fluttered a pudgy hand to her mouth as if to stop any further dreadful exposition. A moment later she cleared her throat and tapped the wheel with the end of her knife. 'That's turned very strong over the winter.'

I stared at the cheese on my saucer and hoped that the odd greenish light in the almost subterranean parlour would mask the flush of my cheeks. My heart was pounding so hard I feared that the housekeeper might hear it. It was a ridiculous thought, but even I was surprised at the way my body had welcomed the news of Vaughan Pritchard's return.

'A *young woman like yourself*.'

The old woman didn't know me at all. If she thought her

warning would induce me to skulk in the shadows fearing for my virtue, she was very much mistaken. A young woman like 'myself' had nothing to lose. I'd cast that die many years back and lost again and again. With pleasure.

I remembered what Vaughan Pritchard had said to me as we faced each other across the frozen river. '*I was told that Grace had a new governess, but if that's who you are then you're not what I expected. Not at all.*'

Suddenly I felt my appetite rise. I took a bite of cheese. It was fierce and sour and it caught the back of my throat.

Mrs Gurney leaned forward. 'You won't take Grace out walking, Marta. Not for a while.'

'Is she also not permitted to see her brother?' I pinched myself beneath the table. The question had been too fast, too pert. It was true that I had wondered about the nature of the relationship between the Pritchard children, but it was best to give the impression of indifference.

'Dawson reckons there's rain coming from the west.' The woman avoided my question. She drummed her fingers on the edge of the table. 'The lamb has a weak chest. Maggie thinks she's starting a chill. Now, is that all understood between us? It's for the best.'

I looked up meekly. 'I will take my direction from you. After all, it is you who employed me.' I studied her expression. I saw relief. It was clear that the true meaning of my answer had evaded her. Both of us could defy orders.

⚜

I stood by the schoolroom window and watched the hillside above the house where rows of drystone walls made a patchwork of the land. The road that had brought me to Fyneshade clipped along the ridge. Soon it would bring Vaughan Pritchard back to his home. I knew it was too early. Mrs Gurney had said he was to be expected this evening, but I could not stop myself. The pleasure of anticipation was almost as great as fulfilment.

I shivered. It was not cold that touched me; indeed, the weather had turned mild. The snow had melted away completely, leaving the courtyards and garden pathways rutted and muddy. I had taken Grace outside just twice since the day I met her brother. In his absence there was little profit in such tedious expeditions, and besides it was impossible to walk in the grounds without soiling my clothes. I was not willing to risk the hems of my two good dresses.

Through the schoolroom window, the afternoon sky was grey and lumpen as the sugared porridge that Mrs Gurney took every morning at breakfast. Crows circled overhead, their harsh conversation echoing off ancient walls. Fyneshade was a maze of stone.

I turned to Grace expecting to see her hunched as usual over a drawing, but she was looking at me. The skin around her nose was raw and crusted – faithful Old Maggie was right about the chill. Today she had styled her charge's hair into two plaits that sprouted from the top of the girl's head, each one finished with a blue satin ribbon. On any other child the effect might have been charming, but it made Grace a grotesque.

She grinned and tilted her head to one side.

'V.'

She formed the sound and giggled, tossing her head so the ridiculous plaits swung. Then she held up her latest piece, the head of a hawk.

'V.' She nodded at me.

I was at her side in a moment. Taking the drawing from her hand, I stared at black eyes that seemed to lock onto my own. I had seen Dido only once, but the bird on the page was Vaughan Pritchard's champion. It was an accomplished rendition.

'Vaw vaw vaw ...' Now Grace rocked back and forth on the chair in excitement. 'Come.'

She knew of her brother's return? I wondered if perhaps Old Maggie had told her, or more likely one of the maids. From the schoolroom window I had seen Eavis and another mole-like creature cross the courtyard below with bundles of linen. When they passed through the arch leading to the back of the house, I knew they were going to the stable block. They were not long about their duties. Some ten minutes later I watched them return empty-handed.

Grace tugged at my skirt and pointed at the drawing. 'Vaw vaw come.'

Was she telling me this, or merely expressing excitement?

Since the night of the disappearance I had not mentioned the feather or the message. I had discovered that a gentle approach worked best with the girl, but that was not my only reason for caution. I had come to recognise something in my pupil that – while not approaching intelligence – could be described as cunning. I did not want to give her a power over me. I would take care.

I held the paper to the light. 'This is very good.' I formed my mouth into a pretty 'o', gasped aloud and clapped a hand to my lips in the playful, theatrical manner I knew Grace liked.

'But I think I know this bird! It is Dido. Am I right?'

She giggled again.

I knelt beside her. 'Do you like Dido?'

'Pretty.' Grace sucked on her thumb.

'Yes. She is very pretty.' I stroked one of the ludicrous plaits. 'Just like you, dearest, with your hair in such lovely ribbons.'

The girl wriggled with pleasure, snorted and rested her head on my shoulder. The moment was perfect.

'Do you ... *see* Dido, when Vau ... your brother is here at Fyneshade?'

She nodded again and continued to suck on her thumb. The wet sound so close to my ear was revolting.

I sighed. 'I would like to see Dido too. Do you remember the feather you brought to me?'

Grace stiffened and shifted a little. I sensed a wariness in my pupil and redoubled my efforts to soothe and cajole, moving my hand from her hair to her shoulders. I held her close.

'That feather came from Dido. I think your brother asked you to bring it to me because he knew how much I liked her.'

Grace shuffled away. Removing her thumb from her mouth, she rubbed the delicate lace cuff of her sleeve across her nose and then she began to pick at the wrinkled skin around the nail. She wouldn't look at me.

I forced myself to speak sweetly. 'I would so like to see Dido again but she will be in the stables and I do not think I am allowed to visit her there.' I leaned on the desk and pretended to think, placing my hands on my forehead. 'What can I do? If only there was a way.'

'Wall.' Grace whispered the word and patted my back.

I looked up to find her staring at me. I feigned a puzzled frown. 'Wall?'

She nodded solemnly.

I waited for a moment and then, clapping my hands, I pounced.

'Oh! You are the best girl and so clever. You are the only one who knows about the secret passages in the walls, aren't you? You know all the ways.'

Instantly her pale eyes filled with confusion and fear. She turned to look at the door and plucked her jutting lower lip.

'Don't worry, dearest.' I turned her back to me and gently cupped her face in my hands. 'I won't tell anyone.' I smiled. 'In fact, it could be *our* secret, just like Panjan. You do want to see him again, don't you?'

She gave a fierce nod.

'Good, then I will make Panjan play again if you take me through the walls to your ... to see Dido.'

⁂

I waited at the window. A frail milky patch in the sky over the stable block betrayed the moon's place, but tonight her face was veiled.

It was late when the carriage finally rumbled into view and circled the inner courtyard. I watched the flat roof pass beneath my room and disappear through the archway leading to the stables. After the clang of the metal gate I stood there for some time hoping for more but the night was full of silence and shadow.

Eventually, I dragged the curtains across the window and went to my bed. The sheets were cold – damp almost. I thought about the bundles of cloth I had seen carried to the stable block earlier that day. Vaughan Pritchard was sleeping now in good linen. As I lay there, my body thrummed with a restless energy that did not come from one of Grandmere's rituals.

Throwing back the coverlet, I went to light my bedside taper from the embers still smouldering in the hearth. A question had begun to turn in my mind and there was a simple way to test the answer. I had used it before at Fyneshade. The embers glowed and sparked as I raked an iron across them and then I plucked five hairs from my head.

I hesitated, rolling the black hairs between my fingers. Country divination was for simpletons. Grandmere would have mocked me, and yet . . .?

I plaited the hairs together, cast the twist into the fire and inscribed the shape of a five-pointed star with my thumb. I whispered the question and instantly, the entire hearth blazed with golden flames flecked with red. The fire disappeared almost as soon as it had come, but as I watched the faintly glowing embers, I considered the meaning of the answer I had been given. Red signified passion.

Taking the taper, I went to the window again, drew back the curtains and opened the box seat. My tin of trophies rattled as I eased it from its hiding place. Beneath it I saw the drawing of the hare that Grace had left in my room. I was not sentimental, but the drawing had a quality I could not cast away. Grandmere had taught me of the kinship between hares and women like us.

I freed the tin from the shawl, opened it and placed each trinket carefully on the rug before me. The tiny shepherdess, the buttons, the locket, the pearl earring and Panjan's key glinted in the light from the taper. The silver coffin plate was at the bottom and it was blackened. I used the hem of my nightgown to make it shine once more and ran my finger over the scrolling inscription.

Hic dormit Charles Van Meeran

I had said that I wanted a keepsake of our trysting place and

Nathaniel had laughed when I prised that plate from his own grandfather's coffin. The earthly remains of Charles Van Meeran rotted in a wooden box in a musty alcove next to the stones where we lay.

With his red hair, green eyes and pointed chin, Nathaniel had reminded me of a fox, but I had glimpsed a creature more powerful in the eyes of Vaughan Pritchard. Closing my fingers about the coffin plate, I gripped so hard that the metal dug into the flesh of my palm.

I felt alive for the first time since I had come to Fyneshade.

16

The next day was full of oddity and obstruction.

Mrs Gurney informed me at breakfast that my pupil was indisposed and would be confined to the nursery. If I had not seen evidence of Grace's infirmity for myself, I might have thought that the housekeeper was lying again. But when she took a handwritten book from the dresser drawer and showed me her mother's unfailing recipe for linctus – a boiled concoction of aniseed, black pepper, dried hyssop, honey and watered brandy – I knew she was telling the truth. I recognised a version of Grandmere's distillation against congestion.

Although the book was battered with a broken spine and the handwriting a spindly scrawl, it was clear that the housekeeper regarded it as a treasure. After we had finished our bread and butter, she allowed me to look through the yellowed pages, offering a homely commentary on old family recipes that had proved successful.

When Jennet came to clear our dishes, Mrs Gurney rose from the table. Clutching the book to her breast, she said she would go directly to the still room to prepare Grace's medicine herself. I asked if I might be permitted to visit my pupil, but the housekeeper shook her head.

'Rest. That's what she needs. Old Maggie says she had a bad night. The linctus will soothe her throat and the brandy will help her to sleep.'

Mistaking my expression for concern, Mrs Gurney smiled and patted my hand.

'Don't fret yourself, Marta. The change in the weather will have brought this on. Happens every year. And every year I keep some aniseed by and I dry some hyssop to be ready. She'll soon be right again. You can take a day to yourself. That might be a rare pleasure, I daresay. I'll ask Jennet to make up the fire in the library – I know how you like to read.' She glanced at the rattling window. 'Besides, you won't be going out.'

Dawson's prediction had been right, although the rain that had lashed the walls and gardens of Fyneshade since the early hours could, more rightly, be described as a deluge.

Mrs Gurney's suggestion that I might take pleasure in a day to myself could not be further from the truth. I spent most of that morning restless and unsatisfied, pacing alone in the library listening to rain thrumming on the windows and the howl of the wind winding about the walls.

The book lying open on the couch purported to be a 'moste true accounte' of life in a French convent, but the sacrilege of the nuns and priests within its holy sanctuary was tame fare.

Besides, I could not read when every nerve in my body was coiled like a watch spring. I went to the window and looked over the formal lawns. Today I could barely make out the gate lead-ing to the river path. As I watched the trees bend in the gale, I thought of Dido flying so close to my head that the beat of her wings moved my hair.

My belly tightened. Vaughan Pritchard was my Panjan and Grace was my key.

There was a sudden shivering cascade of notes from Sophia's harp. I turned sharply, but I knew I was alone. The curtains swayed in the draught that found its way through the gaps in the old casement. I wrapped my arms around me and returned to my watch.

Eventually it was time for my midday appointment in the parlour. As I went along the passage there was nothing to sug-gest that anything had disturbed the house's usual state of quiet suffocation.

Two maids lowered their heads as I passed them on the stairs. One carried a feather-plumed duster and the other held a rag and tin of wax. I knew their faces, but not their names. Like the others at Fyneshade, they were plain girls, squat and spotted like suet puddings.

The great hallway echoed with the sound of the downpour that lashed the stone steps beyond the door. I paused before the long mirror over the hearth. It was an ancient thing, the glass criss-crossed by dark jagged blooms where the silvering had failed.

The woman staring back at me had white, unblemished skin, straight dark brows and a heart-shaped face. The hollows of her cheeks spoke of breeding. Beyond the thorny crackles in the glaze, her black eyes glittered like good French jet and her hair, plaited into two thick braids coiled about her ears, had a pleasing lustre.

Little Magpie.

I had taken trouble over my appearance earlier but that effort had been wasted.

From somewhere above I heard the creaking of floorboards. Turning from the mirror, I looked up to see Eavis crossing the gallery carrying folded towels and a steaming bowl. She went to the left and passed through the swagged archway leading into the passage to Panjan's room. It was unusual to see someone going to that part of the house on a domestic errand. Apart from the cleaning maids and Mrs Gurney with her keys, the icy north-west corridor was unused.

It came to me that last time Vaughan Pritchard had returned to Fyneshade, it was Eavis who seemed to serve him.

I went quietly and swiftly back up the stairs. Passing through the draped curtains, I expected to see the broad-backed laundress ahead of me, or if not her, then at least some sign of her – an open door perhaps, or the sound of a voice. But the passage was hushed, closed and cold as ever.

As I walked from the archway to the far end where a gloomy painting of two children, stiff and doll-like in the clothing of an earlier time, filled the wall, I listened at every door and heard nothing. Like Grace, Eavis had disappeared. But I *had* seen her. I was not mistaken – a medicinal scent that I had never detected here before lingered in the air.

The silence was broken by the sound of clocks chiming for midday. I knew Mrs Gurney would be waiting for me in the parlour. I went back down the corridor, but now, walking in the opposite direction, I saw an alcove on the left-hand wall that – on account of its angle and a cabinet positioned close by – had been hidden from view before. The narrow space was no more than four feet across, almost rectangular in shape with a slit of window and a hanging tapestry. I took a step forward. The odd scent was stronger here, trapped between the ancient uneven walls.

In the thin light, I saw a little puddle on the boards before the tapestry. I went forward and bent to touch the water. It was warm. And when I moved the corner of the tapestry aside, I saw the lower edge of a door. From its size and shape I thought the alcove might be the base of a turret. I stood and held back the fabric to see the door more clearly. It was made from wide oak planks set into arched stonework. On the left side there was an old metal lock, but no ring or handle. I pushed at the wood but the door didn't move. Eavis – I was certain she had come this way and spilled water from the bowl while negotiating the door – had locked it behind her.

We dined on boiled gammon at midday and his name was not mentioned. Apart from that sighting of Eavis, and her subsequent disappearance, the dreary affairs of the house seemed quite untouched by Vaughan Pritchard's arrival. But for the sight of his carriage crossing the yard beneath my window, I would not have suspected his presence.

When we had finished – I barely touched the pallid meat, but I had a way to clear my dish – Mrs Gurney pointed at the window.

'The river has risen. Dawson says the valley road has flooded already. If this keeps up it'll reach the lower gardens.'

She did not seem unduly concerned, but I sensed an expectation that I should engage on the topic. I pushed the last scrap of meat under the table and felt a rough tongue on my fingers.

'Are we in danger, Mrs Gurney? Must we build an ark?'

'No, Marta, it happens every year.' She shook her head. 'The snow didn't help, mind. With the house being set down so low it's natural that water should collect around it. But if you were to ask me, it's the damp that affects Grace so.'

I smiled. 'How is she now? Has your mother's recipe eased her chill?'

Mrs Gurney dabbed at her lips with the tip of a folded napkin. 'Maggie says she took it down easily enough. Never fails, that one ... although, of course, I've made my own adjustments to Mother's recipe. Grace has been asleep for most of the morning without disturbance.'

Now I thought I might catch her. Feigning puzzlement, I rested my hands on the edge of the table. 'But I saw Mrs Eavis carrying a bowl of warm water earlier. I thought she must be taking it to the nursery.'

The housekeeper shook her head. 'Grace has been sleeping soundly. No one has visited her. Maggie gave orders to keep the child peaceful. It's for the best.'

'Well, that is most confusing. I definitely saw Mrs Eavis with a bowl of water.' I studied the housekeeper's face. The indulgent smile that had begun when I enquired after my pupil's health wavered as I continued. 'Naturally I thought she was carrying it to Grace as it smelt medicinal, although I did think it was odd that she went into Panjan's passage with it when the nursery is in a quite different part of the house.'

Mrs Gurney looked away. 'Mrs Eavis has many duties at Fyneshade. I'm sure she was busy with some task or other.

In fact, I . . . yes, I do remember that there's some brass that needs attending to. I mentioned it to her just last week. It was copper polish you smelt – we use lavender and sorrel leaves.' She rolled her eyes. 'That will be why the dried sorrel was left out on the side in the still room this morning. Now—' She rose and headed purposefully to the door. 'You might have a day at leisure, Marta, and I don't begrudge you, but I cannot afford such luxury.'

❦

The afternoon yawned ahead. With little else to do, I decided to return to the library and the confines of the convent which bore little relation to the place of Grandmere's education. As I crossed the hallway to the great staircase, I caught the scent of flowers. This was a heady sweet smell, quite different to the bitter tang of the steam rising from the basin carried by Eavis.

I went up and passed beneath the stone archway into the library passage. Just as the last time Vaughan Pritchard came home, the space where his mother's painting hung was filled with papery, heavy-scented blooms. It was the only sign of his presence, but it was proof enough.

Halfway along, a maid was bent double gathering fallen petals from the boards. Here was an opportunity. I went to her side as she crouched with a pan and brush.

'Were these brought to Fyneshade by the master's son?'

The girl ignored me, so I tapped her shoulder. Startled, she flinched, stood abruptly and shook her head. I recognised her as the shrunken mole-like creature who had accompanied Eavis across the yard to the stables yesterday. Close to, I saw she had surprisingly pretty wide-set eyes that were almost violet. Clasping the pan and the brush to her waist, she tried to dodge past me back down the passage, but I blocked her way.

'I know he has returned. Last time he came, I believe he brought flowers like these.'

She darted away, but I caught her wrist.

'Come now. It is a simple question. These were brought to Fyneshade by Vaughan Pritchard, were they not? They are for his mother whose portrait hangs on the wall just there.' I twisted the girl around, gripped her head and forced her to look up at Sophia. 'There she is. Tell me!'

The maid began to whimper. It was a peculiar high-pitched whine.

'Leave her alone!' The voice came from behind. I turned to see Jennet advancing towards us. 'You're frightening her.' Jennet's unprepossessing face was flushed with anger. 'She can't hear. Let her be.'

I released the girl and she rubbed at her brown buttoned cuff. Darting a fearful look at me, she scurried back down the corridor.

Jennet moved to block my way. 'Suki can't speak, neither. So, there's no point in asking her anything.'

I tried to compose my features to an amenable expression. 'I did not know that.'

She folded her arms. 'That's no surprise, seeing as you've not bothered yourself much with the likes of us since you arrived, miss.'

I noted the scornful pause before she said 'miss'.

Turning, she began to walk away. I called after her.

'Wait!' She did not stop or look back. 'These flowers. Where do they come from? Who brought them here?'

Jennet shrugged. 'I don't know anything about that.' She carried on down the passage, but when she'd gone a little way, I heard her mutter in her broad flat accent, 'And anything I do know is not to be spoken.'

I was running through a wood. It was night, my feet were bare and brambles tore at my dress. Ahead, I saw a faint light and blundered towards it. The trees vanished and I came upon a fine house standing in a wide, circular lawn. The house was in darkness. Rows of blank windows loomed above me but firelight flickered in the panes of a tall window garlanded with roses just along from the entrance. I ran up the steps and hammered on the panelled door but no one answered. I went to the window and peered into the glowing room. Two children sat in front of a fire with their backs turned to me. I beat my hands on the glass but they didn't move. I tried to call out to them but I was dumbstruck. At last, I heard a dry scraping noise as the great door finally began to open. Instead of relief, what I felt was fear.

I opened my eyes and stared at the figured plaster ceiling above my bed. The sound came again, a brittle, rasping noise left over from the dream that was dissolving swiftly. I tried to gather the shreds of the nightmare together but all I could remember was a sense of peril.

I sat up and pulled the coverlet around me. No light showed through the chink in the heavy curtains. Rain tapped on the glass like the fingers of an exasperated schoolmaster. The only light in the room came from the chamberstick burned to a drowning stump at my bedside. The guttering flame jittered in an icy draught that pinched at the bones of my face. I reached for the water tumbler on the stand.

A small hand caught my own and gripped tight.

17

Grace stood beside my bed.

Struggling to master my fright, I took up the candle stump, shielding the tiny flame against the draught in the room. The girl was in her nightshift and wrapped in a lumpen patchwork blanket that fell from her shoulders to her knees. The light brought an eerie, moonish glow to her fleshy face. The candle spat and exhausted itself. Grace giggled as, blindly, I rifled through the bedstand drawer for a replacement.

In the darkness it was difficult to strike a light. I fumbled with the silver case and dozens of matches spilled onto the blankets. Grace snuffled. The bedsprings grated as she settled heavily on the coverlet.

At last I managed it. I set the new-lit candle on the bedstand and looked at my visitor. Grace had her back to me. Holding one of the bedposts, she swayed from side to side and kicked out her slippered feet. Wisps of her hair moved in a draught. I glanced at the door, certain that I had locked it when I retired. It was shut.

Pulling the coverlet around me, I leaned forward and whispered, 'Grace?'

She turned. Her slanted eyes caught the flame and for a fleeting moment I thought of a cat. She rubbed a clenched fist beneath her nose and then she offered it to me. Unwilling to take her sticky hand in my own, I held back, but then she pulled her feet onto the bed and clambered towards me, all the while clutching the patchwork blanket around herself.

'Vaw.' She raised her fist, opened it and a feather fell amid the matches. She prised my hand from the coverlet and yanked hard. I snatched it away, but now Grace slid from the bed and padded into the shadows beyond the huge fireplace on the far side of the room.

I took up the new feather. White-tipped and barred with black and grey, it came, most surely, from Dido.

Boards creaked in the darkness. Then the rasping sound that had lingered from my dream came again. I considered the possibility that I was still sleeping. Perhaps this visitation was part of the same nightmare?

More scraping echoed in the dark. I heard stone grinding against stone, a dry brittle noise. Now the draught in the room was strong enough to move my hair. The air suddenly filled with the damp, musty scent of age.

This was no dream. I was fully awake.

'Grace?' I called softly.

There was no answer. I threw back the blankets, took up the candle and crossed to the fireplace, raising the flame high to give off as much light as possible. Grace was nowhere to be seen; instead, running from the far side of the hearth to a place in the wall where the stonework jutted into the chamber, there was a gaping black hole.

The doorway in the wall, for that was what it was, was half my height. I had wondered why the wall in this corner of my room bulged and arched beneath the intricate plaster ceiling, thinking it to be no more than a symptom of age. Which, in a manner, I now understood it more clearly to be.

Passages and secret ways were not uncommon in houses like Fyneshade. Nathaniel had told me once of the priests who had hidden for days in spaces no larger than a brandy barrel. His uncle's house on the hillside above Croyle was said to have harboured such men. Of course, that was long before the dutiful Van Meerans came over from Holland.

'Grace knows all the ways.'

I remembered the drawing of the hare that had appeared on my bed. Was it likely that she had come to my room that night through this secret door? I bent to peer into the darkness. There was a narrow passage ahead. Just inside, a dusty tangle of looped cobwebs, silver-grey in the candlelight, shivered in the draught.

'Grace.' I said her name again as loudly as I dared and it echoed back to me. I waited a moment and then I called again. At last there was a dry scuffle and she shuffled back into view cradling a finely costumed doll no longer hidden now beneath her patchwork blanket. I had never seen her with any toy before but the way she stroked its hair and crooned as she held it close to her cheek showed that this was an object of veneration.

'Vaw.' She attempted her brother's name again and turned the doll to face me. It was a pretty porcelain thing with dark curled hair, pouting lips and heavily lashed black glass eyes.

She tucked the doll under her arm and reached out a sticky hand. 'Come.'

Despite the cold, I burned beneath my shift. The feather was an invitation. I stretched out my free hand.

But then I snatched it back. I would not be summoned at midnight in my shift. I was not a plaything like the doll in Grace's arms. My breath rose between us.

At cards it was a mistake to play your hand too soon and too eagerly, but was the risk too great? How would Vaughan Pritchard interpret my refusal? And what if this was my only chance? What if he left tomorrow?

I stared at the looped black hair that hung from the doll's head. I had pinned and coiled my own hair this morning, but now it was held in a single simple plait. It would take a long time to prepare myself.

The window shook as raindrops heavy as pebbles pelted the glass. I remembered Mrs Gurney's talk of flood. As long as the barrage continued, Vaughan Pritchard was trapped here, just as I was. I was not fool enough to imagine that he sent for me after midnight for the sake of conversation. Anticipation would sharpen his pleasure in my company. And my pleasure in his.

I chose my card.

'Dearest.' I bent to take Grace's hand and pulled her gently back through the gap and into my room. 'Have you come to take me to . . . Dido?'

Grace nodded. She patted the doll's head. 'Vaw.'

I thought I understood. 'Is this a gift from . . . Vaw?'

She sniffed loudly. 'Pretty.'

'Is she?' I tilted my head and narrowed my eyes. 'But it's too dark in here to tell. Come, we shall need another light so that I can see her.'

I drew Grace back towards the bed. At first, she resisted, dragging her feet on the boards, but when I encouraged her, softly repeating my desire to see her new prize, she came with me.

Cradling the doll like a baby, Grace sat on the coverlet sniffing loudly as I lit a second candle from the drawer and fixed it into a brass chamberstick.

'There. That's so much better.' I turned. 'Now I can see. How pretty she is. Look at her beautiful silken hair.' I sat close and stroked the pale coarse plait that hung limply over her shoulder. 'Just like yours, little one.'

Grace rocked on the bed and grinned as I continued.

'And I can see her dress. What a fine lady she is.'

My pupil swiped at her nose and began to bounce next to me, all the while clutching the doll to her breast.

'Vaw. Vaw. Vaw. Vaw . . .'

Rapidly she became excited, repeating the name so loudly that I feared someone might hear.

'Hush! Hush now.' I pressed a finger to her wet lips and she quietened. I drew back my hand and, with some reluctance, pressed the same finger to my mouth.

'This is our secret, Grace. No one else must know.'

I held up the feather. 'Did Vaw give the pretty doll to you when he asked you to bring this to me?'

She nodded. I paused for a moment, wondering when and how the siblings had met. I decided that the question would be answered soon enough and pressed my case. 'And now he would like *you* to take me to see . . . Dido? That's right, isn't it?'

Grace stared at me. 'Wall.' She freed a hand from the doll's velvet skirts and pointed towards the fireplace. I smiled and stroked her cheek.

'You are very clever to do this, to lead me to Dido. But I cannot go like this.' I brushed my hands over my cotton shift. 'I must dress myself, just like your beautiful doll, and make my hair as pretty as yours.' I shook my head sadly. 'But it is too late.'

Grace put a hand to her mouth. Her eyes were suddenly round and fearful.

'Vaw.'

I patted her knee. 'Yes, little one. We will go to Vaw, but not tonight. Will you come to me in the dark *tomorrow* to show me the way?'

She opened her mouth but no sound came. She clutched the doll to her breast with a fierce desperation. It came to me that the toy was a bribe.

I bent to brush my lips across her damp forehead. 'Shall we go to see Panjan, dearest?'

18

When Grace came for me after midnight again, as I knew she would, I was ready.

I had spent a second day at liberty after Mrs Gurney informed me at breakfast of Grace's continuing infirmity. Other than a persistently dripping nose, my pupil had seemed very much herself last evening. I decided that fatigue was the most likely cause of her frailty, and I was glad of it. Another day of confinement to the nursery would be helpful to my cause.

I retired early to my room complaining of a headache and I set about preparing myself. The Queen of Sheba could not have taken more care of her toilette and costume as I did that evening.

I washed every inch of my body in the cold water from the morning washstand and I rubbed rose oil from a blue glass phial in Grandmere's spice box into my skin. Banking the fire to a steady blaze, I sat naked before it, running my fingers through my hair as it dried, threading it with the scent of the perfumed oil.

When it was almost dry, I brushed it until it shone like glass, but tonight I did not plait or twist it into loops. Instead, I allowed it to fall to my waist.

The dress I had selected hung outside the wardrobe. I hoped that the stench of naphtha trapped inside the old wood would not cling to the fabric. I knew that the good mourning gown showed my skin and figure to advantage, but when I dressed and examined my reflection in the oval mirror on my dressing table, I found myself wishing that it was both just a little more and a little less. The material could have been finer. The cut could have been more fashionable. There could have been more width to the skirt. The jet beading at the collar could have been more opulent. The grey circles beneath the arms could have been less pronounced, the hem could have had fewer knots and jags where the fabric had caught on a nail or a splinter. The neck could have dipped just a little lower.

I frowned as I brushed lint from the bombazine. It was the best gown I had and the red silk petticoat beneath was fine. It would pass.

I would pass.

A familiar shiver ran through me. Suddenly, I thought of Nathaniel; his long white fingers, his green eyes and his red hair. The tiny thing I had buried in the wood ... My eyes glittered strangely in the looking glass.

When I told him of the child, his eyes had slipped uneasily from mine and I saw fear tighten his face. I knew then that he was not worthy of my body or the gift it had made.

I slid his childish ring from my finger and set it down before my reflection.

Smoothing my hair over my shoulders, I went from the mirror

to the far side of the hearth. My back had been turned for a few moments last night when I went to check that the house was quiet before our visit to Panjan's room. When I returned to collect Grace, the door to the passage was closed.

Now the stones were sealed and locked tightly together. I ran my fingertips over the wall. No matter where or how hard I pushed or pressed, I could not open the door. I stood back and studied the wall. There was no outward sign of an entrance here. The outline was lost in the patched jumble of stones and I could not detect a trace of the draught that had come into the room with my pupil.

I lit three candles and took the chair from my dressing table to set it before the hearth. Then I waited. Just after midnight, when the ringing chimes of all the clocks at Fyneshade sounded faintly in my room, the wall shuddered. As I watched, it seemed to quiver in the candlelight. I heard the grating sound of stone moving against stone and the black skirt of my dress billowed in a draught as slowly, the wall opened into itself, revealing Grace dressed in her nightgown and wrapped in the same patchwork blanket.

Framed in the dark entrance, she smiled and clapped.

'Vaw.'

I rose from the chair and she held out her hand. This time, I took it.

'*Grace knows every inch of this house. She could find her way round it blindfolded.*'

I remembered Mrs Gurney's words as I followed Grace's

patchwork back through a maze of passages and tunnels. Before dipping through the low stone doorway, I had taken up a chamberstick, but it was clear that my pupil did not need light to navigate the way. She seemed to find her way by touch, often reaching out to stroke stones or panels as if to reassure herself of our place in the labyrinth. Occasionally, she would pause, flatten a hand against a passage wall and cock her head to listen before speeding ahead. It was as if the house spoke to her. Grace showed no fear of the dark, of the winding passages, of the damp, of the smell of decay or of the creatures that scuttled in the dust. I brushed cobwebs from my face and from my hair, but she paid no attention to them. In fact, they did not seem to touch her at all. In this hidden world where Fyneshade was turned inside out, Grace was my teacher and I her pupil.

In places the passages were tall and narrow, in others I had to duck when the ceiling pressed low. At one point, when we inched along a confined space without any roof visible or tangible in the darkness above our heads, I thought I recognised the plain timbered back of the magnificent panelled screen in the great hall. I had the impression that we were descending, although only once did we come across a crude set of steps studded with ancient nails that tore at the hem of my dress. There, as at a dozen other times during our journey, I was glad of the candlelight.

At last, after what had seemed an hour, but, in truth, had probably been no more than a few minutes, Grace led the way from a cramped, foul-smelling passage into a more open, cavern-like space. I heard the sound of running water and when I raised the chamberstick I saw moss growing on the rock around us.

'Vaw.' Grace rubbed her nose with the trailing end of her blanket and pointed to the shadows. I stepped over a grille in the flagstones for a clearer view and the candle glinted on black water rippling beneath. The stable block ran alongside the river. I could not begin to understand the tortuous, invisible path we had taken through the entrails of the house, but I knew that Grace had led me true.

I watched her pad over the slippery flags and then I followed. A flight of uneven stone steps was carved into the back wall. Grace waved at them and then, giggling, she turned to me. 'Shhh.' She put a finger to her lips.

I nodded and smiled. Grace pointed at the steps again. 'Dido.'

It was the first time I had heard her speak the bird's name.

'Is ... is she up there?' I angled the chamberstick to light the stones.

Without answering, Grace turned from me and began to climb. I pinched up my skirts and followed, joining her on a platform some thirty feet above the cavern. To the left, set into the rock, was a recessed door with a rope handle. Grace tugged at the loop and I had to stand back as the door opened outward, almost knocking me aside. Instantly, the sweet, leathery smell of horse and hay rushed out at us.

Grace took my hand and led me up another short flight of steps. I heard a clatter of hooves. The horses in Fyneshade's grand stables snorted and danced on the cobbled floor as their visitors emerged from a half-sunken door shielded behind a wooden stall. Grace shrieked with delight and ran forward to throw her arms around the neck of a stocky bay pony. Alarmed, I darted forward to drag her away, but the animal lowered its head and snuffled her hair. It was clear that they were old friends.

This welcome was not extended by all the occupants of the stables. A crashing noise came from the far end of the stalls.

Disturbed by our presence, one of the animals kicked and lashed out at the panels. I watched a magnificent grey stallion rear over the side of his stall, massive hooves pounding the wood. Even from twenty yards off, the candlelight showed the roll of his muscles and the wild glint in his eyes. His fury was infectious. Soon other horses began to stamp and call out.

Grace released the mild-natured bay and crouched on the cobbles, hands clamped to her ears. She began to wail and the piercing sound made the horses even more agitated. Soon the noise was deafening. The stables rang with the sound of their hooves. Huge shadows bucked and capered around us. The candle trembled in my hands at the sight and sound of the havoc we had unleashed.

Light whirled on the plaster walls. A tall man strode to the centre of the stables and the lantern in his hand swung again, flooding every corner with a golden glow. Having grown used to the gloom, I shielded my eyes. Grace, still wailing, was now curled into a ball at my feet.

Heavy footsteps crunched towards me. I flinched as Vaughan Pritchard raised the lantern. It was clear that the commotion had roused him from sleep. In haste, he had pulled on rumpled breeches and flung on a shirt which hung open to the waist. His boots were rolled at the knee and unfastened.

Pale eyes skewered me to the spot. At last he took a step back. The lantern light carved dark hollows in his angular face as he smiled.

Catching the rope trailing from the big grey, he dragged its head low. The stallion pranced and snorted, but soon it relented and submitted to control. As I watched, surprised by his lack of fear, he flattened a hand to the animal's shuddering flank and rested his forehead against its arched neck. He seemed to whisper into its mane. After a few moments more, it was at peace.

As if taking their cue from an overlord, the other horses steadied and quietened. The only sound was the scuffle of hooves and Grace whimpering into her blanket. Vaughan Pritchard took up the lantern and held it so that he could see me clearly.

'Do you ride, governess?'

He made a shallow, mocking bow and angled the light to show an archway beyond the stalls. 'My rooms are above.'

Without another word he turned and walked away. After a moment I followed.

Of course.

19

Dido was hooded. The tasselled leather cap was caught at the neck and her blinded eyes were marked by whorled metal studs that glowed in the firelight. Motionless, she perched on a stand behind a wing-backed chair drawn up to the hearth. The only sign that she knew of our intrusion was the flexing of her ridged yellow talons.

Vaughan Pritchard bent to take a log from a pile and cast it onto the embers. There was a hissing sound and then green-tinged flames spurted from beneath it. He straightened up and turned to look at me.

Uncombed, his thick black hair tumbled over his forehead; the skin of his face was still crumpled by the sleep we had interrupted and his linen shirt was not yet fastened. I found it hard to look away from the dark tangle that fanned across the muscles of his chest, but I forced myself to meet his gaze.

I was aware of a vein pulsing at the beaded collar of my dress.

'I thought my invitation had been declined.'

His eyes moved from my face to Grace, who was holding my hand. She was staring, open-mouthed, at the hawk. I raised my chin.

'Was it an invitation or a summons?'

'It was whatever you chose to make of it, governess. Sit.'

He motioned to a settle by the fire and went to a long table drawn against the wall at the other end of the room. I released Grace's hand, smoothed my skirts, brushing dust and cobwebs from the folds, and went to the settle.

His place of exile was far grander than I had imagined. The ancient chamber was hung with paintings and tapestries, taken, no doubt, from the house. Overlapping rugs, presumably from the same source, covered the flagstone floor. Velvet curtains covered three windows set at intervals along one wall. Between the first and the second window was a carved wooden chest. Soft light glowed from the fire and from lighted candles in five heavy gold chambersticks arranged along a beam above it.

I bit my lips to bring colour, twisted on the settle and watched him fill two glasses from a crystal decanter. He returned to the hearth, one in each hand.

'Leave!'

He barked out the word. Startled, I thought he was speaking to me, but then I realised the command was meant for Grace, who had crept to Dido's perch and was reaching out. Immediately she sprang back. Shaking her head, she started to smack the back of her hand as if to punish it for its wickedness.

He passed me a glass almost filled to the brim with wine. Glinting in the firelight, it reminded me of Panjan's ruby eyes. He caught his little sister's arm. 'Come here.'

Pulling her around the wing-backed chair, he forced her to stand between us in front of the fire. 'What have I told you, Graceless?' He ruffled the top of her head and she wriggled with pleasure.

'Touch.' She shook her head so vigorously that the plait whipped about her shoulders.

'Good girl.' He put his glass on the stone hearth and bent to take her shoulders in his hands. He brought his pale eyes level with hers. 'Never touch Dido.'

She nodded, but then turned to me. Her arms flapped at her sides.

'Dido?' She glanced at the bird and flailed a patchwork-draped arm towards it. 'Pretty?'

I sat forward. 'Thank you for bringing me to see Dido, little one. She is a rare beauty, and you are very clever to show me the way here.'

Vaughan Pritchard looked at me over her shoulder. Complicit in that moment, we understood one another perfectly.

Grace smiled. She began to hum monotonously. Freeing herself from her brother's hands, she twirled slowly on the rug. How I longed for her to be gone. From the way Dido stamped and plucked at the metal bar of her stand, I imagined she also wished the child away. Tiny silver bells attached to a leather band around her foot jingled.

When Grace had turned several times and the burbling from her lips had still not found its way close to anything resembling a tune, Vaughan reached out to stop her.

'Enough! You'll make yourself dizzy and fall into the fire. And what would the sheepdog and Gurney say then?' He glanced at me, a smile pulling at one side of his face. Although Vaughan

Pritchard was not many years older than me, there were deep lines running from his nose to the sides of his mouth. I noticed that his lips were wide, firm and well formed. Without taking his eyes from mine, he spoke again.

'Go to the bedroom, Grace. You can play with Rosa until ... it's time.'

She pulled at the ends of the blanket, fanning it out about her like a pair of wings, and stood on the tips of her toes. Pouting her lips and popping a little bubble of spittle, she twisted about and peered at the other end of the room. Turning on the settle, I now saw a doorway beyond the table. The girl shook her head and swiped a hand across her nose.

Vaughan Pritchard stood up. 'If you do not go to the bedroom now, I will. And I will throw Rosa into this fire.'

Grace didn't move.

'Very well; she will burn.' He began to walk slowly towards the doorway. It was enough. Shrieking as if this were a game – and something in her brother's manner told me it was not – Grace darted past him and ran to the far end of the room. A door slammed and, at last, we were alone.

The warmth of the wine slipped down my throat. Vaughan Pritchard sat again in the chair opposite. He was a striking man. Even in this light his eyes appeared so unusually clear and blue that they were almost a fault. I watched him over the rim of my glass as he bent to pull off the riding boots. His hair was as black as mine, clipped at the back, but allowed to grow longer at the sides and over the forehead. It fell forward as he freed himself from the crackled leather. His legs were long and well formed and his back was broad.

He looked up and caught me staring. 'Take your fill, Marta. I do not imagine such pleasure is available in my father's house?'

I was Marta now, not governess? I raised the glass. 'Such indulgence is allowed but once a week, and then the wine is watered, sir. Like the company.'

He tossed the boots to a corner and took up his own glass. 'To pleasure.'

I mirrored the toast and added my own. 'And to indulgence.'

I sat back and drew up my legs to fold them beneath me. The hem of my petticoat ruffled prettily from beneath the black bombazine. The red drew attention to my bare ankles. Nathaniel had called them fine. He had loved the jut of bone above the tender inner flesh. I was conscious of Vaughan Pritchard watching me as I guarded my wineglass and settled to a more comfortable position. Our ease in each other's company was interrupted by a thump from the direction of the bedroom.

I turned. 'Grace! Will she be . . .?'

'She will be perfectly occupied. She knows better than to defy me.' My host turned the crystal in his hand. It caught the firelight and rainbow sparks danced on the walls.

'I thought you had defied me, but here you are.'

We both knew why I had come. There was little point in playing the ingénue, but I sensed that this was a man who enjoyed the chase. It would be delicious to set him a trail.

I smiled. 'You said yourself that I might interpret your message as I wished. I did not think I had received an *order* therefore I did not *defy* you.' I took a sip of wine. 'Besides, the valley has flooded. You will not be able to leave Fyneshade for some time, sir.'

'Brava.' He raised his glass again. 'This is a tedious prison, but I hope that our renewed acquaintance will prove to be mutually ... entertaining. I am glad you have *chosen* to come to me.'

'Grace led me here. She knows all the ways, as you wrote in your note.'

Vaughan Pritchard nodded. 'I showed her the passages in the walls.'

'You do enter the house, then?' I cradled the glass in my hand, interested in this coin of information. 'I understood that you were forbidden.'

The lines around his mouth tightened as he stared into the fire. 'Many things are forbidden at Fyneshade.' His voice was flat and cold now. He twisted the stem of the glass and did not look at me.

I knew at once that I had strayed into territory that would not benefit my present cause. I took a sip of wine and ventured on a new topic.

'How did you fare in the north?'

He frowned and continued to stare into the flames.

I prompted again. 'At the river you said that you were travelling on to Carlisle?'

'There was a tournament.' He turned to look up at the bird, which was now quite still on the stand behind him. 'Dido is a rare beauty, as you say. Not many houses keep a mews or hunt in the old ways but where gamehawking is still a valued sport there's none to match her. She won me a great prize.' He smiled and tipped back his glass. 'As I knew she would.'

I stared at the grey and white hawk. Sensing my interest, she turned her head towards me. It seemed cruel to keep such a proud creature in darkness.

'Why is she hooded?'

'To keep her calm.' He spoke very slowly as if addressing a child. 'Birds like Dido hunt by sight. When she hovers two hundred feet above a field, she can detect a mouse creeping in a hedgerow. She can bring down a heron released three miles from the point of cast-off. The merest flicker of movement – a change in the light, a shadow on a hillside – can capture her attention. Excite her. Draw her.' Vaughan Pritchard leaned forward. 'Make no mistake, she is beautiful, but she is also vicious, Marta. The hood is most necessary to curb her instincts. Without it, naked if you will, Dido would reveal her true nature.'

The log in the hearth popped. Golden flames tipped with scarlet danced into the throat of the chimney. Warmth flooded my belly. It was not from the wine, although I raised the glass to hide the flush that burned on my cheeks.

'I wonder . . .' Vaughan Pritchard studied me.

'You wonder what, sir?' I took a mouthful of wine.

'I wonder at your true nature, Marta. There are not many governesses who would . . . *choose* to come to me as you have.'

I swallowed. 'Do you have great experience of governesses, sir?'

He barked out a laugh. 'None like you.'

Nathaniel had offered me much, yet I had won so little from him. Vaughan Pritchard was a far greater prize. And worth playing all for. But it would be a mistake to allow him to imagine that I did not understand the game we were playing before the fire in his room above the stables.

'My lessons are never tedious.' I reached to the back of my

good mourning gown. 'But it is always more satisfying when a pupil is equal to the subject.'

Dido's bells jingled as she stamped on the bar. Shifting position, she threw out her wide grey wings and buffeted the air, but the leather thongs attached to her legs held her to the metal.

Vaughan Pritchard turned, whispered softly and immediately she quietened. He returned his attention to me. 'My lady is bored. The hunt is everything to such a magnificent creature.'

I placed my glass on the rug beside the settle and stood, one hand still hidden. Turning slowly, I held my hair aside and showed him the hooks that I had already loosened. Half of the bodice hung open now, revealing my naked back.

'I am no hedge mouse, sir.'

I heard the scrape of the chair on the stones as he rose abruptly. In a moment, I smelt tobacco. I felt his lips on my neck and his long fingers move under the fabric and over my skin.

20

And so, we began.

For two weeks the rain continued to fall and the waters rose until Fyneshade was an island of turrets and stone. Each night when the house was silent, Grace came to my room and led me through the passages to the stables. And each night Vaughan Pritchard was waiting for me. We found, that first time, that our tastes were well suited. Although the master's son was a man of experience, he discovered an equal in knowledge and daring.

At first, he complained that he missed the pleasure and prizes of gamehawking, but as the water-bound days of his capture continued he found other distractions.

Two days after my first true meeting with her brother, Old Maggie and Mrs Gurney deemed Grace recovered enough to return to the schoolroom. This was no obstacle. Panjan was a powerful inducement to secrecy, and the doll, Rosa – kept, as

I now knew, in a box beneath the canopied bed in the stables – held equal sway in my pupil's affections.

As long as access to these pretty toys was guaranteed, Grace was happy to be our silent Mercury.

When Old Maggie succumbed to a more severe form of Grace's infection, I did indeed wonder if we were blessed by the gods. The old woman's lungs creaked like an ancient door as she struggled to draw breath and her voice was a rasping croak. Good Mrs Gurney insisted that rest and a stronger infusion of her mother's linctus would ease the ancient nursemaid's condition and she was pleased when I offered to take this steaming concoction to Old Maggie each evening after our meal in the parlour. The nursery was, after all, along the passage from my own chamber.

Mrs Gurney would not have been so grateful had she known of the drops of opium I added to the cup.

We fell into an easy pattern. When Grace came for me, I was ready. And when she led me back to my room after my hours in the stables, I washed her face and neatened her hair so that Old Maggie, if she were to rally, would not suspect her lamb to have strayed. Each time, before Grace disappeared through the wall beside the hearth to return to the nursery nearby, I knelt to press my finger to her lips to seal the pact of our secrecy.

I did not begrudge the hours I spent with her in the schoolroom now. It gave me a chance to rest and anticipate the night to come. Mostly, while Grace drew, I sat by the fire and allowed my thoughts to roam. The books I had found on the secret shelf in the library were a poor substitute for the liberty of midnight.

'Marta!' Mrs Gurney tried again. 'Marta! Did you hear me?'

She tapped expectantly on the table. I looked up from my dish – cold tongue was today's offering. Even Lancer had rejected it from my hands.

'I am sorry, I was considering books that might appeal to Grace.' I smiled. 'While she draws – and as we both know she does that so very well – I thought I could read aloud to her, perhaps Mr Dickens or Miss Austen? It would be beneficial.'

I had been thinking no such thing, but Mrs Gurney would not want to hear the thoughts in my head. In fact, I am sure that she could not comprehend that such things were possible. Or pleasurable.

The housekeeper nodded. 'I suppose that might be very good for her. Now, did you hear what I said?'

I shook my head in apology. 'My mind was elsewhere.'

'You really have been in a dream these last days, Marta.' Mrs Gurney tutted. 'I hope you're not another one to have taken Grace's chill. Old Maggie's barely able to stand with it.' She dabbed at a spot of grease on her broad starched breast. 'What I said was that the floods are clearing. The rain's eased off these last two days and once the lower road is dry again Dawson can go to Tideswell.'

I gave her my full attention now. If the roads opened, Vaughan Pritchard would surely leave to continue his sport. It was a continual wonder that since his arrival, his name had not been mentioned to me once. The man who was present in my every waking thought was a ghost in his own house.

'Is there anything you need?' Mrs Gurney continued. 'For Grace's lessons naturally, but also for yourself? I know we live quietly here, but I wouldn't want you to feel that you can't send for things that a young lady like yourself might want. Lace, for example, buttons, gloves. Black, of course, until . . . well, until . . .' She attempted a smile of sympathetic consolation.

'Until my period of mourning is ended?' I folded my hands in my lap and cast down my eyes. 'It is good of you to ask me that, Mrs Gurney. As you know, I was very close to my Grandmere.' I pronounced that with such a heavy French inflection that it sounded, to my ears, a parody. I knew it would discomfort the housekeeper, who, as far as I could ascertain from our many conversations together, was not aware of a world beyond Buxton. In some obscure way I wanted to punish her for bringing me bad news.

'You are kind. I would welcome fresh paper and charcoal for Grace, but there is nothing I need at present. Oh!' I paused. 'Perhaps black ribbon. Wide. If Dawson could bring me some, I would be most grateful.'

'Good. I'll add that to the list.' Mrs Gurney peered at me. 'Are you sure you haven't taken the chill, Marta? You're pale as a bedsheet.'

I was reminded of one of Grandmere's stories. Twelve princesses were imprisoned by their stepmother in a tower surrounded by the sea. Jealous of their youth and beauty, the older woman wished to hide them from the eyes of men. She set a spy, an ancient crone, to live with the princesses and was puzzled to hear that every morning the girls were too exhausted to rise. Moreover, the soles of the golden slippers at the ends of their beds were completely worn. No matter how many new pairs were sent to the tower, the old crone found the same every morning: slumbering sisters and shredded slippers.

The answer to the riddle was simple. Each night a magical

doorway opened in the tower and the twelve princesses descended to a fairy hall where they danced and danced until their dainty slippers were worn to tatters.

'I am quite well, Mrs Gurney.' I rose from the table. 'Just a little tired perhaps. My sleep has been interrupted these last few days.'

❦

'Where I go tomorrow is no business of yours, Marta.' He rolled from me in the bed and reached for his brandy.

I stared at the canopy above us. 'Is it really so inquisitive of me to ask about the world beyond these walls? You yourself refer to it as a prison.'

He took a mouthful of brandy and set down the glass. 'A prison with the most delightful chains.' Taking a handful of my hair in his, he began to wind it about his wrist. I shifted to let the sheet fall from my shoulders and stroked the back of his hand.

'When will you return? Permit me to ask that, at least.' I looked up at him. 'The days are very long and very dull at Fyneshade.' I knew that the candlelight shone in my black eyes and I saw the wolfish look in his own.

'Soon.' He wound me towards him. 'Sooner than I would usually return to this place of purgatory. I think you have cast a spell on me, Marta. Tell me, are you a witch?'

'Witches exist only in stories for children. And you are no child, sir.'

'The time for formality is long past.' He pulled my hair tight. 'My name is Vaughan. Use it.'

'Very well, *Vaughan*.' I smiled. Grandmere had taught me the power of names. The fact that he had given me permission to use his first name – indeed, asked me to do so – was the sign I had been waiting for. The bond between us now was not that of master and servant. I decided to test this new intimacy.

'You were not named William for your father, then?'

He shrugged. 'It was my mother's family name before marriage. There were no boys in the line and she wished to preserve the connection.'

This apparently easy discussion of his parents took me forward. I had crossed a border and new territory lay there for the taking. I considered my next steps in this unclaimed land.

'I am glad your mother prevailed. Vaughan is a more distinctive name.' I tilted my head. 'You do not look like a William.'

He tugged on my hair. A thick black bracelet coiled about his wrist now. 'And what does a William look like?'

'Old. I have never met your father so I have no idea if he suits the name or not.'

Vaughan stared at me. A twitch pulsed below his right eye. 'Three score years and ten. That is our allotted time according to the Bible, Marta. By that reckoning my father will soon be in debt.'

Sir William was an elderly man then? A future as a dusty widow, pensioned off to a little dower house and a little life was surely not my fate?

'Your fate will turn on the letter P.'

I cannot deny that I had begun to imagine myself in possession of a more agreeable prize than Sir William Pritchard. I sat up in the bed, took up my own glass and rolled the amber liquid around.

I took a sip of brandy. 'I do not believe he knows of my appointment, Vaughan.' I enjoyed using his name. It accentuated our intimacy. 'Mrs Gurney took it upon herself to employ me. It would be unfortunate if Sir William were to return to Fyneshade and find fault with her decision. Old men are capricious. If you are saying that he borrows time, then perhaps I do too.' I allowed a pause. 'What if he were to dismiss me?'

The answer was silence. I slid a look at Vaughan's face to see if my dart had found its target, but apart from that tic, trembling like a flea sealed beneath the skin, he was still and unreadable. I tried again. 'I have been at the house for nearly two months and there has been no word from your father. Is he travelling abroad?'

Vaughan's face darkened. He freed my hair from his wrist and turned away. 'You need not trouble yourself. My father is not likely to return.'

As I studied the breadth of his shoulders and the way the muscles of his back curved like wings in the light of the candles, I knew that it was not fortune or position alone that drew me to Vaughan Pritchard. I saw the marks left by my fingernails across his flesh. My skin was also striped by passion. The high collars and long sleeves of mourning were useful. I had thought that I would never meet someone like Nathaniel, but where he was fire, Vaughan was ice.

I leaned closer and traced the vivid line of a scratch with the tip of a finger. 'If Sir William has been away for so long and is not expected to come back, why will you not enter Fyneshade?' I knew that my next question was dangerously loaded, but the brandy and our new informality made me reckless. 'Why do you hide here in the stables? Do you fear him?'

Now he turned to me. The glass was knocked from my hand and brandy spilled across the sheets as he forced me back against the carved wooden headboard. 'I do not hide from that man,' he snarled into my face. 'He is nothing to me. Nothing.' I felt spittle on my skin but I could not wipe it away. Gripping my shoulders, he shook me. 'I do not fear my father.'

I struggled to breathe. His hands were now about my throat. I tried to prise them away, but his fury had a vicious strength.

'I ... I meant only ... I merely wished to be sure ...' I stared directly into his eyes. 'I did not mean to offend you, Vaughan. This house, the circumstances of my employment ... I wished only to understand.'

At last he released me. He took my glass from the sodden sheets and refilled it from the bottle at the side of the bed.

'Here.' He handed it to me and I thought it a sort of apology, although I knew him too well by now to think him capable of admitting regret. He filled his own glass and we sat in silence for a while listening to the wind buffeting the walls. It was impossible for his outburst to have been overheard by anyone except, perhaps, Grace. We were quite private here. Vaughan's rooms above the stables formed part of a large gabled block that jutted out near the river. His own groom and Dawson shared blind-walled accommodation on the far side of the courtyard where the lights from our windows could not be seen.

In the room beyond, Grace was occupied with her pencil and with Rosa. Once, after our time together, we had found her asleep before the dying embers of the fire, drawings of Dido spread around her. She knew better than to disturb our pleasure or to touch the hawk that 'watched' over her when we withdrew.

I studied our reflections in the Venetian glass that stood opposite the bed. Our dark hair and pale skin were a match, but now there was such a space between us. I regretted my bold questions. I had moved too early in the game.

Vaughan reached for the bottle and finished the brackish dregs of the brandy in sullen silence. I lay back and considered my error. As I studied the narrow silk pleats of the canopy overhead, I decided that it would not be wise for our evening to end in rancour. I searched for a more amenable, less imprudent topic.

Shifting to my side I propped my head on one arm and quizzed him gently about Dido's recent victory in the north. Gradually he thawed, describing the contest and the estate where she had triumphed. Vaughan stared at his reflection in the mirror as he conjured towering peaks, tumbling rivers, forests, valleys and vast tracts of land. I had a strange impression that he saw himself reflected in a way I could not see.

'A man could live like a king there.' He smiled at the glass.

I sat up and moved closer, nestling my head against his shoulder. 'And what of his queen?'

'She will rule his heart.' He threaded a coil of my hair through his fingers.

My own heart leapt as I inferred his meaning, but I was disappointed when he rose from the bed and took his night robe from a chair.

'It is time. Wake Grace.'

I was dismissed. Gathering my clothes from the floor, I cursed myself again for assuming an intimacy I had yet to earn. I dressed in silence, but as I went from the bedroom, he caught my arm and twisted me to face him. 'I believe you must be a witch. Have you cast a spell over me? Before you have even gone I find that I am planning our next meeting.'

His kiss was hard, painful almost. Releasing me he smiled. 'Soon, Marta. Be ready.'

I reached out for him. There was a scuffle from behind and I turned to see Grace standing in front of the fire. She sucked her thumb noisily and her cat eyes flicked between us.

Vaughan Pritchard left the following evening. His departure, like his very presence at Fyneshade, was not mentioned by Mrs Gurney. He was a superstition to her.

It was almost dark when, hidden by the curtain, I watched his neat black carriage roll out from the stable arch opposite my room and pass through the yard. If I had hoped to catch sight of him I would have been disappointed, for felted blinds were drawn at the small square windows.

21

The jewel-studded ball rolled along the grooved channel in the golden cushion until it disappeared into the hole beneath the monkey's tail. Mournful ruby eyes seemed to search for the bauble before finally, very slowly, Panjan closed his paws across his pointed face. Music played for a few moments more, then the room was silent. The performance was over.

I knelt beside Grace, who was still staring, open-mouthed, at the automaton. She twisted the material of her nightgown between her fingers and breathed loudly.

'Again.' Her knuckles showed white as she pulled at the cotton.

'No more tonight, little one.' I stroked her hair and tucked the ends of her small patchwork blanket around her shoulders. 'There, that's better.'

Vaughan had been gone for five days now, but each night I had taken Grace to see the monkey. These midnight excursions to the north-west corridor were a tedious trial, but while Vaughan was absent it was important to retain the confidence and compliance of his sister.

There was a draught in Panjan's room. The candles wavered in the brackets and our shadows shivered on the walls. I turned Grace to face me, but her eyes remained stubbornly fixed on the monkey. Taking her chin between my fingers, I moved her head so that I could look into her eyes.

She snuffled and twisted away to view the automaton. I resisted the impulse to slap her dull face and tried again.

'Listen to me, dearest. You have seen Panjan's little performance three times this evening.' I stroked her cheek.

The girl took a deep breath and began to flap her arms. The blanket fell to the floor. She opened her mouth wide and I feared that she was about to cry out. Instead she flung her arms around me as if I were Rosa and whispered into the folds of my wrapper, 'Back.'

From this I understood that she was at last willing to return to her room.

'Good.' Disentangling myself from her sticky embrace, I retrieved the blanket, wrapped it around her shoulders and smiled. 'Very good, Grace. We will go back now, but remember ...' Smiling, I pressed a finger to my lips.

She nodded and walked slowly to the door, muttering that single word, 'back', into her blanket.

I locked Panjan's room and pushed the key into the pocket of my wrapper. The tips of my fingers brushed the stick of chalk. After that last visit to the stables I had realised that I was beginning to know the way to Vaughan's room and now I intended to mark the maze in the walls to be certain. Knowledge was power and there was so much more to discover within the confines of Fyneshade.

The only obstruction to my freedom was Grace, who had proved surprisingly defiant when I asked her to show me how to open the secret door in my room. No matter how carefully I watched, she kept the trick of it hidden.

The corridor was silent and, apart from the circle of light cast by the candle of my chamberstick, it was in darkness. I turned at a familiar scratching noise. In a moment, Lancer joined us, pressing its nose into Grace's hands. The dog looked up at me, hopefully. It did not expect my affection, but scraps from Mrs Gurney's table had forged a bond between us.

Distracted, Grace fell to her knees and circled its neck with her arms. She began to croon and rock on the boards with Lancer clasped tight to her breast.

'Dearest!' I whispered, fearful that this embrace might lead to a game of chase along the passage. 'Let go. You can play with Lancer tomorrow.'

With some reluctance she untangled herself from the dog and stood up.

'Back.' She pointed into the shadows. After rubbing Lancer's nose, she plodded away, the dog trotting at her heels. I followed.

When we reached the little alcove where I assumed that Eavis had entered a turret, Grace paused and turned to look at me, then her gaze slid to the small enclosed space.

'Back,' she repeated herself. It was not unusual. Words often seemed to stick to her tongue like treacle to a spoon. What was unusual, however, was the way her eyes glinted in the light from my candle. I felt myself appraised. Once again, I had a fleeting impression of intelligence swimming behind the limpid pallor or – to be more precise – something close to guile.

It was a ridiculous notion. A moment later she was turning

circles on the boards and humming tunelessly. Lancer abandoned her and padded into the alcove and began to paw at the foot of the tapestry curtain.

'Black.'

Grace's voice was suddenly loud, perhaps loud enough to rouse someone. Setting down the chamberstick, I clasped her shoulders to stop the twirling.

'Shh!'

'Black.' She said the word quite distinctly and pointed at the dog which was now scratching along the bottom of the hidden door. Burrowing her chin into the folds of her blanket Grace shook her head and shivered theatrically. Although it was cold in the passage, I did not think it to be the cause of her discomfort.

Black?

Was that the word she had been saying all along?

I remembered Mrs Gurney's gabbled story about Eavis and copper polish. Lavender and sorrel indeed!

I went into the alcove, held back the tapestry and pushed at the arched wooden door. It was locked just as last time. Lancer lowered its head and snuffled along the narrow gap between the wood and the flagstones.

As I watched the dog, I realised that while Vaughan was away, I could exploit my freedom to explore other parts of the house. It would be useful and practical to discover new ways to bait Mrs Gurney. At the very least, it would be amusing.

I turned to Grace. She was standing quite still now and staring at me.

It was too late to force my pupil to show me, but as long as I had the key to Panjan, I had the key to everywhere within the walls of Fyneshade.

Grace and I returned to the north-west corridor very late the following night. The promise of five performances from the monkey – I had counted them out on every finger of my left hand – and the chance to hold his golden key was quite enough to persuade her to take me beyond the hidden doorway.

At first.

When I locked the door to Panjan's room and bent to remind her of our bargain, she stared mutinously at her feet.

'Come now, we made a promise to each other.' I wrapped my voice in silk.

'Black.' She whispered the word. I had heard her mutter it several times today in the schoolroom. The first time, I had looked up from my book to find her staring at me rather than scribbling.

'When friends make promises to each other, they do not break them. We agreed that you would show me the way behind the door tonight, little one.'

Grace scuffed her slippered feet on the wide oak boards and did not look up. It came to me that perhaps she did not know a way after all and had played me for a fool.

'Is there a way into the turret or were you lying?' My question came out sharper than I had intended.

Grace shook her head and fiddled with her nightgown. I could not determine how this answered my question.

'Well?' I patted her shoulder but it did not elicit a response. I wanted to pinch the answer from her, but I knew this would increase her obstinacy. 'Very well. If you do not take me there tonight, I will throw Panjan's key into the river.'

Straightening up, I lifted my candle and began to walk back down the corridor.

'Black,' she hissed loudly to my back.

I stopped, expecting her to join me. When she failed to do so, I turned. Grace lingered outside Panjan's room and pointed to the opposite end of the passage. 'Come.'

Puzzled, I watched her stocky form disappear into the shadows.

At the far end of the passage, the moon-white faces of the children in the painting floated above us. In the candlelight, the flushes of red across their pearlish cheeks, no doubt intended by the artist to signal vitality, suggested fever.

I raised the chamberstick. There was nothing here to suggest an entrance to a hidden passage. The stone walls were square and crisply cut to the angle and there were no tapestries or curtains to disguise a door.

Grace bent in the corner. I heard a click and she lifted the boards to reveal a square black hole, a little less than two feet wide. Without waiting, she sat on the edge of the trapdoor and then she slipped down inside.

'Grace!' I peered into the gap, worried that she had fallen, but the light showed a flight of narrow wooden steps. Guarding the candle, I bunched the wrapper at my knees and followed my pupil. Unwilling to leave evidence of our expedition, I took hold of a leather strap attached to the back of the trapdoor and pulled it shut behind me.

There were not many steps, six at most, and Grace was waiting for me at the bottom. We were pressed together now in a small angular space beneath the boards. Grace pointed at a ragged hole in the stones behind her. Dipping her head, she squeezed past me and crawled into the opening. Again, I followed to find that once through the gap I could stand almost upright in a narrow, arched passage. Ahead I saw the white hem of Grace's nightgown and the patchwork squares of the blanket wrapped around her shoulders disappearing into the gloom.

We seemed to be in a very ancient part of the house. The way through the walls here was hewn from great stone blocks and the dry floor was thick with dust that rose into the air as we walked. I felt it in my nose and in my throat and I tasted antiquity on my tongue. This passage was dead; there is no other word to describe the atmosphere that closed around us. No creatures scuttled from the light of my candle, no cobwebs hung in garlands above us; there was no creaking or sighing of wooden boards underfoot.

Grace paused where the passage divided into two forks. She steadied herself for a moment, one hand on the wall, before plunging into the smaller of two entrances. I crouched low and went after her. The new passage led upward. After a few yards the sloping floor became winding stone steps.

I counted as we climbed. At the twentieth step, Grace turned to me, a finger to her lips. I thought we would continue upward for the light showed that the stairs spiralled above us like the shell of a snail. Instead, Grace ran the palm of her left hand over the wall. A section of stones swung silently outward. A gust of fresh air caused my candle flame to flutter. My hair moved on my shoulders as the clean, sharp draught swept over us. I recognised the scent it carried, but for the moment I could not place it.

Grace stared up at me. For once she did not seem eager to lead the way. Her eyes wandered to the doorway.

'Black.'

She rolled her hands together beneath the blanket. Over and

over she turned them, all the while repeating the word to herself in a whisper. She did not seem frightened; that would be too strong a word to describe her demeanour with accuracy. No, my pupil appeared unwilling.

I stepped past her and lowered my head to see what the doorway had revealed. The view was partially obscured by a fall of heavy, sack-like material. Handing Grace the chamberstick, I pushed at the edge of the fabric and found that the door had opened in panelling midway along a great vaulted gallery.

No candles were lit here, but moonlight streamed through a huge mullioned window at the far end. I held the panelled door ajar and listened. The only sound was the slow, regular tick of a clock. When I was certain that the vast space was quite deserted, I took the chamberstick from Grace, caught her hand in mine and stepped into the vaulted gallery, pulling her behind me. The fabric shielding the door creaked as we moved it aside.

In all the weeks I had been at Fyneshade I had never seen this place. The walls were lined with dark tapestries that fell from the cornice of an ornate plaster ceiling to rug-covered floorboards. Heavy gilded chairs with fat cushions and splayed legs were set at intervals along the walls and, where space between the tapestries allowed, huge paintings were suspended from the panelling. A vast marble fireplace supported on either side by pale columns that twisted towards the ceiling interrupted the long run of the wall opposite.

This was the faded grandeur of another age. I was reminded of the great house above Croyle. Nathaniel had taken me to see it once when his uncle was absent. The tiny venal eyes of smug-faced Van Meerans spanning two centuries had watched us from the walls as their descendant showed me his future. Walking through the rooms together, it had been easy to imagine a life in such a fine place, and to imagine the changes I might make in due course. Almost as easy as it had been for Nathaniel to cast me aside.

'Black.'

Grace tugged at my hand and tried to pull me to the right, but first I wanted to confirm a growing suspicion. Fighting her reluctance, I led her past the fireplace and the battalion of chairs to the window. The curve of the river below shone like a scimitar in the moonlight. I was right. This was the north wing, the part of the house locked for the winter.

And now I recognised the scent in the air here. It was the medicinal aroma that had lingered in the alcove when I had followed Eavis and her steaming bowl. A clock began to chime. Three bell-like notes echoed in the chamber. Grace freed her hand from mine and plucked at the sleeve of my wrapper.

'Black.' She pointed to the shadows furthest from the window.

'Yes.' I nodded and raised the candlestick. 'It is very dark here.'

'No.' Grace frowned as if I had said something quite foolish. 'Bad.'

This part of the house was indeed unused, as Mrs Gurney had told me. As we moved back down the gallery my candle showed a thin layer of dust on the furniture. The tapestries and cushions were shredded by moths and the arms of the candle brackets on the walls stood empty.

As we went carefully and quietly, even Grace seemed aware of our trespass. Arms outstretched, she walked on tiptoe, an exaggeration of caution, and she peered about as if expecting to be discovered at any moment.

At the far end of the gallery four doors were arranged in sturdy symmetry on opposite walls. The doors were much like any other at Fyneshade. A little heavier and broader perhaps, but the north wing was the oldest part of the house, built when utility and security took precedence over beauty. Grace stood silently behind me. After a moment she tiptoed from my side and tentatively reached out to one of the doors. She stopped herself sharply before her fingers made contact with the wood. The sudden flinching retraction of her hand was like a burn.

'Black,' she muttered again to herself.

I stared at the door. It was studded with rows of nails and a large iron key with a trefoil bow stood proud in the lock. Entering the room would be easy. A flicker of unease began to dance in my mind. What lay behind those broad oak planks?

And yet . . .

I knelt at Grace's side. 'Dearest, this is very important. If I . . . *we* go into the room, will anyone know?'

She swayed from side to side and stared up at the ceiling.

'Grace!' I set down the chamberstick and took her hands in mine. 'Answer me. Is there anyone in there?'

She looked at me directly and shook her head slowly.

'What *is* in there?'

Her blue eyes were solemn and huge. I wanted to shake an answer from her, but it was hopeless. Resisting the desire to punish her stupidity, I retrieved the chamberstick and stood up. I reached for the metal ring of the door and twisted it, but it was locked.

'Bad.'

I turned. Grace was twirling on an old rug, the steps of her ungainly dance following the looping pattern of the Turkish weave. She started to hum.

When she glanced at me, I put a finger to my lips. 'Shhhh.'

She nodded and continued to spin in silence.

I reached for the key. It turned easily in the oiled lock. There was sharp click and when I applied a little force the door began to open.

22

The smell! That was the first thing that came to me. As I stood on the threshold of the black room, I was enveloped by the faint but unmistakable reek of rotten meat.

Last autumn, boasting of the hard bargain she had driven, Aunt Clare had bought a side of salted pig from a trader passing through Croyle. The cloth-wrapped carcass was delivered to our cottage on a bitter October day and she had taken it down to the cellar to hang on a hook from the rafters. The meat was intended to last us through the winter months.

Two weeks later, blowflies began to appear, scores of them, buzzing in corners, flitting around our skirts and settling on the table when food was served. Soon after, the smell came – the sweetly disgusting odour of putrefaction. I knew it immediately from my hours in the crypt with Nathaniel. When the ancient lead-lined coffin of a Van Meeran cousin had begun to leak a pool of treacle-thick liquid onto the stones we were forced to move our trysting place. In truth, I sometimes wondered if that puddle of stinking slime was liquified outrage at our desecration of an old woman's rest.

I had gone straight to the cellar and found that pig carcass bloated, green and riddled with maggots. The rancid meat had not been properly cured. Aunt Clare had bought badly and she never forgave me for knowing it.

'Bad.'

Grace pressed close and buried her face in the skirt of my wrapper. She was right, the stench was foul.

The doorway was partly curtained off from the room. A glow crept beneath the hem of the draped black satin before me. Covering my nose and mouth, I listened intently. There was a faint spluttering sound. Shielded by the curtain, I was now aware of the peculiar warmth flooding from the room. I could feel the chill of the gallery at my back, but ahead there was heat. I listened intently. I could not be sure that the sound was not that of a crackling fire. But why would a hearth be lit in a deserted wing?

I had come this far. There was no point in hiding behind a curtain at the last. Uncovering my face to grasp Grace's hand in mine, I held out my chamberstick and stepped beyond the curtain.

A dark, richly patterned chinoiserie carpet covered most of the floor, the walls were lined with black-figured silk, swagged curtains in the same mourning hue were drawn across a wide window and the fabric hangings of a four-poster bed opposite the hearth were of a midnight velvet trimmed with gold thread that glimmered in the firelight.

The room had a funereal opulence.

I blinked, surprised by the light. Candles flickered in

brackets over the softly glowing hearth and there were more in the branches of a gilt stick set on a table near the huge bed.

Grace wrested her hand from mine. She rubbed her nose and went to a chair set against the wall furthest from the bed. Planting herself firmly on the gloomy cushions, she began to swing her feet. It was obvious that she did not intend to move from this position.

I raised my finger to my lips. She nodded and copied me. In a corner of the room, just along from the chair where Grace sat, there was a closed door in the fabric-covered wall. Quietly, I went to stand next to it. I listened again but heard nothing. There was a key in the lock. I turned it to be sure that no one could surprise me and, out of magpie habit, I slipped it into the pocket of my wrapper. The tips of my fingers brushed the chalk again. When Grace led me back later, I would mark the way.

Perhaps because I was becoming accustomed to it, or perhaps because our intrusion had brought fresh air from the gallery, the odour was fading. I looked about the room. Other than the great bed, the only other item of note was a long, low object stationed in the shadows below the window. I went nearer and saw that it was a large wooden frame, perhaps six feet in length, criss-crossed with buckled leather straps that flailed over the sides onto the rug. I moved the chamberstick closer. There seemed to be a rounded leather bolster at one end and two metal stirrup-like cups at the other. Strips of leather attached to the cups suggested their purpose was to bind.

I had read of such instruments in the books from the library's hidden shelf. For some, pain and pleasure, torture and delight kept easy company together.

I turned at a sound from behind. Other than Grace, the room

was deserted. The noise, something between a snore and the pant of a dog, came again from the curtained bed.

From this angle I saw a large china bowl on the boards beside the bed and an untidy heap of soiled towels. And now, beneath the stench of decay, I detected again the lacing of something medicinal. I looked at Grace. She was still in the chair on the far side of the room. Sucking on her thumb, she stared up at the ceiling. With her free hand she seemed to be tracking the intricate patterns of the swirls and loops in the plaster.

The sound came again, louder.

I went to the bedside, reached out to part the velvet hangings and immediately had to step back at the fetid smell released by the movement of the fabric. I stood apart for a moment to allow my belly to settle. Something moved inside the bed. Mastering my revulsion, I set the chamberstick next to a glass and water jug on the bedstand and dragged the hangings aside.

The sheets were a stained, disordered tangle. In the midst of them, grotesquely twisted, etiolated and emaciated beyond the point where life could be thought possible, there was a man. An old man.

He gasped and arched his back, contorted limbs jerking like those of puppet controlled by a cruel child. I saw open sores where he had lain too long and the degradation of a body that had lost control of itself. Head trembling, the old man looked at me.

All the remaining energy and purpose of his life was locked into pale blue eyes that burned, most horribly, with understanding. I felt the hairs rise on the back of my neck. I did not fear the dead; the living were another matter. As I looked on his face, I realised there was dread in those familiar eyes.

A hand slipped into mine. I looked down at Grace, who was peering into the shadowed bed. Pouting, she held the end of her plait and twiddled it about and then she stood on the tip of her toes for a better view. At last, as if quite certain there was no mistake, she nodded.

'Papa.'

23

Next morning as I went down to the parlour, questions chased through my head like a pack of hounds.

I had been lied to. That much was clear.

Sir William Pritchard – alive, but barely so – had been here at Fyneshade all along.

The decrepit invalid I had seen last night would never leave that room and had not done so in a very long time. Mrs Gurney's stolid manner had convinced me that she was too dull and too stupid to tell me anything other than the truth. I had been tricked by my own sense of a natural superiority. This was almost as infuriating as discovering her deceit.

But what did it mean? Why did she lie about my employer? And what of Vaughan?

'My father is not likely to return.'

Was he complicit in this charade?

Last night when Grace left me, I thought on these questions

for a long time. Eventually, as light fringed the edges of the curtain at my window, I decided to add the secret of Sir William Pritchard to my cache.

I stifled a yawn as I went to the stairs. Another tedious breakfast with Mrs Gurney lay ahead. It would almost be amusing to confront her with what I now knew about the wretched master of Fyneshade, but that information was valuable currency. And besides, it would lead to questions I would not want to answer.

I caught sight of myself as I passed the mirror at the end of the passage to my room. There were faint shadows beneath my eyes and my cheeks were pale. I pinched them to bring colour and I bit down hard on my lower lip.

No, my reflection agreed with me, *it would be foolish to squander such treasure.*

Satisfied that my face would not betray me, I continued to the upper landing. Far below I heard voices. Taking care not to be heard I descended until I reached the gallery above the great hallway. Mrs Gurney and Eavis were talking together at the foot of the stairs. The harsh voice of the laundress carried easily to the floor above.

'I'm telling you, I know what I've seen.'

I froze. Was it possible that the woman had discovered my visit to the black room? Holding the hem of my dress, I crossed the gallery to a place where I could see and hear better. I slipped behind an oversized vase and watched the lacy top of Mrs Gurney's head move from side to side.

'That can't be. She wouldn't.' She shook her head again. 'I can't think of it.'

My collar seemed to tighten at my throat. I had been silent

and careful last night. How could Eavis know? Had the woman spied on me?

I leaned out a little way. Eavis had her back to the stairs. She towered above Mrs Gurney, whose hands were clasped defensively to her breast.

'The stains!' Eavis stepped closer to the housekeeper. 'Do you want to look for yourself? You'll see. He's had a woman in there. And there's more—'

'No!' Mrs Gurney held up a hand to stop any further sordid revelation. 'I believe you.'

Eavis's grizzled head turned as she made certain that the pair of them were alone. 'We both know who. Thinks herself better than the rest of us, she does.'

Mrs Gurney pulled at the collar of her dress. 'You have no evidence for such an accusation.'

'I do. It's down in the laundry. I had to remind Suki to fetch the rest of his linens yesterday. I know she's been in his rooms, *with* him.'

'Well, it's not something I can . . .' The housekeeper puffed out her cheeks. 'I don't believe it of her. I grant you she's not like the rest . . .' She faltered as a maid limped across the hallway with a coal scuttle. When she had gone, Eavis snorted.

'No, she's not like the rest of them. What were you thinking bringing someone like her to Fyneshade?'

'She came with the best of references. She *is* younger than I expected and quite a . . .'

'Beauty,' Eavis continued where Mrs Gurney left off. 'If that dark, stringy sort is to your taste. And we all know he don't much care who—'

'Enough.' Mrs Gurney raised her hand again. She peered to

the left and right, fearful of eavesdroppers. Eavis shrugged and took up a basket lying on the floor at her feet.

'I've told you now. I'll leave it to you. The pair of you sit together nice and dainty at your table three times a day. There's plenty of time to find out if the governess is a whore.'

❧

Mrs Gurney could not bring herself to look at me. She buttered her bread as if she wished to murder it and then she laid down the knife and stared at the faded floral wallpaper behind me. She sighed heavily and shook her head. The lace lappets of her cap flapped about her chins.

I composed my features to express pleasant concern. 'Is there something wrong, Mrs Gurney?'

The lappets flapped again as she raised the bread to her mouth. She chewed with a slow determination and still she did not look at me.

'Are you ill?' I reached across the table and placed my hand over hers. 'Have you taken the chill that has afflicted Grace and Old Maggie? If so, perhaps I could help you make up your mother's linctus. It eased them so very much.'

I saw confusion on her plain, duplicitous face.

'I am quite well, Marta, thank you for your concern.' She stared frankly at me. I realised she was searching for signs of depravity.

I smiled. 'But I sense that you are troubled, Mrs Gurney. If there is anything I can do, you have only to ask.'

The housekeeper cleared her throat and took a deep breath. 'The thing is, Marta, I need to know ...' She released her hand from mine and took up her teacup. The china rattled as she did so.

'Need to know what?' I played the innocent and nibbled at my slice of bread and jam.

'It's a delicate matter and I don't know how to begin. You see, I have to ask if … if …' She drowned her question with a mouthful of tea. 'Such a difficult thing to ask, but I must for the sake of …' She faltered once more.

I sat back and folded my hands neatly in my lap. 'It is little Grace, isn't it? You are concerned for her?'

Mrs Gurney opened her mouth, but nothing came out. I reached for her hand again.

'I see it in your eyes. It is only natural that you should have questions about her progress. It was, after all, you who took the risk of bringing me here. I am more than happy to discuss her.'

Relief bloomed like cherry blossom across Mrs Gurney's cheeks as I described the many ways that Grace was flourishing under my careful tutelage. I told her again about the artistic gifts that raised the girl above her peers; I assured her that my pupil's sweet nature and gentle temperament were beyond anything that could be required in a young lady of good station and I emphasised every benefit of our joyful time together. Warming to my subject, I allowed small tears to trickle from my eyes.

'Forgive me, dear Mrs Gurney. I find I am quite as in thrall to little Grace as you have been all these years.' I rose from the table. 'And now, if you will excuse me, I will go to her in the school-room. Today we are going to read from a book of fables.'

'Of course, Marta, off you go.' The housekeeper beamed. I was certain that my performance had convinced her of the impossibility of Eavis's accusation. Brushing crumbs from the skirt of my dress, I went to the door.

'Oh.' I paused at the steps and turned. 'I meant to ask *you* a question. There is something that has bothered me, something I thought you should know. I ... I have wrestled with my conscience on the matter, but I think I must tell you.'

Mrs Gurney started to clear our breakfast dishes so that they were ready for Jennet. She replaced the lid of the jam pot and wiped the butter knife with her napkin. 'Go on, Marta.'

'Well, I am sure it is nothing or something quite easily explained. I would not wish to cause trouble.' She looked up from the table as I continued.

'As I think you know, I did not sleep well last week. I believe my concern for Grace – her infirmity – was the cause of my wakefulness. Several evenings ago, very late – past midnight, I went to my window for air and I saw ...' I shook my head. 'No. No, it is nothing. You must forget I have spoken. I do not wish to concern you with a trivial matter.'

'You saw what, Marta?' Mrs Gurney was quite still, the little knife pointed upright in her hand.

I raised my own hand to my heart. 'I saw one of the maids crossing the courtyard beneath my window. Before she went through the archway to the stables she turned to look up and I saw her face in the moonlight. It was Suki.'

Lancer barked and bounded down the gravel path between the avenue of ornamental trees. Grace tried to catch hold of its tail, but the dog jagged to the side and she blundered after it, laughing and fumbling her hands. Her fair hair shone in the spring sunlight and the sharpness of the air brought a ruddy glow to her cheeks. If anyone observed us from the house, we would present a most delightful scene – the caring governess determined to bring cheer and variety to her pupil's routine.

After luncheon I had asked Old Maggie to prepare Grace for a walk in the grounds. Now, suitably muffled, we were heading down to the gate leading out to the riverbank. I intended to study the exterior of the north wing to be certain of the position of the black room.

The path beside the river was no longer waterlogged, but it was still rutted and muddy. I lifted the hem of my cloak and pinched up the dress beneath to guard the fabric as I made my way to the place where Fyneshade's northern wing came into view. Grace and Lancer trotted amiably behind me, the dog occasionally disappearing into the osiers and brambles when its nose caught the scent of an animal or bird.

As we came to the bend in the river, I remembered the first time I had seen Vaughan here with Dido. A sudden warmth and tightening in the pit of my belly told me how much I would welcome his return.

'Soon, Marta. Be ready.'

Soon was not a number of days or a date on a calendar. I envied Dido.

We passed the willows whose trailing branches had been held fast in the ice. Pale greenish catkins shivered from those same branches now. The season was turning. A crescent moon was visible in the clear blue sky. In two weeks, it would be full; the Egg Moon of April when life quickened in the land and the wombs of its creatures.

Lancer pushed past me on the riverbank and I had to steady myself against a tree to keep my balance. The dog loped to the edge of the water and began to drink. Today the river was still and grey. I had gone a little further along this time. Ahead of me there was a low stone bridge that had been hidden before by a bend.

I turned to look back at the house. The northern wing was a jagged dark mass silhouetted against the sky. The only break in that shadowy bulk was a broad window set high in the wall facing the river. The panes caught the sunlight and rippled with gold. I knew it for the window at the end of the long gallery.

There was a soft splash behind me and I turned, thinking it to be Lancer frisking at the edge of the river, but it was Grace. The girl had stepped from the bank into the water. Arms outstretched, she was trying to reach the opposite bank.

'Grace!' I darted over to her. Catching at the sodden hem of her coat, I dragged her back to the safety of the bank, knelt in the mud and twisted her roughly about to face me.

'Stupid girl.' I shook her. 'You could have drowned.'

She tried to wriggle from my grasp, but I held tight.

'Never do that again! Do you understand?' I gripped her shoulders. 'Just look at your boots; they are ruined.'

Grace stared dumbly at her feet.

'And your coat! What will Old Maggie say?'

In truth, that was the question I feared. How would it appear if I delivered the little princess of Fyneshade back to the nursery in such a state? Having taken great care to present myself as a loving and watchful governess, it was infuriating that the child's idiotic incomprehension of danger should undermine me. And now my cloak was soiled, my dress too.

Grace stiffened and looked over my shoulder. Pulling an arm free, she flailed it at the river and wailed.

'Hush.' I covered her mouth to stop the noise and twisted about to see what had attracted her attention.

On the far side, some fifty feet away, two women were walking along a rush-lined pathway. At first my view was obscured, but then they were framed in a clearer space where the osiers grew in wide-set clumps. Their dull brown clothing was not remarkable in any way and I could not see their faces. They walked in silence, their long shadows stretching across the still water to my side of the river. The women halted and I saw through the gap that one of them carried a cloth bag. They embraced and then the smaller of the pair, the one with the bag, carried on alone, drab shoulders hunched, mousy head bowed low.

The other stood and watched her companion for a time and then she turned to retrace the way they had come. As she did so, Grace squirmed free and called out. The woman turned to the source of the sound and she saw me watching through the reeds.

Jennet's eyes blazed with anger. I felt her hatred rush at me across the water.

And I knew that Suki had been dismissed, just as I had intended.

24

Suki's name was not mentioned by Mrs Gurney, but her disgrace was uppermost in the housekeeper's mind as we sat in the library after our meal. Now that the evenings were lengthening, she liked us to take tea and cake together where the light lingered. I was given to understand that this was a sign of favour. Two candles burned in the silver stick on the table behind our couch. This gentle light and the fading glow from the long window encouraged an intimacy between us.

'You'll bear in mind what I said about Mr Vaughan?' Mrs Gurney leaned across and patted my hand. The gesture was the clearest indication of my innocence.

'Only today I found out ...' She shook her head and prodded a fork into a slice of seed cake. 'Well, what I found out isn't fit to repeat, but you mark what I say, Marta.' She looked up, muddy eyes full of anxiety. 'Keep yourself to yourself when he's about. Don't go near the stables. Mrs Eavis made a dreadful mistake taking ...'

Taking Suki there with her.

I could see the words in Mrs Gurney's mind, even if she didn't say them.

She poked the cake into her mouth and continued. 'That's all I'm saying on the matter. I know he's the master's son and all, but while things are . . .' She considered how best to finish that sentence. 'While things are as they are, I'm glad to be in a position of responsibility here at Fyneshade.'

I reached down beside the couch to feed Lancer the last few crumbs from my plate. The cake was pleasing and it had been hard to deny myself. 'While Sir William is away, you mean, Mrs Gurney?'

'That's right.' She nodded but didn't look at me. 'While the master is away.'

Not very far away, I thought. Why was he hidden in that room and why would she go to such pains to keep the secret from me?

Behind Mrs Gurney, the day was fading into the west. Through the tall window at her back, the ornamental garden leading to the river gate was a herd of mounds and shadows.

I laid my napkin down on the small table before us. 'Is he really so very wicked? Young Mr Pritchard, I mean.'

I could not resist. The sight of the prim housekeeper's discomfort was delicious. It would be amusing to report this conversation to Vaughan when he returned. He had already complimented my imitation of the woman's broad vowels and homely speech.

A draught caught the embroidered point of my napkin. The 'P' fluttered back upon itself to reveal the less elegant stitching of the underside. At the same moment, several notes shimmered from the harp.

Mrs Gurney turned to the instrument and then she looked

back at me, her eyes hard and unusually sharp. 'I am not prepared to discuss him, Marta. He is not welcome inside these walls, that's all you need to know.' She set down her plate. 'He's due back in three days . . .'

I gripped my hands tightly together in my lap.

'. . . which isn't at all usual. He's usually away for longer. I'm only telling you so that you can guard yourself. Don't go near him or the stables.'

Mrs Gurney rose from the couch. 'It's winding night. If you'd like to come with me, I'd appreciate the company.'

'Of course.' I stood and smiled. 'Have you found the monkey's key yet?'

Patting the chatelaine at her waist, the housekeeper frowned. 'No, I'm afraid it's still missing. We'll have to send to the clocksmith in Buxton if it doesn't turn up. Fortunately, for the moment, Grace seems to have forgotten Panjan. Old Maggie thinks it must be you who's distracted her.'

We lay tangled together in front of the hearth.

Vaughan pushed my hair from my face and traced the line of my cheek. His fingertip moved to the skin of my neck, lingering in the little dip at the base of my throat before continuing its downward journey.

'You remind me of her.'

'Who?' I reached for his hand and stopped its progress.

'Dido.' He smiled. 'There is something of the hawk in you, Marta. Beneath the feathers, your bones are fine and delicate, but you are powerful. How else would you ensnare me?'

I looked over his shoulder at the hooded bird. Dido was quite still on the metal stand, but the firelight made her shadow move on the wall.

'You are also cruel.' He held up the hand caught in mine. Wide black ribbon trailed from his wrist.

He reached for a silver box on the hearth. Flicking open the lid, he offered it to me. I sat up, allowing strands of black hair to fall in across my naked body.

'A vice I have yet to acquire.'

'Is there room for more?' Vaughan held the end of a small cigarette to the flames. 'You are a witch, Marta. You compel me. I have never been so eager to return to my father's house.' He brought the cigarette to his lips and inhaled.

Remembering our last conversation on the matter of Sir William Pritchard, I knew I had to go carefully.

'And I was eager for your return. The time went slowly. I have no true companions at Fyneshade, as you yourself have observed.'

'Not even my sweet sister?' Vaughan smiled.

I glanced at the closed door to the bedroom and wondered if my pupil was ever disturbed, or even conscious of the sound of our passion. This evening, when I entered the stables, Vaughan had hardly looked at her. Ordering Grace to the bedroom, he had taken me quickly and without care. His hunger for my body was exhilarating.

Vaughan blew a ring of smoke into the air. The tobacco was rich, laced with an exotic scent that hinted at spices and the incense Grandmere had burned in a tiny gold crucible at times of ritual.

He stared into the fire and frowned.

'I have thought of you often in the last days, Marta. You have haunted me like no other woman. I . . .' He pushed at his hair. 'I have come to believe that you deserve more from me. The truth, for example.'

I remained perfectly still.

'Last time we met you asked about my father. I was angry, but not with you.' He drew on the cigarette. 'What has Gurney told you about him?'

'Only that he is away.'

'Away.' Vaughan laughed bitterly. 'He's certainly that. The man I knew left many years ago.'

I examined this statement, opening its compartments like a paper fortune puzzle. Did Vaughan mean that his father was absent in body or in mind? In which case, was he aware of the invalid who lay in the black room?

The answer came more swiftly and bluntly than I had expected.

'My father, the great Sir William Pritchard, is in a sanatorium, Marta. He brought such shame upon Fyneshade that even the servants cannot bear to mention his existence.'

The unexpected crack in Vaughan's voice suggested a depth of feeling I had not imagined him capable of.

Here was news indeed, but I needed to test it.

I sat up, allowing my hair to expose my naked body. When Vaughan turned to look at me, he could not hide his desire.

'A sanatorium?' I feigned confusion and sympathy. 'I did not imagine your father to be an invalid. What is his disease?'

'Spite.' Vaughan cast the stub of his cigarette into the fire and lit another. The scent of spice filled the air as he stood, went to the wall and took his grey coat from a hook. 'Here. Wear this, for now.' He smiled. 'You are too distracting.'

I draped the coat around my shoulders while he retrieved his gown from the chair where he had discarded it earlier.

'Let me tell you about my father.'

I did not speak or move. When a cat hunts with success it waits still and silent until its prey has forgotten its presence.

Vaughan inhaled and held the breath, all the while staring into the flames. At last, he exhaled luxuriously and began.

'My father was a handsome man. You wouldn't believe that if you were to see him now, but it was true. He knew that wherever he went he attracted the admiration of women and the envy of men. Regard was everything to him. He was tall, well formed, a daring horseman and, most importantly, he was landed and rich. William Pritchard was thought to be one of the finest catches in the country.

'My mother ...' I noted the smallest pause, '... caught him. She came from an old Welsh family. The Vaughans were once princes, but their fortune had diminished long before she was born.

'The Pritchards were also Welsh, but they were *not* an old family. Trade was the root of their wealth and a source of embarrassment to my grandfather. When his son fell in love with a nineteen-year-old beauty from noble stock but no great dowry, he was inclined to allow the marriage. His son would be tamed and the blood of the princes would flow in the veins of his grandchildren.'

Vaughan tapped ash from the end of the cigarette onto the hearth. He stood and went to sit in the wing-backed chair.

'The marriage was a mistake. There were seventeen years between them – for her that was a lifetime – and their temperaments were not suited. When my father rode to hounds my mother preferred to read or play music. Although she was young, she did not enjoy balls at the great houses of the county where my father expected her to glitter like an ornament bought to adorn the Pritchard name. Instead she delighted in domesticity and motherhood. He soon became bored.'

I thought about the bland-faced girl in the painting. How simple she must have been to make such an error.

Vaughan drew again. He breathed deeply, rolled his head on his broad shoulders and continued. 'While his disappointing wife buried herself in the nursery, my father sought entertainment elsewhere and did not bother to hide his transgressions. There were arguments, accusations. My parents became strangers to each other.

'I was five years old when William Pritchard decided that life as a husband was not to his taste. This was just after his own father died and he inherited the estate and the means to escape it. He was a wealthy, handsome man and the world was now his for the taking. At first he went to London, where he found the company he desired. Then he went to Europe – to France, Switzerland, the cities of the Italian states, Greece, Turkey, Russia even. He indulged his appetites for eight years, the last two of which he spent in Paris.'

I thought about the singular books I had found in the library. Many of them were printed in French.

'His absence was a happy time for me. I had the love of my mother and the run of the house. She decided that I should be educated at home. Tutors came and went.' He smiled. 'I was not a good pupil, Marta, but I learned . . . *enough* for a boy of my station. And beyond the schoolroom, where presently you spend so many hours with my sister, I discovered so much more.'

Presently? I held that word close and explored its possible meanings while Vaughan continued.

'There was one particular servant, Grindlow the head groom, who had lived at Fyneshade all his life, like his father before him and his father's father before that. Grindlows had served the house long before the Pritchards bought it. He taught me how to ride, how to snare a rabbit and how to fish in the river. Thomas Grindlow was more of a father to me than my father ever was.' Vaughan gestured lazily with the hand that held the cigarette.

'These were his rooms, Grindlow's. Here in the stables, he kept a hawk.' He turned to look at Dido, hooded and motionless. 'His bird was a common kestrel, but it was he who taught me the art of falconry. And most importantly . . .' he sat forward to tap more ash onto the stones, '. . . good old Grindlow showed me the secrets of the walls.'

Vaughan rose to take a log from a pile beside the hearth. He cast it onto the fire and watched it catch. His night robe hung loose and open and the flames gilded his body. I resisted the impulse to draw him to me. Instead, silent like Dido, I waited for more, excited by the inferences I took from his frankness.

Without looking at me, he continued. 'My father finally came back to Fyneshade when his gambling debts had risen beyond his income from the estate. I was thirteen. My mother never discussed such things with me, but I know that in those years abroad he squandered my inheritance.

'William Pritchard returned a bitter and vicious man. Years of dissipation had taken their toll and, just as he was no longer very rich, he was no longer very handsome. His body had coarsened, his features were a blurred impression of the man he had been and his blood was thickened by drink. He barely knew I existed and I was happy to be ignored. My mother also refused his company. He had long forfeited his right to call her 'wife', but they were bound together. Divorce is shameful, and also costly. They lived here quite separately. He took up residence in the north wing and had his room decorated to resemble a particular Parisian bordello – *Le Palais Noir*. At great cost to the estate, the walls were papered with black silk from China.

'Within a year of my father's return, four servants at Fyneshade were forced to leave penniless, each of them with a child in their belly. There were others out on the estate. The women were not willing. There were stories of cruelty and force. I believe my mother sent money, but it was no compensation for lives ruined. People grew wary. Female servants refused to be alone in my father's company. Those years abroad had twisted something in him. There was a madness in William Pritchard, an appetite that could not be sated.'

Vaughan turned to me. 'I believe the French disease that eventually sent him to the sanatorium had already affected his mind. And then . . . then . . .' He lapsed into silence. After a moment, he went from the hearth to the table at the far end of the room. I heard clinking and the gurgle of liquid.

'Here.' He handed a glass of wine to me and sat again in the chair. When he did not speak, I took a sip of wine and waited, unwilling to prompt. At last he leaned towards me.

'And then, late one night, his mind addled with anger, drink and desire, he left the north wing and made his way to my mother's room. He forced himself on her. The next morning, I saw bruises on her face and marks on her throat and hands that she could not fully disguise. Neither could she hide from me what had happened.' He turned the crystal glass in his hand. The wine glowed like Panjan's eyes. 'Do you love your mother?'

'She died when I was too young to know her, Vaughan.'

'And your father?' His pale eyes shone. I could not tell if I saw tears there or the effect of the firelight.

'He too is dead. The same fever took them both.'

'Then we are both orphans.' He took a mouthful of wine and wiped his lips with the back of his hand. 'Or as good as.'

He sat back. 'I do not clearly remember what followed, Marta. Fury clouded my memory. I know I went to my father's room. We argued and, at some point, it brought about some kind of fit and he fell, cracking his head on the stones of the hearth. The one thing I recall with complete clarity is looking down at him jerking on the floor, eyes rolled back into his skull, spittle foaming at his mouth. And then I ran from the north wing. I told no one what had happened. Instead, I took a horse from the stables and rode to the boundary of the estate. Later that afternoon, my father was found by a servant and a physician was sent for.

'Sir William Pritchard should have died. Instead, he lingered in the twilight of consciousness for a month. Every night I prayed that the next day might be his last and I am certain I was not alone in that entreaty.'

Vaughan looked into the darkness of his wine.

'If there is a God, he is deaf. Five weeks to the day of the . . . accident, my father recovered enough to summon our family lawyer. From that hour, I was exiled from the house. My things – my books, my clothes, even my childhood toys – were piled on the steps beyond the great hallway. My own mother escorted me to the gates and, when they were locked to me, she reached through the bars to touch my face. That was my father's greatest punishment, Marta, to divide us.'

I moved closer. 'What did you do, Vaughan? Where did you go?'

'Not far. Thanks to Grindlow, these rooms above the stables became my home. I have lived – if you can call it that – here for the last ten years. Apart from a miser's stipend, I have no fortune of my own. I have relied on my wits and latterly on the success of Dido. Fortunately, she is unmatched. My champion has won me a fortune.'

Aware of the mention of her name, the hawk stamped on the bar and batted her wide grey wings. Suddenly she seemed to fill the stone-walled space. I watched her arch her neck and settle, her feathers sleek once more.

Vaughan took up the bottle and refilled my glass. Wine brimmed over to the stones.

'I am a prisoner of my own fortune, Marta. The changes made to my father's last will and testament are clear on the matter. If I am ever discovered within the house before the death of Sir William Pritchard, then I will lose everything. The estate will go to a distant cousin. I will not jeopardise my last victory over him; the risk is too great.'

I twisted a button on the coat huddled around me. Having seen the man in the black room, it was clear that Vaughan would not have much longer to wait before receiving the keys to his kingdom. It occurred to me also that he must have broken the terms of the will. I set down my glass.

'But you have been inside. You have used the passages that Grindlow showed you.'

He rubbed the side of his face. I heard the rasp of his finger-nails in the stubble that shadowed his jaw.

'Of course I have, Marta. How else would you be here?' He

stared into his wine. 'I went to the chapel on the night before her funeral. It was high summer and she was surrounded by flowers. In the heat they were not enough to hide the corruption.'

'You mean your mother?' I moved closer and rested my hand on his. 'But I don't understand how she could allow . . . ?' I faltered. It was clear that the insipid woman in the painting was not a deity to Mrs Gurney alone. I began again. 'Your mother must have been desolate that day when she led you to the gate.'

Vaughan looked away. 'She had no choice. By that time, she knew that she was carrying a child. Less than nine months later the birth of my sister killed her.'

He raised his glass. 'To dear little Grace. A creature born of madness and violence.'

25

Fighting to stifle my yawns, I concentrated on the stones at my feet. There was a crack in the slab that started under the heel of my boot and zig-zagged under the hem of Old Maggie's skirt in front of me. Grace showed no sign of fatigue from our previous night's adventure. She held the nursemaid's hand and hopped from foot to foot as Mrs Gurney stood at the chapel's lectern and read aloud from the Book of Ruth.

Ignoring the drone of her voice, I thought about Vaughan and wondered at his ignorance of Sir William's continued presence at Fyneshade. If he went through the walls as he claimed, then surely he would know? Last night, surprised by his frankness, I had guarded my knowledge and my tongue. Further interrogation was required until I could decide what to do and how I might benefit from it.

It was a bright clear day and I was glad of it. Sunlight streamed through the window behind the plain altar. A mottle of colours filtered by the old stained glass formed a rainbow pool around the lectern, bringing an unlikely carnival to the housekeeper's starched white cap and collar.

She coughed delicately and turned the page. "'And he said, Blessed be thou of the Lord, my daughter: for thou hast shewed more kindness in the latter end than at the beginning, inasmuch as thou followedst not young men, whether poor or rich.'"

Even if Sir William Pritchard had squandered part of his son's inheritance, Fyneshade was still a great estate. Once he inherited, Vaughan would be a rich young man.

Richer by far than Nathaniel.

I considered what Vaughan had told me about his parents and his exile. He had adored his mother, that was quite clear. It was here in the chapel that he had last seen her *surrounded by flowers*. Now I knew why he worshipped her memory with fragrant blooms each time he came back to the house that was not yet his home.

A shaft of sunlight fell upon an old memorial set on the wall to the right of the lectern.

Sacred to the memory of John Hatton Gt. Mafter of Fynefhade
Hif Virtue fhone a Light upon Darknef.
Also hif wyfe, Elizabeth, Mistreffe of this Houf
Never waf there a Woman more Beloved.

While Mrs Gurney stuttered through the final verses, I allowed myself to think upon the many ways a future mistress of Fyneshade might be loved by its master.

The service was short as usual. We had not stood ten minutes in the chapel when the housekeeper invited the assembled household to recite the Lord's Prayer before returning to duties in the kitchens and elsewhere.

I was not expected to tutor Grace on the Lord's day, but we were still yoked together. It was fatiguing to be the constant companion of a child of limited comprehension. Usually on Sundays we spent the afternoon in the library and were allowed the luxury of a fire in that great hearth. Today we would walk in the grounds.

Mrs Gurney closed the Bible and stepped away from the lectern. She clasped her hands in front of her. 'Before you go, all of you, I would like . . .' She stared at her feet and the ribbons of her cap quivered. At last she found the words she was looking for. 'I would like us to say a quiet prayer for Suki Martin.'

There was a low murmur and then a silence that was almost deafening in its observance. Unable to pray, I looked up to the vaulted ceiling. Carved wooden figures supported the beams that fanned overhead. Directly above me a dusty brown angel riddled with worm holes clutched a harp to her breast. I traced the line of the beam to the opposite wall and was surprised to see that her counterpart was a grinning demon with cloven hooves and a pointed tail.

'He is a devil.'

Mrs Gurney's warning crept into my mind. Why would she say such a thing? Given Vaughan's account, surely the housekeeper would have sympathy for the banished son of Sophia Pritchard? Instead, she and the rest of the household seemed to live in fear of him. It was as if his very presence at the gates was contaminating.

Mrs Gurney jangled the chatelaine on her belt to signal the end of our prayers.

'You may go.'

Boots shuffled on the stones and a low hum of conversation came again. I was about to tell Old Maggie to prepare Grace for an afternoon walk when I felt a quick painful jab in my arm. Muffling a yelp, I twisted about to find Jennet standing just behind me. There was a glint of silver as I caught sight of the little fork she pushed back into her sleeve.

She lowered her head and walked meekly away through the chapel's double oak doors. As I watched her brown back move down the passage, other maids and kitchen servants filed past. Some of them turned to look at me, their eyes hard and suspicious.

The shadowed path leading up through the woodland to the ridge above Fyneshade was overgrown with twisted hawthorns. Grandmere had respected the hawthorn tree above all others. She had used the flesh of its berries in tinctures for a wounded heart and she had brought its branches, heavy with sweet-scented white flowers, into the cottage in May. She said that the hawthorn tree was the guardian of the gateways to fortune and should be welcomed when it flourished.

I pulled the hem of my cloak from the thorns on a low trailing branch and wished that these trees grew elsewhere on the estate. Lancer thudded past and disappeared into the twisted, moss-pelted thicket. I heard the thrum of the dog's feet on the mud and the scatter of stones as it raced ahead.

Grace lagged behind. The girl had a stick in her hand and was thrashing at the briars surrounding us. It would have been better if she had stayed at the house, but there was no way of leaving her without causing suspicion. We had walked in the formal gardens several times now and even if someone had observed us going through the gate to the river it was natural to use Lancer's fascination with water as an excuse.

Today we had followed the river and crossed over the stone bridge into a muddy sloping field. Here, the path I sought led up to a band of woodland below the ridge. Once we had entered the field, I felt easier. Fyneshade was blind on this side. We would not be observed now.

I bent to free my cloak from the hawthorn and waited for Grace to come level with me. Her boots were covered in mud and the branches of the trees had snatched at her hair, pulling it free from the braid so carefully arranged by Old Maggie. I would have to neaten my pupil's appearance before delivering her back to the nursery.

Grace dawdled and thwacked again. She rubbed her cheek and looked at me.

'Hurt.'

There was a little cut below her eye where she had been nicked by a springing thorn branch. I had been lucky it wasn't higher.

'Come.' I smiled and held out my hand. 'Not far now, dearest. Think of the view we will see from the top of the hill.'

Vaughan was waiting, just as he had promised. When I stepped out from the edge of the woodland, he was standing some way above watching Lancer, who was running excitedly back and forth.

Wispy clouds threaded the sky. Vaughan's long shadow fell from the stony path that followed the crest of the ridge. Wind snatched at his long coat and baffled it about him. It was bleak up here. At the summit huge rocks jutted from the bare-faced hillside. From a distance they could have been mistaken for the ruins of an ancient castle.

I scrambled to join him and realised I could see Fyneshade strung out far below. The sun made the ancient walls glow like honeycomb. The remoteness of the house was starkly apparent from here. It hunkered low in the valley fringed by forest to the west and wind-blown slopes to the east. There was no other dwelling place in sight.

'Dido is disturbed by dogs.' Vaughan didn't look at me. 'Why did you bring him?'

The hawk crouched on the crook of his raised arm. Although she was hooded, she could sense Lancer's presence. Curved beak open, her head followed his sound. Her grey feathers were ruffled and angry.

I went closer. Even though she was blind I was wary of Dido's size and power. I saw her yellow talons tighten on the dark leather gauntlet as I approached.

'I could not avoid bringing them.'

'Them?' Vaughan turned now, just as Grace plodded to my side. His eyes were like glass washed in a river.

I knelt and smoothed the girl's knotted hair. 'Look over there.' I pointed at the jumbled rocks. 'If you can climb to the very top, you will have the finest view of all. Perhaps you could touch the sky?'

Grace peered at the stones and grinned. The sight was tempting, just as I knew it would be. She paddled her hands and headed towards the rocks. The dog bounded after her.

I stood, pushed back the hood of my cloak and allowed the wind to catch my hair. The keenness of the air would bring colour to my skin and sharpen the darkness of my eyes.

'It is not easy to do as I wish, Vaughan. I am her companion, even on Sundays. I am here as you asked.'

He wore no hat today. The wind whipped his hair back from his forehead revealing the dark point at its centre. He reached into a pocket and offered Dido a bloody titbit. She ripped it from his gloved fist.

He watched the jerk of her head as she swallowed and his grim expression softened to indulgence. 'So you are, Marta, just as I asked. I wanted to see you in the day. Apart from that first meeting at the river, we have only met by candlelight. I found that I had a curiosity to truly see you.' He looked from the bird to me.

'And are you satisfied?'

He smiled now. 'The view is magnificent.'

The hawk bobbed on his arm as he turned to make a sweeping gesture. 'All this land belongs to Fyneshade – as far as the eye can see. I come here often with Dido, to exercise her. We are always alone. For once, I hoped to enjoy your company without my sister as your shepherd.'

I went closer, careful to remain out of Dido's reach. 'And I have thought that too, Vaughan. I marked the way to your rooms, although I have gone through the walls so many times now that I believe I know the way to the stables without chalk to guide me.'

'Clever Marta. You have the makings of a champion.' He tilted his head. 'But if you know the way, why do you rely on my sister?'

'Because she will not show me how to open the walls. I cannot discover the secret of the door in my room. It is the one thing she has constantly denied me.'

'Ha!' He grinned and the deep lines around his mouth widened. 'Little Grace enjoys her power and her secrets. I taught her well.' He leaned close. 'Look by the hearth, at the bottom near the wall. There is a round stone that does not quite match the others. Step upon it. The wall will open. The principle is the same throughout the house. Once inside the walls, you need only to push at a doorway for it to open. Grindlow showed me and in time I showed Grace.'

He reached for Dido's head and in a quick, practised movement he removed the studded hood by the tassel. The hawk's yellow-rimmed eyes widened as she straightened on the glove to examine the world around her.

I stepped back. 'Why did you do that?'

'Because she needs to hunt. Wait and you'll see.'

'No . . .' I stepped back again as Dido stretched out her wings. 'I meant why did you show Grace the passages?'

Vaughan pulled at a trailing leather strip caught in his fist. Dido arched her neck and cried out a harsh single note.

'Because she is my sister and had a right to know. Because it has been useful to have an ally in the house, and because it amused me to think of her escaping the clutches of those women.' He stared along the ridge. Grace was happily scrambling among the lowest stones seeking a way to the summit. Lancer yelped and dashed around the outcrop, grey tail wagging like a flag. 'Tell me, what have you noticed about the servants at Fyneshade?'

When I didn't answer immediately, he turned his attention from the hawk.

'Come, Marta, you are not the woman I think you are if you disappoint me.'

I met and held his gaze. 'And you must know by now that I

will never do that. In answer to your question, they are all female and they are all . . . undesirable.'

'Undesirable.' Vaughan laughed. 'You are quite the exception at Fyneshade, my heart.'

My heart?

This was progress. I wondered how to steer our conversation to questions of my own.

'I was not what Mrs Gurney expected. She has said as much on several occasions. I believe she was hoping to employ someone older and—'

'Plainer,' Vaughan interrupted. 'Of course that's what she wanted. The woman has filled the house with freaks. If she could have employed a bearded lady as governess to my sister, she would have done so.'

I laughed now. 'She was mistaken when she employed me, but very successful in her other appointments. Why so?'

'Because of my father.'

I frowned. 'But he . . . he . . .'

'Was a bitter and jealous man. After the fall, my father suffered spasms that crippled his body. He was still proud and despite everything, vain. He had a contraption made – to a design he had seen abroad – to straighten his limbs. He thought he would ride again. I imagine he thought he would do many things. For a time, he made progress. He was even able to walk a little way.'

Vaughan loosened the leather straps that bound Dido's talons to the glove.

'But the improvement did not last. Within a year, he was bedridden once more, a dribbling sore-covered wreck. Do you remember last night I told you that his disease – one of many – was spite?'

I nodded.

'I am not a saint, Marta. Once, there were many pretty young maids at Fyneshade who took pity on the young master banished to the stables. When it came to my father's attention that I enjoyed the company of women, and they mine, he gave orders that the house should be filled with the lame and the ugly. Gurney is a loyal servant.

'Now watch.'

He strode from me and surveyed the hillside below the ridge. For a moment he stood very still and then he twisted and threw up his arm, casting Dido to the air. The bird soared into the sky. High above us, a dark crescent, she rode the wind.

Vaughan shielded his eyes and followed her flight. I went to his side and did the same. Dido's wings did not seem to move as she circled the crest. The hunt was silent and beautiful.

As I watched, I made up my mind to cast for myself.

'You asked me what I had noticed about the servants at Fyneshade, Vaughan. There is something else. I presume Grindlow is dead?'

Vaughan nodded. 'He died six years ago. He had no son and Dawson replaced him.'

'But apart from Dawson and your own groom, neither of whom come into the house, there are no other men at Fyneshade. Is that by accident or design?'

Vaughan's attention was locked on Dido, who now hovered as if suspended on a single point so far above us that had I not known she was there I would not have noted her.

Finally, without losing sight of the hawk, he replied.

'It is no accident, Marta. I have already given you the answer – pride. After what happened, my father could not bear another man to look upon him. For William Pritchard, to see pity in a man's eyes would be crueller than the most degrading disease. He even dismissed his physician. For many years Eavis was his nurse; no one else had the stomach to look at him. Ah!' Vaughan broke off and pointed. 'Now see her go.'

I looked up. Dido was plummeting, straight and fast, her wings pinned back. Below her I caught movement on the lower slopes. Something dark dashed across the stony hillside. At the last, mid-flight, the hawk folded back on herself, talons extended.

The creature – a blurred shadow – jagged towards us, but it was too late. Dido fell upon it, wings stretched wide to envelop her prey. I saw her head rise as she called out her victory and then she jabbed and jabbed again at the body beneath her.

'Come.' Vaughan started off down the slope, his coat flailing in the wind. I began to follow, but I remembered Grace. Turning, I was surprised to see her standing at the summit of the rocks, Lancer at her side. She was watching me. I raised my hand in a gesture of approval, but she didn't move.

'Marta!' Vaughan called again and I went to him.

Dido spread her wings and hissed. Her beak was red and the feathers around her eyes were spattered with blood. Caught by the wind, tufts of brownish fur tumbled on the stones around her.

'Here.' Vaughan stretched out his arm and whistled. Dido threw back her head and stamped on the body beneath her yellow claws, then she rustled and rose to his gauntlet.

'Good girl. Good.' He spoke in a low soothing voice and reached into his pocket. Clenching up his fist, he set another strip of fresh meat on the leather. Dido ducked her head, as if submitting to his mastery, and took it.

I looked down at her kill. It was a hare. Huge, lifeless, other-worldly eyes stared at me and two barely formed young spilled from a gash in her belly.

Vaughan moved closer and held his arm so that Dido was almost between us. I tore my eyes from the mess of entrails and death before life and he smiled.

'Come to me alone tonight, Marta. Test your marks and find your way through the labyrinth.'

26

Vaughan was no longer next to me. Stretching drowsily in the bed, I realised that the sheets where he had lain were cold. I wondered how long I had slept and a moment of fear came upon me. The servants at Fyneshade rose early. Since Suki's dismissal Jennet had not served me, but what if a girl had already come to my room with water?

Quite awake now, I stared into the blackness of the canopy. The room was in darkness. To the right of the bed, no light betrayed the faintest outline of the curtained window. It was clearly some way before dawn. Gathering the sheets around me, I sat up.

'Vaughan?'

The answer was a scrape, and then the flare of a match. He was sitting in the furthest corner of the room. Half of his face seemed to float eerily in the glow from the little flame as if disconnected from his body.

'You have slept for an hour at least.' He set the match to three candles in a silver stick on a chest beside him. 'I did not have the heart to wake you.'

He was dressed in his night robe. Something pale bundled in his lap trailed to the floor.

I pushed my hair from my face. 'What time is it?'

'Early. You need not flee my company yet.'

'Good.' I pulled back the coverlet and smoothed the rumpled sheets beside me. 'For I do not wish to go.'

I thought about our passion earlier that night. Sometimes we were savages tearing at each other's flesh, at others we moved so delicately that every nerve was strung taut as a bowstring. It had become a game of daring between us. My audacity delighted him, as his invention pleased me. We were equals.

'I do not wish to leave you, ever, Vaughan.' I allowed the sheet to fall away. The invitation was clear. 'The days at Fyneshade are long. The nights pass too quickly.'

He smiled, but he did not come to me. 'When I am master here, I promise that I will have our bed moved into the house.' He shook his head. 'God knows when I will be able to keep that promise.' The lines around his mouth tightened.

Our bed?

This was a new and emboldening prospect.

Throwing off the sheets, I moved closer to him.

'Vaughan, I must ask something. You know the ways through the walls as well as Grace; better in fact as you showed them to her. Why have you never come to me?'

'Ah! That is a clever question, governess.' I was relieved to see him smile. 'The truth is that I fear Gurney.' He raised a brow and I laughed, thinking this to be a jest.

'It is most amusing, I know, but it is also true. The wretched woman found evidence that I had been within the house and she threatened to inform our family lawyers if I ever trespassed again. A sum of money was involved. I could barely afford it, but I paid for her silence.'

'Mrs Gurney blackmailed you?' I could not hide my surprise. The woman I knew was as far from a Machiavel as a shrew to a fox. But then I remembered her lies about Sir William and the night when she had drugged me. I was coming to see, to my chagrin, that I had underestimated her.

'She had no concern for the chastity of her women. I think she feared that I might contaminate Grace in some way.' Vaughan shrugged. 'Two years ago, I was away sporting with Dido when our father was finally removed from Fyneshade. The disease had gone too far, even for Eavis. Gurney made the arrangements and in her message she took great pleasure in describing the disgrace and secrecy of his leaving: the covered wagon that came at night; the rough doctors who bound his rotting, twisted body to a board.

'God! The shame of it. What a family we are.' He looked down at the bundle and then into the candle flame. For a fleeting moment, I thought I saw tears in his eyes, but he blinked and shook his head.

'If anyone were to know my father was mad ... You are the only person I have ever told that miserable tale to, Marta.'

I sat quite still. The night had revealed a part of Vaughan's nature for which I was unprepared. After a moment he continued.

'Once he was gone, for a short while I used the passages again, just as I had in the days after he first cast me out. I visited Grace until Gurney's accusations, but now my sister must come to me.' He leaned forward. 'Don't you see, Marta? I cannot allow anything to stand between me and my inheritance. I cannot risk discovery again. I cannot lose Fyneshade.'

I considered his predicament, which was also my own. The man I had seen in the black room was surely close to death, but how was Vaughan to know that?

'Be patient. The disease you told me of moves swiftly at the end.' I reached out to him and the candle flames danced just beyond my outstretched fingers. I expected Vaughan to take my hand, but he did not move.

'You're wrong, Marta. A man cannot live on patience. My father appears to be an immortal. He could linger for years more, damn him. Eavis informs me that, despite everything, the doctors at the sanatorium say his heart is sound.'

'Eavis speaks to you?' This was new. I wondered how to unravel the unexpected information, but Vaughan answered me.

'She's one of the few that does. When I am here ...' he gestured to the room, '... Eavis dirties her hands with the things that Gurney cannot bear to face, including my linens. Any necessary communications with the house are passed through my father's former nurse and vice versa. Eavis despises me almost as much as Gurney. They enjoy the power they wield. Two queens of a small forgotten realm.'

He smoothed the fabric in his lap. I had thought it to be sheets from the bed, but now I saw that it was finer stuff than linen. The candlelight brought a sheen to the material. Beneath Vaughan's fingers tiny pearls were sewn in rows.

'One day, there will be a new Mrs Pritchard. A new lady mistress at Fyneshade.' My heart fluttered like a moth as he looked directly at me. 'That day can only come when my father is dead. Do you understand me, Marta?'

Understand?

There was so much to examine in that brief sentence that I was relieved to find he did not expect a response. Instead, he rose and shook out the fabric. It was a dress made from milk-pale silk studded with iridescent pearls and trimmed with lace. He held it towards me. 'I would like you to put this on.'

'Is this some new game?' I wrapped an arm around the bedpost and smiled, all the while holding his eyes in mine. 'Why?'

'Because it would please me to see you clothed in something other than black. Take it.'

He pushed the dress at me. It almost fell to the floor, but I caught it. The fabric was so delicate and frail it felt like water slipping through my fingers. It was old – the high-cut waist, curved neckline and bell-like sleeves were the fashion of an earlier time. Lace panels at the hem and the neck were grey with age and there were creases and dusty lines where it had been folded. Tiny holes in the sleeves suggested that moths had feasted on the silk.

I stood and held it against my body. 'There. Do I please you?'

Vaughan tilted his head in appraisal.

'The old style becomes you. Come, I am anxious to see how you wear it. Put it on for me.'

The fabric whispered as I stepped carefully into the fragile skirt and raised the bodice. Several beads came loose and pattered to the boards when I pushed my arms into the lace-edged sleeves. The bodice gaped at the neck. The dress had been made for a woman whose body was more rounded than mine. I held out my arms and the fabric fell from my shoulders.

'Turn around.'

I did as Vaughan instructed and he tightened ribbons threaded into eyes sewn down the back. Satisfied that the dress was now a better fit, he placed his hands on my shoulders and steered me to stand before the Venetian glass at the foot of the bed. The silk and the beads shimmered in the candlelight. It was almost impossible to see where my skin ended and the dress began. My hair lay black against the pallor. I pushed at the lace that didn't quite cover my breasts, but Vaughan stopped my hand.

'Leave it. You are leaner and your colouring is quite different, but it looks well on you. As I thought it might.' He stared intently at the glass; indeed it would be more accurate to say he seemed to stare *through* it. For the second time, I had the odd impression that he saw something quite different to our reflections.

'There is one last thing.' He stepped back into the shadows. I heard the creak of old metal hinges as he opened a chest. 'Close your eyes.'

Ah, I thought, here it was, some new and daring game of love. I shut my eyes. 'Will I be pleased, Vaughan?'

'Your pleasure in this matter is entirely irrelevant, my heart.' I heard his step behind me. 'Keep your eyes closed until I say you may look.'

His fingers moved through my hair like a comb. I felt him place something very light on the top of my head. It fell before my face and fluttered over my shoulders almost to my wrists. I felt cobweb kisses on the skin of my arms. Quite suddenly, the smell of naphtha filled my nose.

'Now you may look, Marta.'

I opened my eyes. In the glass, a veiled woman stared back at me. Tattered gauze fell from a brittle crown of pearls and twisted gilt leaves that glinted in the flickering light.

In the glass, Vaughan reached out to touch my shoulder but

suddenly he drew back. Something in his eyes suggested that the gesture had alarmed him. He turned from me quickly and took up the candlestick.

'What do you think?' He held it higher so that we both might see better.

My black eyes gleamed through the veil. I was aware of a vein pulsing in my neck.

'It was my mother's wedding dress.' He set the candlestick down and folded the veil carefully back from my face. His fingers trembled as he did so. 'Do you like it?'

This ancient rag belonged to Sophia Pritchard?

My mind scrambled for the answer that would please him most. Before I could reply, he bent to kiss me. I felt his teeth on my lips and the tip of his tongue moving against mine and at that moment I thought of Nathaniel. Forcing him from my mind, I caught Vaughan's face in my hands and we embraced before the glass. At last he broke away and stared over my shoulder at our reflection.

'You did not answer my question.'

'It is exquisite.'

He smiled. 'I know it is not cut to the present style and needs alteration and repair, but it has always been my wish that one day, when my father is dead and I come into my inheritance, my bride will wear this gown and veil.'

I nodded, unable to speak for fear of breaking the spell between us. This was the moment foretold, the moment I had known would come. Vaughan Pritchard was mine. His next words confirmed my victory.

'We have known each other barely more than a month's worth of nights, yet I think I know you better than I know anyone. It was fate that brought you to me, Marta, not Gurney's mistake.'

I reached out a hand to the glass. More pearl beads scattered to the boards as I flattened my palm against that of the woman standing before me.

I saw two versions of myself in the Venetian mirror. One of them was clothed in the milk-pale dress, the other was veiled in darkness.

My vision swam for a moment, but Vaughan's voice brought me back.

'... away tomorrow. It cannot be helped – there is a tournament in the Borders. Dido will win me a fair sum.'

He turned me to face him. 'I will miss you, Marta. I wish ... I wish that you could come with me.' He grinned and for the first time, I saw the boy he had been. 'That would be a fine thing would it not, my lady?'

I lowered my veiled head. 'It would not be seemly, my lord.' Affecting a modesty we both knew to be false, I continued, 'Not while I am governess to your sister.'

I pushed at the wall and the door opened into my room. Using my chalk marks, I had navigated the way to and from the stables with ease. A faint line of purple fringing the hem of the curtains suggested that dawn was not far off. I listened for a moment but the house was quiet. It was still too early for the servants to be about their duties.

Shielding my candle, I stepped lightly on the small rounded stone at the corner of the hearth. I had found it exactly as Vaughan had described. Without knowledge of its purpose, a person would not pay attention to the unusual smoothness and regularity of this decorative detail. Now I knew, it seemed to me the most obvious thing.

I watched the stones swing silently back into place and then I went to the window. Setting the chamberstick on the boards, I drew back the curtains to look out at the courtyard and the archway leading to the stable block. I wondered if Vaughan slept now, and if he did, was I in his dreams?

The country girls of Croyle held that it was unlucky for a groom to see his bride in her wedding gown before he met her at the altar. I did not share their belief, and although I did not share Vaughan's admiration of his mother's dress, I would wear it for him.

And I would do more.

I took a deep breath and pressed my forehead against the glass. A dull ache had begun to throb in my temples. I needed to rest, and yet every time I lay in my cold bed I found that I could not sleep for the thoughts that raced wildly through my head. Tonight, those thoughts ran to a fixed point, but that was almost more exhilarating.

Murder was too strong a word. The death of Sir William Pritchard would be a mercy, both for him and for his son. I had seen Grandmere ease a person from the world, out of kindness, and I had the knowledge and the means to follow her example. Her spice box contained all the ingredients I needed to shepherd Vaughan's father to the grave.

'When my father is dead and I come into my inheritance, my bride will wear this gown and veil.'

A jab of excitement punched below my ribs as I thought of Vaughan's face reflected in the mirror over my shoulder. At that moment I had seen him struggle to master his feelings for me. Indeed, he had been unable to mask his surprise at this, possibly unwelcome, revelation. I enjoyed Vaughan's company, his body and his skill, but I did not love him. Love was for fools. I had learned that lesson long ago. Nevertheless, we were well matched and he would make a tolerable husband, until he strayed, as all men do.

No. I did not love Vaughan Pritchard. I loved Fyneshade.

I stood back and scanned the sky. The waxing moon was about to slide beneath the humped back of the hill above the stables. In the half-light of dawn her face was flushed pink not silver. When April's Egg Moon was complete and perfect, I would take Grandmere's bowl from its hiding place beneath the window.

Somewhere deep in the house a clock began to strike and soon it was followed by the call of many others. The chimes lasted a minute or more. Five o'clock – there was an hour still before Fyneshade awoke. I turned from the window, took up the chamberstick and went to my bed.

At first, I could not understand what it was that lay on the cover propped against the pillows. I stared at the dark shape and for a moment I thought it to be a cat curled and asleep. Raising the candle, I saw a mass of tangled black hair.

Warily, I reached out to touch the thing, but it did not move. Now I pushed. It fell to the side and I saw it was Rosa, Grace's doll. Her beautiful porcelain face smashed beyond recognition.

Egg Moon

27

I dipped a spoon into the glass bowl and allowed a tiny globe of jam, red as Panjan's eyes, to slip onto the half-slice of bread. I could take nothing more this morning. The butter, yellow and sweating on its saucer, revolted me and my stomach lurched as Mrs Gurney carved at her slab of bacon, knife squealing on the china. The sight of grease pooling on her dish was bad enough, but the fatty, charred stench of the meat was unusually strong in the confines of the parlour.

I took the smallest bite from a corner of the bread. The sweetness of raspberry was all I could bear, but even that brought bile to my throat. I swallowed hard and put the bread down. My stomach churned again.

A frail old man, hidden away from the world, was all that stood between me and my destiny. It would be a great thing to be the wife of Vaughan Pritchard and mistress of Fyneshade.

I would be a great thing.

The sound of the knife clanging on china came again. I looked up to see Mrs Gurney's hand poised above her dish. She set the knife down.

'Got your attention now, have I? You've been in such a daze this morning, Marta. I don't think you've taken in half of what I said.'

I shook my head. 'I am sorry. My sleep is still disturbed.' I looked to the narrow window where sunlight brightened the sill. 'Perhaps it is the change of the season? The weather is so improved. Grandmere always held that our souls respond to the turning of the world.'

'Did she?' Mrs Gurney tutted, as I knew she would, but today I was reckless. The housekeeper flattened her hands on the table. 'I daresay that's something she heard in France, for it's not something we'd say here in Derbyshire. Did you hear what I said about Master Vaughan?'

Now I was alert.

'He's leaving today,' she continued, 'and he's not due back for a month. Dawson says he's going back north, something to do with that bird and his sport. When he's gone, you'll be quite free to take Grace anywhere in the grounds, far as you like. As you say, the weather's much kinder and Old Maggie tells me that Grace enjoys her rambles in the garden and down by the river. Does her the power of good, it truly does, and you were right to see that.'

'A month?' I lifted my cup and considered this news. Mrs Gurney neatened the cutlery on her greasy dish and looked at me.

'Do you like to ride, Marta?'

The question was so unexpected, I almost spluttered weak tea across the wood. Instead, I smiled. 'We did not keep a carriage at home. I'm afraid I have the most limited experience with horses, Mrs Gurney.'

'That's a pity. Grace likes to ride in the summer. Dawson says she has a good seat.' Mrs Gurney beamed with pride. 'There is a particular pony, Rummy, a nice little bay he is, in the stables. She's very fond of him.' She leaned forward. 'Seeing as how . . . well, as he's . . . as the stables are . . .' She gathered herself to the point. 'There's no reason why you shouldn't take Grace to the stables to see her pony later in the week. It's been such a time. Even if you don't ride out together, she'd like to see him, I'm sure.'

'Of course.' I set my cup down on its saucer. 'She could draw a most excellent likeness of . . . Rummy, is it?' Mrs Gurney nodded and I smiled again. 'Besides, a visit to the stables would be interesting for me. I have not yet been there.'

❧

I haunted the schoolroom window while Grace scribbled in a sullen silence that I did not have the inclination or patience to interrogate. I tried to ignore the scratch of her pencil and the thumps when she kicked, irritably, at the legs of her desk. I concentrated on the archway and thought about Mrs Gurney's announcement.

'He's not due back for a month.'

Why had he not told me last night? The question rolled about my head – a marble in a game of bagatelle. At least he had expressed a desire for me to accompany him, however ridiculous. To be a mistress in private is a very different thing to being a whore carted about the country like a battered portmanteau.

My fingers froze on the draughty stone sill as I kept a close watch on the courtyard below. If I had been sharper this morning and less surprised by this news, I would have used a headache as an excuse to observe the stable arch from my room. It would not, entirely, have been a lie and at least I would not have had to endure Grace's bad temper.

Late in the morning Vaughan's carriage bowled across the courtyard and out through Fyneshade's main gateway. Unusually, he rode alongside the elegant black brougham. His mount was the grey stallion that had betrayed my arrival the first time Grace led me through the walls to the stables. Vaughan allowed his groom to steer the carriage through the narrow stone gateway first; the big grey arched its neck and pranced on the cobbles as he reined him back.

I flattened my hands to the glass.

Vaughan sat tall in the saddle. Hatted, straight-backed, the black tails of his riding coat draped over the horse's flanks, he was easily the master. The silver tip of the familiar riding crop in his gloved left hand twitched against the animal's muscular shoulders. The touch was lighter than a kiss, but it carried the threat of punishment.

My breath obscured the pane. He did not look up at the schoolroom window or back at the house as he followed the carriage beneath the gateway. Even though I could not see the road, I lingered there for some time after he had gone.

My thoughts ran on the night we had spent together. We had been intimate and easy in each other's company. Indeed, Vaughan had never been more open. The talk of his father's death and inheritance, the dress, the veil . . .

'One day, there will be a new Mrs Pritchard. A new lady mistress at Fyneshade. That day can only come when my father is dead.'

Grace ambled behind me across the rear courtyard. Every time I tried to draw her attention to a point of interest – a bird, the rainbow effect of light reflected from the windows, even Lancer's long shadow – she turned her face away and blew a noise through her lips.

It was clear that she had taken exception to my independence. When we were high on the peak with Dido, Vaughan had been careful to explain to his sister that her assistance to guide me to his room that night would not be required. I had marked the firm, gentle way he gave this instruction with surprise, and with gratitude.

I confess there were times when Vaughan and I lay together that I found myself wondering about Grace. If she was not always asleep in the other room, what did she make of the sounds that she must have heard?

There had been one occasion, just after Vaughan's second return, when we had taken our pleasure on furs spread before the fire. Finally, exhausted, we had fallen asleep, our limbs tangled together. I had dreamed then that my pupil sat in the wing-backed chair, watching us. It was unsettling, but merely a dream. We parted, as usual, before dawn and Vaughan had roused Grace from his bed.

Truly, I had not thought myself to be inhibited by my constant chaperone until Vaughan had told his sister not to guide me. Her absence had been both a relief and a release.

Yet Grace had come to my room all the same, and when she found that I had gone without her she was angry.

'Little Grace enjoys her power and her secrets.'

Vaughan had laughed when I told him of her stubborn refusal to reveal the mechanism of the walls. But I understood. For Grace, the hidden passages were a possession. For a long time, she alone of all the inhabitants of the house had owned the key to a secret world. She had controlled the ways, but now there was another.

Grace Pritchard was jealous.

This called for delicacy. She was my reason to be at Fyneshade. If I lost her affection, I would lose all.

I trod carefully. After Vaughan's departure I sat with Grace in the schoolroom and tried to engage her with soft words and praise, fully expecting her silent enmity to fade. It did not.

Now, as a peace offering, I was taking up Mrs Gurney's suggestion of a trip to the stables. I caught hold of Lancer's collar and pulled the dog to my side. It looked up at me, mouth agape, tail thumping at my skirts, and I recoiled from its breath. The stink of dog had always repulsed me. I had allowed the animal to follow us this far because I knew that Grace delighted in its company, but Mrs Gurney had given strict instructions that it was not to enter the stables.

'Dawson,' I called through the metal gate. Lancer jumped up, its great paws flailing at my cloak. I managed to hold it away.

'Mr Dawson!' I rapped on the bars and called again. 'I've brought Grace to see Rummy, but I need your assistance with the dog.'

I heard the creak of a door beyond the archway and the crump of boots on the cobbles.

Dawson rounded the curve of the wall. He bent to unlock the gate and immediately grabbed at Lancer, who broke free from my hand and tried to dash through to the stable yard.

'I'll tie him out here.' Dawson held the dog firmly by the collar and nodded at Grace, who was flapping her hands and peering through the archway. 'He'll be waiting here for you when you come out, lass. And there's another who'll be happy to see you. He's in his regular stall.'

Grace nuzzled the pony's neck and stroked its mane. Her large hands were not delicate or gentle, but the creature submitted to her affection with sturdy patience. She chuckled with delight as it butted against her shoulder. I had been right the first night I came here: Grace and Rummy were old friends.

There were four other docile horses in the stables this afternoon, but Grace was only interested in the fat little bay. The sweet smell of horse and straw was very strong in the confined space. The stones trapped the cold and steam rose from the mouths and nostrils of the animals as they pulled hay from the racks on the walls.

'Here.' Dawson took an apple from his pocket and gave it to Grace. 'He'll like this.'

'Surely it is too early for apples?' I smiled at the groom. He shrugged, his attention fixed on the girl and the pony. 'I store 'em through winter.'

Dawson spent words like a miser. Even when he'd brought

me to Fyneshade in the Pritchards' monogrammed carriage he had only spoken to point out the house in the valley at the final approach.

I tried again. 'Mrs Gurney tells me that Grace enjoys riding. I understand she has some skill?'

'Um.' Dawson nodded. I had the impression he wished I was somewhere else. His dark eyes softened beneath boot-brush brows when he spoke to Grace but he never looked at me. I noticed that he was careful to keep a distance between us.

Some devil within urged me to provoke him. The thrill of being here, so close to the rooms I knew so well, was a dangerous temptation.

I fluttered a hand vaguely towards the beamed ceiling. 'Mrs Gurney also told me about the younger Mr Pritchard who, I believe, lives here. I understand that he has gone away for a month.'

Dawson bent to collect a nugget of apple that Rummy had dropped to the cobbled floor.

'Um.'

That infuriating answer again. The man's reticence was a lure to my reckless demon, his reluctance to communicate increasing my determination. Besides, as the only companion of Vaughan's groom he was likely to know more than Mrs Gurney.

He passed the half-chewed apple to Grace and I stepped closer. 'Where has he gone? I think he has taken the bird. Dido, is it? Another contest perhaps?'

Now Dawson looked at me. His eyes narrowed.

'I don't take an interest in him, ma'am. Not in the hawk or his travels. His groomsman, Ricketts, sees to all that. Mrs Gurney, now, that's different; she has to take an interest in him – and I reckon with you two being so close in the house with the little one she's already told you everything she knows.'

He went to Grace's side and fished another apple from a pocket. 'Here y'are, lass.'

We stood apart in an uncomfortable silence as she petted the pony and presented the apple from her flattened palm. She giggled at the tickle of Rummy's whiskered muzzle. As the pony munched slowly, the sweet fermented smell of overripe fruit turned my stomach.

'A true innocent.'

I was surprised to hear Dawson speak of his own volition. He turned to me and added gruffly, 'We're all very fond of her. Now, if you don't mind, I'll be getting on. If you'd close the gate when you're done, I'll see to the lock.'

He raised a smudged finger to the brim of his hat and went to the door leading out to the stable yard.

The gesture, rather than his manner, suggested the respect due to a superior. Next to Mrs Gurney, I was the most senior servant. She was the housekeeper at Fyneshade, its mistress in all but name. For now.

'Grace,' I called softly but she did not turn from the pony. I had given some thought to my strategy to win her over. If Rummy failed to sweeten her mood, I had other cards to play.

I went to her side and rested a hand on her shoulder. 'I know you are angry with me, dearest.'

She shrugged as if to flick me away, but I held tight. 'I will always be your friend, little one. I hope you know that?'

Grace buried her face in Rummy's mane and blew.

I moved my cloak aside and reached into the pocket of my gown. 'Now, what could this be?'

I shook my hand and allowed the items in my palm to chink as they tumbled together.

'I wonder what your brother would say if he knew about Rosa. She was such a pretty doll.'

I closed my fingers and rattled the contents of my hand again. 'He would be very sad if he knew about what happened to her. What do you think he would say if I showed him these? Look what I have here, Grace.'

She turned warily from Rummy and I opened my hand. Rosa's black glass eyes, perfect tiny facsimiles of my own, rolled in my palm. The effect was as gruesome as I had hoped.

My pupil gasped.

'Poor Rosa,' I whispered. 'Now she is blind and it is all because of you.'

Grace covered her own eyes, unwilling to look at the chinking horror in my hand.

I slipped the eyes back into my pocket and knelt beside her. She was snuffling and possibly weeping now behind pale fingers. That was good.

'Hush, hush now.' I stroked Grace's hair. 'I want us to be friends again, just as we were. I promise that I won't tell your brother about Rosa ... and what you did to her.' Grace peered out at me through the cage of her fingers. I was right, her eyes were cloudy with tears.

'Friends keep secrets for each other, don't they?' Gently, I dabbed at the watery trail leaking down her cheeks.

She nodded.

'We have the best secret of all, don't we, little one? If you come to me tonight, I promise I will be waiting ...' I crossed my heart on the cloak. 'And where do you think we might go, just the two of us?'

Grace brightened immediately. She clapped her hands and pouted to form the name.

'Pa ... Pan ... Panjan.'

'Clever Grace.' I nodded, smiled and huddled her close. 'We will go to see Panjan. Just you and me.'

28

The water tasted of metal.

I set down the glass and ran a hand over my belly. It was just as before with Nathaniel. In the earliest days my senses had been heightened to a pitch of almost unbearable acuity. Now, when I sat, I could feel the buttons of my dress press into the flesh of my back. Noises made my ears ring. Scents revolted me; food and most especially the sharp musty smell that rose from the bodies and drab brown dresses of Fyneshade's maids made my stomach roll. The roots of my hair ached when I released the coiled plait from its pins. My forehead throbbed with a dull and constant pain, and beneath my bodice my small breasts were swollen and tender.

I was carrying Vaughan Pritchard's child.

Or was I? I had always been sensitive to stench and taste – too dainty according to Aunt Clare – and now my courses had come with the Egg Moon.

I took up the blood-spotted rag, slipped from the bed and went to the window. In the clear night sky, the face the moon turned to the world was milk-white and whole. I tried to remember what Grandmere had said about the ritual; the warning. The blood of the querent should never be mixed with the blood of another. I stared at the rag. Was this my blood, or the blood of the child I had made with Vaughan?

My monthly visit was usually light, but this clout was barely stained. The time was right, however; my courses often followed the moon. Grandmere said it was a sign of her favour. In confirmation, a familiar grinding ache pulled at the depths of my belly.

Was it possible to hold a child in my womb and continue to bleed?

Tonight, more than ever before, I needed to consult the bowl, but it was a risk to do so without knowing if the blood was pure. I knelt and removed the tapestry cushions from the box seat. Opening the lid, I moved my shawls and linens aside to take out the bowl and the spice box. I needed salt.

My trinket box rattled as I pushed it to one side. I had a fresh trophy to add to my collection, one that would not fit in the box. My new treasure lay hidden beneath the bed. I went to fetch it and, before hiding it away, I opened it. Moonlight spilled across the paper.

Mrs Gurney's mother had written in a looping childish hand; her recipes and simple remedies were blotched and ugly. I ran a finger along the first line of her *'soverin cure for the goute'*, a concoction of ginger, nettle, celery and *'rype cherry in seeson'*.

I had nothing written in my own mother's hand.

I leafed through the fragile yellowed pages and halted when my eye fell on a page of indecipherable scrawl. For a moment, I wondered if this was written in code or some other language, but then I realised what it was. Taking the silver hand mirror from my dressing table, I held the glass to the moonlight and read.

Recepe to ban a babe

I sat back surprised. Mrs Gurney's mother had dealt in areas that were forbidden. No wonder she had written backwards in an effort to evade detection. I wondered how many girls she had helped with this *recepe*.

I angled the mirror to see if her knowledge and methods agreed with my own. The tincture included parsley, motherwort, pennyroyal, fennel, rue, tansy, yarrow and poppy oil. I had used just four of these, with wormwood, to rid myself of Nathaniel's whelp.

Flattening a hand against my belly, I wondered again if I carried. If so, this child would be born and christened with its father's name.

I folded the tattered book in a petticoat and hid it at the bottom of the box seat, mounding other items on top. Looking up, I saw that the moon had risen high in the sky. Light streamed through the window, over the seat and across the boards. This was the time of power.

I glanced at the wall, certain that Grace would not come. Last night's visit to Panjan had been a success. We were friends again. After winding him to perform four times – his antics were now a trial to be endured – we had returned to my room, where I told her the pretty story of the princesses whose slippers were worn thin by their midnight dances and who slept through the day.

'Dearest,' I had said. 'If we play every night in the walls our slippers will be frayed to threads and Old Maggie will set a spy on us to see where we go. Where *you* go.' Grace's pale eyes had widened in alarm as she contemplated this unpleasant possibility. It had been most satisfying.

Before she left, I had made her promise that in future she would only come at my invitation. She nodded and crossed a finger over her heart, just as I had done in the stables.

No. She would not come tonight.

I stood before the window and unfastened my wrapper. Turning slowly, I allowed the silver light to bathe my body. I raised my hair so that the moon could bless the flesh of my neck and back and then I knelt for a time, emptying my mind, offering only devotion.

When I felt the faintest thrum of her power, I rose, went to the bedside and returned to the window with the water glass. I tipped half of its contents into the bowl, along with a twist of salt. I took up the blood-spotted rag. If I dipped it into the glass and squeezed it over the bowl, there would be blood enough to perform the divination.

I studied the stained clout in my hand. I had thought myself careful, but I had been mistaken before. A woman needed to lay with a man only once to conceive. It was more than four weeks since I had first lain with Vaughan. If this was not my monthly visitation but a flag of a different kind, then what?

It came to me that there was a way to ensure the blood was pure, but it was not something Grandmere had taught me. This would be a refinement of my own design.

Setting the bowl on the window seat, I went to my dressing table and took a hat pin from a drawer. There was a faceted green glass jewel at the blunt end and a point sharp enough to pierce braided straw at the other.

I jabbed the point into the ball of my thumb. In seconds, ripe red beads crept from the wound. I stretched my hand over the bowl and allowed five drops of blood to fall into the water. Silver became rose as blood spread like liquid smoke. I licked the tip of my finger and swirled the water around. Whispering the greeting, I raised the bowl, offering salt, my blood and my body to the full moon through the glass.

I set the bowl before me on the boards and drew a figure in the air with my left hand. Closing my eyes, I brought the tips of my fingers to my forehead and concentrated. My hair crackled and rose about me. I spoke the words of supplication and repeated them five times, once for every point of the pentacle I had drawn and once for each drop of blood.

I asked the questions and felt the air of the room stir. My hair began to wind itself around my face; something cold and damp pressed against my skin. Suddenly, there was a great cracking sound.

Fearful that the bowl had broken, I opened my eyes and scraped the hair from my face.

The bowl was whole. The liquid within, however, was black and thick as treacle. Six dark droplets glistened about it on the boards as if the water had been stirred by a careless hand.

I stared at the bowl and tried to understand answers that were not there. Pushing back my hair, I looked up at the moon, and then I saw it.

A hundred panes in the diamond-shaped lattices had broken in two. Each one of them was now shattered by a single slanting crack. I stood and stepped slowly away from the window where a huge 'V' formed by the faults in the glass was clearly visible.

I looked again at the six black stains on the boards.

I had my message.

29

I had, originally, imagined myself as Sir William Pritchard's bride, but that was not my destiny.

Or his.

His end, when it came – six days and six nights after I consulted the bowl beneath the Egg Moon of April – was a small affair.

Vaughan's father was awake when I pulled at the curtains draped around his bed. As before, the stench of disease rolled out to greet me and my stomach rolled. Obscurely, I thought of Eavis and her steaming bowl. The woman was paid to nurse this living corpse and yet she allowed him to rest in his own filth. I remembered the tale she had brought to Mrs Gurney. When I was mistress of Fyneshade there would be no need to keep Eavis beneath its roof.

I paused, alert, at the soft creak of a board close by. Turning, I searched the shadows for evidence of company, but I was alone. Ancient timbers and stones muttered to each other and their continual conversation was most apparent when the living inhabitants of the house were silent.

The contraption designed to straighten Sir William's limbs stood below the window. The curtains had not been drawn and in the clear light of the waning moon I saw cobwebs on the frame and on the leather straps. He had not used it for a very long time.

This was not murder, it was charity.

The little candle in my chamberstick guttered in a draught. It had lit my way through the walls and shown me the chalk marks I had left when I last came to the black room with Grace. I had thought it was curiosity that prompted me when I scraped those lines on the wood and on the stones. Now I knew it was fate.

I returned to my task. Setting the candle on the boards, I drew the bed hanging aside.

The old man's pouched and rheumy eyes sought mine, his body twitched and his crusted mouth worked at words that did not sound. I reached for a claw-like hand. There was no reason for cruelty. He was about to do me the greatest favour and I was minded to be gentle.

'Sir William.' I smiled, bent close and whispered, 'I have brought you medicine.' I took the blue glass phial from my pocket and raised it to catch the light. 'This will ease your pain.'

I released his hand and reached to the pillows at his head. The man was so frail and shrunken in the sheets that it was easy to prop him higher in the bed. All the while, his fearful eyes – very blue like Vaughan's – never left mine. His mouth gaped like that of a baby bird.

Truly, it would have been an easy thing to tip the contents of the phial into Sir William's mouth and hold his head to make him swallow, but to muddle my medicine with water and press the glass to his lips seemed a more tender and compassionate ministration.

The water jug and glass I had noted when I last came to the black room were still on the bedside stand as I'd hoped. Filling the glass, I twisted the stopper from the phial and added its contents to the water. Dark threads coiled through the liquid and I caught the faintest scent of damp, new-cut foliage.

Used correctly, monkshood was always fatal – and fortunately every part of the plant was effective. I had found some growing by the river three days ago while out walking with Grace and the dog. The flowers would not come until the end of summer, but its hand-like leaves were potent enough. Combined with extract of foxglove and opium, both from Grandmere's spice box, my tincture would kill the man staring at me from the bed.

I smiled at him and swirled the glass in my hand to ensure that the poison mixed with the water.

'Here.' I pressed the rim of the glass to his lips and tipped it a little. 'Drink.'

He gulped and choked as his mouth filled with death. I held his chin high and tipped again. His fingers scrabbled at the soiled sheets and he tried to move his head, but I held him.

After a very short time, Sir William realised that the liquid would drown him if he did not swallow. All the while, his eyes fixed on mine as he drank. Fear turned to resignation, and resignation faded to oblivion.

When he had taken the full glass, I closed his dull eyes, patted his hand and dabbed his lips gently with Aunt Clare's lace handkerchief. Then, to be certain, I took up a pillow and pressed it to his face until his fingers stopped twitching.

30

I awoke to sunlight. The day promised to be sharp and clear as the 'V' etched into the panes of my bedroom window. Stretching out in the warm sheets, I listened to Fyneshade. Nothing suggestive of alarm came to me.

As I lay in the bed, I considered the fragility of the thread that bound a body to a soul. I had been at Grandmere's bedside when she died, but then my mind had been clouded by grief. Detached from Sir William by any emotional bond, I was more inquisitive. It had been instructive. The snapping of his thread had been the work of moments, yet when he was gone from that corrupted shell, it was his absence – the sudden and total emptiness of flesh and bone – that told me most of life.

I wondered where a soul like his might go. If it ever truly left, that is.

When I had made quite sure that my work was complete, I replaced the tainted glass with one from my room – carried specially for the purpose – and then I moved Sir William's pillows and placed his chicken-foot hands beneath the sheets. After returning through the walls to my room, I had slept quite soundly.

There was a soft knock on the door. A shrew-faced maid entered with a jug of warm water. She nodded at me, limped to the washstand in the corner and then she crept back to the door without uttering a word. Just as always.

I wondered if I might find myself altered, but the face reflected back at me from the glass of the washstand was unchanged. There was no visible trace of my conduct on my person. It was almost disappointing.

When I dressed in my good black bombazine, I wore the red petticoat beneath it in secret jubilation.

I stood at the top of the stairs above the hall. Below me, two maids scurried across the black and white tiles. I heard a door slam and then Eavis appeared from the arch leading through to the scullery steps. She crossed the hall and began on the stairs. Halfway up she raised her head and saw me standing above. Hatred flared in her eyes, but she managed to master herself before closing the gap.

When we were level, she nodded at me.

'Good day, Mrs Eavis.'

I stepped aside to let her pass and stared at her broad grey back. There were dark circles in the cotton beneath her arms and the lingering smell of medication followed in her wake.

'I trust all is well … in the laundry?' Some devil put the

question into my head. The woman's suspicions were nothing to me now. Soon Vaughan's stained linens would be the least of her concerns.

Eavis stopped but she didn't turn. Her harsh voice came loud and clear. 'The work is foul. As I imagine you might know.'

I watched her cross the landing and turn to the north-west corridor.

The morning after my second visit to the black room passed much like any other. The thrill of anticipation carried me through the tedium of two hours in the schoolroom.

At midday I dined with Mrs Gurney. That is to say, I dined with the shell of the woman who had prattled across the table almost every day since my arrival at Fyneshade. All the bustle and energy had gone from her stout little body. Now she was hunched and silent – a misshapen bundle of striped cloth, much like a pudding set to boil on a stove.

I considered the best way to greet the news that surely was about to be imparted. I was interested to see how Mrs Gurney would tell me of the death in the house of a man who was not supposed to be here.

She stared dumbly at the pork chop on her dish. Occasionally her fingers strayed to the silver cutlery to move a knife or fork a tiny distance across the wood as if to assure herself of their reality. Finally, she looked up and I saw that her face was as pale as the lacy lappets of her cap.

'Are you quite well?' I set down my fork, although I had eaten nothing.

Mrs Gurney swallowed loudly and shook her head. If she intended to answer my question, the words could not escape from her lips. I reached across the table for her hand.

'Whatever is the matter, my dearest? I trust I can call you that after all the time we have spent together.'

'You are too good, Marta.'

She took a great shuddering gulp of air. A tear teetering perilously in the corner of her left eye brimmed over and slipped down a flabby cheek.

'I just don't know . . .' She buffed at the wet trail with the back of a hand. 'I don't know what to . . .' Incapable of continuing, she started to sob.

'Mrs Gurney!' Swiftly, I went from my chair to kneel at her side. The trailing hem of my red petticoat peeked out from beneath the hem of my black dress. It surprised me to remember at that moment that Judas had red hair, just like Nathaniel.

I rested a hand on her solid lap. 'I hope we are friends. Please, share your burden with me, Mrs Gurney. I am here to help.'

'I can't, not now.'

Stifling a sob, she took my hand in hers and held tight. 'You are a good, sweet thing. Don't leave, Marta, whatever comes. Don't leave Grace. She needs you so. Promise me that.'

Leaving Fyneshade or, indeed, Grace was the very last possibility in my mind.

This was the moment. I soothed her damp hand. 'Why would I leave when I am so happy here?'

At this Mrs Gurney threw her apron to her face.

'Don't.' The word was muffled by cotton and tears. 'You don't know . . .'

'Hester!'

The name was barked from the parlour doorway. Eavis glowered in the shadow of the stairwell. Unmoved by the tableau before her, she folded her arms.

'Shall I send Dawson to fetch Reverend Abney?'

Mrs Gurney emerged from the apron. The stony presence of Sir William's nurse seemed to remind her of her position and her dignity. Sitting straight in the chair, she dabbed her face, neatened her cap and pulled at the cuffs of her dress. She seemed embarrassed.

'Abney would be best. Not Walpole at Bakewell. He's been around too long.' She pushed her untouched chop away and cleared her throat. 'We should inform Dr Foldine too, and I must write the message for Dawson to take to The Angel for forwarding by express. That will be the start of it, mind. And the end.'

A look passed between the two women.

Eavis nodded slowly as Mrs Gurney, her quavering voice strengthened by purpose, continued.

'They won't be here until late afternoon. Everything must be ready.'

The nurse shrugged. 'It had to come.' She turned to the panelled stairwell and her hollow voice echoed back to the parlour. 'You'll need to open the north wing, Hester.'

Mrs Gurney stared at the doorway, her lips twitching at an unspoken answer. I patted her arm and frowned in a way suggestive of puzzled innocence. 'What did Mrs Eavis mean just then? Is someone ill? Is that why you are sending for a reverend and a doctor?'

Rising from the table, the housekeeper rested a hand on my head like a blessing. 'Poor Marta. You'll know soon enough. Now,

Grace will be waiting for you. If you'll excuse me, I'm afraid I won't be able to join you this evening. I have urgent things to attend to.'

31

I leapt to the schoolroom window as the rumble of wheels sounded in the courtyard below. The carriage that rocked to a halt before the steps leading up to Fyneshade's doorway was small and shabby, not the elegant brougham that Vaughan had followed on his grey.

The groom dismounted and went to open the door. I was certain the visitor was either the Reverend Abney or Dr Foldine, but because of the angle I could not see who stepped out.

The summoning of a doctor did not worry me. Grandmere's recipe to ease a soul from the world was devised to leave no trace.

I glanced at Grace. A score of abandoned drawings lay scattered on the boards around her chair. I went to her side and tapped her shoulder.

'Dearest, I must leave you for a moment. Not long, I promise.' I smiled and placed a fresh sheet of paper before her on the desk.

'When I come back, perhaps you will have drawn Rummy for me? I would like that so very much.'

She grinned and set to work. As did I. Walking silently to the end of the passage, I stood behind the elaborate fan of drapery obscuring the way to the landing and stairs. Although I could not see from here, I could listen.

Soon there were voices from the hallway below – a man and a woman. At such a distance, the words were unclear but I thought one of the speakers to be Mrs Gurney.

On the surface, affairs at Fyneshade seemed little changed. Clocks struck the hours, the halves and the quarters. Maids busied themselves in the passages and at the hearths in the rooms of use. Yet I had the strongest and strangest impression that this was all a façade. Although I had never bothered to make friends among the servants – to be frank, I still found it difficult to tell the sparrows apart – it seemed now that they took pains to avoid me. When I passed a maid on the stairs or in one of the many corridors, their faces were taut as if a new, immovable skin was pulled across the bones. If I forced them to speak, their answers were clipped, but declaimed aloud to ensure that the exchange was above suspicion. It occurred to me that the house had become a stage for an audience of one.

I welcomed the visitor as a sign of change.

From my hiding place behind the curtain, I concentrated on the sounds from the stairwell. The muttering grew louder as they mounted the steps, but still I could not make out more than one word in five. At last, when they reached the landing just below, where a corridor led to the doors of the north wing, I caught Mrs Gurney clearly.

'. . . to be expected, I suppose. It's been such a time since you last came.'

'He would not allow any physician to attend him?'

This question, asked in a querulous, waspish voice, came from a man.

'Never. The last doctor to call upon Sir William was your good self ... and that was ten years ago. You must prepare for the alteration, Dr Foldine.'

'Am I to take it that he never recovered from the fall, Mrs Gurney?'

'He never left his room, and now he never will, except for when ...' Too dainty to continue that sentence, she stopped and began again. 'It's this way, if you remember, through here.'

'I do indeed, ma'am. If I may say, I was surprised not to be called back. I thought Sir William had decided to call on the services of Bretton in Sheffield. He was fashionable a decade ago, quite the coming man.'

Footsteps crossed the landing. Foldine's voice came again from a greater distance. I strained to catch his words as Mrs Gurney led the way to the north wing. I heard the creaking of the boards as they went.

'Of course, Bretton is dead too, now – typhus – but I did think it odd that Sir William had decided to try a less experienced ...'

Dr Foldine's opinions on a deceased rival were still very much alive. The buzz of his resentment receded until I could not even hear it as a distant irritation. I lingered behind the curtain for a few minutes more. The conversation I had just overheard confirmed what Vaughan had told me. Foldine had spoken of Sir William's 'fall' and of the subsequent dismissal of his services.

'For William Pritchard, to see pity in a man's eyes would be crueller than the most degrading disease. He even dismissed his physician.'

I would have waited for their return had it not been for more sounds from below. Slipping from my hiding place, I went to investigate.

A slightly stooped young man with a face like a sheep stood at the foot of the great staircase. I needed no introductions to know that this was Reverend Abney.

Jennet deliberately turned her back on me as she took his hat. His straight fine hair, the colour of whey, fell in two lank curtains that scraped along the collar of his sullied travelling coat. The man's eyes widened when he caught sight of me on the stairs.

'Mrs Gurney?'

I smiled and brought a hand to my breast. 'No, I am not she. I am governess to Grace Pritchard.'

'Ah, the poor child.' He shook his head and attempted a sympathetic smile. 'This is my first visit to Fyneshade, but I trust that I will be permitted to meet her in due course to offer my most sincere—'

'Reverend Abney, is it?'

Mrs Gurney's voice, shrill with alarm, came from the landing above. She almost flew down the stairs to position herself between us.

'*I* am Mrs Gurney.' She bobbed a small, old-fashioned curtsey. 'Can I offer you refreshment, Reverend?'

Without giving him a chance to reply, she turned to Jennet. 'Bring tea, bread, cheese and potted meat to the library. Reverend Abney has come from Tideswell. Take his coat.'

Jennet accepted the travelling coat and slipped from the hallway.

Anxious to fill the silence, Mrs Gurney burbled on about scones and fresh-baked seed cake. All the while I stood close by on the stairs, deliberately excluded from this meeting.

If the reverend thought it odd to be received in this way, he did not show it. I saw his eyes wandering around the hallway. The panelled walls glowed like fresh-hatched conkers and the hollow shells of silver armour glinted in the shadows beneath stone arches.

'Seed cake? Thank you, that will be most welcome.' The reverend did not strike me as the sort who found pleasure in food.

He stared with a different sort of hunger at the plaster ceiling and wide oak stairs.

He gestured at the space around him. The movement of his hand was like a benediction. 'I have a great interest in architecture. St John's is blessed by many fine monuments and I count it a great honour to be the custodian of the Bower Chapel. Very fine work in alabaster, dating from the fourteenth century.' His eyes continued to roam the hallway. 'Fyneshade is one of the oldest houses in the county and I have long harboured the desire to see it. My great sadness is that it should be under such circumstances, Mrs Gurney.'

Instantly, the housekeeper span on the tiles and headed for the stairs. 'If you'd follow me, Reverend.'

She forged past me without a word. Reverend Abney followed, but he, at least, smiled and nodded. 'Ma'am.'

My stomach pitched – the young cleric stank of sweat and unwashed cloth. When he had gone a few steps higher, I felt his eyes on me, as I expected. I turned and he looked quickly away, guilty to be caught adding the sin of lust to his covetousness.

When they reached the first landing, I called out.

'Mrs Gurney!' My voice echoed in the hallway.

She paused and peered down at me over the rail, unable to avoid this interaction in the company of the reverend. I smiled.

'We have not had the chance to speak for such a time. There is clearly much to discuss. I hope we can meet later when you and the Reverend Abney ...' I wondered what to say for just a moment, '... have taken refreshment.'

She glanced at the unwitting clergyman and nodded. 'Tomorrow, Marta. That would be best. We can talk then.'

32

Despite her assurance, Mrs Gurney did not join me for breakfast the following day. It was exasperating, but I knew that I could not afford to show any sign that I was aware of Sir William's death. When Old Maggie delivered Grace to the schoolroom, my reasonable enquiry as to the housekeeper's health and whereabouts was met with a tersely mumbled excuse.

Shortly after we had settled into the monotony of the morning, the sound of hooves came from the courtyard below. Abandoning my book, I flew to the window to see a man in a greatcoat dismount and dash up the steps. His dusty horse, loaded with leather pouches, scuffed the cobbles and nodded patiently, all the while fretting at the bit in its mouth. I was surprised Dawson didn't tend to the creature, but moments later the rider remounted and steered the horse back through the gateway.

This new visitor had delivered a message. The strapped

pouches flung over the horse's haunches were postal bags, a rare sight here. I took up the book again and tried to find diversion in the tale of a Turkish seraglio. As my eyes skipped along the lines, I found myself thinking about the nature of the message that had just been delivered. I stared into the hearth and ran the sharp black corner of the book cover back and forth over my lips, tasting fusty leather and victory.

Old Maggie appeared at the schoolroom door, just as the chorus of Fyneshade's clocks began the midday chimes. I was sitting at the desk now and reading aloud from the Bible – a portrait of companionable duty and concern. Alerted by the chimes for the quarter before noon, I now performed this charade every day for the nursemaid's benefit.

She held out a hand to Grace, who went meekly to her side. Old Maggie stared at me. 'I'm to ask you to go to the library, not the parlour.' She blinked as if I were an object too brilliant for her gaze. 'Mrs Gurney is waiting for you there.' This was one of the longest sentences the woman had ever addressed directly to me. Surprised, I rose from the desk, but before I could question this rearrangement, the nursemaid turned and ushered Grace into the passage.

Draped in a woollen shawl, Mrs Gurney was sitting at the wide mahogany desk. The curtains had been drawn back to allow as much light as possible to penetrate the gloomiest reaches of the library, but the darkest place of all was the housekeeper's face.

A chair was set ready. I smoothed the skirts of my dress and sat opposite her. A growl rumbled from beneath the desk. A second later Lancer's head appeared next to Mrs Gurney's arm. The dog rested its muzzle on the corner and stared at me, amber-flecked eyes catching the light from the window. It snorted, dipped and arranged its long limbs to a reclining position in a patch of light on the rug.

'Old Maggie told me you wished to see me here.' I smiled in a manner intended to suggest concern and friendship. 'I am glad. I heard you speak of sending for a doctor, and yesterday Reverend Abney came. I hope you are not ill?' I sat forward. 'Forgive me if I presume too much, Mrs Gurney.'

She shook her head and avoided my eyes. Tiny motes of dust floated in the air between us. At last she spoke.

'It is I who have presumed, Marta.' She pushed at something on the desk. I saw that it was the pretty silver chatelaine that usually hung at her waist. The keys had been removed from the silver loop and were spread before her on the tooled leather of the desktop. There was a pile of papers there too.

Now she looked at me directly. Her eyes were red and the skin around them was pouched and raw. This was a woman who had shed so many tears that the reservoirs were almost dry.

'Dear Mrs Gurney! Whatever is wrong?' I reached across and laid a hand on hers.

'Everything, Marta. That's the heart of it. Everything is wrong.'

The moment had arrived. I offered her a silence to fill. She took a breath and sighed.

'I have lied to you.'

I waited.

'There's no easy way to tell this, but I'll try to be plain. I never meant to deceive. It was all for her, for Grace I mean. You must remember that.'

I stroked her spotted hand softly. 'Tell me what?'

'I led you to think Sir William was travelling, but he wasn't. He was never away from Fyneshade. All the time you've been here he's been here too, an invalid, poor soul, hardly able to raise his head from the pillow nor move a muscle in his body.'

Snatching my hand from hers, I brought it to my lips. 'No.'

I found myself absurdly pleased by this moment of theatre.

Mrs Gurney nodded. 'It's true. He didn't even know you were here. As I told you, it was me who took you on for the sake of the little one. Sir William hadn't the first idea of your existence.'

She could not have been more wrong about that. This was becoming a game.

'But why are you telling me this now?'

'Because he is dead, Marta. It was his heart. He died two nights ago and that's why I sent for the doctor and the reverend. He ... he was to be buried in the chapel, next to the mistress, according to his wishes.'

She turned to the harp as if she expected to hear a note from it, but if Sophia Pritchard's ghost was with us, she did not care to reveal her presence. Mrs Gurney pulled a white cotton handkerchief from her cuff and gripped it tight.

'If only she knew, dear lady. And now it's the end for us all.' She scrabbled at the papers on the desk. 'Well, most of us. She'll need you more than ever now. That's why I must talk to you, Marta.'

'Talk to me! Dear Mrs Gurney, I cannot begin to understand what you are saying.' I thought it best to appear bewildered. 'Sir William has really been here all the time?'

She nodded and twisted the white cotton square in her hand. A scrolled 'H' was embroidered on a trailing corner.

'Then, where was he? Where is he now for that matter?'

'In the north wing.'

'But you said it was locked for the winter.'

'He's been ill for such a long time that we . . . we simply grew used to it. We kept it locked and . . .' another twist of the handkerchief, '. . . we kept it from you,' she whispered, ashamed of her duplicity.

'*We?*' I tempered my innocence with a little steel. 'What do you mean by that?'

Mrs Gurney stared at me, her lower lip quivering dangerously. 'All of us at Fyneshade know about Sir William. It's happened over so many years that it's become . . . natural.'

I allowed a little gasp to break from my lips and raised a hand to my breast. 'There is nothing *natural* in hiding the presence of the master of the household. After you, Mrs Gurney, I am the most senior servant here. How could you keep this from me?'

I disliked using the word 'servant' to describe myself, but in a short time it would not apply.

The stricken housekeeper fiddled with a key.

'I was going to tell you everything, Marta. Truly I was. Indeed, I was on the point of it several times.'

'But you did not.' I shook my head, affecting bewilderment and justified anger. 'No! This is unforgivable. I thought you and I were friends and yet—' I broke off and looked at the window, allowing the light to catch the tears I had brought to my own eyes. 'I am bitterly disappointed that you could not trust me. And further, I believe you have made me a laughing stock in this house. It is only now, when your secret must be discovered, that you tell me.'

In truth, my anger on finding that everyone knew of Sir William's presence except me was not feigned. I stood, clasping my hands to my breast. 'I have been most grievously wronged.'

'Please, Marta, sit. Let me explain.' Mrs Gurney waved the handkerchief at the chair. 'It wasn't supposed . . . *you* weren't supposed . . .' She faltered. 'Give me a chance to explain, I beg you. It's important for Grace's sake that you understand it all.'

For a moment I did not move. The dog raised its head to look at me; its ears twitched as if it had been following this exchange and was as curious as I to know more. Mrs Gurney's face was a mask of misery. She opened and shut her mouth like a stranded fish and finally managed to emit a further appeal.

'Please.'

I was quite aware of the effect of the blackness of my dress, my height, my silence, my stillness and the total absence of expression on my face.

'Very well, Mrs Gurney.' I sat down again. 'Tell me.'

33

In the beginning, I recognised her account. I already knew from Vaughan that Sir William Pritchard had married a girl half his age and that the marriage had not been a success. I also knew that he had left his wife and child at Fyneshade while he travelled abroad for many years and that he had returned much altered. But that was where the stories took different paths.

'He was a successful man of middle years by then and I imagine it was to be expected that some of the wildness had gone from him.' Mrs Gurney nodded to herself. 'But he'd been away for nearly eight years and in that time Sophia had become a woman, not the shy girl he'd left behind. While he was gone she'd learned to run the estate, earning the respect of all, from the tenant farmers to the servants here at the house. That's not an easy thing for a young woman to do, Marta.'

The housekeeper turned from the desk and peered at the harp in the shadows.

'She was a kind lady. It was her idea to employ girls who might not find work elsewhere. You'll have noticed that most of the servants have a . . . a *difficulty* of sorts.' Her eyes flicked to my face but she looked away swiftly. 'I've tried to be like her. In all the years since I've often thought to myself, "what would the mistress do?"'

'Would she keep the presence of her husband from me?' I could not resist this tart question.

Mrs Gurney shook her head. Her answer was a barely audible whisper. 'It had nothing to do with her.'

She pushed at a long silver key on the desk and we watched it spin on the leather. It came to rest with the teeth pointing at me. After a moment she resumed her tale.

'Eight years is a long time apart, but the master and mistress met again as different people. Gradually they found happiness. You might almost say it was as if after thirteen years married they were newly-weds once more. He had his room in the north wing decorated in the French style especially for her – although, in all truth, I don't think she much liked it. And of course, Sir William's business ventures abroad had made him a more serious and thoughtful man. We live here so simply that you might not think it, Marta, but the estate is very rich. The income comes mostly from Sir William's merchant companies. Until now those affairs have been attended to by his lawyers, but soon . . .'

She faltered again, but one word sang in my mind.

Rich!

I allowed myself to imagine life as the wife of a wealthy man while Mrs Gurney continued to describe a halcyon past at Fyneshade that bore little resemblance to Vaughan's account. According to her, Sir William and his wife were devoted to one another and they ran the house and the estate with the benevolence of happy monarchs. Soon, I would assume those duties, with Vaughan. Beneath the desk I flattened my hand against my belly where I was now certain that his child lay curled and waiting. I could *feel* it.

'Then Master Vaughan came back . . .'

His name in the sugared posset of Mrs Gurney's recollections sharpened my attention.

'. . . quite suddenly. I never knew what he'd done – none of us did, but it must have been something bad for him to be packed off home with no hope of return.'

'Vaughan Pritchard was sent away to school?'

I asked so that she might clarify the point. He had never mentioned this part of his past.

Mrs Gurney nodded. 'For his own good. He was always a strange child. Spiteful you might say, spoiled too. He had, *has* a cruel streak in him. The mistress blamed herself. She doted on him so very much as a babe that, at first, she was blind to his faults. Then, poor lady, she came to think that in the absence of his father she might have done something wrong. When he was eleven years old, or thereabouts, Vaughan was sent away. To speak frankly, it was the best thing for him. He was already spending too much time with a man who . . .' She pursed her lips. 'You don't need to hear tattle from more than a decade back, Marta, but I'll just say that Thomas Grindlow was not a gentleman.'

'*Good old Grindlow showed me the secrets of the walls.*'

The strings of the harp murmured in a sudden draught. Alarmed, Mrs Gurney turned but the rustle of the papers on the desk proved that the instrument had not been touched by the hands of a spirit. Nevertheless, she shivered and drew her shawl about her shoulders. Her fingers strayed to a very large ornate key. The bow was identical to the shape of Fyneshade's gates. We sat in silence for a time. She appeared to be wary of opening a locked room in her memory.

I prompted. 'What of this man? Grindlow, was it?'

Mrs Gurney nodded again. 'He was head groom here, just as his father had been before him and his grandfather before that. I daresay Grindlows had been at Fyneshade since the building of the walls but Thomas was the last of them, the ones with a right to the name, that is. He was a big man with a nasty temper, and rough with it. He never married but there was talk. A girl was born to Farmer Lacey's widow at Upper Riding.' She pointed at the window as if I might know where she meant. 'There were others too, but nothing could ever be held against him, not for a long time.'

She picked at the handkerchief again, rolling the edge between her fingers.

'Lady Sophia was a good soul, like I said, but I always thought that Thomas was one of the reasons she deliberately employed girls who weren't . . .' She paused. 'And Vaughan, well, he turned out just like him. That's why . . .' She faltered again. Bobbing her head like a hen, she moved the pile of papers to a new place on the desk before continuing the decade-old tattle I didn't need to hear.

'While Sir William was away, Thomas treated Master Vaughan like a son. The pair of them were always together. He taught the boy how to fly a hawk – he had a bird too, just like that vicious Dido – and how to fish and swim in the river. But he also taught him arrogance, language that's not to be repeated and . . .' Mrs Gurney returned her attention to the handkerchief, pleating the cotton to a fan, '. . . much more, I suspect. Although no one could prove it. When Vaughan was sent away to school it was a relief to us all.'

This was new. I drummed on the leather. 'Surely, if the man was such a bad influence, Lady Sophia would have sent *him* away, not her own son?'

'It's as I told you, Marta. Nothing could ever be proved against Thomas Grindlow. And even if it could, no one would speak against him. Besides, the fact that he was the only person Vaughan listened to put the mistress in a difficult position.' She sighed. 'Lady Sophia and Master Vaughan were close, but as he grew, she couldn't control him. Sending him away was for the best. Grindlow didn't want the boy to go from Fyneshade, but for once he had no say in the matter. He wasn't the boy's father, after all.'

I was keenly interested in the story now, but I did not wish to appear eager. I considered how I might lead her to continue without revealing a particular curiosity. I continued to tap lightly on the desk.

'Mrs Gurney, I cannot see how any of this is connected to the secret of Sir William's presence here at Fyneshade. You have warned me on several occasions about his son and perhaps, from what you have said, I begin to understand a little of your concern.' I looked directly at her. 'Suki?'

She nodded, her chins quivering. 'There've been others, but she was his latest, yes.'

'Poor child.' I tilted my head to assure her that she need not explain. This gossip mattered little to me. I knew better than anyone that Vaughan was not a saint. Had he not told me so himself? But he had chosen me above all others. Together we would rule Fyneshade and its lands. I would be the new lady and my portrait would hang in the hallway. Our child would ride a fat pony in the grounds.

I prodded again, careful not to reveal myself. 'But you are circling the point. Why was Sir William hidden from me?'

She clenched her hands into little pink fists. 'He was ashamed, Marta. After all that happened, he could not face the world.' She leaned forward. 'When the boy came home from school, things had changed. For a start, Grindlow was gone.'

Scanning the room as if to discover an eavesdropper, she spoke in a hushed voice. 'Thomas had very fair hair, almost white it was – and so did a baby boy born to a thirteen-year-old scullery maid. She'd been *forced*, poor girl. For all his cunning Grindlow couldn't hide the fact that he was the child's father and Sir William wouldn't be cowed by a bully. He dismissed him.

'Vaughan, now, he couldn't accept the changes. It was bad enough that his father was back, but worse was that he saw his parents were happy. He was jealous. That's the beginning and the end of it. It didn't help matters that Sir William was so distant with him.'

She paused and sucked in her cheeks. 'No, that's not quite right. He seemed disgusted by him. Whatever it was that had happened at the school Sir William knew all about it. For the first time in his life that boy was properly disciplined. It made him angry and it made him dangerous.'

I frowned. 'Dangerous is a strange word to use of a child?'

She snorted. 'Vaughan was no child when he came back from school. He was a devil.'

Devil again? I thought back to the grinning carving on the roof of the chapel as she warmed to her theme.

'First, there was the accident. Sir William went out on the estate one afternoon and when it fell dark and he didn't come back, a party was sent to look for him. Eventually, they found him on the high moor up near Longstone Tor, pinned beneath his horse with his right leg and arm shattered beyond use. The creature had stumbled and broken its neck. They had to put it out of its misery before they brought the master back. The mistress was distraught. She sat by Sir William's bedside day and night and wouldn't allow anyone else to nurse him. In the end she sent for some new medical contraption from London to help him exercise his limbs and it worked well enough. In six months, much to everyone's surprise, especially Dr Foldine, he walked again.' Mrs Gurney bent forward and whispered, 'Thing is, Marta, we all knew that was no accident. The master's horse had been attacked. One of its eyes had been torn from the socket. Ripped out by something . . . with *claws*.'

I plucked at my black skirt and watched the tent of the material settle back to my knee. 'Are you suggesting it was attacked by Vaughan's hawk?'

'I'm not suggesting anything. I'm telling you what was found up there. Vaughan was missing when they sent out the search party. He said he was flying Circe – she came before Dido – out at Bryn Cop on the other side of the valley.' Her eyes narrowed. 'The only thing he asked when they brought Sir William back that night was whether he'd live.'

'That is a reasonable question, is it not?'

'Not when you consider the horse, Marta.'

'But if it fell and lay there for a while it would have been vulnerable to attack from any creature.' I shrugged. 'Did Sir William describe what had happened?'

Mrs Gurney shook her head. 'Along with his broken bones, he'd taken a bad knock to the head. He had no memory of that afternoon, and perhaps that was unlucky given what came next.'

Suddenly the harp shivered into life. This was no faint murmur of strings but a single chord that sang out into the room. Glassy notes thrummed in the air as we stared at each other over papers that did not move.

Lancer let out a long low whine and stood, ears flattened to its head.

I confess it was most odd. A sudden chill on the nape of my neck made me twist to look into the shadowed corners. We were not alone together in the library now, I was sure of it. I wondered about the spirit of Sophia Pritchard. Where was her place in the categories of the returned?

Tail curled low, Lancer slunk from the desk and padded across the library to the doors. The dog whined and scratched at the wood, but when it became clear that neither of us would go to release it, it stretched out along the threshold, nose pointing at the wall.

I turned back to find my living human companion staring at me, her eyes round as twin moons.

'What came next, Mrs Gurney?'

'The baby.' The answer was barely audible.

'Grace?'

'Yes and no.' She slid a wary glance at the harp. 'It was a great joy to us all at Fyneshade when the mistress found she was to have another child. Nearly all of us, that is. Sir William was happiest of all. It seemed to confirm his recovery and vitality after the accident and there was such gladness that the mistress was still able to bear a healthy child. By spring she was round as an egg and so pretty and thriving that you might have taken her for a woman ten years younger.'

She twisted the handkerchief again.

'Master Vaughan wasn't happy. Mostly he'd be out on the estate with Circe, and that was best for all of us. When he was in the house he was difficult. Some days he fell into a rage for no reason. Things were said of him.' She shook her head. 'There were stories.'

I straightened in the chair. 'There seem to be a great many stories, Mrs Gurney, but they are not facts. You told me that you did not wish to spread tattle that was stale a decade ago, and yet—'

'It's no tattle!'

I was surprised by the force of her interruption. 'He'd appear out of nowhere at night. He walked the corridors and lingered at the maids' doors. It was a good thing most of them shared the space in the attic. One of them, Sarah Dunn from the kitchens, woke and saw him standing at the end of her bed. She threw a shoe at him and then she said he just laughed, backed into shadows and disappeared. He was uncanny.' Mrs Gurney nodded at me. 'You know what girls are like, Marta. They were frightened, and the more they talked about him the more frightened they became.'

She pulled at a thread hanging from her shawl. 'I have no actual proof of what came next, but I know the truth of it.' She took a deep breath.

'The master had gone to see to some business in Buxton. He still wasn't ready to ride and Dawson had taken him there in the carriage. They were to stay one night at the Palace Hotel.' She flapped a hand. 'It was summer and all these windows were open. They argued so loudly you could hear it all over the terrace. The things he called her! You wouldn't believe it possible he could know such—'

'Wait.' I raised a hand. 'I am confused. Of whom do you speak?'

'Lady Sophia and her son, that's *whom*. I heard it all and what he said is still here.' She patted the side of her head. 'I only wish it wasn't. He was jealous of the new baby and he blamed her for it, for allowing his father near her. Filthy, horrible talk it was, not fit for a sailor let alone a boy. I can guess where he learned it, mind.'

Mrs Gurney's breast rose and fell. The stripes on her bodice heaved beneath her chins.

'There was slamming and crashing and then I heard the mistress cry, "Get out!" It went quiet after that so I came straight here and found her at this very desk.' She fluttered a hand to the corner. 'Her harp was thrown on its side and a vase, a favourite, had been smashed by the window. I remember her trying to help me collect all the broken pieces but she was so big by then she couldn't reach down to the boards. Her face, Marta! All pale and bloated it was and her lovely eyes were cloudy with tears that wouldn't stop falling.

'"What have I done, Hester?" That's what she said to me. At the time I thought she meant the argument but now I think she meant Vaughan. I told her to rest.' The housekeeper patted the edge of the desk as if it was the arm of her deceased mistress. 'And, poor lady, she went to her room. She didn't come down again that day, but later that night . . . well, it was closer to morning, really . . .'

Mrs Gurney gulped back a dry sob.

'A maid found her at the bottom of the stairs in the hallway. Lady Sophia had tumbled all the way from the first landing and was lying on her side, hands curled so tight to her breast that no one could free them. There was a puddle of blood and at first the silly girl thought it was from the gash on her head but then she realised it was the babies coming. She was carrying twins. The miracle of it all, if you could see it that way, was that the mistress was still alive – just – when the maid found her, but the fall brought on the births too early.' Fresh tears glazed her eyes. 'Later that day, Dr Foldine delivered a living girl and a dead boy. My poor lady followed her little son a few hours later. They're buried together in the chapel. Sir William was always meant to join them, but now ...'

The tears brimmed over and dripped from the housekeeper's jowls to her starched white collar. She dabbed her face with the handkerchief. Her eyes strayed to the papers on the desk and she shook her head.

'The master was with her when she died. When he came back to Fyneshade in the afternoon of that terrible day he found that everything had changed. Dr Foldine told him that he had gained a daughter but lost a son and that his wife was nearing the end. Ignoring little Grace, he went to Sophia, shutting the doors to the room so that the two of them were alone until the last. Just the two of them, Marta, remember that. Vaughan was nowhere to be found that day.'

The housekeeper stared at me. I saw her draw every sinew of her body into a knot of resolve.

'And now we come to the heart of it, Marta.' She glanced at the harp and then back at me. 'It was past midnight when the master came out of that room. He went straight to his study. Next day, instead of visiting his newborn daughter, comforting his only living son or even speaking to the household, he stayed there alone. On the second day, he summoned the family lawyer from Bakewell and the two of them were private for three hours.

'Very early next morning, Sir William called me to him. Truly, Marta, I have never seen a man so changed. I swear that a part of him died with Sophia. He trembled as he ordered me to wait until Vaughan went out that day – as he always did with Circe – and then to make sure that the boy's possessions – his clothes, his books, his childhood toys – were taken from his room, gathered together and piled in the courtyard. Then I was to lock every door leading into the house so that his son could not enter Fyneshade, no matter how hard he hammered or how pitifully he called from outside.'

Mrs Gurney cleared her throat as if to continue, but apparently could not find the words. I clasped my hands together on the desk and bent towards her.

'You say this is the heart of it yet still I cannot understand how Sir William came to be hidden from me. He was lost in the depths of grief, was he not? Perhaps that is the reason for his strange behaviour and yet you seem to imply that—'

'I'm not lying, Marta.' Mrs Gurney wrung her hands. 'I'm not proud of what I did, that's why it's difficult to tell. The master gave me a sealed message for Vaughan. I was to leave it with his things in the courtyard. But before I did that ... I ...'

Her eyes roamed to a point above my head. Sensing an ancient guilt, I pounced.

'You read it!' Arranging my features to an appropriate solemnity, I waited.

'I know it was wrong of me ...' she nodded, '... but it was such an odd time. In all the years that have followed I wish I hadn't. It's been a heavy thing to carry, the knowledge of it all.' She pushed at the empty chatelaine, rolling the silver fob back and forth over the leather. 'It was a brief message, no more than a dozen lines. The nub of it was that Sir William never wished to set eyes on his son again. If Vaughan ever entered the house during his father's lifetime he would be struck from the will and cast penniless into the world. He said that his name was a stain on the family but that as he was his only living son, he could not bring himself to tell what he knew. Sophia had given him the proof before she died.'

'Proof of what?'

'I didn't understand that myself until later.' Mrs Gurney blinked. 'When Vaughan came back and howled like an animal at the door his father went to his room and locked himself inside. Vaughan circled the house, screaming and begging to be allowed back in. The master must have heard him, even shut away in the north wing.

'It was such a terrible day, Marta. None of us knew what to do for the best so we didn't disturb Sir William. We left him and carried on our duties as well as we could. I remember tending to little Grace. Poor lamb, born into such sadness and such a weak scrap of a thing we didn't think she'd live much longer than her mother and brother. Even then I knew she'd been born different.' She shook her head. 'Come next morning, none of us could rouse the master. We knocked and called at the door to his room but there was no answer. In the end we had to force the lock, and it was a good thing we did.

'Sir William was lying beside his desk. His chair had tipped back and everything was skewed and toppled. The master's face was spotted black with ink that had dribbled over the edge from the dipping well.

'He couldn't move. He could hardly speak and his left hand

was clawed up into a fist. We made him as comfortable as we could and called for Dr Foldine, who came before midday. After examining him, he said the master had been stricken by apoplexy brought on by the shock of Lady Sophia. He thought it possible there was bleeding on the brain going all the way back to the fall from the horse the previous year. He said Sir William wasn't likely to last the week, but that was ten years ago, Marta, and from that day the master never moved again from his bed.'

Suddenly, the harp sang softly in the corner. Mrs Gurney nodded as if in answer.

'When he was struck Sir William had been writing, but I couldn't make sense of it. The paper was covered with one word scrawled over and over. He'd written with such force that in places the pen had torn through the page.

She turned to the harp and nodded again.

'That word was "shame". And later, when Dr Foldine left, he asked me why the master was clutching a hank of black hair so tight in his left hand.'

34

'Black, just like Vaughan's it was.' Mrs Gurney stared across the desk, willing me to understand. 'Foldine said he had to force Sir William's fist open to take it from him.' Gulping, she screwed her handkerchief to a knot. 'There, you have it all, Marta.'

I considered how to proceed. Her story was quite different to the one I had heard, but did that matter so very much? I had made a choice about my future when I went to the black room with a tincture of monkshood. In a way, there was more to bind me to Vaughan now than ever before. We were true equals.

My hand went again to my belly.

'Are you saying that you believe the boy was responsible for the death of his mother?'

Mrs Gurney nodded. 'That hair was the proof. Sophia kept it clenched tight in her hand until the end. The last thing she did was to give it to her husband. That's why Sir William locked Vaughan out of the house. Can you imagine knowing that about your own son? Your *only* son? I reckon it drove him mad, what with writing that word over and over and then taking a fit.'

'From which he never recovered?'

She nodded. 'We didn't tell anyone about what happened, not exactly. How could we? I ask you, Marta, how could we tell the tale I've just told you without any proof? Vaughan was barred from the house and *I* . . . we, all of us, knew that if he was ever to set foot inside again then he would be struck from the will. Sir William's lawyer wrote to me to tell me that after the master took ill. I was to keep watch.'

'You became a spy?' I began to understand Vaughan's antipathy to the housekeeper.

Mrs Gurney studied the keys. 'I became a guardian, to Grace especially. The months went on, then they turned to years. There was talk in the county at first, but people soon forgot and moved on to fresh gossip. And that suited us all.'

'And the boy?'

'Vaughan couldn't go far. He moved into Grindlow's old rooms above the stables. Under the terms Sir William had worked out with his lawyer, he was to receive the smallest stipend from the estate. He still does.' Mrs Gurney swallowed loudly. I caught an odd expression in her eyes. 'As long as he doesn't enter the house that money is still paid regularly, but as he's grown it's not enough. *Mostly* Vaughan Pritchard gambles and lives off his winnings from Dido. Meanwhile, Sir William has lingered on half dead and half alive in that room. Gradually, without any of us noticing, it's become the ordinary way of things here at Fyneshade.'

I was quiet for a moment. I allowed the silence to grow to an uncomfortable void between us before I filled it. 'What do you expect me to say, Mrs Gurney? From what you have just told me, ordinary is the last word I would use to describe this house.'

'That's why I wanted a companion for Grace.' Her chins jostled over her collar as she agreed. 'She'd spent such a time on her own and we couldn't teach her the things a young lady might need. I did my best, we all did, but it wasn't enough. When I heard from my sister about you needing a position and being told on enquiry that you were just the sort who might suit here . . . Well, you know the rest.'

It was not *I* who needed a position. It was Agatha Van Meeran who *needed* to part me from her son. The thought of myself as the beneficiary of Mrs Gurney's pity for a fellow servant was unbearable.

'I do not *know* anything, Mrs Gurney.' I was harsh and cold. 'You have kept it from me deliberately.'

She winced. 'Not deliberately, Marta, no. At first, I didn't think you'd stay. It's as simple as that. I was told you were a plain girl – the sort that does well at Fyneshade – but when you came here, I saw you were . . . a clever, fine young lady, and so pretty with it. I reckoned you'd take one look at us all – and at Grace – and leave. But you didn't. And that made things difficult because you're not like . . .' Mrs Gurney stared into the space above my head.

Clearly, she found no way to continue that explanation. Instead, she rested her hands on the desk and leaned forward.

'When I saw how fond Grace was of you and the good you did for her, I made up my mind to tell you about Sir William. Truly, Marta. The longer you were here the more convinced I became that I'd done the right thing in taking you on. I could see you were a good and decent young lady and not one to spread gossip about the state of the master. You deserved to know everything.

But then you met Mr Vaughan by accident. He knew I'd taken on a governess because I asked him and he agreed, but he didn't know that you were . . . were like you are. *He* gave orders that you were not to know of his father.'

Vaughan had discussed me with Mrs Gurney? This was new intelligence. I thought back to the day at the river when we had spoken across the ice. I remembered that he had known me.

'*I was told that Grace had a new governess, but if that's who you are then you're not what I expected.*'

I frowned. 'Surely Vaughan Pritchard has no say in matters relating to the house. From what you have said he is an outcast. Why would you take orders from him?'

She studied the keys splayed before her. I saw the rise and fall of her breast.

'It was such a small thing, Marta. Please don't think any worse of me than you already do.'

Unable to look at me, she began to fold her cotton handkerchief into a small, tight square. 'My nephew's a lead miner over at Sheldon. He's a decent lad and a good father, but a year back he had debts. I . . . I gave him some things to sell. Only small things, trinkets mainly. I didn't think they'd matter or be missed, but I was wrong. Vaughan came across one of them – a tiny mechanical bird no bigger than my hand – in a pawnbroker's shop in Bakewell. He recognised it and when he enquired as to where it came from it didn't take him long to find the connection. Since then he's . . . he's had a hand in my affairs.'

She looked at me now. 'I was stupid and I was wrong.'

I almost laughed aloud. The thought of the woman sitting opposite me as a petty thief was as unlikely as it was amusing. 'Do you mean he blackmails you, Mrs Gurney?'

She nodded. 'I curse the day I gave him the idea. He asks for things from the house and I have to let him have them. He's threatened to accuse me of stealing, my nephew too, if I don't do exactly what he wants. And, for some reason, he wanted to be quite sure that you didn't know about his father.'

Pushing the handkerchief into her sleeve, she continued. 'The day after you first met him at the river he sent word through Eavis that we were not to mention Sir William to you. He was most specific on the matter.' She reached across the table for my hand. 'I've tried to keep you safe, Marta. All along. That's why I warned you. He *is* a devil.'

I thought back to that day at the river. Even then I had been aware of a bond that linked us. And Vaughan had felt it too. He had recognised a fellow spirit. My free hand strayed again to the almost imperceptible mound beneath the bombazine.

Why would he give that order about his father?

I concentrated on the many keys laid between us – each one fashioned to unlock a room that would soon be mine. My eyes fell upon an elegant silver key with a curved bow set to the side like a letter 'P'.

I was always meant to be at Fyneshade. Vaughan was my destiny.

As I was his.

A little gilt clock on a marble table near the window twitched and began to ring out the hour. Soon the sound of Fyneshade's many clocks reached the library. I pulled my hand from the housekeeper's clammy grasp, stood and began to walk to the door. Lancer stood, whimpered and scratched at the wood.

Her voice quavered behind me, 'Where are you going?'

'To my room.' I did not turn. 'This has been a great shock. I must consider my position and my future, Mrs Gurney.'

In the tall mirror over the hearth, I saw her reflection rifle through the pile of papers on the desk. When she found what she was looking for, she waved it at my back.

'But there's more, Marta. You can't leave Fyneshade, not now that everything's to change. It's Grace we must think of. If you care for her, as I think you do, then you'll stay on. Please say that you will.'

In the glass, I watched her flap the paper at the empty chair. 'This came this morning. You must read it for yourself and decide. I don't care so much for my future, but I fear the little one will soon need a friend.'

Opening the door, I allowed Lancer to skid out into the passage. I lingered a moment to give the impression that I might follow – *of course I would not* – but then I pulled it shut, turned and walked back to the desk. I held out my hand.

Mrs Gurney stared up at me, eyes glassy with fresh-sprung tears, and handed me a letter.

'She doesn't even bother to call me by my name.'

For the attention of the present housekeeper

I am writing to inform you of the necessary changes that will take place at Fyneshade following the death of Sir William Pritchard.

Firstly, as a matter of some urgency, the new baronet, Sir Vaughan Pritchard, has asked me to inform you of alternative instructions for the burial of the late baronet. Sir William is not to be interred in the house chapel, instead you will arrange for him to be buried in a convenient church or churchyard at a minimum distance of five miles from the curtilage of the estate.

When you have carried out Sir Vaughan Pritchard's wishes pertaining to the burial, your services and the employment of all servants, apart from the exceptions as explained herein, will be terminated. Once Sir William's body is taken from the house, the new baronet asks that you and all others not mentioned hereafter should remove yourselves from the estate.

I understand that a governess has been employed for Miss Grace Pritchard. It is the new baronet's wish that she should remain at Fyneshade, and, for the sake of his sister, that her employment should continue. I trust this generous offer will be acceptable to her.

In your absence, and before I take up my duties as housekeeper, it is the wish of the new baronet that you relinquish all house keys to her custodianship.

George Dawson, groom, is also to remain to tend to the welfare of the horses and for the reassurance of those remaining in the house, given it is not unlikely that a few days may elapse between the burial of the deceased and the arrival of the new baronet.

Sir Vaughan Pritchard fully intends that Fyneshade shall become his principal home. To that end, he instructs that the contents of his current rooms in the stables be immediately conveyed to the house and to the bedroom of his late father, which, on possession, he intends to make his own. Sir Vaughan asks most particularly that the bed and mirror in the stable rooms be transported with care to his late father's room and that the current furnishings should be removed and burned.

Once you have made these arrangements you will write to me at the address below to communicate the date of all ceremonies and removals required by the new baronet, who will dispense with the services of household servants on the day of his father's interment. I am to assure you that payment will be made until the end of the month and that, in every case, a small additional sum will be added to the amount disbursed in recognition of years of loyal service.

I trust this fair and reasonable offer will give you and all others the opportunity to leave Fyneshade in a timely and orderly fashion.

I am yours,
Elizabeth Balquist, Coldharbour House, Mungrisdale, County of Cumberland.

Postscript. Failure to carry out any of the instructions communicated in this letter will nullify all offers of payment and may incur legal retribution.

I read the letter again to be quite certain of its meaning. The script was neat, formal and slanted to the right. It was a commonplace school-book hand that gave no clue as to the character of its writer. Oddly, this extreme ordinariness added to its menace. Mrs Gurney's life and that of nearly everyone else at Fyneshade had been changed, you could almost say ended, in a few brisk, callous sentences.

And yet . . .?

It would be a lie to say that I had not felt a rush of excitement when I read of Vaughan's desire to make the black room his own.

'When I am master here, I promise that I will have our bed moved into the house.'

That canopied bed was likely where our child, his heir, had been conceived. It had borne witness to the promise Vaughan had made the night I wore Sophia's bridal gown and veil. Surely this was his particular message to me? Why else would he ask that I stay when the house was unburdened of the lame, the deformed and the ugly?

'It is the wish of the new baronet that you relinquish all house keys to her custodianship.'

It was beginning. Everything I had set in motion when I eased Sir William from life into death was falling into place like the gem-studded ball that rolled at Panjan's feet. But there was still much I needed to understand.

I flattened the letter on the desktop. 'Who is this woman, this Elizabeth Balquist?'

Mrs Gurney shook her head. 'I've never heard of her, but it seems she is to take my place here. She's giving orders already.'

I pointed at the top of the paper. 'Does this name, Coldharbour House, mean anything to you?'

'Nothing at all.' She fumbled at the cotton cuff of her sleeve and pulled out the handkerchief again. More tears glistened in her eyes.

I studied the address.

County of Cumberland?

Vaughan's recent victory with Dido had taken place in the north. I remembered the night when he had described the land there with the intensity of a lover. Scanning the copperplate writing again, I found I had a burning curiosity to know more of Elizabeth Balquist.

'Say you'll stay, Marta,' Mrs Gurney pleaded as she dabbed her eyes. 'I'd feel better if I knew you'd be with her.'

I pushed a lock of hair from my brow and frowned.

'How can I promise anything at all? My head is already spinning from the strange history you related, and now this.' I tapped the letter. 'As I said, I must consider my position. You cannot expect me to simply accept these extreme transformations. It seems that everything I thought I knew about this house has been a deceit.'

Mrs Gurney's lips trembled. 'Not all of it. There's Grace and your affection for her. Think of the child, Marta. When we're all sent away from Fyneshade, who will care for her?'

I was careful with my answer. It was important to continue the appearance of confusion. 'But why would he do such a thing, Mrs Gurney? To dismiss everyone is such a drastic step.'

This was not entirely a pretence. Although I would not miss any of them, it did, indeed, seem an excessive command.

'It's all there in that letter, I reckon.' She took it from the desk and peered closely at the sloping script.

'It's cruel. Sir William always wanted to be buried with his wife and now ...' She blotted a tear from the paper with the cotton. 'Vaughan hated him, and he hated us all for what happened here. Now he's come into the estate he's taking revenge. He must have planned this for a long time. Oh, it's set out in fine words and charity so no one can take exception. Some might even call him generous. Here ...' She pointed to the foot of the page. '"Fair and reasonable", she calls it. But it's spite. I don't care for myself, Marta, but most of the others now, the poor girls who need ...'

Now Mrs Gurney began to sob. Unexpectedly, I experienced a flutter of pity for the broken woman before me.

'What will you do? Where will you go when you leave?'

She gulped out the answer. 'To my brother in Sheffield, most likely. He's a grocer there and well set. He'll give me a place. As I said, it's not me I worry for. I've had a good life here, all things considered, and I've tried to do good where I can. No, it's the others and poor Grace.'

Reaching a damp hand across the table, she gripped my arm. 'What will happen to her when we're gone? She won't know a soul. I don't believe her brother will take much trouble in finding someone suitable, if he bothers at all. I'd feel easier if I knew that you were here too. That at least would be a comfort.'

She stared dismally at the letter. 'Please stay on like she asks, even if it's just long enough to make sure that Grace is to be well treated. I know how fond of her you are, and she of you. I count bringing you here as one of the good things I've done.'

Mrs Gurney was silent for a moment, then she stared at me. 'And now you know *everything* about him you'll be on your guard. You'll be safe, Marta, won't you?'

Mother's Moon

35

At dawn on the day Sir William Pritchard's coffin was to leave Fyneshade dark clouds massed above the valley and an east wind blew. By the time Reverend Abney and eight representatives of Sutter & Sons of Tideswell arrived at the gates with a carriage, three open carts and a glass-sided hearse, the view to the court-yard was veiled by rain.

The black-coated men dismounted from the first cart and swarmed towards the steps. The carriage door swung open and Reverend Abney followed them, one hand clamped to the drip-ping brim of his hat.

I turned from the schoolroom window. Grace was engrossed, as always, in a drawing. This morning, for the last time, Old Maggie had washed her, dressed her in a sober dress and combed and neatened her hair. The bulge of stiff black satin ribbon tied at the end of the plait dangling over my pupil's shoulder was the flag of a surrender.

In my heart, I was surprised to discover a sliver of sympathy for the ancient nursemaid, who, later today, would follow Sir William's coffin and leave the house for the last time, along with everyone else who had worked here. After all the clocks struck their noonday chimes, Grace and I would be alone within Fyneshade's walls with just the dog for company.

I had waited a night and a day before I gave Mrs Gurney my answer. Caution and bewilderment would have seemed a most natural response to everything she had told me and I was careful to play the innocent. When, finally, I had told her that for the sake of Grace I would stay, she had cried and, most unexpectedly, hugged me close.

By then, she had set everything in motion. Letters had been sent and arrangements had been made. Sir William's body was to be taken from the house and conveyed to the churchyard at Tideswell. For nearly two weeks his lead-lined coffin had sat in Fyneshade's chapel. Mrs Gurney seemed to take comfort from the fact that, for a short time at least, he had lain near the blessed Sophia.

I freely admit that I admired the housekeeper in those last days. In her practical, almost maternal way, she had managed to comfort the servants and keep them steady in their work until the last moments of the old order came upon us. She had even managed to secure positions for some of the younger girls on the farms and in larger households of the district.

On the surface life continued little altered, but the atmosphere of the house shivered. It seemed to me that Sir William's death had damaged a precarious balance. If Fyneshade had been made of glass and not stone it would have splintered.

Nothing was said but it was clear that news of my continued

employment had spread. When I encountered a single servant their face closed and their eyes slid from mine. When two of them stood together they fell silent as I passed, then, I heard the hiss of their whispers like cockroaches in the skirting.

If ever I felt a stab of guilt that it was my own hand that had wrought the changes about to fall upon them all, I thought of my future and of the destiny foretold for me, and I smiled.

Now I watched Grace as she bent over the paper, carelessly swinging her legs beneath the wooden desk. I wondered how much she understood. It appeared that the alterations had hardly touched her. Despite the fact that I had tried to prepare her for the events of today, she did not seem to care. It came to me that this odd creature would soon be the aunt of the child I carried. I pressed the flat of my hand to my good black dress and tried to determine the sex of the baby that grew there. Grandmere had used a clouded green stone suspended on a fine golden chain when asked to divine whether an unborn was male or female. She had held the gem over a woman's belly like a pendulum and waited for it to move. If it circled to the left the child was a girl.

Vaughan would be anxious for a son. Although I hoped our first-born would be a boy, it mattered little. I was young enough to bear again – if necessary.

The door to the schoolroom opened to reveal Old Maggie, dressed in a threadbare black travelling cloak. Her face was almost lost beneath the arch of a large black bonnet tied with a bow that hung like a dead crow at her neck.

I went to the desk and rested a hand on Grace's shoulder.

'Is it time?'

Old Maggie nodded. Incapable of forming words, she simply held out her hand.

'Come, dearest.' I patted Grace's arm. 'We must go down to say our farewells.'

Draped in black velvet, the coffin stood on a long table in the hallway. I surmised that Sir William's feet faced the door. From the rail of the gallery, I saw the eight black-coated attendants sent by Sutter & Sons waiting beside it while Reverend Abney spoke to Mrs Gurney.

Like Old Maggie, the housekeeper was dressed in a dark travelling cloak. Her usual white cap had been exchanged for a black beaded version and she turned the brim of a veiled bonnet in her gloved hands. She nodded when the reverend gestured to the coffin and the dark lace lappets, weighted by jet, swung at her jaw.

The galleried landing above the hall and the stairs were lined with the women of Fyneshade, all of them dressed in mourning, all of them carrying or standing over a bag. All of them silent.

The air was heavy with the scent of fusty cloth and wood polish. Mrs Gurney had been determined to leave the house a shining testament to her stewardship.

As we came down, I felt everyone turn to look at us. Old Maggie was holding Grace's hand and I followed, head bowed low in a show of sorrow and respect. The women parted on the landing and on the staircase to allow us to proceed slowly to the hallway. Grace was quiet, but she stared at the servants pressed around us and sometimes she waved. She halted in the middle of the flight to stare up at the galleries that turned on the floors above. She flapped again and made a small mewing sound. I followed her gaze but there was no one.

When we reached the chequered hallway, Mrs Gurney and Reverend Abney skirted the coffin with great solemnity and came to stand with us. Reaching out, Abney placed a hand on Grace's head. Her nose wrinkled.

'Poor child. Now she is an orphan.' He smiled sadly at me, pushing a limp strand of hair from his eyes. 'Does she understand?'

'I have tried to explain . . .' I shook my head, '. . . but it is difficult to know what she fully comprehends of this sad, sad situation.' I heard Old Maggie gulp. 'I have done my very best to prepare her for what is to come.'

It had been decided that Grace should not accompany her father's body to Tideswell church. Mrs Gurney and Old Maggie had agreed that it would be better – 'less unsettling for the lamb' – if she said her farewells at the house and then returned to the schoolroom with me.

Reverend Abney removed his hand from Grace's head and nodded, shedding tiny scales of desiccated skin onto the shoulders of his black coat.

'It is very good of you to remain here with her.' He bent closer, lowering his voice. His breath was stale. I fought to remain still as he breathed upon me. 'I understand that the new baronet and his household will not be in place for some days.'

'Yes.' I placed my hand on Grace's shoulder. 'It is my understanding that we will be alone in the house until Friday. Those are Sir Vaughan Pritchard's wishes communicated through . . .' I faltered and glanced at Mrs Gurney.

Her fingers tightened on the brim of the bonnet. 'You may as well say it, Marta, for it's the truth. His wishes were communicated by the new housekeeper, Mrs Balquist.'

'Indeed.' I nodded and cast my eyes to the marble. 'I am sorry,

Mrs Gurney, I did not wish to add to your sorrows on such a day by mentioning her name.'

'Oh, Marta!' I felt her hand on my arm. 'You have been a true strength and support. It is my great regret that we have known each other such a short time, but when I leave today ... when we *all* leave today ...' she looked up at the crows flocked around us, '... I'll take comfort in knowing that the little one is in such good hands.'

She released me and her black cloak and skirts billowed around her as she sank to the tiles to enfold Grace in a final embrace. The scent of naphtha and lavender rose into the air as she clutched the child to her breast. My pupil stared over Mrs Gurney's shoulders at the coffin and the shabby men standing guard and seemed to endure rather than enjoy the housekeeper's muffled endearments.

Embarrassed by this display of affection, Reverend Abney sidled away. From the corner of my eye, I saw him stroke a hand along one of the stone pillars and crane his neck to admire the extravagance of the ceiling.

At last, Mrs Gurney released Grace and stood up. She cupped the girl's face and tilted it to her. 'You'll be good for Marta now, won't you?'

Old Maggie sniffled at my side but Grace did not reply, her attention locked completely on the velvet-draped coffin. The coats of the men who lined each side were soaked with rain and even at a distance I could smell a sour frowstiness rising from them. They held their dripping crepe-banded hats before them in a show of respect.

The housekeeper looked at me and shook her head. In the past days, I had respected her efficient dignity but now I saw the strain on her fleshy face and realised that she too was fighting back tears. Placing the bonnet over her black lace cap, she went to the crackled mirror to adjust the position and fold down the netted veil. She cleared her throat and came back to my side. 'The keys are laid out on the parlour table. Go down when we're gone. There are some other things for you, as you'll find.' The beads on her lace cap clicked and glittered through the veil as she shook her head. 'I shut Lancer down there too. I didn't think it would be right to have him running free at such a time.' She leaned closer. 'You'll remember *everything* I said, Marta?' Her voice was very low and the question, audible to me alone, was a warning.

I nodded. 'I will. Thank you.'

'Don't thank me, Marta.' The housekeeper's pale eyes shone like moonstones through the netting. 'Just remember.'

Linking her hands beneath the bulge of her ample breast, she turned to survey the hallway. 'I always thought I would be carried from Fyneshade in a box.' She took a deep breath. 'That was silly of me, wasn't it?'

I did not have a ready answer if one was expected. Fortunately, at that moment the chinoiserie longcase clock on the landing clicked before playing the chimes to mark the third quarter of the hour. It was almost noon.

'We must go.' The housekeeper took a few steps towards the coffin, but then she twisted about and returned to my side.

'I almost forgot. There is one thing, Marta.'

I gave a mournful smile. 'Anything, Mrs Gurney. You know that.'

She touched my arm. 'Do you remember my mother's recipe book?'

I nodded.

'I couldn't find it anywhere. It's as if it's disappeared off the face of the earth like Panjan's key.' Instantly, I felt the force of Grace's attention. She slipped her hand into mine and stared up at the housekeeper with an expression of intense interest.

'Pan . . . Pan . . .' She began to stutter the infernal thing's name. I gripped her hand, fearful of what more she might be capable of saying.

'K . . . K . . .' She leered up at me. 'Key.'

'Forgive me.' Mrs Gurney brought a hand to her veil. 'I didn't wish to remind her of him at such a time. It will be hard enough for you these next days without Grace fretting for that monkey.'

'Hush, little one.' I squeezed my pupil's fingers tightly and assumed a puzzled frown. 'It is no matter; please continue, Mrs Gurney. You have mislaid your mother's recipes?'

She nodded. 'I've looked everywhere. They're all I have of her. It's a small thing to ask, Marta, but if you come across the book, I'd be grateful if you sent it on to me. This is my brother's address in Sheffield.'

Delving into a pocket within her travelling cloak, she produced a fold of paper and handed it to me. 'I'd be obliged, Marta, very . . . very . . .'

Suddenly she flung her arms around me. Surprised, I couldn't move, but then, aware of the many eyes upon us, I returned the embrace, aware that the woman's shoulders were heaving beneath my hands. Old Maggie's sniffles had turned to muffled sobs now.

At last Mrs Gurney pulled away. She nodded at me and then she went to stand at the end of Sir William's coffin, facing the silent flock gathered on the stairs.

She raised her head and began to speak in a voice that, although cracked at first, gained strength and resolve.

'And so, the time has come for us to leave Fyneshade. I'll say my farewells to those who have chosen to accompany Sir William on his final journey after the service at Tideswell church. To the others, those of you who are going direct to new positions or hoping to find employment, and I pray to the Lord that you will find a good place soon, I wish you well and thank you for your service and your loyalty. None of you will ever be without a reference, remember that. You know where to find me and I'd gladly give you all the highest recommendation.'

She turned to the Reverend Abney. 'The prayer?'

'Indeed, ma'am.' Stepping forward, he removed his tall hat and looked up to the women massed on the stairs and pressed to the rail of the first landing overlooking the hall. He began to intone the familiar words.

'*Our Father, who art in heaven, hallowed be thy name. Thy kingdom come . . .*'

The women joined him and the prayer echoed in the gloomy hallway. When it was over the drumming of the rain on the steps outside was the only sound. Until Grace laughed.

It was shocking and horrible, even to me, to hear her cackle and clap her hands at such a moment. I bent to hush her. Taking hold of one hand, I pulled her close, hoping to stop the noise. Instead of quieting, she beat at my legs and yelped like an animal. Kneeling, I turned her to face me, pressing a finger to her lips.

'Shhhh.'

In answer, Grace lashed out, knocking the pins from the coil on my head. I saw a loop of black hair fall free and winced as her nails scraped the side of my face.

I felt all eyes turn upon us. What a pretty memory to take from Fyneshade! If we had not been under such scrutiny, I would have returned my pupil's fury threefold, but now I hugged her close, crooning words of gentleness into her hair. Old Maggie circled and touched a consoling hand to the girl's back, but Grace shrugged her away. I stared up at Mrs Gurney over Grace's shoulder.

'This is too much for her.'

She nodded and the beaded lappets rattled beneath her bonnet. 'We must go before the lamb is upset any further. It's for the best that she's not to accompany us to the church.'

'I fear you are right.' I pulled Grace closer, more to silence than comfort her.

Reverend Abney dragged his eyes from my tussle and signalled to the men from Sutter & Sons that it was time to take up their load. They bowed, raised their hats to their heads and turned to their duty.

As Grace squirmed in my arms, the men heaved the coffin to their shoulders and waited for the reverend to take his position. Fyneshade's huge double doors were thrown open and Abney stepped out into a wall of rain. Sir William's coffin swayed after him with Mrs Gurney at its rear. Once they had gone beneath the porch arch to the steps, the other servants took up their bags and followed in dark, silent procession.

At the threshold, Old Maggie turned to look at Grace. Her former charge was still now, her face hidden against my breast. The ancient nursemaid lingered for a moment and then she stepped through the doorway.

As Grace quietened, I watched the sombre stream flow down the stairs and out through the doors. Some of the women stole furtive glances at us but mostly they kept their eyes fixed on the doorway through which Sir William's coffin had been carried.

When the last of them went through the arch, I pushed Grace from me and stood up. Instantly, she ran to the door and I hurried after her, catching her hand before she could dart down the steps. I need not have worried; Grace was standing beneath the dripping porch, enthralled by the scene playing out before us.

The glass-sided hearse carrying the coffin was moving across the courtyard to the gateway. The black plumes of the horses in the traces were limp and sodden with rain. Reverend Abney's little carriage jerked and rolled forward in pursuit and behind it two of the open carts that had come from Tideswell were already filled with the pall bearers and those who had chosen to attend the funeral. A shifting jumble of black umbrellas formed a sort of canopy above the carts as they began to rumble after Abney's carriage. A small queue of dripping women waited to mount the third cart while others, not many, thanks to Mrs Gurney's offices, waited with their bags by the gate until the cortege passed and they were released to the road and an uncertain future.

'I know what you did.' The voice hissed in my ear. I turned. Jennet and Eavis stood just behind me under the vaulted porch. Grace twisted about to look up at them, her pale eyes alert and watchful.

'And I know what you are.' Jennet took a step closer. 'You think you're very clever, don't you, miss? Different to the rest of us.'

There was no point in arguing. I had won, the matter was closed. I decided to continue as the innocent. 'This must be a very difficult day for you, for you all. I am sorry.' I shook my head. 'I understand that Mrs Gurney has found you a position in Matlock, Jennet, is that not so?'

She spat at me. That was my answer. Careful not to be drawn, I wiped my cheek and was surprised to see red on my fingers along with spittle. Grace had drawn blood. Jennet's eyes blazed with such ferocity that I thought, for a moment, that she too might lash out, but Eavis caught her arm.

'Take your seat on the cart, girl – before it leaves without you.'

'But I can't go before I've—'

'No.' Eavis pulled her roughly from my side. 'She'll pay, don't you worry. Go.'

Jennet heaved a bag to her shoulder. Without looking back, she trudged through the rain to the cart and sat among the crows. Eavis continued to linger at my side.

'You will miss your place.' I nodded at the cart.

The ugly nurse bent to take up the large cloth bag at her feet. 'And where's your place, Marta?'

It was a ridiculous question, but I decided to answer for the sake of pretence. 'Here at Fyneshade. I am to care for Grace, just as before.'

'Is that what you think?' The woman snorted. Shrugging the bag to her shoulders, she went down the steps and continued to the cart to take the last seat beside Jennet. The two women faced away from me. I watched their rigid black backs as the heavy dray horses dipped their heads and heaved.

When the third cart had grumbled beneath the stone arch and the last of the women had followed on foot, Dawson crossed the puddled courtyard and locked the great gates.

Fyneshade was mine.

36

I stared at my face in the speckled mirror where minutes before Mrs Gurney had adjusted her hat. There was a small bloody crescent beneath my left eye. I would take pleasure later in cutting Grace's fingernails. I wound the lock of hair she had knocked loose back into place and secured it with pins.

'Ma petite pie.'

Apart from the tiny gash of red, the woman who looked back at me was indeed a magpie, a beautiful, sleek-winged, black and white creature with eyes that shone with triumph. I had stolen the greatest prize.

The new baronet had chosen me. In a way, I had begun to think of the night Vaughan dressed me in his mother's bridal gown as our true wedding. It was then that we had made our vows. Of course, a public ceremony would have to come in due course – and sooner rather than later – but for now I was content.

I leaned closer and examined the tiny imperfection beneath

my eye. The skin was delicate there, but also quick to heal. By the time Vaughan returned to Fyneshade, it would hardly show. I loosened five of the buttons at the neck of my gown, allowing a delta of white flesh to show in the black. Beneath the mourning gown there was now a little cleft between my breasts. Was it possible that already my body was changing? I had always had a horror of the brood mares of Croyle whose waists were thickened by carrying. If the baby was a boy, I would take pains to ensure that he was an only child.

There was a flicker of movement at the side of the glass. I stepped back to better observe Grace's reflection. The girl was standing at the foot of the great staircase, her attention fixed at a point somewhere above. As I watched, she nodded, lowered her head and shuffled from side to side, kicking her feet together as if she had been admonished.

I went quickly to her side. Grace's hand stole into mine as I stared up at the stairs and the galleried landings above us. We were quite alone.

She rubbed her belly with her free hand and raised it to her mouth. As we stood there all the clocks of Fyneshade began the midday chorus.

Grace tugged my hand.

I looked down at her. 'Are you hungry, is that it?'

She nodded. For a moment I considered denying her food as punishment, but then I thought of the time we were about to spend alone together. It would be better, for both of us, if we remained on good terms. Besides, the events of the morning probably *had* been strange and unsettling for her.

'Come with me then, Grace.' Turning from the stairs, I led her by the hand to Mrs Gurney's parlour.

Lancer whimpered and scratched at the wood as we went down the narrow stairs. When I opened the parlour door, the dog barked and flung itself past me into the narrow space, colliding with Grace who, delighted, fell back onto a step and draped her arms around its neck.

Leaving them together, I went on down to the room where I had spent so many tedious hours. The red-tiled floor was scrubbed and clean. Newly dusted rows of gleaming blue and white china lined the dresser. A little fire glowed in the hearth and a copper kettle was set beside it. The familiar teapot stood sentinel over two cups and a milk jug on the side table and beside them, beneath a glass dome, a golden cake waited to be cut with the knife laid ready on folded white napkins.

Nothing was different and yet everything had changed. Mrs Gurney's absence was a palpable presence. I went to the table where her chatelaine lay at the centre of a carefully arranged circle of labelled keys. A letter was weighted beneath the ornate silver ring that had hung at her waist.

For Marta

It was in Mrs Gurney's childish hand. I opened it and unfolded a single sheet. As I did so, another smaller letter slipped out and fell beneath the table. I read the housekeeper's message.

Marta

There's enough in the pantry cupboard to see you and dear Grace through the next few days. You'll find cheese, ham, preserved fruits, bread and honey. I asked also for a saffron cake because I know she's partial to sweet things, like you. There's milk, butter and cream in the cold pantry behind the scullery. All the keys are here ready for her. The clocks have been wound, but you might remind her it is among the duties. All those keys are in the dresser drawer. Remember that Dawson is across the yard if you have need of him. God bless you, Marta. I know I do.

Hester Gurney

The letter enclosed arrived early this morning

I bent to retrieve the fallen letter. I recognised the blandly threatening copperplate script. *For the attention of the governess.*

The seal was not broken. Presumably Mrs Gurney could not bear to read her replacement's message. In her place I would have done so. Ripping open the envelope, I scanned the curt instruction.

The new household will arrive at Fyneshade at one o'clock in the afternoon of the Friday following the interment. Sir Vaughan asks that you and Miss Grace be ready to greet us.

EB

Furious, I screwed the note into a ball and threw it onto the hearth where it bloomed like a flower before succumbing to the flames.

Us?

Who was this Balquist woman? How dare she give me orders as if I were no more than a common servant. I took up an iron and poked the blackened paper until it dissolved into flickering cinders. When Vaughan returned, I was of a mind to ask him to dismiss her for my sake. But as I watched the letter crumple to ash it came to me that this was part of the game we were playing, part of our careful charade.

It was natural that Vaughan should want to replace the servants of the old regime, and natural also that he should appoint a new housekeeper. Would he confide his intentions of marriage to a servant? The thought was so absurd that I began to laugh.

Drawn by the sound, Grace stepped down into the room and Lancer skidded across the tiles to my side, grey tail wagging and thumping against the legs of the table. Excited, it began to yelp and bark. Catching something of my mood, Grace clapped her hands and giggled.

'Come here, lamb.' I reached out my hands and caught hers. Together, laughing, we spun around and around on the red brick tiles while the dog capered at our skirts.

<hr/>

I came to a decision about Grace. Despite her earlier behaviour, it was better to consolidate our friendship. Allies were useful. Once I was mistress of Fyneshade, Vaughan's sister, with her knowledge of the secrets of the walls, would be a valuable friend.

We spent a pleasant enough afternoon together in the library. Grace was good-natured now and her attention was consumed by her drawings. I let her sprawl before the vast crackling fire – what would Gurney have said to such a shameless extravagance? – while I read.

Later we dined on cake and honey. It was a fine thing to sit before the glowing hearth, licking sweetness from my fingers while imagining the luxuries of days to come.

When the clocks struck ten, some way past the girl's normal time to be settled, I took her up to the nursery further along the passage from my own room. Without maids to light the corners and corridors, the house was quite unlike itself. Creaks and groans I had long ceased to hear were magnified as we made our way along the library passage. The sudden scuttle of mice at our approach was proof of their bold and reckless occupation of what they had taken to be a deserted place.

The shadows were deeper than I had ever known them. As we crossed the landing, light from my chamberstick made no dint on the gaping blackness of the hallway below. Pausing to illuminate the way to the next flight of stairs, I was aware of an unfathomable space at my back that could have opened to the very centre of the earth. I had the strongest impression that the darkness was not empty. Fyneshade was an ancient house and it did not surprise me to be watched. Nevertheless, I was grateful for Lancer's solid company. I held Grace's hand as we went up the staircase, our shadows rippling on the steps, and decided that tomorrow I would light many candles to ward off the night.

I had visited the nursery on just a handful of occasions before. It was Old Maggie's territory and her silence had always made me feel like a trespasser. This time, after lighting half a dozen candles, I took the opportunity to examine it closely; after all, my own child would be here soon.

Although old-fashioned in style, the room was clean and comfortably furnished. From the direction, I assumed the windows looked over the terraced gardens. Grace's toys – a balding rocking horse, some sad cloth puppets, a box of building bricks and several plain-faced dolls – were stacked on a chest. We would buy new playthings for our child.

I spun a little papier-mâché globe, taken perhaps from the schoolroom. It sat loosely on its wooden axis and the motion was uncertain. My geography was fair. Before I came to Fyneshade, I had imagined teaching my pupil to recognise the patchwork of nations that rolled beneath my fingers, but Grace's world was always destined to be small.

Moving to the alcove beside the large stone fireplace, I explored the cupboard and drawers. Old Maggie had left everything neat and laundered. The linens were scented with lavender and I noticed that the devoted nursemaid had embroidered Grace's initials on her handkerchiefs, petticoats, smocks and dresses. The girl had been loved.

An enamelled trinket box stood on top of the chest of drawers. Opening its rose-strewn lid, I released a dreary little tune. I turned to see if the simple tinkling notes attracted Grace's attention but the girl was sitting quietly on the edge of her bed, tugging at her stockings.

The box contained a string of pearls. Although their lustre had dulled through lack of use, the pearls were large and fine. It came to me that they were likely to be the ones worn by the child's mother in the insipid portrait in the library passage. I ran the tips of my fingers over the milky gems and felt them warm to my touch as if I had brought them to life.

I set a small fire in the grate and moved the cage across to shield the flames. Then I helped Grace into a fresh cotton nightgown, tying the loops at the neck into a bow. While Lancer dozed by the fire, I sat beside her bed for a while, but once I was certain she was asleep I rose quietly, took up my chamberstick, and went to the door. I turned to check her one last time. A regular soft-throated growl was proof that she slept.

Reaching for the handle, I opened the door. My intention was to let Lancer go out first, but now the dog was sniffing at the bed coverlet.

'Lancer, here!' I hissed, but the creature ignored me. Instead, it pulled at something. As I watched, the dog dragged a white arm from beneath the bed. The limb was attached to a china doll much finer and larger than Rosa.

'Leave it!' I whispered firmly. Setting down the candles, I went to take the doll. The dog let go with some reluctance. Its tail curled between its legs as I examined a perfect porcelain beauty. Where Rosa had been dark, this one was fair. Real golden hair had been used for thick plaits that framed a heart-shaped face. The large, long-lashed blue eyes, delicate nose and pouting rose-bud lips were a cruel parody of what Grace might have been.

I had never seen this toy before. Its unruffled condition suggested it was new. The scent of violets rose from the crisp white lace of its dress.

Lancer stared at me, then it yawned and padded to the door. I frowned as I looked at the doll's pretty pink and white face, but when Grace stirred and muttered in her sleep, I decided to put it back in the place where the dog had found it.

Returning to the library, I selected a new book from the secret shelf. I had begun to suspect that this scandalous cache might just as easily have belonged to Vaughan as to his father. The thought amused me. Pouring myself a glass of marsala wine, I lay on cushions before the fire and read of Moorish corsairs and Spanish virgins until all the clocks chimed for midnight.

Grace crept into my bed that night. I do not know what time it was when she came to me, just that it was very late or, more accurately, very early. My candle had long burned out and the only sound was the constant thrum of rain on glass. She woke me as she snuggled close, but I hadn't the will to take her back to the nursery along the dark, cold passage. I turned away and soon she began to snore.

While Grace found it easy to sleep again, I did not. Just when I was at the slipping point, half between consciousness and dream, something intruded. In a moment I was fully awake, straining to listen in the darkness. Beyond the rain and laboured breathing of my pupil, I heard nothing.

And then it came again – the distant, fragile chords of a harp.

37

Sunlight slanted across the boards when I awoke. Grace was no longer in my bed, but I had not dreamed her company. There was a depression in the sheets where she had lain and she had left the door wide open when she had gone. I pulled my wrapper over my nightgown and went to the corridor. I called her name and waited, but there was no answer.

I went along to the nursery, expecting to find her asleep in her own bed again but the room was cold and empty. The fire I had set hours ago had long since burned to ash. I was about to leave when I remembered that fine doll discovered by Lancer. Kneeling, I reached beneath the bed, but when I felt nothing, I flattened myself on the faded rag-rug to peer into the shadows. Except for balls of dust and rusted springs that had worked their way free of the mattress to hang like twisted tree roots, the space beneath Grace's bed was empty.

Straightening up, I examined the room in daylight. It was just as I had seen it last night. Clean, orderly and just a little tired. I glanced at the toys lined up on the chest, but the doll was not among them. Neither was it in the long cupboard in the wall beside the bed. The shelves were stacked with more linens and when I opened it, a sweet smell came rushing out. There was nowhere else to store a doll of that size. It was odd.

The disappearance annoyed me. No, that is not quite correct. In some obscure way I found it unsettling. A few hours earlier, I had lain awake in the darkness straining to catch the sound of a draught moving the strings of a harp and it was then that I truly recognised the doll's insipid beauty. Those rose-bud lips, flushed pink cheeks and vacant blue eyes reminded me of Sophia Pritchard, the last mistress of Fyneshade.

Fortunately, my pupil had not strayed far.

When I went to the landing over the gallery and called her name, I heard her high-pitched bleat of reply. A moment later Lancer came thundering across the boards from the entrance to the corridor to Panjan's room. The dog yapped and circled me, before lolloping back the way it had come.

Grace was sitting outside the locked door to Panjan's room. Arms folded, she was staring at the panelled wood as if willing it to swing open. I considered chivvying her back to the nursery to wash and dress before seeking breakfast, but then I thought about the doll. Fyneshade was an emptied shell. There was no one here now to care what hours we kept or what we did. The golden monkey was still useful and today I did not even need to conceal our visit.

I went to Grace's side and bent close.

'Do you want to see Panjan?'

She nodded fiercely.

'Very well. Sit here with Lancer and I will fetch the keys.'

I waited until the automaton had performed that interminable routine four times before I asked. As usual, Grace was enthralled by Panjan's glittering mechanical melancholy, but when I retrieved the key from the gilded cushion and made a great display of putting it into the pocket of my wrapper, she balled her hands into pudgy fists and knocked them together.

'More.'

'Poor Panjan will be tired.' I shook my head. 'We must not wear him out. Come . . .' I headed to the door. 'There is still some cake in the parlour and lemon curd.'

'More!' She shouted at my back like a petulant Roman emperor. I turned. Grace glowered at me from beneath thick pale brows.

'Again!' She stopped beating her knuckles together and flailed her fists, as if to ward off an invisible enemy.

I pretended to think for a moment. 'Very well. I will allow Panjan to perform not once, but *twice* more if you give me something in return. Do we have a bargain?'

The girl nodded. I returned to the automaton's side and fitted the little golden key into the lock. As I twisted it to start the clockwork, I felt Grace's eyes on me.

At last the monkey's paws closed over its ruby eyes. I held up the key, as a temptation.

'Now, it is my turn. Where did you get that pretty blonde-haired doll with the white lace dress?'

Grace's fingers fluttered to her lips and she breathed very

loudly. I moved the key back and forth. Her eyes followed its progress. 'We made a promise just now, did we not, dearest? I will make Panjan play one more time if you tell me about your new doll.'

The girl pressed the flat of her thumb to her lips, splaying them wider. 'Shhhh.'

'Ah! A secret is it?'

She shuffled and nodded.

Smiling, I stepped closer. 'But we have secrets too, little one, do we not?' I pointed the key at Panjan. 'Do you want to see him play for us just one more time today?'

Grace nodded. Her eyes slid greedily to the monkey.

'Very well. Who gave you the doll? Was it Vaughan?'

Grace shook her head.

I had been sure that the doll was another gift from her brother. I asked again to be sure.

'Not Vaughan?'

'Not.' The plait down her back whipped from side to side.

'Who then?'

'M . . . Ma . . . Mama.' Once the word was out, she clapped her hands over her mouth. Eyes wide with alarm, she scanned the corners of the room, ridiculously fearful of being overheard.

Mama? It was impossible. I considered this puzzle for a moment and discovered a probable solution. Grace was loved by the women who had cared for her. Was it likely that years ago they had given her the doll with the charming pretence that it was a gift from her mother? I considered the way Mrs Gurney and Old Maggie had always clucked over the girl, and thought that it was.

Such a fine piece would be cherished and revered as a

memento. I could easily imagine the ancient nursemaid taking the doll from its place of safety for one last time out of pity for the orphan she was abandoning to my care.

Suddenly, I remembered the sweet scent in the nursery linen cupboard. It was the fragrance of violets. Of course! That was where the doll had been kept.

Smiling, I bent to fit the key into the lock in the gem-studded cushion. As the music began to play, Grace clapped her hands.

'Again!'

❧

The day was bright and clear. The rain that had accompanied Sir William Pritchard to his appointment in the churchyard at Tideswell had been replaced by a glazed blue sky shredded with high cloud. Later that cloud would dissolve in sunlight.

Without anyone to count the hours or expect us to live within the confines of a routine, Grace and I were free. We dressed with little care and breakfasted in the library, taking our cake and curd to the window seat overlooking terraces. Grace hummed as she chased crumbs around the saucer with the tip of a finger. The sound was a flat drone but after a while I recognised Panjan's tune in the midst of it. When she had finished the cake, she pushed the saucer away and continued to hum, all the while staring out through the window and twiddling her plait. Old Maggie would have disapproved of the gobbets of curd transferred to her hair from those sticky fingers.

Afterwards, I allowed Grace to choose what to do and I was not surprised when she simply collected her papers and pencils and returned to the library. I had come to understand that my pupil had little imagination. Her drawings were competent, excellent even, but they were copies, not creations.

As I watched her sprawl on a rug, her stocky body barred by sunshine, I decided to explore the house. Before I left Grace with Lancer – who was stretched out alongside her – I took an embroidered shawl from the back of a couch and draped it over the harp. The draught would not bother me tonight.

Today Fyneshade was silent and magnificent. Light streamed through the tall windows of the hall, gilding and enriching everything it touched. The oak staircase glowed like Baltic amber, silver glinted in the shadowed corners, the golden tassels of the red velvet curtains framing the door dripped like honey to the shining marble tiles.

The chiming of clocks began to sound and the thought of all those valuable time pieces singing out made me smile. This was a treasure house.

As I stood at the head of the stairs, considering where to go first, I found myself stroking a stone column at my side. I found a little sympathy in my heart for the covetous Reverend Abney, who yesterday had done the very same. A place like Fyneshade would never belong to him, or he to it. I was fortunate indeed.

Instantly, I knew where to go. Vaughan had ordered that his bed – our bed – be taken to the black room.

The towering carved doors leading to the north wing were unlocked. I passed through them onto a landing that mirrored the one at my back. The black room was on the floor above, off the gallery I had last seen the night I helped Sir William from the world. The scent of polish was strong again as I mounted these stairs. Mrs Gurney had been very determined to leave every corner of Fyneshade a credit to her care.

The door to the black room was open. I paused before I crossed the threshold, wondering if I might experience some dread or superstition as a consequence of my actions, but I felt nothing. Pushing aside the curtains, I stepped into the room.

Last time I was here, the air had been thick with disease, but now it was filled with the scent of roses. A large glass bowl brimming with dried petals sat on a Spanish leather chest midway along the wall and opposite it, Vaughan's bed with its canopy of pleated blue silk had replaced the towering velvet-hung monstrosity that had been Sir William's living tomb.

The straightening contraption had gone from the window. In its place I saw the elegant Venetian mirror where Vaughan had shown me my future. In the glass, light from the window sparked a rainbow from something lying on the blue cover of the bed. Turning to see what caused the pretty effect, I was surprised. A necklace heavy with diamonds was arranged on the velvet. There was a sealed note beside it addressed with a single word.

Beloved

Snatching it from the cover, I tore the seal.

'*M – my heart. These jewels belonged to my mother. I give them to you with gratitude and in celebration of marriage.*'

I felt the flutter of my heart in my throat. The necklace had been laid out on the bed for me like a promise. Vaughan had ordered it so, but I wondered who had positioned it for him. Not Mrs Gurney, I was certain of that. When I looked again at the hard, glittering jewels, I thought of Eavis and her spite. No wonder she had baited me yesterday. How she must have resented this final instruction.

Taking the necklace, I went to the mirror again and, with a little difficulty, fastened it around my neck. Framed by the black neckline of my dress, the diamonds looked well against my skin. Turning to admire them from a different angle, I saw the way they accentuated the spark in my dark eyes.

'M – *my heart*'.

Any lingering questions I had were irrelevant now. I was certain that Vaughan's feelings for me were quite genuine. I wondered if that might, in time, become cloying. It was no great matter. I smiled at my reflection. In due course I would be a great lady with Vaughan at my side. And one day, who knows?

A wealthy, titled widow with a legitimate heir would have a freedom to exploit.

I would place the necklace and the note – resealed with care – back just where I had found them. When he returned Vaughan could fasten the jewels at my throat. As I thought of his pale, clever eyes, his hard features and his long fingers, my body told me that it was not just possession of the house I longed for.

I *knew* Vaughan Pritchard, and he me. We were perfectly matched. If tomorrow rode towards me on a chariot drawn by four dragons it could not come quickly enough.

38

I was ready. Beneath the gown, my body was fragrant with oils from Grandmere's box. My washed hair was wound in a coil that nestled at the nape of my neck. Tonged black ringlets hung loose at the sides to frame and enhance the whiteness of my skin. I had dabbed my lips with carmine pomade and rubbed just a little more onto the arches of my cheeks, careful to preserve the effect of nature over artifice.

I confess, I was not entirely certain what the day would bring. The Balquist woman had occupied more space in my thoughts than a servant deserved. And I was curious about the new household that would come with her. In time, they would serve me, but for now they would see me as an equal. I had decided to be aloof from them all until Vaughan revealed the truth. It would be better that way.

Before Grace and I went down to the hallway, I dropped belladonna into my eyes to make them larger, blacker and even more brilliant than I knew them to be. It was an old trick and one to be used with care and a steady hand, but today was special. Grace sat on the bed and watched while I arched my neck and tipped the tiny glass phial.

The black bombazine was the best I had. Earlier this morning I had taken it from the closet and examined it in the brilliant sunlight that streamed through my chamber window. Apart from smuts on the hem and the sleeves, which I brushed away, it was presentable.

While preparing for Vaughan's return, I had laid the dress over a chair positioned in the window so that the sun might rid it of the faint odour of the closet and the occasions I had worn it. Curling my hair, I had caught sight of the gown in the mirror. With the skirts spread wide and the bodice resting on the back of the chair, arms hanging, it looked like the shell of a woman. The tip of the 'V' etched into the panes of glass pointed at her heart.

For the first time since we had been alone, I had taken trouble over Grace's appearance. Today her clean hair was bound in one thick intricate plait threaded with black ribbon. I knew that Vaughan would care little about mourning costume for his father, but, for the sake of appearance, I had dressed her in a dark purple taffeta gown with a high neck, long puffed sleeves and a skirt that stood proud of her body.

It was, perhaps, a garment kept for the most special occasions. A birthday, Christmas, Easter – the annual festivities that measure lives. I had come across it in the nursery during my exploration. It was hardly worn and, judging from the size, brought within the last year or so. Grace had wriggled in protest as I attended to the line of buttons at the back. The fabric was stiff and formal and the dress was just a little too tight, but when the time came, I imagined we would make a pretty picture together.

That time was close at hand.

Blinking, I placed the phial on the nightstand. Grace fidgeted on my bed, kicking her legs and shrugging her shoulders. I knew she was uncomfortable. The taffeta scratched her skin and I had drawn the plait tight from the crown of her head. She scowled at me and I felt a small sympathy for the plain creature who would soon be my sister-in-law, not my responsibility.

She thumped the coverlet.

'Hurts.'

Today above all others, I needed her compliance. I smiled. 'Vaughan will be here soon. I am sure you want to look your best for him. Would you like me to make you beautiful, Grace?'

She stopped squirming and nodded.

'If you promise to behave very well for me, I will share a secret with you. A lady's secret, not something for little girls. Will you be good?'

Grace nodded again.

'Very well.' Taking her hand, I led her to my dressing table. I took up the carmine pomade and unscrewed the lid.

'This is a magical potion.' I tipped her face towards me. 'If I dab a little here.' I dipped a finger into the pot and brushed it across her petulant lower lip. 'And here . . .' I dipped again and rubbed a tiny amount of pomade into her cheeks, '. . . you will be the prettiest girl in the room.' I stood back, pretending to admire her.

The effect was surprising. Grace stood in a shaft of sunlight that blurred her features and gilded her hair. Just for a moment, with her pouting, newly pink lips and lightly flushed cheeks, she looked eerily like the doll I had found under her bed. And very much older than her years.

I rubbed the carmine from her lips so that just the faintest stain remained and screwed the lid back on the pot.

'There. You are a princess.'

Grace studied herself in the mirror and grinned.

'Come then.' I reached for her hand. 'We will go down. He will be here very soon.'

Lancer basked in a square of sunlight on the marble tiles. As Grace and I came down the stairs together, the dog stretched, yawned and padded to the girl's side. Burying that long grey nose into the brittle, unfamiliar taffeta, it sniffed and shook its head.

The first of Fyneshade's clocks began to chime the tune for the hour. Soon the hallway was busy with whirring and jangling. The lacquered chinoiserie longcase clock on the gallery landing was always the last to join the chorus. Once it had struck its single doleful note we stood in silence.

I considered where to present myself to the best advantage. If I went out onto the steps, the light might reveal faults in my dress. If I lingered inside near the door, I would appear to be a dutiful servant waiting, always waiting, and serving.

Keeping hold of Grace's hand, I crossed the hall to open the double doors. My first action on greeting the new household would not be that of an inferior. As warmth and light spread across the chequered floor, I continued to think about where to stand so that I might have the advantage. Just as an acceptable solution occurred to me, I heard the rumble of wheels. Grace freed herself and ran clumsily to the oriel window looking out onto the great courtyard. Lancer barked and followed.

'Not there!' I called after her, but the girl's attention was locked on the scene outside. I joined her, determined to draw her back to the staircase. Grace's nose was flattened against the glass. She batted my hand away as I reached for her own.

Through the window I saw a smart black brougham, not Vaughan's, circle the cobbles. It was drawn by a sorrel mare, mane plaited with green ribbons. Close behind it came three more carriages, larger and cruder than the first, followed by two lumbering farm carts, one loaded with what appeared to be jumbled household objects, the other with people. Where I had expected the dun livery of servants, the second cart was a patchwork of colour. As it came closer to the house, I saw that the bonnets of the women it carried were decorated with flowers.

The brougham came to a halt. As the door opened, I was momentarily blinded by the flash of sunlight on polished lacquer. I heard the rattle of steps as they rolled to the ground and I saw a yellow-gloved hand on the side of the door.

A woman descended. From my vantage point I watched her walk forward a little way and pause to look up at the house. She was dressed in black and grey. The hem of her pale skirt and the pleats on her dark sleeves were banded with tiny beads of jet that winked and glittered in the brilliant sunlight. Unusually, her head was bare, but her hair – plaited and pinned to a coronet in lieu of a bonnet – shone almost white against the black of the carriage. Even from here, I could see that she was tall, unusually so. Unlike most women of similar stature, she did not stoop her shoulders or make any attempt to disguise her height. Quite the opposite in fact. Her hair seemed to have been deliberately arranged to emphasise this difference.

I waited, my breath caught in my throat. No one stepped down from the carriage to join her. As I watched, she brushed her skirts and raised a yellow hand to the edifice upon her head.

I moved around Grace to see the courtyard more clearly, but neither Vaughan's carriage nor his fine grey were present.

Where was he?

People were climbing down from the carts now and the occupants of the carriages – men and women, servants from their dress – were standing in knots on the cobbles, talking and pointing at the house. Some of them carried flowers. The babble of cheery conversation seemed out of place. Usually silent, the courtyard had become a village fair.

Elizabeth Balquist, for I was certain this was my correspondent, stood straight and tall as she examined Fyneshade. And then, holding her skirts, she began to climb the steps. Lancer barked and ran to the open door. The huge creature bounded down the steps towards the woman, who paused mid-flight. I knew she would come to no harm, but what would she think? I watched her bend to ruffle the dog's ears.

I was almost grateful.

'Grace!' I pulled her from the window and dragged her, protesting, back to the staircase where I had decided to stand to greet the arrivals.

Indeed, I *was* there – on the fifth step with Grace at my side – when the woman passed beneath the porch arch and into the hallway, Lancer padding at her side. She walked briskly to the centre of the hall and appeared to study the walls and the furniture, but I knew she had seen me.

'Good afternoon.' I smiled down at her. 'Welcome to Fyneshade.'

39

I was pleased by the way my voice filled the space. The woman was forced to look up at me. Now we were close, I saw that she was older than I by a decade at least. I was less delighted by the fact that her skin was so pale and delicate it was almost translucent and that her eyes were a striking, tawny shade. They glowed like amber beneath her silver-gilt hair. All things considered, she retained a sort of beauty.

Smiling, she revealed large teeth that were well formed and white. 'I am Elizabeth Balquist, the new housekeeper.'

There was a faint trace of an accent in her voice. I put a hand to Grace's back and pushed so that she stepped down to stand in front of me. Resting my fingers on her taffeta shoulders, I smiled again.

'This is Miss Grace Pritchard, Sir Vaughan's sister, and I am—'

'You are the governess. I know.' Balquist turned away. She went to the door, followed by Lancer, clapped her hands and called out.

'Bring them.'

There was a clatter on the steps and then four men and two women bustled into the hallway, each of them carrying an extravagant arrangement of flowers and leaves.

'There and there.' Balquist pointed to the places where the women should set down their loads. 'And here at the foot of the stairs, one on each side.' Ignoring us, she waved vaguely in our direction. 'And over there.' She flapped a hand to indicate another place near the door. 'Then take your places outside.'

The flowers were white and their spring scent already laced the air. I was reminded of the times when Vaughan had come back to Fyneshade with cloying blooms for his mother. Something fresh and clean about these sprays made the hallway seem even brighter. They added a festive note in celebration of new times. These flowers were for me.

Without moving from the stair, I called out, 'Where is the master? Is he with you?'

'Soon.' Balquist did not bother to look up. 'We are here to prepare for the arrival.'

Her clipped speech was coldly efficient. It was clear that this harpy did not intend us to be friends. I vowed that in the days to come, I would take steps to enlighten her. Before Elizabeth Balquist left Fyneshade, she would understand the meaning of her position.

The dog pricked its ears and barked twice. Leaving Balquist's side, Lancer padded to the door and stared out into the sunlit courtyard. That long grey tail wagged slowly. Now I caught the sound of the carriage wheels.

'Ah!' At last, Balquist deigned to look at me. 'It is sooner than I thought. We will go to the steps. You will bring the child. She will like it.'

Torn between anger at the woman's haughty command and my desire to see Vaughan, I tightened my grip on Grace's shoulders. She looked up at me. There was confusion in her eyes and a sheen of perspiration in the hairs of her upper lip.

'Come!' Balquist clapped her hands again as if I were a maid to be chivvied.

Grace made the decision for me. Breaking away, she stomped down the stairs and ran to the door. I followed slowly; there was nothing else I could do. Balquist watched me cross the hall. I did not look at her, but I felt the keen appraisal of her strange eyes. When I passed under the porch, I heard the tap of her heels behind me.

Grace and I stood side by side just outside the grand doorway. The new servants lined the steps now, men on the right and women on the left. The women carried flowers and there were sprigs of green in the men's buttonholes. This welcome party extended a little way across the stones of the courtyard. Through the gap, I saw Vaughan's brougham following the curve of the wall. His magnificent grey, unsaddled and tethered on a leash, pranced behind it. The creature tossed its head and rolled its eyes as the brougham came to a stand some twenty yards from the house at the end of the avenue of servants. Vaughan's groom Ricketts, face hidden beneath a hat, signalled at Dawson, who had come through the arch to the stables.

I heard the door on the far side of the brougham open and the crunch of boots on gravel.

Vaughan patted the grey's rump as he rounded the carriage. He looked up at the house and immediately he saw me. There was not a clock in Fyneshade's many rooms that could have measured that moment. Time seemed to stand on a precipice as our eyes met. Every part of my body was drawn tight by the invisible cords that bound us together. He paused, smiled and gave a small, curt nod. Raising a hand, he pushed a wing of inky hair away from those cool eyes. It was a salute. No one else there would have noticed the gesture, but I knew it was for me.

His long grey coat swept dust from the courtyard as he turned from me to the carriage. The door opened and he held out his hand. A woman emerged, blinking, into the sunlight. She steadied herself against the side of the rocking brougham, and then, taking Vaughan's hand, she stepped down to the courtyard.

Squat and dressed in a pallid, tiered confection that emphasised her girth, she tapped Vaughan's arm with a fan. He bent to listen, nodded and whispered into her ear. I heard her giggle like a child. Turning her attention to the house and the servants marshalled on the steps, she beamed and flapped open the fan to cool herself. Someone had tried to make the best of her thin sparrow-coloured hair, but the task had evaded their skill. It hung in limp tendrils about a wide, heat-blotched face where currant eyes darted nervously.

I was aware of a movement behind me. Balquist snatched a posy from the nearest woman and knelt beside Grace.

'Take this to her. She will like it.' She thrust the pretty purple flowers into my pupil's hands.

Grace stared at the violets and then at me, but Balquist placed a large hand on her head and turned it to face the woman.

'Take them to her. Go!' She rapped the back of Grace's legs and compelled her to move.

I watched the girl stumble down the steps and along the phalanx of grinning servants. The stiff purple taffeta, shiny and wrong in the sunlight, made her look even more ungainly and lumpen than usual. Scuffling to a halt, she stared up at Vaughan. He bent to talk to her and she nodded, all the while shuffling from foot to foot. Now Vaughan gestured at the frump beside him. Grace thrust the posy awkwardly at the woman.

'How charming.' The reedy girlish voice continued, 'This must be your sister.'

'Indeed it is. Grace, where are your manners?' Vaughan bent again to murmur into the girl's ear. Instantly, she flung her arms around the dumpy stranger. There was more, but the sudden ringing in my ears made it difficult to hear. I reached out to a pillar as the stones of the courtyard seemed to tilt in the harsh, brilliant light.

Balquist stood up beside me. I was aware of her height and her scent – a sharp citrus cologne. My stomach pitched.

'Are you quite well?' There was no sympathy in her voice.

'It is merely the heat. The day is very warm.' Drawing a deep breath, I forced myself to ask the question.

'Who is that lady?'

Balquist's eyes did not leave the touching family reunion playing out before us.

'She is the new mistress, of course. My lady and Sir Vaughan were married three days ago.'

40

I fought my own body as I stood beside Balquist on the steps. Colours swirled before my eyes like the patterns in a child's kaleidoscope and my ears were muffled by the roar of an invisible sea. I counted beneath my breath and concentrated on a single stone as I struggled to remain upright. I had felt her tawny eyes upon me as she spoke those terrible words and I knew she enjoyed what she saw. I would not give her the pleasure of my pain.

I smiled and smiled until the bones of my jaw ached. I clapped with the rest of the servants as the couple climbed the steps together arm in arm. I laughed at the shower of white petals that greeted them at the door. And I tasted ashes and dust when Vaughan stepped into the house without even glancing at me. He came so close that I breathed the familiar scent of the oil in his hair.

I watched them walk towards the flower-decked staircase. Framed by the porch, they were a portrait of devotion. Vaughan's long fingers rested on the back of his pudgy bride and when she looked up at him, I saw the adoration of a cossetted lap dog; one that had grown fat on sweetmeats.

Just before they reached the stairs, the woman halted. 'We must have Grace with us. I'm sure she would like to show me the house.' Her high girlish voice had a piercing quality. It was all I could do not to scream and stop my ears as she continued, 'After all, my dear, we are family now.'

Vaughan turned. He looked directly at me and smiled.

'Marta, bring Grace to us.'

The girl had trailed behind the couple from the courtyard. Now she stood between Balquist and me, rubbing the back of her hands together. Balquist, who had hold of Lancer's collar, nodded, as if giving me permission to obey the master's command.

I reached for Grace's hand and led her across the black and white tiles. She trotted along beside me until we were level with the couple. I heard the tick of Lancer's claws on marble as Balquist followed. The sharp stench of her cologne overpowered the sweetness of the blossoms. My stomach rolled again as I dipped my head.

'My lady, Sir Vaughan.' I could hardly say his name.

The bride smiled. Her teeth were small and discoloured. She reached for Grace's hand.

'We are going to be great friends and I know you will like your new maid, Elsa. She is a lady's maid, not a nursery maid. Would you like that?'

When Grace didn't answer, the woman's beady little eyes sought mine. Lowering her voice to a confidential whisper, she spoke directly to me. 'It must have been very difficult for her

– all the changes. We are most grateful that you agreed to stay. Vaughan has told me how fond you are of his sister.'

Handing me the fan, she returned her attention to Grace, cupping the girl's face in her fat ringed fingers.

'Have you been a good girl for your governess?'

This simpering was intolerable. I looked up to find Vaughan watching me. There was amusement in his voice as he answered his bride's question.

'My sister is always good, Mariah. She is a very biddable girl. I very much doubt the governess had a moment's trouble with her. Now, let us go. There is much to see. Fyneshade has many secrets.' He rested a hand on Grace's shoulder. 'You can lead the way.'

Grace grinned up at her brother. For the first time ever, I caught the true likeness between them. A glacial quality in their pale blue eyes. The purple taffeta rustled as she turned and began to climb the stairs. I stepped forward, but Vaughan raised a hand.

'No. We will go as a family, just the three of us.' His eyes strayed over my shoulder. 'Besides, I know that good Mrs Balquist has some questions about the house.'

When they had gone up the stairs and disappeared into the library passage, Balquist called loudly to Fyneshade's new servants, who were still gathered outside on the steps and the courtyard. Lancer, the betrayer, pressed close to her side, eyes fixed on her face. They looked well together.

As the men and women swarmed purposefully about us, she took my arm. 'The keys. Where are they?' The beaded bands on her sleeves and bodice rippled in the sunlight. I looked at the yellow-gloved hand curled about my wrist and was reminded of Dido tearing at the belly of the hare.

Bile flooded into my mouth. I swallowed with difficulty and

managed to answer without disgracing myself before them all. 'Mrs Gurney left the keys in the parlour.' I pointed to the passage off the hallway. 'The first flight of steps on the left leads to her . . . *your* room.'

Nausea came again, rising like a bitter wave in my throat. Pulling my wrist free, I backed away. 'I . . . I am unwell. The sun . . . I must go to my room.'

I twisted about and stumbled blindly to the stairs. When I was alone, I vomited all my rancid hope into the basin on the washstand.

When Grandmere died, I went to my room and sank into a fathomless, dreamless sleep. My anguish was so great that my mind closed itself as a defence against madness. That afternoon, for the second time in my life, I slept like the dead.

It was late when I woke. I listened to the distant sounds of the new household finding its way. There were thumps from the corridor beyond my room, the patter of footsteps on the boards, snatches of conversation, laughter even. Then silence.

I lit a candle stub and rested my hands over my belly. Vaughan's child had no place in this house or my body. When I thought of him now, any affection had shrivelled to something black and vile. A heart cannot break – that is a tale for cow-eyed virgins – but it can rot.

I stared at the ceiling, tracing a crack that wandered across the figured plaster. The dancing flame on the nightstand made it seem to move. Every time I thought I'd chased the fissure to its start, it branched off in a new direction.

Grandmere had been wrong. My fortune did not turn on the letter P. I had been misled by my own vanity, my desire, my envy, my craft and most of all, by Vaughan Pritchard.

As I lay there, chasing the fractured path in the plaster, I considered many ways to take revenge upon him. Upon *them*. Grandmere's spice box contained enough poison for the entire household. But I wanted more. There were other ways to inflict lasting pain. As a wedding gift, I intended to give Vaughan and his bride a lifetime of suffering. Dark magic is always bought at a cost, but the price is worthwhile.

I sat up. The fan was beside the basin. Mariah had given it to me herself. I went from the bed to collect it, but as I neared the stand, the sour stench of my own vomit repulsed me. Taking the water jug to the basin, I diluted the foulness and then I carried it to the window, intending to fling it into the night.

As I drew back the curtains, the waxing moon slipped from behind a cloud. Through the splintered glass, I watched her skate, swollen and shapeless, on a wisp of cloud. In less than a week she would be complete once more. There was an irony to the fact that the full moon of May was the Mother's Moon.

I set the basin on the seat beneath the window. Gathering the skirt of my dress, I stepped up onto the box and reached to the metal clasp of the long casement.

'Surely you would not take such a drastic step?'

My hand froze on the catch. My heart unfurled, battering against my ribs like the wings of a crow. I breathed deeply, fighting for a command I could not be certain to attain.

I turned. Vaughan leaned against the wall in the deep shadows on the far side of the hearth. The rounded neck of his shirt, loose beneath his night robe, was very white in the moonlight. He must have come through the wall. How long had he been there?

I linked my trembling hands before my belly. 'Would you like me to throw myself to the cobbles, Vaughan?'

I was glad my voice did not betray me.

'That would be a little dramatic, even for you, Marta.'

'We are both players.' I stepped down from the window. 'You must be a talented actor indeed to keep disgust from your face when you ride your fat mare. What would your wife say if she knew you were here?'

Ignoring my question, he moved from the wall. 'I have come to say farewell. You cannot think that I would allow you to remain at Fyneshade.'

My time here had outrun its course, but to hear it presented so bluntly was shocking. In my addled state I had entertained a dim awareness of continuing as governess, serving in spite and silence until I had my revenge, but now I saw the impossibility of that future.

Vaughan crossed to the nightstand. He took the brass chamberstick and used it to light the three-branched candle tree on my dressing table. Then he dragged the chair to me.

'Sit.'

Placing the candle tree beside the hearth, he gestured lazily at the bed. 'Unless, for the sake of old times, you would rather lie.'

'There is only one liar here.'

'And only one murderer, my heart.' Candlelight glinted in his eyes. 'If you will not sit, I will.' He settled himself on a chair beside the hearth.

'I must thank you for that. It was neatly done.' His drawl was an insult. 'Once I was certain to inherit the estate, the path was clear. Dido helped – Lord Tallentire wanted that hawk so much.

Every time I flew her at Mungrisdale she won. Dido's victories are famous on the great estates of Cumberland where falconry is still revered as a gentleman's sport.'

He smiled. 'Ah, I see I must explain. I am a gentleman and my wife must be a lady. Mariah is Tallentire's daughter. I have courted her for a year. We kept our secret until the time was right. Tallentire wanted a champion and I wanted a rich wife. I gave him Dido in exchange for his only child to seal our bargain.'

Vaughan examined his nails. His lazy voice came again. 'I always said she reminded me of you. Vicious, but easy to tame – and often blind. I'll miss Dido, but I can train another.'

I gripped the back of the chair. 'I will tell her. I will tell your wife of our promise.'

'What promise would that be, Marta?' He feigned puzzlement. 'I made no promise to you.'

'The dress!' I spat the word at him. 'You told me that it was always your wish to see your bride in your mother's gown and veil. You gave it to me yourself that night in the stables when we . . . when you . . .' I hesitated. I began to doubt myself. I could not recall the exact words of his proposal.

'It is true that I came to a decision that night.' He shrugged. 'And you are quite right about that dress. It was my intention to take it to Coldharbour House for Mariah, but sadly she does not have the . . . posture for it. You confirmed that for me when I asked you to wear it.'

Vaughan shook his head. 'I believe you deceived yourself about a promise, Marta, yet still you murdered my father.'

His cold eyes held mine. An icy finger traced my spine from my neck to the tender dip at the base of my back.

'You have no proof.'

Vaughan reached into the pocket of his night robe and took out his silver case. Leaning forward to light a cigarette from the candle tree, he continued to stare at me.

'Grace led you to the black room, just as I asked her to. It was a game to her. She likes our games and, of course, you were so very easy to lure. What is it they say about cats and curiosity?' He drew on the thin cigarette. 'I'm sure it will come to me. Once you found our father you killed him. Just as I knew you would. And you found the diamonds and read my letter to Mariah too? Oh, you are so predictable, my heart.'

He laughed. The sound scraped beneath my skull.

'I have one question though, and for once I have been unable to predict your answer. Would you have told me what you had done, or did you think it better to let me believe he had died naturally?'

I looked away. Of course I would not have told him if . . . if . . .

'My sister will miss you at first.' He interrupted my theory of a future that was never to be. 'In her own way she is quite fond of you, but dear Mariah has already won her favour. Grace has a weakness for pretty dolls, as you know . . .'

I thought of the golden-haired doll that Lancer had dragged from beneath the bed.

'M . . . Ma . . . Mama.' The stupid girl had been trying to say Mariah.

Vaughan exhaled a cloud of aromatic silver-blue smoke. 'Over the years Grace and I have become very close. It may surprise you to hear that, Marta, but it is true. Family is everything, after all. There was a time when I thought that perhaps *she* might go to the black room for me, but it seemed grotesque. And it is regrettable that my sister's . . . condition makes her clumsy and a little unpredictable. I could not trust her entirely.'

'Why not you? You could have gone to him at any time. Were you afraid of Gurney?'

Something dangerous flared in Vaughan's eyes, but I was determined to goad him.

'Yes, I think you were. The thought of losing everything was enough to keep you away. That is the desperation of a coward.'

'Desperation?' Idly, Vaughan examined the cigarette. It was maddening. I lashed out again.

'And what of that ridiculous tale of the sanatorium when you knew all along that your father was here?'

Returning his attention to me, he smiled. 'As you did, when I told it to you, but you did not rush to correct me. That was when I knew I *had* you, my heart.'

How I hated those words in his mouth now.

'You must have known I would discover your lie.'

'Of course.' He shrugged. 'What would it matter by then?' He enjoyed my wretched comprehension. 'Do you play chess, Marta?'

When I did not answer he leaned forward. I smelt tobacco and brandy on his breath.

'You should. It is a game of strategy. The queens are the most powerful players on the board. One is white and the other black. I enjoyed watching you both today on the chequered tiles of the hall. My queens.'

'Balquist?' I could hardly choke out the name.

He nodded.

'Who is she to you?'

'She was Mariah's lady's maid, but we, *I*, have found other uses for her. Elizabeth is also an excellent chess player. It was her suggestion that it would be best if my father were to die when I was far from Fyneshade and beyond suspicion. The matter became more pressing in January when she told me that Tallentire had received an approach from the Earl of Faugh, whose son, Viscount Farlam, was certain to inherit.' He drew again. The tip of his cigarette glowed red. 'Then you arrived at exactly the right time. An answer to my prayers.'

In that moment I thought I saw it all. Vaughan's cunning, his betrayal and the trap he had set for me. How easily he had snared me, just like Mariah. I almost pitied the woman.

'You used me.' It was a revelation spoken aloud, not a question,

Vaughan shrugged. 'I think it would be more accurate to say we used each other, my heart. You were very willing as I recall.' He waved his cigarette at the chair. 'I wish you would sit. I have something to show you.'

I shook my head.

'I prefer to stand. And I will stand when I tell your wife every-thing. *Everything*, Vaughan. I have been wronged. You took advantage of a servant, and not for the first time, I hear. People will believe me. Besides, you have no proof that I murdered your father.'

He turned. In the shadows behind him a dark, rectangular object leaned against the wall.

'Open it.'

He handed me a ribbon-bound file. I reached out to take it, but the malice that suddenly sharpened his hard features made me draw back my hand.

'Why?'

Vaughan laid the file between us and drew again luxuriously from his cigarette before crushing the stub beneath his foot on the stones of the hearth. He moved the candle tree to shed a pool of a light. 'This will help you see more clearly. It will be easier if you sit, my heart.'

He pushed the file with the tip of a slipper. Briefly, I saw a monogram embroidered in golden thread – a V and M linked together. It was not my name he wore. I blinked. The smoke clouded my eyes.

I took up the file, sat stiffly in the chair and untied the knot in the ribbon. The boards fell open and a sheaf of papers cascaded from my lap. I recognised Grace's heavy scrawl on some of the sheets that fanned across the boards. Bending to collect them, I saw what she had done.

'My sister is a very talented artist.' Light flared as Vaughan struck a vesta against the side of the silver case.

The drawings were explicit and anatomically correct. A naked woman rode an ancient man in a heavily draped bed. In some pictures the woman's face was obscured by a mane of scribbled black hair. In others she turned, leering to face the artist, her face – *my face* – contorted into an ecstasy of carnal abandonment. The man was shrivelled and bony. His head lolled back and his mouth gaped wide. In one picture, the woman had placed Sir William's twig-like hand between her legs. In another she held a whip.

'But this is not … not …' Horrified, I flung the file from me. 'This never happened. None of it.'

'Not to my father, no.' Vaughan blew a ring of smoke that rose into the air between us. 'Grace can only draw what she has seen. I merely suggested some small … refinements.'

He smiled. 'Now, Marta, I liked you for your imagination. What if we were to imagine the case if my sister's work were to fall into the wrong hands? Perhaps Grace's new lady's maid, Elsa, might find these drawings? Horrified, she might take them to Mrs Balquist, who, equally revolted, might take them to her very innocent mistress, who, in tears of genuine distress, would bring them to me.' Vaughan raised a brow. 'I know from Dr Foldine that my father died of a weakened heart. That alone is terrible enough, but to know that you had exposed a child to such obscenity, depravity ...'

'No ... no ... NO!'

Taking up three of the drawings, I ripped them into pieces. I snatched at three more and did the same, screwing the paper into balls that fell about my chair. At first, Vaughan watched in silence, then he tossed the cigarette to the stones, reached across and gently stopped my hand. I pulled away and lashed out, but he caught my fingers in his, crushing them so tightly that my nails drew blood from his palm.

His face did not alter as I dug deeper and deeper.

'These are not the only ones, Marta. There are others, dozens of them. Many of them much, much worse.'

Releasing me, he took the file from my lap, closed it and tied the black ribbon into a bow.

'It is late and Mariah will be sleeping now. I must be careful not to disturb her.'

He stood and began to walk to the door. At the foot of the bed, he stopped, turned and tossed a jangling pouch to my feet amid the screws of paper.

'One hundred guineas – more than I have given any whore, but you have earned your wages, my heart. You will leave tomorrow morning. Elizabeth ... *Mrs Balquist* expects to receive your resignation at breakfast. When a queen is taken the game is over.'

41

I left in the darkest part of the night when I was sure that the household slept. Grandmere had told me that ghosts prefer the hours between midnight and the dawn. She had told me many things.

If Sophia Pritchard observed my departure, she did not strum a sad tune to bid me farewell. Lancer was the only creature who watched me walk down the stairs and across the hall. The dog padded to my side and sniffed at my heavy tapestry bag. I ruffled its head without affection and gathered some loose grey tufts from beneath its collar. Yawning, the animal returned to its nightly resting place beneath a long oak buffet set with old silver.

Leaving my bag at the doorway, I went quietly and swiftly to the parlour where I had spent so many hours with Mrs Gurney. I did not know what I would find, but I hoped Balquist had left something of herself there. When I opened the door and stepped down, the sharpness of her cologne filled my nose. My belly tightened, but I did not retch. The scent was proof she had been here.

I lit a candle from the embers of the hearth and scanned the room. The keys had gone from the table. A jug of white flowers stood in their place. Everything was crisp and ordered. It was too much to hope that Balquist had left her vulgar yellow gloves here, but there must be something I could take.

I raised the candle and searched the shelves of the dresser, where rows of familiar blue and white china gleamed in the dancing light. Nothing had changed. Opening the cupboard, I saw the remains of the saffron cake left by Mrs Gurney. My belly clenched again. The happiest days I had spent in this house were the days when Grace, the ugly, ungrateful bitch, and I were alone together.

Shutting the door, I turned to study the room more closely. There was a strange glinting beneath the table, as if a dozen black-eyed mice watched me from the shadows. They did not scatter when I lowered the candle. Instead, I found what I needed.

A handful of tiny jet beads from Balquist's grey skirt was enough. I pushed them into a leather purse along with Lancer's coarse hair. In my bag, I had already stored Mariah's fan, Grace's drawing of a hare and a square of cotton on which I had cleaned Vaughan Pritchard's blood from beneath my nails. I had collected some other mementos too. It had been easy in the silence and darkness. These valuable trinkets were now lodged in my box of secrets.

I went back up to the hallway and threw open the doors. The dog raised its head, but it didn't bother to stand again. It was raining now. A sharp gust chased a scuttle of damp leaves over the threshold.

Raising the hood of my cloak, I took up my bag and walked out onto the steps without fastening the doors behind me. An ill wind was coming to Fyneshade.

Let it blow.

Rose Moon

42

The sea was grey and listless. Fingers of yellow-flecked foam clawed at the pebbles on the shore and dragged them, rumbling and growling, back to the water. If I closed my eyes, I could almost believe the land was breaking apart beneath my feet.

Tonight, if the cloud lifted, the Rose Moon of June would shine a path to France across the waves. When I was done, I intended to go there. I spoke the language fluently and I had the means to live well.

Turning from the sea, I pulled up the hood of my cloak and entered one of the stinking passages leading into the town. I would buy the last ingredient I needed at the dimly lit apothecary on Middle Street.

Deal was a wretched place. A warren of squalid, fetid little streets lined with taverns and brothels that served the naval shipyards. Sunlight never seemed to penetrate the gridwork of cobbled lanes and alleys that turned their back on the sea. It was probably best that way.

And it suited my purposes.

The morning I left Fyneshade, I walked for several hours until I was able to board a public coach on the high road leading to Bakewell. The other passengers, a man and his two daughters, exchanged glances as, mud-spattered and sodden, I clambered aboard. Knowing that they would remember me, I moved swiftly on to Matlock, and thence to the city of Derby where I took a room in a backstreet tavern. The mattress stank of sweat and piss, and the narrow window looked out to blank wall. A day later, I travelled by coach to London, a journey that carried me two days further from Fyneshade, but even there in the grimy, teeming vastness, I did not feel that I had gone far enough.

It seemed to me that France, the land of Grandmere, was calling me home, which was how I came to the Kentish coast, a place so remote from Fyneshade it might almost have been on the far side of the papier-mâché globe in the nursery. It was near enough, however. The ritual would work while we walked the same land.

A reputable house would not have taken a woman alone like me, but Mrs Firmin's sprawling establishment was not quite respectable. Although, on the surface, it seemed clean and decent enough, I was not blind to the purpose of the rooms on the upper floor where women received callers from midday to the earliest hours of the morning. Their painted cheeks, vivid hair, reckless dress and geegaw jewels were a uniform, much like that of their drunken clients from the shipyards.

If I met them on the stairs, Mrs Firmin's whores stared at me, no doubt wondering what I was doing there. I felt their black-rimmed eyes on my back when I went down for my daily walk beside the shore. Secure in the knowledge that I would not be here for long, I rejoiced that I had not fallen among them.

I had told Mrs Firmin that I was a widow and the mourning I was forced to wear confirmed that condition, as did the cheap ruby ring now on the third finger of my left hand. I offered her a vague but affecting story of my wish to be near my late husband's naval brothers, for poor Edward, a second lieutenant in Her Majesty's navy, had died at sea. It mattered little whether she believed me. For three weeks now, I had paid my rent and made no demands on her time or services. Tomorrow I would be gone.

The bell over the door jangled as I entered the apothecary shop. A man in a dusty ochre-coloured work coat looked up from the ledger on the desk.

I nodded and went to the counter.

'Do you have artemisia absinthium?'

He moved a pair of wire-framed glasses further down his nose. 'Wormwood?'

'Is that the same?' I feigned ignorance. 'I have been recommended artemisia for my digestion. I have a delicate constitution; my friend suggested that it would help.'

'Wormwood helps a lot of things.'

The man stared at me and then he turned to survey the jars on the wall behind him. He pulled a narrow wooden ladder to his side and climbed it to reach a glass jar on the highest shelf.

'How much do you need?'

He placed the jar on the counter and I saw the name scrolled in gold across the glass. When he lifted the domed lid, a sour miasma rose into the air between us.

'Enough to fill this.' I pulled a phial from my pocket.

'That's more than I'd normally prescribe.' He frowned. The glasses twitched on his thin nose.

'My condition is persistent.' I pushed the phial towards him. 'I wish to be assured that I have enough.'

He peered at me again above thickened lenses. 'This amount will be sufficient, miss. I am certain of that. Shall we say five shillings?'

We both knew the price was too high, but I nodded. Taking up a little copper spoon, the apothecary filled the phial while I counted coins from my purse.

Before I left the shop, I turned to find him watching me. The accusation in his eyes was intolerable.

'It is not *miss*, I am Mrs . . . Van Meeran.'

The bell jangled behind me as I slammed the door.

My trinket box rattled as it fell from the shawl to the bed. The lid opened and some of the contents spilled onto the worn patchwork counterpane. The rubies chinked against a diamond-studded ball. When I left Fyneshade I had taken Panjan's eyes and his precious toy along with Grace's pearls and a tiny filigree clock with thirty sapphires set into the dial. My future was assured by these valuable items. I had also accepted Vaughan's guineas. To have left them behind would have been a feeble gesture, the scratch of a kitten.

Since arriving in Deal, I had spent many evenings counting my trophies and wondering about my past and my future. Such sweet little victories – Aunt Clare's earring, the buttons, the prim little shepherdess. Even the coffin plate was a pleasant reminder of Nathaniel. I was not sentimental about the thing I had from Vaughan.

I gathered the jewels and the trinkets together and put them back in the box. Tonight, it was Grandmere's bowl I sought in the folds of the shawl. Easing it free, I glanced at the window. My room occupied the eastern corner of the boarding house with a narrow view of the flat sea at the end of the lane. The cloud had thinned during the afternoon and now the rising moon was just visible as a lick of silver on the horizon.

It was not bad luck for me to view her through glass.

The other trophies I needed tonight were hidden at the bottom of my tapestry bag. I arranged the fan, the beads, the drawing, the grey hairs and the bloodied handkerchief before the hearth and struck a vesta against the stone.

Although the June night was warm, the ritual called for fire. I watched the flames flutter into the throat of the chimney and then I went to the bed to cover the patchwork with a heavy blanket I had bought from a street pedlar. I poured a glass of wine and laid out the herbs and the bowl on the boards before the fire, alongside the offerings.

Parsley, rue and pennyroyal had been easy to find in the hedgerows about Deal. A phial in Grandmere's spice box contained thick black poppy oil. Wormwood was more difficult. I had taken a risk in going to Middle Street, but I knew I was not the only woman who had made such a purchase from that dingy shop.

Crushing the leaves together in Grandmere's bowl, I added five drops of poppy oil and the wine from the glass. Having taken this path before, I knew the exact quantities to use and how long it would be before the pains began.

I went to the door and listened. Familiar sounds came from the floors above. It was odd, at that moment, to hear laughter and singing, but I was glad that business was brisk. I did not wish to be disturbed. I turned the key in the lock and stepped from my wrapper to stand naked before the rising moon.

Taking the bowl to the window, I greeted her and then I dug my fingers into the damp blackened mess and forced it into my mouth. The wine took the edge of the bitterness away, but, just as last time, it was still difficult to swallow the foul-tasting mash. When I had chased the last of it around the bowl, I held the rim to my mouth and finished the wine.

Then, I lay on my bed and waited.

I bit down on a rolled cloth to stop myself from screaming. It had not been like this before. Nathaniel's child had slipped easily from my womb, but Vaughan's bastard thrashed in my belly like an eel. The pains came in waves that caught me up and threw me down again to await the next assault. When the blood came it was dark and thick.

I reached for the rag I had prepared and clamped it between my legs. The movement was agony. My body bucked again as pain gripped me like an armoured gauntlet, squeezing the last dregs of a life from my body. The blood was still coming. The hot metallic scent of it rose around me.

Moaning, I rolled from the bed and crawled to the fire, dragging the blood-soaked rag. The embers were glowing and now the milk-light of the risen moon, the Rose Moon, spilled into the room. It was time.

Despite the gnawing pain, I cast fresh coals onto the embers and blew. I whispered the words of supplication and I drew the sign in the air with my left hand. When nothing happened, I repeated the curse and the sign.

Instantly, the fire spat and the blue-hearted flames flared with a ferocity that rattled the coals. I ripped a handful of hair from my head and threw it at the fire. The blaze seemed to form itself into a fiery hand, snatching the gift and tossing it about before consuming it completely. The animal smell of burning hair – sour-sweet and fatty – rose from the hearth. I gasped and bent forward as the stabbing came again. My body glistened with sweat as the heat intensified. Now my head throbbed and the room spun. Struggling to rise, I toppled forward to crouch on all fours like an animal. I could not fail, not now I was close.

I stretched out a hand.

Lancer's grey hairs went first, then Balquist's beads. I cast them over the coals and watched them melt into tiny molten droplets. Mariah's fan opened and fluttered with a filigree of fire before it blackened, sparked like a starling's wing and crumpled to ash. Grace's drawing rose into the throat of the chimney, flames licking at the edges. Then, fully alight, the paper singed and curled inward. The hare's eye fixed mine as it burned. Lastly, I tossed the little cloth spotted with blood from Vaughan's hand into the fire. But I still had something better of his. The most powerful weapon of all to curse a man.

I took up the rag that had caught the stinking clotted remnants of the child we had made and cast it into the fire. Instead of smothering the flames, the rag sizzled like meat on a griddle. As I watched, it burst into a ball of brilliant light that burned so bright I had to turn away to shield my eyes. When I looked back, the rag had shrivelled to a blackened lump the size of a fist.

The last thing I remembered, before my senses deserted me, was the sight of the moon through the window. She was not rose – she was red.

43

The screech of seagulls was the first thing I was aware of. The harsh sound came again and I wondered how such birds came to be at Fyneshade. I tried to open my eyes but they were gummed together. When I moved in the bed, every part of my body ached as if I had been crushed beneath the wheels of a carriage.

'She's come to herself!'

Footsteps thumped around the bed. 'Mrs Firmin! Did you hear me? She's come right again.'

Pain shot across my skull as I rubbed my eyes. The world came dimly into view. I was not at Fyneshade. Hand on hip, a girl dressed in a red bodice and petticoat stood at the doorway. She nodded at me and wrinkled her freckled nose.

'Feeling better are you? A right dance around the maypole you've given us all.' She turned and bellowed, 'Mrs Firmin!'

Returning to the chair next to my bed, she collected her

needles and green wool and went back to the door. Before going out she turned to look at me, not unkindly.

'We've all been there, dearie. You only had to ask one of us and we'd have helped. It's not as if it don't happen all the time.' She checked the passage and lowered her voice. 'The old cow's not happy. She had to call a crow and that's not good.'

Fragments tumbled in my mind like the pieces of a wooden puzzle. A fire, a dog, a fan, a hare, the moon, a man . . .

I moaned and curled into a ball in the bed as the memories locked together.

'Water? Is that what you want?' Setting down the wool and the needles, the girl took a jug from the washstand and filled a glass.

'Here, drink it slow.'

She held the glass to my lips and tipped it. At first, I could hardly swallow, but as the water filled my mouth, I realised the burning pain in my throat was thirst. I began to gulp greedily, catching her hand to keep the glass in place.

'There, I reckon that's better. We didn't think you'd come through at first. Tell you what else I think—'

Before she could finish, the door swung wide and Mrs Firmin lumbered into the room. She jerked her head at the girl.

'Out. And shut the door behind you.'

When we were alone, the woman clumped around the bed and sat in the chair.

A mass of dark red hair, some of it her own, was piled on the top of her head and her busy floral dress was cut low to reveal the mounds of her large breasts, the skin wrinkled and brown like fruit that has gone days beyond ripeness.

Her small dark eyes creased with cunning as she began. 'There was a lot of blood. Everywhere it was – smeared on the boards near the fire and on that bed. You were lucky I found you when I did. You could have died in here. All things taken into account, that might have been more considerate.'

Mrs Firmin leaned forward. I smelt tooth rot laced with gin.

'You've been very stupid, Mrs Van Meeran – if that's your true name, on which point I have my doubts. You've cost me dear, and worse than that, you could've called the law on me. It's very fortunate for us both that Dr Betteshanger is an old acquaintance and a friend to this house. Otherwise . . .' She whistled through the remains of her teeth and huddled forward, revealing the shrivelled chasm of her chest. 'To speak plain . . .' her coarse voice was low, '. . . what you did is a hanging offence. Murder is murder, even if the babe hasn't seen the sun.'

I turned from her to face the wall.

'Oh, don't mind me, you rest yourself.' A hand caught my shoulder and pulled me roughly. Mrs Firmin's fleshy face was so close to mine I could see red veins beneath the powder and the dark hairs on her chin.

'You'll listen to me, *Mrs Van Meeran*, when I tell you what I found in this room when I sat by your bed. Quite the magpie aren't you, with all them pretty things hidden away with the junk?'

She had my attention now.

'See, I'm not unreasonable. I . . . *we* are prepared to let you leave here at the end of the week with ten of them lovely shiny guineas I found in your bag.' Her black eyes narrowed. 'Dr Betteshanger's time and his discretion don't come cheap, but I reckon them big rubies, the pearls, the ball and that nice little clock will go some way to cover it. We've come to an arrangement about his . . . fees.'

I gripped the edge of the coverlet and tried to speak to her, to scream at her, but my voice wouldn't come.

The woman patted my hand. 'There, don't fret yourself. It's all worked out for the best. Dr Betteshanger said that once you'd come to yourself again, it would only be a few days more before you could pack your bag and go on your way. If you're wondering, I've already got your dainties safe. It wouldn't do to leave such valuable items lying about where anyone could find them.'

She stood and rubbed her heavily ringed hands together. 'Seeing as you're not quite yourself yet, *Mrs Van Meeran*, I'm prepared to let you have this room until Friday. That will be another two guineas. Then you're out.'

Mrs Firmin started for the door, but she paused at the foot of the bed, scratching her scalp beneath the hairpiece. 'There's one more thing, and I wouldn't be a good Christian if I didn't pass it on. Dr Betteshanger told me to tell you that if you try that trick again, it'll kill you.'

Thunder Moon

44

The coach swung on the bumpy road and I had to steady the newspaper in my hand to see the close-packed print again.

COUNTRY HOUSE DESTROYED
TRAGIC DEATHS RECORDED

My heart leapt anew each time I read the story. It was the one thing that had sustained me through the last weeks, when my life and all the plans I had made collapsed around me like a house made from playing cards. I had snipped the story carefully and neatly from the newspaper and in moments of darkness, I allowed myself to feed from it.

The fire that destroyed Fyneshade, killing the new baronet, his bride of just one month, his younger sister, the housekeeper and a faithful guard dog 'whose piteous howling was heard, with horror, by those assembled in the courtyard as the great and ancient house – one of the finest in the county – burned with a ferocity that turned night to day,' had occurred on the night when I performed the ritual.

I had known, of course, that a cursing carries a high cost, but in the last days I had sometimes wondered whether I would have sought such deep vengeance if I had known I would lose so much. At those times, I thought of Vaughan's last visit to my room and was almost happy.

A woman alone in the world, with little more than intelligence and imagination to sustain her, has few pathways from which to choose. It seemed to me that I had been a good governess to Grace, and fortunately Mrs Gurney agreed. Indeed, she was very willing to attest to my ability and good character.

When I wrote to her in Sheffield, expressing shock and sympathy at the death of poor dear Grace, I explained that her warning about Vaughan's 'defects of character' had proved to be accurate and that, despite the marriage, I had been forced to leave Fyneshade shortly after he took up residence with his bride. I told her that, in a way, I owed her my life and would always consider her to be a true and loyal friend. I enclosed her mother's recipe book with my letter, claiming to have come across it when I prepared the parlour for the late Elizabeth Balquist. My message concluded with the hope that she might provide me with a reference, for I intended to continue as a governess, dedicating my future service to the memory of Grace.

Mrs Gurney's fulsome reply and excellent reference arrived at my shabby lodgings in Rye almost by return.

And now I was travelling to a new position.

I had been interviewed in Harley Street by a wealthy,

self-consciously handsome young man who initially affected to be more interested in the pages of his sporting journal than in me.

The post would be 'dull', he freely admitted. His country estate in Essex was remote and very quiet, although the house itself was more than comfortable and surrounded by excellent gardens. The day-to-day running of affairs was managed by his senior man-servant and a capable housekeeper. My only duty, he explained, would be to care for the children of his deceased brother. As their guardian, he was concerned for their welfare, naturally, but he did not wish to be involved with the small details of their small lives. He did not, in fact, expect to hear from me.

I knew he found me attractive, even in my old mourning gown. After I accepted the unusual terms of the engagement, I felt his eyes on me as I left the room. It was a pity, I thought, that he did not intend to make regular visits to his nephew and niece. Perhaps, in time, that might change?

At the appointed place, the coach rocked to a halt and I was met by an open fly sent from the house. The day was warm and very pleasant. The air was sweetened with the scent of flowers as we rolled along the country lanes. With this freshness, a sudden sense of optimism came upon me. On impulse, I took the snippet of newsprint from my bag and, without reading it again, I let the breeze snatch the past from my fingers. As I turned to watch the paper curl and flutter into the sky, I saw a fragile lacy ghost suspended in the blue above the trees. The Thunder Moon of July, named for the storms of summer, would be complete within a week.

The fly turned into a shady oak-lined avenue and gradually the house revealed itself. I was surprised by a jolt of recognition. I had never been here before and yet there was something familiar about the circular lawn, the roses at the wide entrance and the tall cool windows.

A woman stood at the top of the steps outside the door. She held the hand of a small girl dressed in a shimmering white smock. Rooks cawed in the gilded sky and the wheels of the fly crunched on gravel as we circled the lawn to a halt.

'Good afternoon and welcome.' The woman beamed up at me and the girl, a tiny beauty, made a pretty curtsey.

I dismounted, held out my hand and smiled. 'Good day, Mrs Grose. I must apologise for being a little late.'

'You're here now, that's the main thing. We've been so excited, haven't we?' The child smiled bashfully and hid her face in the housekeeper's skirts.

The woman petted her indulgently. 'Flora's shy, but you'll have a friend for life once she knows you. Her brother's just the same.'

At a sound from the hallway, she turned. A man came out into the light. Twisting back to the fly, I pretended to concern myself with my belongings, certain that the sudden pounding of my heart must be audible to all.

The finely dressed man was tall, auburn-haired and absurdly handsome. A mature and thrillingly dangerous version of the boy I had left in Croyle stood before me. It was as if Nathaniel had been plucked from the face of the earth and finished by an unholy hand. I took my little handbag from the seat of the fly and, gulping a secret breath, I faced him again.

He smiled. 'Welcome to Bly.' Wide green eyes held mine.

'I am Peter Quint. And you must be Miss Jessel.'

'I was not gifted like Grandmere and she had died too soon to complete my education, but when I chose to, I could hear the echoes of long-dead souls. I knew there were many types of ghost. Most were harmless . . .'

If you are curious to see what sort of ghost Martha Jessel became, an answer lies within the pages of *The Turn of the Screw* by Henry James.

Acknowledgements

Fyneshade is a ghost's story, the spectre in question being Miss Jessel, one of two tormented fiends who may or may not (depending on your reading of the book) haunt the vulnerable governess narrator of Henry James's *The Turn of the Screw*.

If you are familiar with this classic and deeply unsettling novella, then you will know that Marta is about to pay very dearly for her sins. In her own catalogue of the returned, she is destined to become the sort of revenant she fears most: the damned.

'The worst – and thankfully they were rare – were angry. Their souls were consumed with bitterness and hatred so heavy that it chained them to the earth. The more these dead saw of the living, the more powerful they became, feeding on their own envy.'

In *The Turn of the Screw*, Miss Jessel (we never know her first name) is a rarely glimpsed but dreadful apparition, unlike her partner in corruption, Peter Quint, whose spectral presence is surprisingly substantial and menacing. We learn much about the diabolical Quint but little about Miss Jessel, which set me thinking – what sort of a person was she and how did she become that wretched lurking horror? *Fyneshade* is my answer to those questions.

It seems only right that my first acknowledgement should be to Henry James for writing a story that has haunted me since I first read it at around the age of fifteen, the ghost story that inspired the book you have just finished.

If you have not yet had the shivering pleasure of reading *The Turn of the Screw* but are impatient to learn a little of what happened to 'Marta' after her arrival at Bly (where *Fyneshade* ends) then may I suggest that you track down a 1961 film called *The Innocents*. Directed by Jack Clayton, partly scripted by Truman Capote and filmed in stunning black and white by Freddie Francis, it is both luminously beautiful and utterly terrifying. For me, it is the most elegant and perfect expression of gothic on screen and I'm happy to admit that I tried to capture something of its shimmering, otherworldly quality in the blackest shadows of Fyneshade.

I must thank my husband Stephen for introducing me to *The Innocents* many moons ago and for so much else. Without his belief, support and enthusiasm, I wouldn't have written this book – or anything else! He knows only too well that my natural operational mode is 'sloth' and his tact and forbearance when confronted by my procrastination, work aversion and general disorganisation is the stuff of legend.

I must also thank friends who have always encouraged me and who have shared the highs of lows of my writing career to date. Special mention here to Lisa who read the first iteration of *Fyneshade* in weekly instalments. Lisa – your genuine hunger for more was just the spur I needed! Thanks also to Susan, Sue and Helen, and also to Leah, who knows how much I love Thackeray's Becky Sharp and immediately spotted her in Marta.

I'm lucky to have made some wonderful friends in the writing community over the last few years and their support has been invaluable. I won't list them here for fear of missing someone out, but I hope you know who you are.

So many people play a role in the making of a book that I

often think they should get their own credits at the end, like a film. I'd like to say a huge thank you to the wonderful and welcoming team at Viper. Miranda Jewess – you are the most forensically brilliant and ghoulishly delightful editor. When I lost my nerve at one point and tried to be 'nicer', you showed me the foolish error of my ways. Thank you to Hayley Shepherd who knocked my tortured 'Jamesian' prose into shape and to Emily Frisella, who expertly and gently guided the editorial process. Huge thanks also to Profile's Alia McKellar as I know you were a champion of *Fyneshade* from the start, and to the excellent Therese Keating.

I can't finish without including my fellow Viper authors who are not only fiendishly talented but also extremely good company. As is my spectacular agent, Eugenie Furniss.

And that's a wrap … except the one final, heartfelt thank you to Edward Bettison, whose beautiful but deliciously wicked cover design for *Fyneshade* is a work of perfection.

About the Author

Kate Griffin studied English literature at university and developed a healthy obsession with Victorian gothic novels. She has worked as an assistant to an antiques dealer, a journalist for local newspapers and for the Society for the Protection of Ancient Buildings. *Kitty Peck and the Music Hall Murders*, Kate's first book, won the *Stylist*/Faber crime writing competition. She is also the author of three subsequent Kitty Peck novels, and the co-author of the forthcoming *The Blackbirds of St Giles* with Marcia Hutchinson, under the pseudonym Lila Cain. Kate lives in St Albans. Find her on X @KateAGriffin.